Splinters of My Soul

A novel by

Kimberly Morton Cuthrell

SERENITY LEGACY PUBLISHING

Dedicated to:

My ancestors, grandparents, parents, husband, children, sister and brother.

Table of Contents

Prologue

Tiffany Brown-Carson tossed a small black rose on top of the silver casket. A single tear slid down her face, not for the man whose life ended so gruesomely, but for the children of Cloverdale who had been damaged by his mere presence.

The sun grazed the back of her neck. Rubbing her face, she gazed out at the retreating forms of the few people who had ventured to Crystal Lake Cemetery just to make sure the man was truly dead. Unfortunately, placing him six feet under wouldn't wipe the memories from their minds, remove his horrible deeds from their nightmares, or alter the fact that the city had turned its back on them.

A large wooded area surrounded the clear blue waters. The burial ground was adjacent to a small lake—a quiet place for people to fish. Tombstones were lined neatly on the five-acre stretch of land. The gated cemetery was clean, a peaceful area for the dead to rest or the living to think about their very existence.

Tiffany spun on her heels, trampling the fresh cut grass under her feet as a cool gentle breeze swept her way. She paused, inhaling the sweet scent of fresh flowers as a black limousine passed in front of her; another group of family and friends were on their way to say their last goodbye to a loved one. She glanced at her brother, Tony, whose gaze was locked on the casket as it lowered into the ground.

Glancing back over her shoulders, Tiffany observed two men, one tall and gangly, the other short and stocky, who had started the tedious job of covering the grave. The men worked steadily in unison as the scorching sun beamed on their dark green uniforms. It seemed more work to lay the man to rest than he deserved.

Tiffany wished she could have spared everyone the trouble. If she had the guts, she would have buried the man alive and lit a match, giving him a personal cremation befitting every crime. His murder should have been carried out before the innocence of so many children had been taken, before so many lives were ruined. No one would have considered it a crime, at least no one in the Cloverdale Assisted Housing Community.

It all began in one summer, on a hot June day. A summer that had promised to be everything that kids from the community could expect. A summer of dreams and hope. A summer that should have fulfilled all expectations but it was a summer that was the beginning of the end for the innocence of many people. Through some twist of fate, she stood accused of killing a man everyone outside of Cloverdale held in high esteem. But the people of Cloverdale knew the truth. Her brother knew the truth. Her uncle knew the truth. She certainly knew the truth. But she wasn't talking. And that could land her on death row.

Chapter 1

We don't cheat. We're just better than they are, Dr. Tiffany Brown-Carson thought remembering her conversation with her brother, Tony, as she stepped out of the office into a brightly lit hallway. She strolled past the medical-records room, the bathroom and the lab, putting the rest of her uneaten lunch in the tiny silver refrigerator that still housed yesterday's lunch and of the day before that.

Tiffany giggled softly as she strolled up the hallway with a wide smile across her lips. Tony and Heather wept like puppies when they lost the card game before. She planned to make that little tiger-eyed heifer weep just one more time.

She turned the corner and a peal of laughter died on the tip of her tongue. The hairs stood at attention on the length of her arms. Her gaze swept across the entrance to the medical center, past the rows of waiting patients and straight to the strange scene unfolding before her very eyes.

A crowd walked in as though they were joined at the hip, inching through the glass doors, then fanning out like soft strands of hair on a bedroom pillow. The silence of so many was eerie, setting her teeth on edge.

Patients who had been seated for a long time stood. The crowd parted like the Red Sea, allowing a slender woman wearing a tattered trench coat to stroll through, carrying a tiny child curled in her light brown, skinny arms.

The woman's weathered and tear-stained face didn't cause for alarm. The sight of Christy, a little girl she mentored at the outreach program, being cradled like a newborn babe wasn't enough to set the tone for what was yet to come. But the blood seeping through the bright floral dress, trailing down the little golden brown legs, dripping onto the tile made Tiffany's heart slam against her chest.

9

Conversation among her patients died away like a bubble evaporating in the air. People holding ground at different places in the waiting room watched every move intently.

Tiffany stared at the crowd, eyes scanning the somber faces hoping that someone would answer. Not a dry eye looked back at her.

Cautiously, Tiffany extended her arms, reaching out for Christy. Karen Thompson, the girl's mother, walked as though in a daze, ignoring the gesture, strolling past patients, nurses and the receptionist without a backward glance.

Someone reached up, switching off the television, silencing the afternoon news. Somehow, this incident wouldn't make it on the airwaves. The things that happened in Cloverdale stayed in Cloverdale.

Gently, Karen gave Christy over to Tiffany. Murmurs wafted softly from the crowd.

"Another one? Somebody had to see something," blurted an old lady with a raspy voice who had been waiting in the lobby for thirty minutes.

A hush fell over the room.

Tiffany rushed to the closest examination room, carrying Christy while Karen grazed her heels. Laying the little girl on the tissue-covered table, Tiffany slipped on a pair of latex gloves and went to work. The sound of her heart racing filled her ears, mixing with the shallow sounds of the little girl's breathing.

Karen's hair was pasted to her light brown face. Tears streamed endlessly toward her chin, then dripped onto Christy's body, which she stroked lovingly. Her eyes, filled with a world of pain, finally focused on Tiffany. "Somebody. . . some *animal* hurt my baby."

With that, she collapsed. Nurse Patterson sprang forward but missed Karen as she slumped to the floor in a soft heap, sobbing.

Gently removing the blood-soaked clothing from the little girl's thighs, Nurse Patterson dashed on the other end checking the girl's pulse and pressure. "Weak, but it's there. She's hanging in."

Nurse Brooks walked in, took Nurse Patterson's place, her full pink lips parted and grew slack as her ivory hands trembled uncontrollably. "Again?"

No one said another word.

Nurse Patterson worked feverishly with Karen as Nurse Brooks assisted Tiffany with Christy.

"Somebody found her in the alley near Latham Park, down the street from Cloverdale," said a hefty woman standing in the crowd, who had managed to inch her way into the examination room. She curled up on the floor next to Karen, rocking the distraught mother from side to side.

"Why my baby, *Petrina*?" Karen asked, staring into the woman's light brown eyes.

Tiffany braced herself, taking shallow breaths. *Oh God, oh God, oh God*. She had trained at Duke Medical School and completed her residency at Wake Forest Hospital preparing for moments like this. Medical training and the actual presentation of such a horrible deed were two separate things.

The wheels of her mind clicked. Stop the blood. Clear the area. Gauge the best possible course of action.

"This is the fifth child this month, you know," Tiffany said as her heart wept with pain and sorrow, but her mind remained stable and clear.

"The others weren't as bad, though," Nurse Patterson replied, her dark brown eyes scanning the medical supplies.

The fact that the blood only appeared from the waist down told Tiffany plenty, but nothing could prepare her for the sight of Christy's injuries.

"Dear *God*," Tiffany uttered as her eyes widening with horror. With antiseptic pads, she began cleaning the area and trying to stop the flow of blood.

Karen slowly recovered.

"Why didn't you take her to the hospital near Latham Park?" she demanded of Nurse Petrina Mathis, the head nurse in charge, who was also Karen's best friend.

Nurse Petrina inched back toward the wall, her gaze glued to the table and the activity on the lower end of the girl's body. "Karen ain't got no insurance. She said she missed the deadline to submit her renewal paperwork for her *public aid insurance*. We knew you'd treat her anyway."

"Why didn't you call the ambulance?" Tiffany glanced at the blood pressure meter attached to the green band around the little golden brown upper arm.

"Now you know don't no ambulances come down here in Cloverdale," Nurse Petrina snapped, light brown eyes peering as Tiffany continued pressing gauze to the girl's labia. "She'd be dead before they'd get here."

Truer words were never spoken.

"Police ain't even trying to find the man who did the last ones," Nurse Petrina said straining to see over Nurse Patterson's shoulder for a better view. "No one cares what happens to poor people. 'Especially poor black folks livin' in the ghetto."

Tiffany glanced up at the nurse whose hand trembled as she held onto the little girl's nearly lifeless one. She stroked it gently along with the loosened ponytail as though the action alone would bring things back to normal. But Christy would never be normal again.

With swift strokes of gauze, which turned from pink to red within seconds, Tiffany glanced at Nurse Patterson. "Call the paramedics anyway.

She's going to need surgery right away. I don't have the facilities to do it here."

Nurse Patterson laid Christy's hand gently on the table, then scurried away.

"They found her near the alley," Nurse Petrina slurred, wiping her face with the back of a trembling hand. No one knew whether the action was due to a need for a fix, or anger for what had been done to another innocent little girl.

Tiffany gently moved the pad, trying to see if there was any hope for the tiny vaginal walls, which had been ripped as though an alien or a wild animal had attacked. A tear around the anus caused even more alarm. Had the man also done damage to the girl there?

The bleeding had slowed, but the throbbing membrane at the center of Christy's uterus would need her attention right away—the paramedics wouldn't make it in time.

Though Tiffany wanted to give the little girl a chance at a normal life, with each passing second, a harder choice came to the forefront: save her life and let her deal with the aftermath later. A woman could learn to deal with not having children. She couldn't deal with anything if she landed in the morgue.

"I'm going to operate."

Nurse Brooks stole a quick glance at Tiffany as Nurse Patterson's head whipped around, bushy eyebrows drawing in. "Doctor?"

"Yeah, I know," Tiffany said while still racking her brain for other options. "But I don't have a choice and neither do you." Tiffany looked over her shoulder. "Everyone clear the room except for Nurse Petrina," Tiffany said glancing at Nurse Petrina. "Stay in here. Administer the medication to her," Tiffany commanded Nurse Petrina knowing without a doubt Nurse Petrina knew exactly what medication. Nurse Petrina was always on point leaving Tiffany with no concerns.

Tiffany's eyes darted around at the standing bodies. "This place isn't prepared for major surgery, but we should have enough to do what needs to be taken care of right now."

Nurse Brooks carried the sobbing mother out of the room and back toward the anxious crowd. The door swung shut behind them.

Nurse Petrina administered a dosage of medication to the little girl, which would soon render Christy totally unconscious. She wouldn't feel when the smooth edge of the knife pierced her soft skin or when the needle tugged at the soft folds of flesh as stitches were applied to her fragile body.

"Who in the world would do this?" Tiffany asked, searching Christy's golden brown face for an answer that she knew wouldn't come soon. Her long sandy brown hair spread over the white cloth.

The child's eyelids fluttered open. Soft brown eyes focused on the light. Then Christy's gaze locked on Tiffany before she whimpered in pain.

The sound stabbed at Tiffany's heart even more than the sight of the injuries—which were more than any woman could withstand, let alone, a child of eight-years-old. Small, delicate hands reached for Tiffany, ignoring the nurse's efforts to keep her still so the anesthesia could kick in.

Tiffany, pulling on another set of gloves, leaned in as the girl tugged on her white lab coat, parted her lips and uttered a single name barely audible . . . .

Chapter 2

Dr. Anthony "Tony" Brown strolled out of his office in Brown Orthodontist Center, making a mental note to call his wife a little later. He would give her tips for the card game at his sister's place later that night. They couldn't lose for the fifth time in a row. He didn't care what his sister, Tiffany, said. She and her husband, Vance, had something going on with the *cards god*. No one could win that much!

Bright blue paint on the walls of his dental office served to make patients feel more at ease. At least that's what the decorator had said. Sports, health and entertainment magazines made a trail around the wooden circular table in his modestly decorated lobby. Patients ranging from three years old to seventy waited for their names to be called, while soft mellow tones flowed through the speaker system.

The heady smell of jasmine flowers, picked by his wife, lingered in the air mingling with the acrid scent of fluoride that drifted out when the examination room doors opened. Somehow the fluoride always kicked the jasmine in the tail. The place would always smell like a dental office no matter how many fruity sprays his wife bought or the constant stream of floral arrangements she sent each week.

As he entered the file-clustered area where his receptionist, two assistants and the clerk called their "workstation," a familiar, but distressed voice echoed through the hallway.

"Come on, baby, this has been our third time coming here," said a short, portly woman as she leaned over to her husband. "You've got to get that tooth pulled, Derrick."

"I know, baby," the man whined, placing a large brown hand over his cheek, a common move by patients trying to ease the pain. Tony hadn't seen it work yet.

She leaned in; one eyebrow raised. "Are you *scared*, Derrick?"

The man's hand fell from his face as he shot straight up. "Who? Me? No!"

"What's the problem then?" she teased, pursing her small cupid bow lips in a disapproving frown.

"Melinda, how are my pictures gonna look if my tooth's missing?"

A single hand whipped out, landing squarely on her wide hips as she peered at him. "Who are you trying to impress? Me or somebody else?" she snapped. "How do you think you're going to look with a mouth full of rotten teeth and stinking breath?"

"My breath doesn't stink," Derrick growled.

Tony scanned the room, noticing the smiles and grins on nearby faces.

Derrick's gaze swung to his wife's face, now turned into a scowl, waiting for a response. Poking her lips out before pulling them back into another major frown, Melinda said, "You don't have a choice. That tooth is coming out today! I can't take it anymore."

Tony grinned, checking Derrick's chart. The woman had made reference to the bad odor that flowed out the man's mouth every time it opened. He agreed with the wife's diagnosis—Derrick's tooth would have to make a hasty exit. *If* only they could convince the man to stay in the chair this time. Tony didn't stop the couple. The comedy routine had calmed some of the other patients.

"We have too many bills for you to be calling in sick," she said, waving her hands above her small head. "You're not going to lay around the house another day. Cleophus, do you hear me?"

16

Derrick yanked her back down in the black chair. "Don't call me by my middle name." He looked around at the staring eyes with matching smiley faces.

Her head swirled on her shoulders. "That's your name, ain't it?"

"I told you not to ever use that name," Derrick mumbled.

"And I told you to get that tooth pulled."

A giggle escaped Tony's mouth as he observed a kid laughing so much he slid out of his chair.

"Stop tripping, Melinda."

"You better not let my lights get cut off." She folded her arms across her large bosom. A few snickers escaped as patients tried to hold in laughter.

"I haven't *missed* that many days," he shot back, his hand now back in place on the left side of his face.

"Wait 'til I tell the kids that their father is too *scared* to get his tooth pulled," she said slyly. "You know *little* Derrick pulled his tooth out last month. He was ready for the *Tooth Fairy* to come."

"Yeah?" Derrick mumbled angrily. "And what was his motivation? Money!"

"*Arrrgh.*" Melinda tossed her hands. "I give up."

"Derrick Hunter," Samantha, Tony's dental assistant said as she held the door open with her foot. Tony's light brown eyes glared at Samantha, who barely hid a laugh behind her pale hand as she plucked the chart from his hands.

"Derrick, she's calling you." Melinda nudged him with her elbow. "Go ahead. And don't sneak out either. I'm coming back there to check on you. This doesn't make any sense."

Tony saw Derrick's gaze land on the pictures above the water fountain, the magazines on the roundtable and the cream vertical blinds;

17

basically, everywhere but on Samantha who stood in the doorway, waiting for a response.

Samantha paused for a few seconds before repeating his name. She turned her head in the direction of every corner in the cozy lobby, waiting for the burly man to respond.

Tony stood by, waiting to see if Derrick would turn tail and run—again. He should've taken bets with the staff. They still believed Derrick would overcome his fear. Ah, the power of dental anxiety. People would walk around with a tooth hanging halfway out, gums throbbing with pain and still wouldn't come to see Tony. He was in the wrong profession. He should've been a gynecologist like his sister. Now that was a steady stream of work without all the emotional tug of war.

"Mr. Derrick Hunter," Samantha repeated again as her light blue eyes darted across the grinning figures in the lobby.

Derrick stood, his expression grim, bony knees knocking together loud enough to start their own band. "Let's go, Melinda. I'll reschedule and—"

Melinda pressed down on the arms of the chair projecting her body forward. She stood, trembling with uncontrolled anger as she braced herself and placed her hand back on her wide hips, squinted, then pointed her index finger at Derrick.

"With who?" she spat, inching closer, so they were almost nose-to-nose. "You know Dr. Brown's the only dentist in town who'll put up with your dumb ass."

Derrick dipped his head sheepishly.

"And he's the only dentist that'll accept that lame insurance your job offers. It doesn't cover squat. Sooner or later all of your teeth are gonna fall out."

The man glowered at her. "Then I won't need a dentist, will I?"

18

Melinda reached out, popping him upside the head.

"Ouch!"

Waiting patients pointed at Derrick as they covered their mouths to prevent themselves from laughing out loud. Soon no one was successful as the amusement spilled over.

"Excuse me, sir," Samantha said, moving to stand between the happy couple. "Are you Mr. Hunter?"

"Yes, he is and he *is* ready," Melinda replied as she pressed her folded arms to her chest, patting a tiny high heel on the gray and white marble floor. The sound resonated under contemporary jazz music.

"Stop tripping, Melinda."

Melinda fluttered her hand at him as if shooing a pesky fly.

Looking back over his shoulder at his wife as he trudged to the examination room, Derrick's grimace resembled a criminal returning to a cell after visitation hour.

"Good morning, Mr. Hunter," Tony said, glancing down at Derrick's hands. They were shaking like leaves on a windy North Carolina day.

"Dr. Brown, reschedule me," Derrick pleaded, pressing his back against the door and putting a death grip on Tony's lab coat like a child visiting the dentist for the first time. "I'm not ready."

Tony coughed, struggling for air as he plucked the man's fingers from around the white cotton material, which had stretched to a point it nearly choked him. "Please have a seat, Mr. Hunter."

Slowly dragging his big feet toward the chair, Derrick kept his gaze on the small metal instruments displayed on the tissue-covered tray.

"This is your third time rescheduling," Tony said, inhaling deeply, trying to maintain his cool. "I understand you're uncomfortable. I'll give you something to make the area numb before we start. You won't feel a thing."

Tony opened Derrick's chart and looked at the X-rays. "I'll explain the procedure to you as I go along. I want you to relax."

Derrick shook his head vigorously, pressing his back into the leather chair like a little child about to receive a butt whipping. "I—I—I can't do this."

Tony reached down, lifting an object from the tray. "I want you to take this mirror. Look at your jaw."

Derrick shoved it away. "I know it's swollen. And it hurts!" Tony kept the mirror turned toward the man. "I'll reschedule," Derrick mumbled, hopping out the chair, then sprinting for the door.

"It's up to you, Mr. Hunter," Tony replied with a weary sigh. "I can't force you to do something you don't want to do. But as your dentist, I strongly recommend that your tooth is removed today. The pain isn't going away."

Derrick whirled on his heels, yanked open the door and ran smack into Melinda's scowling face, nearly knocking her over.

"Where are you going, Derrick Hunter!" Melinda shrieked, placing a single hand on the wooden section of the doorway, blocking his way as her eyebrows twitched angrily.

With a trembling hand still on the metal knob, he looked at his wife and stammered, "I—I—I was coming to get you."

Tony glanced at the clock. Time was passing rapidly, but Derrick moved in slow motion. Tony *thought* he had the day mapped out. His time was devoted to twenty patients on the schedule, two hours to do at the community center, a call to his wife, then a card game at his sister's. If the first half-hour was an indication of how the rest of the Friday morning would go—he was in for a ride.

Chapter 3

Sergeant Paul Smith sat in the conference room at the Charlotte police station reading a brochure from his insurance company. He scanned the sections on accidental deaths and benefits for the third time, making sure he didn't overlook any vital details.

Focusing on a way to get rid of his wife, Smith didn't concern himself with her funeral arrangements. When Morgan died, she would get the bare minimum. But how long would it take to get the cash? He closed his eyes, imagining the luxury items he would now be able to buy and a life without the *religious fanatic* he had married.

"Hey, I'm going back to Cloverdale," Sergeant Clark said, grabbing his black coat from the back of Smith's chair. "You coming?"

"Yes," responded Officer Brian Clark.

The sun beamed down on his black uniform as the two community patrol sergeants walked to their cars. Every third Friday morning, they had to meet at the police station where nothing of any importance happened. At least nothing Smith cared to remember.

"Goodness, I'm glad that's over," Clark said, wiping his pale, smooth forehead with a light yellow handkerchief. Smith paused and stepped in the opposite direction of Clark, trying to ignore him while he took one last puff on a cigarette.

Brian Clark had been the community patrol officer in Livingston Elderly Village for five years. For the past three months, he had to rotate to Cloverdale to work for a week shadowing Smith, preparing for the eventual transition to full-time service in the projects, a place Smith considered the bane of his existence.

"How's it going, Smith?" Clark asked. His muscular chest protruded through the uniform. His green eyes sparkled with a youthful glow the man didn't have a right to claim.

Irritated at being torn from his plans for Morgan's early demise, Smith replied, "Seems like Cloverdale will be all yours in a few weeks."

"Yes, but I'm not in a rush," the younger man said, stroking thin fingers through his bright red hair. "I like the old folks. They're funny. They don't wear Depends—some of 'em need to wear *dependants*."

Smith laughed, keeping in step with Clark. "Cloverdale is a lot tougher than Livingston. I wish I could've patrolled there. I guess the only thing you had to worry about was folks digging too many holes to plant flowers," Smith said with a loud guffaw.

Patrol cars zoomed by them. Clark stopped at the curb before crossing and turned to Smith. "How are your kids?"

"Those ungrateful bastards?" he said, grimacing as he kept in step with the younger man. "They only come to the house when I'm not there. They're grown now and settled into their careers. I paid for their education, put food in their stomachs and a roof over their heads and I've never received a thank you or a dime."

"When's the last time you saw them?"

"When they went off to college. They never kept in touch." Smith scratched his head, blonde curly hair moving in unison with his thick fingers. "I don't know what's wrong with kids today. They aren't like they used to be." He paused as though trying to tailor his words. "They keep in touch with their mother, though." He vaguely waved at another officer who blew his horn and drove past.

"I'll say a prayer for you and your family."

Smith's eyebrows twitched as he held back a smart remark.

"What about Morgan?"

Smith shrugged. "She's doing all right. She pissed me off the other day." His lips spread into a sneer. "She knows I'm about to retire and she turned down a promotion."

"Maybe you two need to talk about it, pray about things first."

A frown crept on Smith's alabaster white face. Clark's belief in God puzzled him. How could anyone believe in someone they'd never seen? "How is your wife?"

"Lindy's doing well," Clark said with a wide smile gracing his small arched lips. Obviously, the man had fond memories of the woman, which irked Smith even more. The only good memory Smith had of Morgan was the first time he popped her cherry. Breaking her in had been the highlight of their marriage. It had been all downhill for him since then—until he arrived at Cloverdale.

Clark cast a cautious glance in Smith's direction. "You know she's the community social worker at The Safe Haven Outreach Program. A lot of people volunteer there like . . . Tiffany, Tony and other kids who grew up here in Cloverdale." He paused. "Tiffany's a doctor and Tony's a dentist now. They've done great things with Lindy at the program."

"Yeah. I think somebody told me that," Smith replied, rubbing his cleft chin. He needed a shave. A picture of Tiffany flashed in his mind forcing him to contain his lustful thoughts. He knew Tiffany mentored the kids at the program. He popped his knuckles. "I don't see how Lindy sits and listens to sob stories from those tenants. Most of the people in Cloverdale don't want help, they only want a handout. It's bad enough their kids come to the community center without paper or pencils, begging for tutoring. I'm not putting any of my money in that school-supply account." Smith forced air out of his nostrils. "I've done my share when I hosted a fundraiser for the kids ten years ago. I'm not wasting my time or money again."

Clark rubbed the back of his neck with his heavy hand. "Lindy thinks some of the kids *and* their parents have potential," he said, scanning Smith's face.

"Potential?" A bitter laughed trilled off the tip of Smith's tongue. "I don't know who she's working with, but I seriously doubt that they're from Cloverdale. They aren't worth the time."

Clark followed him toward their patrol cars. "Everybody deserves a chance, Smith. Somebody gave you a chance once."

The number thirty-four was written near the patrol car's door handles and in the back window. "Nobody ever gave me anything," Smith growled, then softened his tone at the puzzled expression on Clark's face. "Nobody."

Another patrol car zoomed past them. Clark turned in the direction of the blue flashing light, traveling down the street. "Trouble in paradise."

Smith wrapped his lips around his cigarette and exhaled a small curl of smoke. "I know you're glad you eased your way into a sergeant position."

"God is good. I'm glad the chief recommended me. I was delighted to know that my hard work and efforts didn't go unnoticed."

A stab of envy ripped through Smith's heart. "It took a few deaths in Cloverdale before that same chief even agreed to give me a raise." Smith bit his bottom lip, trying to hold back his sharp tongue and keep in the fact that he knew more about those deaths than he could ever tell. "Well, in a few weeks you and your wife will be able to have a tag team role with the tenants." He snickered. "I'd like to hear what you have to say after you've been here a while."

Clark exhaled as he pulled out his car keys. "If you hate these people so much, why did you accept the position in Cloverdale?" he asked as his eyes widened.

Smith's thin lips fell into a smirk. "No one else wanted the position. Besides, it came with a promotion and a sign-on bonus. Death benefits." He drummed his fingers on the roof of his patrol car.

Clark frowned, then shook his head.

Smith stared at him, becoming more certain by the minute that the Irish man couldn't be as clean-cut as he seemed. He figured Clark disguised his devious behavior by flaunting religious beliefs. Smith was convinced that the man had a good game plan, probably a better one than Smith had for years. If a rape occurred or a drug trafficking ring got pulled in, no one would expect good old Bible-thumping Clark.

A billboard overhead showed an attack on Senator Davis who wanted to raise taxes for the third time in one term.

Smith grimaced. "I hope my tax money isn't wasted on those lowlifes."

Beads of sweat formed on Clark's forehead. He hauled out his handkerchief again and wiped his face. "I don't mind if it's spent for a good purpose."

Smith shook his head. "I do. I don't see how any good can come of it."

"Cloverdale has several tenants that are successful—Tony, David and Tiffany Brown just to name a few," Clark said with a grin as he slipped behind the wheel.

The man would never see the point. He must have heard about them from Lindy, because Smith had never mentioned the three family members who broke out of the projects, despite everything he had tried to do to keep them there.

Minutes later, Smith cruised down Central Avenue, passing a car lot, grocery store and a taxicab stand while Clark rode closely on his bumper. A dark cloud stretched across the once bright sunny blue sky, bringing droplets of rain in the middle of June. Preoccupied with ways to reel in cash, he ran a red light and swirled into another lane, without noticing his actions.

Within minutes he pulled up to the community center. Smith ran a hand through his blonde hair. The rain pelted the windshield at a steady pace. He reached behind him, picking up an umbrella from the back seat.

He laughed, watching the Cloverdale tenants rush outside to snatch nearly dry clothes off the line. Some had been thrown across the white fiberglass line without the little wooden spikes to hold them in place.

"Too poor to buy pins. They're pitiful," Smith said as Clark pulled up beside him, following Smith's gaze. "They can't even afford a dryer. I wonder if they have a washing machine, or if they wash clothes in their tubs or sinks. Lindy can't help them. You can't help them. *They* put themselves in this condition."

Smith ran inside the community center, passing the water fountain, the bathroom and the fire extinguisher and walked straight to his office. Clark shadowed Smith's footsteps while shaking the rain off his hands and wiping his face.

Clark dropped down, sitting in a wooden chair. "I keep telling you that all people in the projects are not bad."

A strong stale smell of coffee drifted past Smith's nose. Starbuck cups were piled up in the trash can.

Clark cleared his throat. "Tiffany's a doctor, Tony's a dentist and David's a computer engineer. That has to count for something."

Footsteps tapped up and down on the floor in the hallway. Smith stared at his white door, hoping no one knocked on it. He would love to end the day without another complaint.

Smith drifted off in a daze as Clark continued to express his point about golden years news. With the mention of Tiffany's name, a picture of a petite woman with a creamy caramel complexion and a curvaceous form flashed before him. A stirring in his pants made it uncomfortable to sit as he got a stiff one. Tiffany Brown. Correction—Carson-Brown, married to a lawyer. Boy did that little bastard luck up. But Smith had taught her a lesson before she went off to college. And he really wanted to ram that lesson home, but she disappeared from Cloverdale that summer before Smith could really sink his teeth into her. He would have to rectify that—soon. That summer he had hit pay dirt in more ways than one. David and Tony were prime for the taking too. Did Tony tell his sister what happened to him that night?

The reality of Tony and David going to college also flashed in Smith's mind. The boys were smart kids in high school, but he had doubted they could handle college without tutors. It irked him that they had proven him wrong. It also upset him that they made more than he—or his children.

"Smith. Smith, did you hear me?" Clark asked as his bushy eyebrows shot upward into half-moons. "What are your plans after retirement?"

Smith rolled his eyes. "If Morgan doesn't take that promotion, we'll be in a financial slump." He elevated his legs on top of his desk, crossing one foot over the other. "I've borrowed so much money against our house that I don't think we have enough equity to get anything out of it."

Clark pondered that for a moment. "I hope everything will work for the best for you and your children."

"I'm not thinking about my *children*," Smith snapped. "With the way they treat me, they'd better not ask me for a *thing*. And if Morgan wants to make sure she's all right, she'd better take that promotion." Smith turned to the green-eyed man, sneering as his gaze landed on the man's flat mid-section. Something Smith hadn't had in years. "How are *your* kids?"

"They're doing well. We're having dinner at The Melting Pot restaurant tonight."

Smith scanned Clark's ivory face, trying to detect the slightest clue that would reveal the man was as treacherous as himself. "You know you'll really have your hands full. Cloverdale's the third-largest project here in Charlotte."

"Yeah, I know. I've read the report."

Smith folded his hands and placed them behind his head as he leaned back in the chair. "I'm going to give you a little heads up on this *low-life* neighborhood. There are 120 apartments that house over 800 tenants, scattered over several acres of land."

"My report said only 550 tenants."

Smith's eyes narrowed. "You can throw that report away," he said. "The office manager doesn't have an accurate count of how many people live over here. The tenants don't tell Floyd when they allow their friends, boyfriends, or girlfriends and other family members to live with them. If you ask me, I think people like to *freeload* off project people. And I think project people freeload off middle-class folks like you and me."

"What about the monthly tenant reports? That should give an accurate update."

Smith's lips curled into a thin line. "I don't think you heard me. Nobody's trying to keep up with these hoodlums." Smith bellowed with laughter, then leaned toward Clark, chest pressing against the brown wooden desk. "When Floyd completes those monthly reports, he only keys in the tenants' names that are on the housing application. Sometimes he cross-references the names of the children who come to the community recreational center." Smith tapped his ink pen on the desk. "Floyd's not trying to move that big fat beer belly too much," he said, roaring with laughter.

"What about the yearly update reports?"

A door slammed in the hallway. Smith paused before he spoke. "Do you honestly think Floyd's gonna knock on every door and ask the tenants how many people are living in their apartments? These tenants never come to meetings and Floyd doesn't pressure them." Smith snickered. "Floyd's the laziest man alive; he figures if household members aren't causing any problems, then there's no need for him to worry about what goes on behind closed doors. He leaves the real problems to us."

Clark propped his right foot on his left knee.

Smith giggled and added, "And I don't blame him."

Clark shook his head, glancing at the piled-up newspapers and magazines in the corners. "What about your *officers'* monthly reports?" He stretched out his legs. "Officers Jenkins and Price should have an accurate update."

Smith peered at the white clock with large red numbers on the wall. He frowned, ignoring Clark's implications. "Seems like you'll have your hands full when you come on board, especially with the traffic flow of hustlers and prostitutes on The Hill." Smith snickered. "Don't waste your time cleaning up that spot. As soon as you arrest those folks, they'll be back before you sit down to eat dinner."

Clark shifted his butt on the hard wooden chair. "Why's it called The Hill?"

Smith turned opening the tan blinds. "You see that bald field all the way over there." Clark stood, glancing out the window. "The grass has been trampled on so much it refuses to grow. But if you're over there you can see when someone's approaching the area." Smith tapped his fingers on the glass. "It's higher than everywhere else. That's why they call it The Hill. It's hard for cops to trap the people because it's a large open space that leads to several alleys, abandoned buildings, woods and a creek."

Gunshots fired. Clark flinched, bumping into Smith's desk. Smith closed his blinds and turned in his seat.

"Sit down," Smith grunted. "The hustlers on The Hill like to fire their guns in the air. I think they get a thrill out of that, or perhaps they're trying to intimidate the addicts."

Clark slowly sat back down. "I think we need to go check it out. Somebody could be hurt."

Smith almost burst the seam on his shirt from laughing. "You better buy yourself a pair of good running shoes if you plan on chasing these folks. I remember when you were nothing but a young underdog, trying to learn the ropes. How long ago was that?"

Clark's skin flushed a bright red as he stood. "Well, gotta get back to the folks at Livingston before they tear the place down. You know how old folks like to party. Say hi to Morgan," Clark said, closing the door.

Clark's form retreated up the concrete path leading away from Cloverdale. But the man stopped and bent down to speak to a little girl who ran up to him on the path.

Hopefully, the next time Smith saw Clark, the man would be attending Morgan's funeral.

Chapter 4

Two weeks later, Tiffany trudged into her back office carrying a pink insulated tote bag. She dreaded making the call that would confirm her place in the same room with her sister-in-law later that Friday evening.

Heather had hated her from the moment she laid eyes on Tiffany's small caramel frame, hazel eyes and shoulder-length black hair. But it wasn't the physical looks that created the tension. Tiffany's bond with her brother had been a bone of contention for his wife even before Tony made the grave error of asking the woman's hand in marriage. He could have done so much better. But what did she know? She was only his sister. But she was certain that Heather had manipulated her way into his heart. Heather went out of her way to become Tiffany's friend. After the wedding, Heather tried so many ways to break Tony's bond with Tiffany.

Pondering whether to eat now or after the call, she took out the lasagna Vance had prepared, then slipped the cordless phone off the cradle, dialed and was soon greeted by, "Good afternoon, Dr. Brown's Office."

"Hello, Mrs. Spinks," Tiffany replied. "He's expecting my call."

"How are you, Dr. Brown?"

"I'm doing well," she said. The old woman had never used her married name. "And what about yourself?"

"I can't complain. God is good all the time. Hold one minute, please. I'll connect you."

Gently pressing a slender finger on the stereo to silence the classical music, Tiffany closed her file cabinet with her left knee as Mrs. Spinks transferred the call. The walls of her office were adorned with eggshell paint that provided a perfect backdrop for the degrees from Bennett College and Duke Medical School. Behind her on the credenza, her certificates and

31

plaques from Cloverdale Community Center and The Safe Haven Outreach Program took a front seat.

The musty-sweet smell of lavender drifted in the air, giving her office a fresh, clean scent. The office was nice and cozy, a place within the heart of Brown-Carson Medical Associates where Tiffany could relax and hold private conversations without the listening ears of her talkative staff.

Moments later, a rich, radio-quality, baritone voice echoed on the other end. "Hello, Dr. Anthony Brown speaking."

"Tony, why are you trying to sound all professional?" she asked, laughing. "If only your patients knew the trash you talk about when playing Spades."

"What trash, girl?" He chuckled lightly. "I'm *Mr.* Professional."

"You know you hate to lose."

"Hey, cut that out, you're interrupting my date with a turkey sub," he said, chewing. "But I'll make a few minutes for you anytime—when you're not teasing me about cards. We're gonna whip your butt this time. We're not losing another Friday night card game."

"Whatever," she shot back, taking a bite of her lunch, which was a tad bit more upscale than her brother's. "I knew I'd catch you feeding your face. I'm feeding mine, too." Tiffany nodded to the petite nurse who walked in and placed a file on her desk, then she added, "Did you get some *practice* since last week?"

"Tiffany, you and that lawyer husband of yours were cheating. Lawyers always cheat. And now he's rubbing off on you."

"Come on. You know we beat you and Heather fair and square." Tiffany glanced at the pictures near the edge of her cherry wood desk. Her gaze fixated on a silver-framed photograph of Tony and his tiger-eyed, auburn-haired wife. "I can't help it if your wife can't play Spades. She can't cook or do laundry; I don't know why you married that heifer in the first place."

"Don't go there," Tony said. "Speaking of Heather, I have to call her in a few minutes."

Confused by the sudden fluctuation in his voice, she asked, "Why, what's up?"

Tony sighed. "She's been nagging lately. She wants me to stop volunteering with the kids in Cloverdale. She practically insisted I stop taking Carmen and Anthony Jr. with me."

"What!" Tiffany's lasagna froze midway to her mouth. "Doesn't she realize the impact you have on those kids?" She clamped her mouth shut, quickly reining in her temper. After counting to five, she said, "Heather came from an upper-middle-class family and there are some things she'll never relate to."

"She thinks the things that kids in Cloverdale are exposed to will somehow influence our children."

Tiffany glanced behind her at the family portrait of Tony, his *beloved* wife and their children. Tony's tall frame, handsomely chiseled features and smooth chocolate skin glowed with a health that belied their poor upbringing. His pearly white teeth had a brilliance of their own, but his eyes, always so moist and alive, had begun to take on a dull glow when it came to his wife. Tiffany totally understood. If she were married to a conceited, overbearing, nagging witch, she'd feel a little lifeless too.

"Are you serious?" Tiffany asked. "How did she arrive at that assumption? I guess she read that in one of her *pediatric* magazines," she said, not bothering to hide her sarcasm. "You need to tell your wife that everything in life is not picture perfect. I know she wants the best for my niece and nephew, but raising them with blindfolds will cause more harm than good."

She tried to continue eating. "I think your kids need to see both aspects of life. We did and we came out just fine."

Tony cleared his throat. Uh oh, more bad news on the way. What a way to start lunch. She punched the stereo, putting the music back on, but turning the volume down some.

"That's not all," he said resuming his meal, even though Tiffany had now lost her appetite and pushed the lasagna away. "She doesn't like the fact that I still hang out with a few old buddies over there. She thinks they're all bad news. It's not like I hang out with those clowns every week, maybe once or twice a month." Tony sighed softly between bites. "I have to keep up with what's going on in the hood from time to time."

"Somebody needs to keep tabs on Cloverdale." Tiffany glanced out her window as the roar of an airplane swept over the medical center. "There's too much going on over there that goes unheard. Too many people look up to us and need our help. If you stop going, that's going to send the wrong message, a message that we don't care."

"You're right," Tony replied and Tiffany imagined him biting his bottom lip as he did whenever he was worried. "I saw Sergeant Smith the other day."

Tiffany tensed at the mention of the man's name. Her stomach rumbled.

"I was tutoring at the community center. I could feel his eyes piercing on the back of my head." Tony's voice had taken on a hard edge. "When I got up for some water, he stared at me as if he wanted me to be intimidated. I stared right back. I wanted him to know that I'm no longer that scared, little boy he forced to—"

"Forced to what?" Tiffany demanded, her blood running cold.

Seconds passed like hours before he simply said, "I don't know why mama won't move."

Ah, the age-old question.

"She told me she didn't want to leave her friends." The subject of Tony and Smith was closed and she kicked herself for her impatience. "We have to do something about that, Tony. It doesn't make sense for us to live in nice houses and drive decent cars when mama's still living in the projects."

"Tiff, what *can* we do? She refuses to move. I'd pick her up personally and cart her off, the television and blender included if I thought it would work."

Tiffany gazed out of the window beside the large bookshelf. Clouds gathered beyond the horizon.

Finally, Tony broke the silence by saying, "Let's go talk to her sometime next week. She's gonna be busy this weekend with the bake sales for the church."

"I'm all for that." Tiffany grinned as she squared her shoulders. Her little brother always gave in to her wishes. "And since I told you not to marry that woman, now you'll have to deal with that mess too."

"Girl, is that all you have to say?" he quipped, mouth full of food once again. "I know you're over there rolling your eyes and swirling your neck."

She giggled because she had done just that.

"Come on, Tiff, help me out."

"Personally, I don't see anything wrong with you mentoring the kids or hanging out with your friends." Tiffany swiveled in the burgundy leather chair, landing at a better view of her small office. "But I'm not trying to interfere with your marriage. You know Heather gets mad when we do things together. That's why she always insists that our weekly card games take place at your house."

"Well, that shouldn't be much of a problem, right?"

"Wouldn't be a problem if the woman could cook."

"Don't start with *that* again!" he growled. "I don't know what's wrong with her. She thinks I spend too much time with you." Tony exhaled deeply. "Anyway, how's the outreach program coming along?"

"It's going okay." Tiffany stood, stretching before perching her butt on the edge of the desk. "I'm glad the outreach program is only seven blocks from Cloverdale. A lot of girls from the community have joined."

"Hey! Why don't you come to the community center and recruit even more kids? I know the boys would enjoy the new game room and the girls would love to take part in the self-esteem, hygiene and prevention programs you teach."

She focused on the grains on top of the cherrywood desk. Silence streamed through the phone.

"Tiffany, are you there?"

"Yes," she whispered. "You know I'm not going to the community center. You can tell the girls to come to the outreach program."

"Tiffany," he began, "we need to talk about some things."

Fear stormed through Tiffany's body like a hurricane. Butterflies swarmed the empty areas of her stomach as her hands began to shake. Would he question her again about what happened that summer before she went off to college? Well, it seemed that he had some secrets of his own. Why should she be the one to break the silence? Why couldn't she get some answers, too?

He urged softly, "We can do it one day next week . . . ."

Tiffany inhaled sharply before saying, "Don't be late tonight, Tony. You know how Heather gets. I've never seen anyone as slow as she is. I practically had to twist her arm to have dinner at my place last time." Then she added slyly, "You know we're going to put a hurtin' on that tail."

"So now you're speaking for your husband, too?" he shot back. "And is that a threat or a promise?"

"You figure it out."

"We'll bring hot wings and wine," Tony said and she could imagine his full lips spread into a warm smile. "And *you* can tell Vance to leave the lawsuits in his office and bring his best game to the table." Tony chuckled, a sound that always put Tiffany at ease.

"Hush, Tony. We'll see you later."

"I'm going to buy a new deck of cards before we get there. I think you and Vance have those cards rigged."

"Whatever," she shot back, twirling a blue globe paperweight in her soft hands. "We beat you guys with your own deck of cards before. Don't expect things to be different this time."

"If you say so," snapped Tony.

Soft taps landed on Tiffany's office door.

"Tony, I have to go. I'll talk to you later," said Tiffany while hanging up.

"Come in," Tiffany said in a calm tone.

Nurse Petrina strolled through the door. "Excuse me, Dr. Brown-Carson," Nurse Petrina said in a settled tone. "A lady name Karen called for you. She didn't leave her last name. She said you would know who she was." Nurse Petrina cleared her throat. "She said she's Christy's mother. Christy is the patient you saw last week."

"Yes, I know who she is," Tiffany said. "What did Karen want?"

Nurse Petrina's nearly connected. "She wanted me to tell you that Christy was taken to a psychiatric hospital. She said the doctor told her Christy had a severe panic attack from thinking about her rape. She also said Christy's been having nightmares." Nurse Petrina paused. "Karen told me to tell you that Christy has been diagnosed with PTSD. I figured she was talking about Posttraumatic Stress Disorder."

Tiffany's heart slammed against her chest. "Thank you, Nurse Petrina. I will follow up with her."

"You are welcome." Nurse Petrina said walking out of the office.

Tiffany leaned back in her chair, closing her eyes for a few seconds. Unsettling memories of Christy's injured flesh flashed before Tiffany. The vivid memories pierced her soul causing every neuron in her brain to fire off.

The thought of Christy being in a psychiatric hospital caused an unsettling feeling to storm through Tiffany. The agony of knowing a *monster* had raped Christy and now she's suffering from the traumatic experience, sparked a fierce side in Tiffany.

Tiffany had no doubt who may have raped Christy. She had no proof but was destined to find it. She dashed out of her office faster than a rocket. She was tired of crime being overlooked in Cloverdale. Tired of evidence mysteriously missing. Her soul shook at the mere thought that people in Cloverdale were bound by fear and secrets. Guilt clenched her stomach. She had her share of secrets. She was determined to put an end to the madness. Even if it meant risking her life or freedom.

Chapter 5

Smith had done his rounds for that Friday midday and still had to tie up a few loose ends before meeting Morgan later that evening. He grabbed his groin thinking of how fulfilled his last sexual encounter had made him. Who needed a wife? The projects provided him with any outlet he needed.

Rocking in his chair, he frowned thinking of his wife, his life and being fed up with just making ends meet. He couldn't ask for a raise since he had reached the salary cap for his position, creating a need to find other ways—even if it meant someone's death. Especially Morgan's.

Smith and his wife were middle-class people—and middle-class wasn't good enough. He saw how other sergeants, schoolteachers and social workers were living and knew deep down that he was better than most middle-class families. After a quick glance at the potholes in the streets, piled-up debris, broken swings at the playground, and the overall impoverished appearance of Cloverdale, he certainly knew he was better than the project people.

His thoughts turned to Morgan again. Poison would be too risky; chemicals would show up in the autopsy.

A small stab of disappointment pierced his mind as each plan was shot down. There must be a way to bring in some extra cash.

Some officers from another county had paid some project kids in their precinct to steal cars. They gave the kids a little cash for their services, but that was too risky for Smith. In this area, there were too many eyes, too many loose lips. Most of all, he didn't like sharing money.

Maybe he could get an addict to rob a convenience store. But that wouldn't be enough cash. What about getting a strung-out junky from one of the alleys to rob a bank or an armored car? Nah, too dangerous. Addicts were too unpredictable. He had learned that back in the summer of '95. Kids who had a sliver of hope were much easier to manipulate than addicts. Like Tony . . . like David . . . like Tiffany.

Now a chop shop could work. He could get some of the Cloverdale boys to get cars for him. Then his cousin at the DMV could help. Josh knew someone who could change the VIN numbers and alter the serial numbers, then Smith would have someone paint the cars. But then he would have to give Josh some of the profit, too.

Smith sat at the brown wooden desk twirling a pencil and gazing out of the office window. Loud music resonated into his office. He opened his blinds. A nice, clean Mercedes drove down the street. The car had to be about two years old, but it was in better condition than Smith's Buick. The white woman drove down the street with two half-breed children sitting in the back as if taking a joyride. Then she parked in front of the community center. The pencil snapped between his thick fingers.

Smith snatched down the blinds and sneered. "Someone in the ghetto driving a nice car? How can she afford a car like that? Who is she?" He would definitely find out. Smith could find out anything that went on in Cloverdale. Her parents should be ashamed for allowing her to live in the ghetto.

Smith turned on his small radio, then turned from the window, pissed because Morgan wouldn't fight for the higher-paying position. She was qualified, but not interested in the promotion. Smith insisted his wife meet with her supervisor, but she refused. She was an easy going, calm and humble woman, which made him sick to his stomach. That promotion would've put the extra dough in his pockets. But Morgan was the type of woman who let things be and always said, "God knows what's best for me."

Well, Morgan could meet her God a lot sooner than she planned.

The rain began to ease and people streamed out of their apartments. Children ran through the run-down park and crackheads staggered out of the nearby alley. He hoped one of the addicts would hound or tease the children. He could use a good laugh.

Smith slumped down in his chair, propped his feet on his desk and flipped open the insurance brochure once again. He glanced up from the brochure looking out to the alley, then back again.

His thin pink lips spread into a sly smile. He walked out of his office with a concrete decision the moment he gaped at the people in the alley. He was destined to find a *prey* roaming in Cloverdale. Consequences were the last thing on his mind. The precious years spent with Morgan slurped on their way down the drain—along with any consideration for their marriage or her life.

Chapter 6

Two hours later, Tony had finally pulled Derrick's wisdom tooth. They had to put the big guy to sleep to get it over and done. But even before they started, Derrick still dug in his heels, refusing to release his death grip on Tony's jacket. When Melinda yelled at him, threatening that he wouldn't get any nookie until the tooth was gone, dental services were a done deal. Oh, the power of the—

"Good afternoon, Dr. Brown's Office, how may I help you?"

Tony checked his watch before turning to face his assistant. Mrs. Spinks, with salt and pepper gray hair, unblemished skin to die for and a wide, welcoming smile, had been in his office since he opened the doors four years ago.

"Hello, Heather," she said, locking a mischievous gaze with him. "How are

you?"

Tony vigorously shook his head, waving off the call.

Mrs. Spinks grinned, eyes glittering. "And . . . how are the kids?"

Tony glared at Mrs. Spinks, daring her to defy his wishes. First Derrick, then Mr. Ben Lockett a sixty-five-year-old who cried and shrieked holy murder as his teeth were pulled, knowing that five shots of Novocaine meant he couldn't feel a thing—and now Heather? A man could use a break!

"He'll be available in ——"

Tony flashed both hands twice.

". . . twenty minutes." Mrs. Spinks leaned back in her chair, lips spreading into a small sly smile. "Yes, it was nice speaking with you, too."

His assistant placed the phone on the cradle, a smug expression on her youthful face. "You owe me."

Tony waved her off. "That's your job, woman."

"Not to lie for you, but I'll give you a heads up. You forgot to buy tickets for the kids to see the circus."

Tony grimaced smacking a hand to his forehead. His wife had reminded him *three* times. He was in deep trouble. Twenty minutes of break time wouldn't be long enough.

"Thank you," he said, scurrying off to the next patient.

Exactly eighteen minutes later, he strolled into his office past the lounge, examination rooms and the X-ray room as the phone rang.

He snatched it up. "Hello, Dr. Brown speaking."

"Anthony *Mason* Brown, why didn't you call me?" Heather's normally soft, mellow voice came out in an angry rush. "I left you several messages. I wanted us to have lunch together."

Tony paused for a moment, knowing when Heather addressed him by his full name—upset wasn't even the word.

"Oh, I apologize, baby," he said softly, slipping into the black leather chair Tiffany had bought him when he first opened his practice. He smiled thinking about tonight's game. "I was talking to Tiffany and got side-tracked."

"You can say *that* again," she snapped.

Tony slapped his forehead again. He realized he had made a huge mistake by the mere mention of his sister's name.

"You always get *side-tracked* when you talk to her."

"I apologize, baby."

"You need to set your priorities straight. You spend too much time talking to her and worrying about what's going on with her. You're a married man now. Act like one."

"Heather, slow down," Tony said, holding back a sigh. "We were trying to make arrangements for the card game. She still wants to have it at her house."

43

"I'm tired of going over to her house. She can come to *our* house."

Tony's gaze shifted toward his ceiling. "The last card game was at our house and the *three* before that."

"There's nothing wrong with having it at our house again!" she shrieked. "What's wrong with our house? We don't have cooties or roaches. I don't like traveling to Snobville just to please her." Heather let out a long slow breath, obviously trying to reign in her temper. He wondered how long it would last. "I wanted to have lunch with you today, but I see *now* that you were too busy babysitting your sister again."

Tony leaned back in the chair, propping his feet on the edge of the long black desk. "Come on, Heather—"

"Don't come on me, Anthony *Brown*. I'm tired of this mess. Every time I turn around, you're doing something for Tiffany. She's married now and has her own man. You're not her father or her husband. I need you more than she does."

A sudden flash of anger shot from Tony's head to his heart. "Tiffany and I are close. We have a strong bond and there's nothing anyone can do about that. It's how we survived . . . ."

A quick glance at the edge of his desk showed a photo of Heather's long wavy auburn hair, greenish-brown eyes and olive complexion. He instantly thought of happier times—like the day they were married. Maybe that had been the *only* happy time.

"You have a wife and children now. You need to make a choice."

"A choice?" he said, snapping out of the past. "I'm not choosing between you and my sister. That's crazy. I love you and you know that I'm a good man. I take care of you and the kids."

"You need to show me more love then."

Tony brushed a lint ball off the tip of his black shoes. "I'm giving you my all."

"Yeah?" She huffed heavily in the phone. "Well, I want the part that your sister gets."

Tony balled up the notes that held a previous message from his wife. For a split second, he thought about the good qualities Heather had. She was a loving, passionate mother for their children. Spending family time was a key factor in their marriage. Not to mention the numerous hours she spent doing charity work at the orphan centers. Tony often thought she pushed herself too much. And although a highly recommended pediatrician, she couldn't handle stress well. And she couldn't handle Tony too well, either, especially if she thought he would choose between the two women.

"I'm willing to do what it takes to keep peace in my home," he said, running a single hand through his short-cropped hair. "I made an honest mistake. I forgot to call you. If you want to eat lunch with me now, I'll come by there," he said, not bothering to mention that his stomach was already way past full and thinking of which patients he'd have to juggle to keep his wife in a decent mood.

Mrs. Spinks walked in. The smell of fluoride drifted into his office, mixing with the jasmine flowers that his wife placed on his desk. She tapped her wrist, signaling that patients were waiting.

"There's *no* need," Heather said in a petulant tone. "I can't believe you forgot to call me because you were talking to your *sister*. You always forget to do stuff when your mind's preoccupied with Tiffany."

Tony sighed, growing weary of the same argument that happened several times a week. Given a choice: a sister who was loving and supportive, or a wife who nagged so much that his hard-on didn't even want to swim Nookie Lake anymore—love and support won hands down. A man could always handle lack of *nookie*—one way or another.

"Look, I've already apologized. There's no need for us to have a disagreement," he said while thinking—*again.* "You know I don't like to

45

argue, baby. I have too much respect to raise my voice but you're *really* beginning to piss me off."

Her voice trilled to a high pitch. "Piss *you* off? *I'm* the one who should be pissed."

"Listen, Heather. We'll talk about it when we get home."

She inhaled sharply. "What about the card game?"

Tony propped his wide hand on his forehead. "We'll cancel it. You can't speak a civil word to Tiffany anyway."

"Oh no," she shot back. "I don't want your *sister* saying I was the reason we didn't come to her house."

Tony shot straight up in his chair. "So, don't spoil the mood. And if you'd stop being so mean to Tiffany maybe we could focus and win a game." No wonder they had hit a losing streak. Heather was becoming a rabbit's foot—an unlucky one. "You know I love you. I promise we'll have the game at our place next time."

A slight pause greeted him on the other end.

Tony sighed. "Heather, are you there?"

"Yes."

Tony paused before he spoke, the tapping noise of Mrs. Spinks' shoes as she passed his office signaled that she would come in and yank him out of the chair next time. "Baby, I don't know what happened, but you and Tiffany used to be so close. I'm trying my best, Heather. I love both of you."

"It seems like you love her more than me," she whined, grating on Tony's nerves.

Tony slumped in his chair. Realizing it was a lost cause.

Heather's voice lowered and became soft and sexy. "I need you, Anthony, more than you could imagine. You're the only person who has shown me real love."

Tony rubbed his temples gently as a throb of pain pushed its way through, something that happened almost every time his wife called him at work.

"I don't think you have respect for my feelings."

"How can you say that?" he asked softly. "I've bent over backward to please you. I love you."

"I know you do, Tony," she said, conceding just a little. "But you spend too much time caring about your sister. If I didn't know any better, I'd think you all—"

"You *think* we what!" snapped Tony. Anger shot through him like a bullet. "We'll talk about this when I get home!" He clamped his lips, holding back his anger. "But if you're implying what I think you are, we won't talk at all."

"Okay."

"What about the card game?" Tony said, jotting down a note to pick up two packs of cards. "Can we do it at Tiffany and Vance's place tonight?"

"Yes, Anthony," she said, sighing heavily. "But I don't want to stay all night. And—"

Mrs. Spinks burst into his office. "Excuse me, Dr. Brown, you have an emergency call."

Tony pulled the phone from his ear, staring at her.

"Your sister ran out of her office an hour ago and no one has seen her since."

Tony leaped out of his chair, hanging up the phone.

Chapter 7

Friday afternoon, the sun beamed down on the Cloverdale community, shining a light in the darkest secluded areas. Smith had roamed the impoverished streets for the past two hours, still searching for the right man. Since he left the alley earlier that day, he'd experienced a run of bad luck. He couldn't find a single addict to serve his purpose. The two he asked were afraid to carry out the task, but he made sure they wouldn't tell a soul about his plans. Some were too stoned to even listen and others were too jittery to stay still long enough to do anything but stare. "Forget this, I'll do it myself," Smith mumbled.

Smith stood, thrusting his chair against the back wall. A quick glance at his watch showed it was now after one. Officers Jenkins and Price were still patrolling the nearby streets and would probably be near the used-car lot and The Hill. He walked over to the window scanning the area. "Where is a good dopehead when you need one?"

Smith stormed out of his office, slamming the door behind him, pissed off and dreading his dinner with Morgan. As he trudged to the car, heated words coming from the alley behind a hair supply store signaled a fight was on the way. Smith ignored the commotion, refusing to go to anyone's rescue. Arguments were the usual thing for this drug-infected area. Hopping into his car, he cranked it up and inched away.

Two men shot out of the alley darting in front of him like bats out of hell. Jim Boy's pale white face had turned beet red; Jay Rock, a stocky Hispanic, was sprinting fast on his heels. Smith had given them citations for disorderly conduct last month. And they still managed to stay in trouble.

The two men ran as if a lion were on their tails, but the tall, skinny black man who chased them gained ground every time his gray sneakers hit the pavement. Smith didn't recognize him.

Why were they running from that puny guy? The two men could easily jump on the black man and beat him down, or at least knock some sense into him. The man didn't look stronger than a roach. Smith slowed the car and parked. He wanted to see somebody get pounded into a pulp. Now that would bring a smile to his face.

Jim Boy and Jay Rock hurdled over the small wooden fence, leaping over the rubbish on the ground and scurried up the street as if the man chasing them were some type of monster.

Smith scanned the alley. The spot where he parked provided a wide-open view. They ran past the patrol car—again.

He slumped down, watching the events unfold as though he had pulled into a drive-in movie theatre. As they moved further away, he inched down Harris Boulevard, hoping no one would signal him to stop the fight.

The fearful men ran around the playground, trying to dodge the wide-eyed black guy. When they moved left, he moved left. They ran right and the man shifted right. Jay Rock gripped the hood of a car and tried propelling himself over the vehicle. That didn't work.

Another quick maneuver trapped the two men in a corner. The tall, skinny man clenched his fists, rolled his neck from side to side, then paced around his opponents as if preparing for a heavyweight boxing match. He lunged forward, tackling both men to the ground—then whipped the living fire out of them.

Smith jerked forward. "You've got to be kidding me!" he shouted to the men.

"Fight back! Who *is* that guy?"

The children sitting on top of the monkey bars pointed to the men. Smith made a quick U-turn, whipped into the parking lot trying for a better view of the action-packed event. It had always been a kick for him to see addicts fight, break into tenant's apartments, or steal garments off clotheslines. When the tenants chased them away with sticks and bats, it was even funnier. Yes, Cloverdale was a hotbed of excitement.

Smith laughed as the man kicked, slapped and punched Jim Boy and Jay Rock. The fight had definitely become one-sided.

"Get up and fight, you cowards!"

The two boys stretched out on the ground as if they were dead. No one would call the police or the ambulance. Addicts would fight today and be best friends tomorrow.

With every passing moment, Smith became more impressed with the man's boldness, strength and cockiness. The man reached into the pockets of the two men, then quickly shoved something in his own pocket. Was he an addict or a hustler? Experience had taught him that both had amazing speed and strength when it came to running away from the police or fighting for their dope.

Smith left the patrol car, following the man back into the alley. By the time he spotted the scrawny man, he had sat down in the alley, clutching his pocket with eyes completely closed. The man's dry, cracked lips spread into a goofy smile as he enjoyed a few puffs of crack. Smith stood with his back to the corner.

The strong acrid smell of urine rushed into his nose, causing him to choke. The alley resembled a disaster zone. Broken glass, chairs and paper were everywhere. The windows in the nearby abandoned buildings were shattered and the doors were cracked and hung off the hinges. The fire escapes were rusted and bent.

Smith inched closer, scanning left then right, making sure the alley was still empty. He stepped on beer cans, cigarette lighters and glass.

The man's eyes popped open just before Smith reached him. Shoving the clear pipe into his pocket, he kept his beady eyes on the sergeant. "What do you want," he growled, wiping his runny nose with the back of a single hand. "I ain't bothering you or nobody."

Smith squatted. The man pressed his back further into the brick wall.

"Somebody told me that you attacked some guys a few minutes ago."

The man grimaced, keeping his gaze on Smith. "So, what?"

"I'm following up on a complaint."

He squinted. "Who made the complaint? Did those two fools snitch on me?"

"No, the tenants over on Harris Boulevard put a call in."

"Oh, I was getting ready to say . . . ." The man glared at Smith. "A tenant called you this quick? Which one?"

Smith cringed. The man was a lot smarter than he looked. "Come on, man, I can't tell you that."

"So, now what?" he said, lifting his chin defiantly. "You gonna arrest me or what? I ain't afraid to go to jail."

"Calm down." Smith frowned. "Now that depends."

"On what?"

Smith peered up and down the alley.

"Man, take me to jail," he said, thrusting his scrawny arms out, waiting to be cuffed. "I don't have time to sit here and listen to your bull." He trailed his brittle, dirty nails up and down his ashy arm, scratching. "If you're going to arrest me then go ahead." Then he peered down the alley. "'Sides, I don't want people to think I'm a snitch. If they see me talking to you, that ain't a good thing. So, go ahead and pull out your shiny little bracelets."

Smith felt a small stab of disappointment. The situation was not going as planned. "Wait a minute," he said, reaching out to the glaring man. "Tell me what happened first. Maybe I can help you."

"Stop the *bull*! You ain't concerned about nobody 'round here. So, keep your little pep talk to yourself and take me to jail." Then he had the nerve to smile. "At least in jail, I can take a shower, get a free meal and sleep on a clean bed."

Now a shower Smith could agree with. He scanned the man's pockmarked face. "What's your name?"

"Why? If you take me to jail, I'll tell you my name." The man's dark brown hands lowered a little. "But if you're going to jive talk me then forget it."

Smith could feel a prime opportunity slipping away. "Man, why do you want to go to jail so bad?"

"Man, please take me to jail," he insisted, lowering his hands to his sides. "Maybe I can get some real help."

Those words were like a knife in Smith's gut. An addict wanting help? Definitely not the type of man needed for the job. "What kind of help do you need? What're you on?"

"Crack and I shoot up a little heroin every now and then."

Music to Smith's ears. "What's your name?"

The man's jaws slowly parted. "June Bug."

"Man, I hate to tell you," Smith said, gawking over the man's ashy face, "but crack and heroin? You really have it bad."

"So, did I pass the test for jail?"

"What do you mean?"

"I attacked them," he said, shifting nervously back and forth. "Now, take me to jail. I'm not about to sit in this hot alley and talk to you all day."

Smith glanced at the wall. Graffiti covered almost every inch. "Before you go to jail, do you want to take one last puff?"

June Bug whirled to face him. "Wait a minute now. You mean to tell me you'll let me take another puff before you take me to jail?"

"Yeah. I don't care."

June Bug paused as the sound of sirens roared in the air. His body jerked as if he were about to jump up and run. Then he relaxed. "Man, are you high, too?"

"No, but I have plenty of dope stashed away for a lucky guy."

Wrinkles formed on June Bug's forehead and his eyebrows drew in. "A lucky guy? What's that supposed to mean?"

"For real." A small grimace unfolded on Smith's face. "I have lots of dope."

"Man, you don't have to say it that way. I get your drift." June Bug licked his dark crusty lips. "So, what does a *lucky guy* have to do to get that dope?"

"He has to do something very special for me."

Those lips curved into a frown. "Like what, man?"

"Whatever I tell him to do."

June Bug backed up against the wall. "Man, I'm not like that . . . so, if you're trying to get your groove on, you got to go to the other end of the alley. Or up on The Hill."

"Fool," Smith spat. "I'm not talking about screwing you."

"So, what you talking about, then?"

Smith reached into his pocket, pulling out a small piece of crack. Something he kept for desperate times, like the need for getting information from his snitches or a little head from a local prostitute.

June Bug's lips twitched and his eyes widened to the size of saucers. "You gonna give me that?"

Smith jiggled the small plastic bag in front of him. "Yeah, you can have plenty more if you do something special for me."

"Man, you keep on saying *something special*," he said without taking his eyes off the little white rock in the plastic bag. "What are you talking about?"

Smith smiled, leaned toward June Bug and whispered, "Murder."

Chapter 8

Tony sped down Central Avenue in his silver Lincoln Navigator, heading toward the place where his mother still lived. No amount of talking to her about leaving Cloverdale Assisted Housing Community would change her mind.

Two hours had passed since Nurse Patterson told Tony that Tiffany yelled she was going to Cloverdale, leaving all of her patients behind. He had to find Tiffany.

Tony and Tiffany had struggled to escape from the steady rise of crime in Cloverdale and from the corruption that came from sources that were supposed to protect them. But that one summer when he had to help Tiffany disappear had totally strengthened their bond. His promise to his father as the old man lay dying of cancer, had been that he would go to college, protect his mother and sister and be a good husband to his wife and kids. Though Tiffany had never opened up to tell him what happened that summer, Tony knew he had failed her then. He would never fail his sister again.

Tony had fond memories of Cloverdale, but he remembered when Sergeant Smith began to patrol the area, things had become a bit troubling. Tony could feel hate streaming from the man's pores. One summer, in particular, the trouble had turned into a nightmare . . .

Spring had almost come to an end. Summer, with its grilled hot dogs, the Good Humor Ice Cream Man and kids playing in the sand-filled park or enjoying a good spray from the fire hydrant, was right around the corner. On the last day of school, a bunch of students from Cloverdale stood around teasing one another at the bus stop.

Traffic had slowed to a near crawl. Squeals of delight flooded the air as little girls tried to run from boys who were trying to steal a kiss. Tony Brown was one of them. Blessed with a creamy, chocolate complexion and light brown eyes, an athletic sculptured body and pearly white teeth, girls were always coming on to him. But he preferred the ones he had to chase.

Tony tutored at the Cloverdale Community Center. He was a good student and always kept his nose clean. Almost everyone in the neighborhood was proud of his accomplishments in the classroom and on the basketball court and they knew he was bound for college. All he needed was a scholarship from Wake Forest University and his future would all be set.

Tony walked to the corner of Harris Boulevard and Albemarle Road. Smiles broke out on faces with hues ranging from golden, redbone, to dark brown. Book bags and notebooks were now a thing of the past.

"Hey Tony, wait up."

Tony turned to his cousin. "Man, you'd better keep up. You know Mr. Pete will leave us if we're not there on time."

"That old, grouchy, white man?" David said, a frown on his thin lips. "He'd better not leave without me or I'll whip his lily-white ass."

Tony looked at him, laughing, "Didn't stop him last time, did it?"

David fell in step beside Tony, his wide mouth crinkling with displeasure. "They know they should've gotten us a black bus driver. Mr. Pete doesn't like coming into the projects as if we'd do something to his old wrinkled behind."

"Yeah, his main goal seems to be getting in and out of the projects as fast as possible. If he could get away with it, he'd make us jump on while the bus was still rolling."

"If he got paid by the head, then I betcha half of us wouldn't have to run every morning. He'd wait as long as it took." David ran a finger through his faded black hair. His honey brown complexion, muscular body and sparkling dark brown eyes could be seen from a distance. "Remember that time I had to walk to school and my mama came up to the office and pitched a fit?"

Tony nodded just before they reached the crowd playing cards.

"The old grouch said I was lying and then said that there was no one at that stop."

"And they believed him, too."

"Yeah, like twenty-five of us were wrong." Tony shook his head. "That old buzzard."

David's head dropped to his chest. "I saw June Bug smoking crack in the alley yesterday."

Tony exhaled slowly. "Man, I don't know why your daddy will not get off those drugs. My mother can't sleep at night worrying about him. He's the only brother that she has."

David slowly lifted his head and established eye contact with Tony. The sun shone on his face. "I don't think there's any hope for him." The twinkles in his eyes vanished. "I think Star is following in his footsteps."

Tony placed a hand on his cousin's shoulder. "David, I can't believe that your sister is ..."

"That's what I heard. I've never seen her on The Hill. But people keep telling me." David clenched his hands. "Her teachers said she's been skipping a lot of classes."

Tony asked, "How? She gets on the bus with us every morning."

David's lips parted, but no words sprang forth.

Light blue clouds formed a massive layer in the sky. The sun moved gracefully to find a spot to shine through.

Tony and David joined their friends near the stop. Some chattered about their plans to hang out at the community center during the summer while other kids streaming in from the top of The Hill created a long line for the bus.

Tony wiped his forehead with the back of a single hand. It was a hot day in June—so hot that he could've fried breakfast right there on the concrete. He scanned the area, searching for his older sister. He had left the apartment only minutes before she walked out, but she still hadn't made it to the stop. If she didn't come soon, he'd be late for school. He had no intention of letting her walk to school by herself, no matter how grown she thought she was.

He turned back to the dice game in progress. The dice whipped into Devin's pocket. David reached out, claiming the cash on the ground. Three of the other guys stood. Tony's head whipped around just in time to see a black Mustang pull up to the curb.

"Hey, don't take those dice under hostage," snapped Hilton as the sun beamed on his chestnut brown oval face.

"Man, hush," Tony said. "We're surprised you haven't left yet to go on your *summer* vacation," Tony chuckled. It was routine for Hilton to leave Cloverdale every summer to go to camp and return a few days before school started back.

"I'm leaving today. I wanted to shoot some dice with my *homies* before I left." Hilton giggled while looking at his watch, flexing his arm as his biceps protruded. "I've got to go," Hilton said while briskly walking away toward a nearby bus stop where other kids had gathered.

"I think he's on steroids," Tony chuckled. "None of us have muscles like him."

"Shut up, Tony. You know he does pushups like he's preparing for some type of *muscle man* contest," Devin laughed.

"I wish I had muscles like that," muffled David glancing at his flimsy arms.

"Why does he always go to that other bus stop?" Devin sneered.

"He likes talking with Blake." Tony blurted. "They're cool."

"Blake stutters a lot," David said. "But he is cool."

"I know," muffled Tony. "He's in *love* with Hope but she ignores him." Tony laughed.

Devin chuckled. "I know . . . 'cause I'm trying to *push up* on her."

David's lips round lips curled into a sneer. "She's not thinking about you," spatted David, gently shoving Devin's right shoulder. "She doesn't pay nobody no attention. So, Blake is wasting his time."

"Well, Blake thinks she's going to be his wife one day," chuckled Tony. "He knows sign language. I think that's cool." Tony scratched his head. "He said he's going to find a cure one day for himself and work with other kids like him. He wants to be a doctor."

"Maybe he can find a cure to help Hope stop being so nervous." Sighed David. "I've seen her in class shaking a few times for no reason."

"Yeah, me too," Devin mumbled. "She tugs on her hair. I think that's why she has that small *bald* spot in the front of her head."

"Come on guys. *Don't* pick on her." Tony blurted, quickly recalling how Tiffany shared with him the troubling stories about Hope's *cracked-out* mother beating on her. "She can cook *really* good. My mama is teaching her. She wants to be a famous chef one day." Tony smiled. "I wish she would teach my sister how to cook. Tiffany will burn water." Tony laughed.

The window lowered. Sergeant Smith's gaze, sharp and intense, swept across the young men now crowded in a circle. After parking near the mailboxes, Smith strolled past the fire hydrant, dumpster and broken-down cars. His normally pale skin flushed pink with heat. Curly blonde hair, small piercing blue eyes and cleft chin combined with an unfriendly face. His pungent cologne lingered in the air for miles after he walked past. The man must have drowned in the stuff every morning.

Nearby, conversations lowered and fizzled out, suddenly sprinting children found their legs unable to move. The more anxious peered down the street as though wishing the bus would hurry. All turned, watching the tall, slender-built man walk towards them.

One teenager in the center of Tony's crowd murmured, "What's he doing here so early?"

Everyone focused on the black uniform and the man who wore it as if the clothes alone gave him authority to do evil. And the man could do evil. And there was nothing they could do about it.

Sergeant Smith had a way of intimidating people with his height, his deep voice and the fact that his badge did give him some type of authority. But it wasn't the type that the city paid him to have. Some tenants in Cloverdale were fearful of him, but he had a way of making some of them feel that only the criminally minded need to fear him. How wrong they were.

Smith shrugged, popped his knuckles, then gripped the nightstick holstered in his waistband. As he sauntered forward, he gawked at the students, then to the place where the money had been on the ground and then up to Devin's hands now stuffed deep into his jeans pockets. Keeping his gaze on the students and their hands, he came closer, watching everyone suspiciously to see if any drugs hit the ground or to scope out the instant they decided to take off running.

"Tony," Smith snapped. "Come over here for a minute."

Tony stepped out, but turned to his comrades, whispering, "Man, I hope he's not coming over here to harass us this early in the morning." He inched close enough to Smith to hold a conversation, but far enough away to take flight if necessary.

"What are y'all doing, all huddled up like that?"

Tony glanced at one of the single dollar bills that had fluttered from David's hand and landed on the ground. "We're just playing cards and rolling some dice until the bus comes."

The officer flicked a glance to the group, then back to Tony. "I know y'all not playing for money."

"Now, you know better than that," Tony said as an uneasy chuckle left his throat. "We're just goofing around freebie style."

The tall, white man's stare lingered on the students. They stared back at him, recording every detail, ready to serve as witnesses if something happened to Tony. Everyone in the community was used to the police trying to harass them, so they stood still, each ready to jump in if necessary. Often that was the case.

Smith tilted his head and looked at the other boys. "All right then." After a pause, he said, "Who's that kid walking away?"

"Oh, that's Hilton," Tony said.

"Who's that fellow in the blue shirt?" Smith asked as if he was doing a roll call.

"David." Tony grinned at his cousin, whose lips silently moved as though he had said something to Devin. "He moved into the community about a month ago. He's in some of my classes." Tony wiped his clammy hand on the front of his red tee shirt. "I hang out with him a lot. We play basketball for the school."

"Oh, I *see*." Smith rubbed his chin and smiled.

Tony made a quick mental note to mention to David that he should never walk the area alone—at least not on Smith's watch.

"You already know the rest of the crew," Tony said smoothly as another breeze whipped past him, plastering the red tee shirt to his body.

"Yeah, I've seen them around." Then Smith turned to Tony. "And since you're *Mr. Commentator*, tell me what's up with them."

Tony bristled. "Nothing really. They're trying to get out of the hood like I am."

Smith's bushy eyebrows shot up. A sly grin graced his pink lips. "Oh, really?"

"Yes, sir. You see Devin right there in the brown shirt?" Tony pointed while his friends shifted, watching. "He wants to be a child psychologist."

Smith laughed. The harsh sound grated on Tony's nerves. "Maybe he'll be able to help some of these crazy people in the hood," the sergeant responded, angling his head at a different group of boys who stood several feet away. "What about the other guys there, what's up with them?"

"They live down the street." Tony peeked over his left shoulder to make eye contact with David. "I don't hang out with them that much, but they're good kids."

"If they're so good why don't you hang with them?"

"They live on the other side of the projects," Tony replied. "I don't have time to hang out when I get home from school. I have basketball practice and games. Plus Devin, David, Hilton and I volunteer at the center—"

"Yeah. I see you guys leaving there from time to time," he said, gaze sweeping back toward the bus stop. "Somebody needs to teach these lowlifes how to read and write."

Tony thought it was wise not to say what had rolled through his mind. Muffled conversation sporadically floated in the air.

"So . . . a *ghetto* psychologist." Smith chuckled. "What about Hilton?"

Tony signed. "He wants to be a psychiatrist."

"A psychiatrist! *Please*...spare me...and jump my *balls*." Smith roared with laughter. Then he looked at David. "What's his story?"

"A computer engineer."

Smith laughed out loud. "*Whatever*."

Devin gripped David's hand and kept him still.

Tony hesitated, knowing the sergeant would have a sarcastic comment. "I want to be a dentist one day." Tony nodded, visualizing himself in a white lab coat.

"A dentist?"

Tony's chest puffed out a little. "Yes, sir."

Smith bellowed with laughter and didn't bother to cover his wide mouth. "I'm sure there are a lot of kids with messed-up teeth running around this ghetto," he said between laughs.

Tony didn't find anything funny, but swept his anger aside and said, "That's why I want to come back and help." As Smith's laughter died out, Tony asked, "Why are you patrolling the bus stop this morning? You're *never* here this early."

Smith instantly sobered, but he didn't make eye contact with Tony. "I heard some guys were selling drugs here."

"Who told you that?" Tony glanced back at his comrades. "We don't sell drugs. Maybe you need to ask the guys hanging out at the *top* of The Hill."

Smith shrugged, then rocked back and forth on his heels. "I'm following up on a tip." Now his intense blue eyes scanned the area as though searching for something else. Or someone else.

"Come on, Sergeant Smith, you know me," Tony inched forward. "You know I'm about school and community work. We're not drug dealers."

A smirk curved his pink lips. "So you say, Tony."

"I'm not going to sit around the projects all my life."

The man's head whipped around.

"No, Sergeant Smith, I'm for real." Tony glared at the tall man. "And besides, I think there are more good guys living here than you think. People come to our neighborhood from other cities to sell drugs and it makes our community look bad."

"I don't like your tone, boy. You getting feisty with me?"

"No sir, but it would be nice if you actually had a kind word to say about the people you're paid to protect."

Smith's cheeks turned a bright red. Tony's friends could hear the conversation. Some rolled their eyes. Some poked out their lips while staring at the sergeant. They wanted to get back into the game before the bus arrived.

Loud horns blew, warning the students that cars were approaching.

"I know what you mean, Tony, but you know what?"

Tony turned, staring openly at him.

"This community is a *mess*," Smith said, eyes bearing down on Tony. "I don't think there's a lot of hope for you, kids. Most of the people living here are looking for a quick high, a quick buck, or a free meal. Taxpayers like me get the short end of the stick."

Feeling bolder than he should, Tony shot back, "Regardless of what neighborhood a person comes from, there's always the good and the bad. Isn't there such a thing as *white* . . . collar crime? They're not from our neighborhood, right?"

Smith's eyes widened with anger, lips tightening into a grim line.

Tony added, "We may not have opportunities like where you come from, but we still work hard and one day we'll have something to offer."

"Enough about those endless dreams, Tony. Where is that pretty little sister of yours?"

Ah, now for the *real* reason Smith was at the bus stop. Tony followed the man's gaze, searching to see if Tiffany had arrived. "What do you mean endless dreams?"

"Nothing, Tony." Smith avoided eye contact. "You know how tough it is surviving in the projects."

A smile consumed Tony's face. "Do you know I'm an Honor Roll student? And that David and Devin are too?"

"I hear you, Tony," Smith snapped, rocking on his heels. "So, where is your sister?"

Tony hesitated. Then Smith's gaze landed on him, so he said, "She's in the house, but she better get out here before the bus comes."

"What grade is she in now?"

Tony shifted uncomfortably. "Twelfth."

"So," Smith rubbed his chin, "that would make her about . . . seventeen or eighteen, right? She just had a birthday in May, right?"

"Yeah, something like that." Tony's eyebrows drew in. "Why do you always want to know about my sister?"

Smith licked his thin lips. "Just curious, that's all."

"Oh, another one of those hopeless people? My sister received full scholarships to go to several colleges. *She* wants to be a doctor."

"Great, which college did she choose? I—"

"Come on, Tony!" yelled a voice from the crowd.

Smith searched the crowd for the speaker.

"Excuse me, Smith, but our bus is almost here." Tony turned away, anger filling every square inch of his body. Then he spotted her. He glanced quickly over his shoulder, knowing that Smith was watching.

"Tiffany! Come on, girl!" he yelled. "Mr. Pete will leave you!"

Short with a caramel complexion, hazel eyes, a short mane of black hair, Tiffany had a sparkling personality. Tony's friends called her a "brick house" and teased her about her big breasts, plump butt and juicy thighs. Though this was never said within Tony's hearing; they knew he would tackle any guy who *stepped* to her in the wrong way.

Tiffany possessed a soft melodic voice unlike many of the girls in Cloverdale. Tony's friends wanted her, but she paid them no attention. Her heart was set on being a doctor and she was determined not to allow anyone or anything get in her way.

Tiffany rushed down the stairs, up the path and past the mailboxes, struggling to keep the books securely in her hands. Sergeant Smith's gaze trailed over her body as though she had left out of her apartment in the nude.

"Those thighs and breasts look mighty good," he whispered.

Tony whirled to face him, snapping, "Tiffany isn't a two-piece meal."

Smith ignored him, eyes remaining focused on the girl before him.

She stumbled over a crumpled brick; books went flying out of her hands. Tiffany's friends, Karen and Genesis and her cousin Star laughed as they watched her plunge face first to the ground. Tony didn't see anything funny about her falling. He also didn't see anything funny with Smith's obsession with his sister.

Tiffany stood, brushed the red and brown dirt from her jeans and glared at the girls giggling and pointing at her.

The bus screeched to its stop. Tiffany's books were still scattered everywhere. She wouldn't make it.

Tony jerked forward but refused to leave his sister behind.

Smith waved him onto the bus. Tony stood his ground.

The man glared angrily at Tony, who glared right back. Moments passed. Finally, Smith signaled to Mr. Pete to wait for Tiffany—causing him to mumble something that Tony couldn't quite catch.

Sergeant Smith then rushed over, dropping one knee to the ground as he scooped the books into his pale hands. He stared down her yellow shirt as she bent over, then picked up most of the books, dusted them off and handed them to her as though he were a perfect gentleman. "Here you go," he uttered, smiling.

"Thank you," Tiffany said in a shy, sweet voice and soon stepped on the bus with Tony trailing behind her and Smith trailing behind him.

"Oh, you're really going to thank me later," he mumbled, "You just wait. Just wait. I'll get between those thighs of yours."

A sharp stab of fear pierced Tony's soul. Summer was a long time to be tied to his sister at the hip. But until she left Cloverdale that was exactly what he needed to do. With their father gone and their mother working all the time, Tony was her only source of protection.

Unfortunately, he wasn't watchful enough.

Chapter 9

Tiffany had tried several times to go back to the medical center. Cloverdale's treacherous history pierced her soul like an avalanche forcing her to take action. She had tried to force herself to forget her painful secrets and focus on her caliber image as a doctor. Instead, she hopped in her black BMW, leaving her staff members and patients with shocked expressions. She didn't think twice as she zoomed down Central Avenue, circling the Cloverdale community several times.

Driving past Latham Park, she soon passed the community center and the outreach program. She scanned the area, searching for at least an hour.

The sizzling summer heat penetrated through her car windows, battling with the air conditioner to control the temperature inside. Nothing could control the anger roaring within Tiffany; it would take more than a switch to turn it off.

Abandoned buildings and dark alleys surrounded the Cloverdale community. Broken-down cars and potholes took over the streets. The neighborhood was stricken with old brown bricks, rusted gutters and cracked steps, which barely supported the foundation.

Trash lay piled up on every corner, ranging from milk cartons to broken wooden chairs. Garbage collectors were scheduled to pick up trash every Friday, but as usual, the tenants had to wait until Tuesday or Wednesday. The fact that the apartments passed the city's housing ordinance codes was nothing short of a miracle and that the people could even make it out of this place, unthinkable. But Tiffany had made it. So had Tony and David.

The last day of high school, the day that marked her pathway into womanhood and paved the foundation of her dreams had started off on a good note as eighteen-year-old Tiffany entered through the brown doors of her guidance counselor . . .

The wooden panel board about four feet high surrounded the area. Stacks of reference books and a dried up gardenia plant competed for space in the far left corner. Mrs. Pratt, a short, skinny woman with ivory skin and a frizzy beehive hairdo, pushed the oval-shaped glasses up on her pert nose. She had been assigned to the students from the Cloverdale projects because she enjoyed working with them. She was one of the only counselors who cared about the students enough to want to see them graduate from Independence High School.

She often said that her compassion to help people and her ability to overlook stereotypes made it easy for her to discern their potential. And she truly believed all of them had potential. But the old woman really had a special place in her heart for Tiffany, Tony and David.

When Mrs. Pratt found out Tiffany received the scholarship to attend Bennett College, she was as ecstatic as if her own personal dream had come true. The moment Tiffany stepped through the door that last day of school, a smile danced across the woman's lips, wrinkling her face as she scanned the contents of a manila folder before dialing, then putting the call on speaker.

A subtle smell of Sand and Sable perfume floated in the office; a scent that registered in Tiffany's memory bank that flashed a picture of Mrs. Pratt when she smelled it.

"Hello, Johnson's residence. This is Mrs. Brown."

"Hello, Mrs. Brown, how are you doing?" Mrs. Pratt said. "I'm Tiffany's guidance counselor at Independence High School."

"Huh?"

Looking at Tiffany, she grinned. "Please excuse me for calling you at work, but I just wanted to congratulate you personally for the accomplishments of your wonderful daughter. Tiffany's extremely talented and smart."

Tiffany beamed.

"Why thank you, honey." Mama's voice, raspy from working too hard, suddenly lowered. "What did you say your name was again?"

"Mrs. Pratt, Tiffany's guidance counselor."

"Okay, how you doing?"

"Just fine, Mrs. Brown." Mrs. Pratt's bow-shaped lips spread into a soft smile. "I hope you are well."

The crashing sound of a mop bucket hitting the floor, vibrated through the phone. Tiffany's body flinched.

"I'm fine, honey. Just working too much. Arthritis acts up sometimes, other than that I'm okay."

"Aw, I'm sorry to hear that, Mrs. Brown."

"Don't worry about me, honey." Mama coughed a little. "Tell me, what can I do for you?"

"I called to let you know that Tiffany's earned a full scholarship and I'll be driving her to school in the fall since you don't have a car."

"Praise the Lord!" Tiffany's heart lifted at the sound of her mother's excited voice. "We've been blessed in so many ways. Thank you, sweetheart, thank you."

Mrs. Pratt smiled. "I'd like for you to come with us on the way to such a prestigious college."

"I thought my baby was going to a college in North Carolina called Bennett?"

"She is, Mrs. Brown, all I am saying is that . . . uh, never mind, ma'am. I'd like for you to go with us for the ride, Mrs. Brown."

"This will be my first time putting my foot on college ground. I'm so proud of my baby."

Mrs. Pratt looked up as another student tapped on the window of her office door. "Hey, I have to go now; we'll talk more about our drive over the summer. I'm sure Tiffany will tell you; I thought I'd ask you to go too. It's one occasion where the kids want their parents' support."

"I'll be there with bells on. She did mention it, but I'm glad you invited me."

"Okay, I'll give you a call over the summer. Bye, bye," Mrs. Pratt said while holding back laughter.

"Bye sugar and thanks for calling."

Tiffany walked out Mrs. Pratt's office on cloud nine. Something as simple as a ride to school, volunteering at the center, or receiving book vouchers from the local librarians was enough to put a smile on her face. Getting a full scholarship had only been the tip of the iceberg. That good feeling lasted throughout her day as she drifted from class to class.

Then she stepped off the bus later that afternoon and stared right into the lustful eyes of Sergeant Smith. That good feeling left faster than a falling star leaves the cosmos.

Chapter 10

Tony cruised through the streets surrounding Cloverdale, searching for Tiffany's vehicle for the second time. His heart was beating rapidly.

Driving through his old stomping grounds, Tony passed the park, the community center and the drug-infested hill. He turned on the radio, trying to soothe his nerves. That didn't work much. He pressed his slender fingers firmly on his temple.

Spoiled milk, food and rotten fruits circulated from outside into his air vents as he passed a small convenience store. Trash had been piled up outside near the back door. His mind began to wander.

"I've got to stop thinking about the past," Tony said as his mind drifted further to the last day of school . . .

Police sirens swirled in the air from miles away. The nearby streets had become hot spots for drugs and prostitutes and thanks to an influx of new people, Cloverdale projects had suddenly become the harvest center for crime.

Tony, basketball in hand as he inhaled the fresh-cut grass, froze as he stepped off the school bus a few paces behind his sister. Sergeant Smith's patrol car sat parked at the bus stop again. Why was he *still* around? A loud, wailing sound pierced the air, making several heads turn.

Smith had flipped on his siren trying to get everyone's attention.

Cautiously, Tony, Tiffany and David walked towards their apartments. An uneasy feeling settled in the pit of Tony's stomach.

"Tiffany, come to the patrol car," echoed over the loudspeaker.

Tony gulped. Hairs on his arms spiked like a frightened cat.

Splinters of My Soul

Tiffany trembled as she walked past the mailboxes, dumpsters and broken down cars. Her walk from the bus stop to the black patrol car seemed endless. With every footstep she took, the sound of Tony's heartbeat grew louder as though fighting to break free from his young chest. A quick misstep and Tiffany dropped her books—again.

Sergeant Smith jumped out, rushed toward Tiffany. She froze. As Smith slowed to a jaunt, Tiffany squatted to pick up the textbooks. Although this was the last day of school, Tiffany had brought her books home to have something to read during her free time in the summer. The librarian trusted her to return the books. She had always done so. She glanced at Tony, her pretty hazel eyes, gleaming from the rays of the sun.

"Am I in trouble?" She asked, her voice squeaky and a far cry from the soft melodic tones everyone was used to.

Tony winced as Smith stared at his sister, bright blue eyes twinkling as if in love with her. Seconds ticked by in an endless stream of anxiously held breaths before he answered, "No, sweetie, I want to congratulate you." Smith shoved his pale hand into his stitched pocket. "I heard the good news about your scholarship."

Tiffany let out a long breath. Tony and David inched closer.

Tony asked, putting a little bass in his voice, "Is everything all right?"

Smith walked closer to Tiffany, handing her a little plastic card. The man stammered like a lovesick puppy. "This is, um," Smith cleared his throat, "for you to um, buy school supplies for college."

Tony's blood raced frantically through his veins.

Her thin eyebrows drew in as she glanced from Tony to Smith. "How did you know about my scholarship?"

Tony leaned in, hugging his sister, placing his body between hers and Smith's, whispering, "Give it back." Laughter erupted from the crowd of kids as his buddies teased Tony for acting like a wimp, hugging his sister in public.

Tony didn't care. His sister deserved the gift card, but it came from Smith. And that could spell trouble.

Their mother couldn't afford to buy all the things his sister needed for college. Since their father passed away ten years ago, things were rough. The task of taking care of two children with only a part-time job and no college education was difficult. They had survived with their father's income before his death, but without it, their house was foreclosed and they had to move into Cloverdale. Things were good in the beginning, but the influx of outsiders and Smith's obvious dislike for people in the projects made life harder.

Smith mumbled something that Tony couldn't quite catch, but then ended with, "Boy, are you gonna hold onto that little girl all day?"

Tony inched away from Tiffany but stayed in front of her. "We thank you for the card, but we can't accept it."

Smith snapped, "And why not."

"Our mother won't allow us to accept gifts from strangers."

Smith grinned. "I'm not a stranger. Your mother knows me."

Yes, Mrs. Brown did know the man. But she didn't know everything. And that's what bothered Tony the most—the horror stories he had heard . . .

.

Tony gritted his teeth. "Tiffany, give the card back."

"But we need—"

Tony gripped Tiffany's elbow. "Give it back," he snapped at Tiffany while still glaring at Smith. "Now."

Tiffany extended her hand, holding the red card to Sergeant Smith. "I can't accept this card."

Smith glared at Tony, then turned to Tiffany, smiling. "You keep it, Tiffany. If you don't use it, give it to someone who will."

Smith marched toward the patrol car.

A sharp twinge of anger set in. Tony snatched the card from Tiffany's delicate fingers, ran after the man's retreating form, waving the gift card in his hand like a flag.

Smith slipped into the driver's seat and slammed the door, blue eyes flashing with unconcealed fury. Tony pushed the card toward the open window. Smith turned his head, punched the pedal and the patrol car sped up Harris Boulevard.

Tiffany plucked the card from his fingers and strolled happily away toward their friends.

A strong premonition of foreboding nagged in the corner of his mind: Tiffany would have to pay for that little gift—one way or another.

Chapter 11

Smith eased away from June Bug. The smell of the man almost made him lose his lunch.

"Murder?" June Bug responded eyes bucked wide.

Sergeant Smith leaned forward, whispering, "Yeah, murder. Can you handle that?"

June Bug laughed out loud. "Man, I thought you were talking about burning down a barn full of people or killing the President."

Smith's eyebrows twitched. Excitement leaped into his heart. Maybe he had his man. "So, can you handle that?"

June Bug kissed his hands. "Man, look at these hands. These are hands of mass destruction. I've killed people with my bare hands in the military."

The sergeant frowned. "The military?"

"I was a lieutenant." June Bug slowly dropped his head. "I wasn't always this way. Look, I don't want to talk about that anymore." He thrust his hands out. "Take me to jail."

Smith glanced down the alley as a foul odor swept by. "Man, why are you sitting beside this dumpster?"

"Why are you worried about all of that? Do you want to help? Then take me to rehab."

Smith's small notion of hope seemed to be slipping away. "Where you from?"

He leaned to the side, scratching his rear end. Smith cringed.

June Bug pointed down the street to Cloverdale. "I used to live in that complex over there. I grew up in that place. Plus I have two children over here."

"Which complex?" Smith turned his head.

"Right beside Mrs. Brown's apartment." He stretched his flimsy arms as he yawned.

"Oh, I remember you." He smirked, memory finally serving him correctly. "You're Mrs. Brown's brother . . . And you're David and Star's father."

June Bug waved his hands as if he were in a classroom trying to get the teacher's attention. "Yeah, that's me." He chuckled deeply. "Just like I know you're Sergeant *Paul* Smith, better known as the beast who roams these streets."

The sergeant sneered. When did people start calling him that? "What are you talking about?"

June Bug cut his eyes at the sergeant. "Man, what do you want from me?"

"What happened to you, man?" A strong scent of urine drifted with the wind past his nose, causing him to wince.

"I just told you."

"So, where you living now?"

Hands spread, he said, "Right here. But sometimes my sister lets me come to her apartment to shower. She wants me to get help." He grazed his face with his palm, fanning a fly away. "I'm going to church with her on Sunday. Man, I need to change my life. I know God doesn't want me to be like this."

With each word, Smith shifted his gaze to areas of the alley. "So, what about my proposition?"

"What proposition, man? You haven't told me what you want me to do. Besides, I don't know right now. I want to get right with God."

"Man, that's what you all say," Smith said, kicking June Bug's dirty tennis shoes.

June Bug gaped up at the sergeant. "I'm serious. I've lived a tough life, too long and now I'm tired. I know God will forgive me."

Smith stared at the man.

"Forget you! My sister will take me to rehab. *She* wants me to get some help."

The thumping sound of bass from a car ricocheted against the building in the alley, causing the doors on the abandoned building to vibrate. Smith looked around to make sure the alley was still vacant. He extended his hand. "Before you do all of that let's talk about my proposition. Here," Smith said, handing June Bug the crack. "Take a puff of this, then tell me what you think. I've heard it's the best. You'd better take it while I have it. Or, I can just give it to someone else."

June Bug shook his head at a rapid pace, side to side. "Man, why are you trying to tempt me? You know I'm weak. Don't do this to me. *Please*, take me to a rehab center."

Smith grabbed his hand. "Here, take it, it's yours!"

June Bug snatched away. "I'm trying to straighten up."

"Come on, man. I just saw you smoking some crack. Now, take it."

"But I made a promise that it was going to be my last high."

June Bug attempted to stand. Smith put a knee into the addict's ribcage forcing him back to the ground.

"Man, get your knee off me." June Bug balled his hands into fists. "Didn't you see me beat them fools down? You better get out of my way."

Smith backed up. "I'm only trying to give you a *free* gift."

"Man, did you hear what I said." June Bug glared up at him. "I'm trying to get right with God."

Smith heard scrambling from the far end of the alley. He peeked around the dumpster to get a good view. He squinted, peering into the dark part of the alley. A short lady wearing a bright yellow skimpy skirt dropped to her knees in front of a tall man in a black business suit. They couldn't see him because of the dumpster. Smith watched for a second, fascinated by the way the woman's lips wrapped around the man's erection, sucking like a vacuum. The man gripped her head, thrusting into her waiting mouth.

Smith reluctantly turned his attention back to June Bug. "I heard you." He tossed the dope on the man's lap. "But I don't want to waste this. Let *this* one be the last hit; then I'll take you to rehab, I promise."

The man stared down at the little white rock as if it were pure gold, but didn't touch it.

"I can't keep walking around the projects with this in my pocket."

June Bug's legs shook as if he were sprinting on a treadmill. The crack fell on the ground.

Smith snatched the crack up, then shoved it into his pockets. "I'll give it to someone else."

June Bug fumbled with his fingers. "Let me see it again. How do I know if it's really dope? Let me pinch a piece off so I can taste it."

The sergeant looked in both directions of the alley. "Here, take it!"

The man stared at the white rock. "Wait a minute, man. Is this going to kill me," June Bug said, eyeing Smith closely. "You're too quick to give it away."

"Come on, June Bug. What do you think this could be? It's not rat poison."

Sweat poured down the man's dark brown face. June Bug wanted the dope so bad Smith could see it in his eyes. June Bug finally put the crack on the pipe, lit it and pressed his back against the wall. He stretched out his legs and rocked side to side. The high was almost instant.

June Bug stretched his hands out, signaling for more.

The sergeant shrieked, "Not until you agree to do the job!"

With eyes shut, head pressed against the wall, he said, "Tell me what you want."

"Not much to tell, I need something done. I'll pull a few strings to cover you. And you'll get a lot more of this after the deal's done."

June Bug's eyelids slowly separated. "It doesn't sound right, man."

"It'll be alright," muffled Smith. "I'm sure you can do it."

June Bug paused for a few minutes. "Okay, I think I can handle that." He slid his pipe in his pocket.

Then remembering June Bug's earlier requests for help, Smith said, "In the meantime, I want you to meet me every day. So I can supply you with your medicine."

The muscles in the man's face contracted. "What medicine, man?" He pulled the pipe out of his pocket and stared at it. "What are you talking about?"

"Man, I'm talking about the dope." Smith peered through the alley. "Why are you so paranoid?"

June Bug scratched his face. "Whatever, man. There's no telling these days."

Smith rubbed the back of his neck. "Listen. I'll meet you every night at nine, behind the abandoned building."

"Which abandoned building?"

Smith paused for a few seconds, trying to figure out which alley had the least traffic flow at night. "The one on the other side of the projects near the creek."

The cool breeze that surfed off the water at night from McAlpine Creek was enough to prevent even the heartiest of hustlers from venturing through there. Wild animals in that area had carted off children and homeless people. Bodies were found there all the time.

"Okay, man. You'd better be there," June Bug said, struggling to stand. "This is a big step for me."

The sergeant sneered. "What are you talking about?"

"I figure since you're gonna give me dope I don't have to snatch it from another addict or steal something to trade for it."

Five minutes later, they sauntered out of the alley together. Smith placed handcuffs on June Bug's scrawny wrists.

"Hey! Why you—"

"I have to do this just in case someone wonders why I was in the alley so long."

Smith was right. Some of the tenants were still standing outside at the playground, pointing in the direction where June Bug had attacked Jim Boy and Jay Rock. Everyone stared at Sergeant Smith as he put June Bug in the patrol car. Smith was not bothered. He was focused on brewing a murder.

Chapter 12

Tiffany drove away from Cloverdale heading toward her house in Lake Norman. It was past 4 o'clock. She had nearly run out of gas driving through her old neighborhood, peering up and down the streets like a detective.

The sun drifted behind the clouds, allowing a shaft of light to spread across the North Carolina sky. As she passed Latham Park, the place where she had spent a lot of time as a child playing in the sandbox, on the swing set and the monkey bars, she noticed that the equipment at Latham was in much better condition than Cloverdale's park. As she stared at the swing set, she turned the corner and her mind drifted back to her childhood experiences. She tried to focus on the good times. But thoughts of one dreadful summer still pierced her soul . . .

Anxiety took over Tiffany as she went over her to-do list for the one-hundredth time. College meant more responsibilities and she doubted that she would have any time to have a social life. She wasn't the type of girl who liked to hang out with crowds; becoming a social butterfly wasn't in her repertoire anyway, but who knew what people expected on campus? She didn't want them to think she was strange.

Yellow and green floral sheets hung in front of her window. The burnt floor mat her mother had purchased at the thrift store decorated a worn out ceramic floor. Crayon-sketched pictures adorned the wall—some of Tony's best work. She took in a deep breath and exhaled. Her mother was doing the best she could to provide for the family.

Tiffany closed her eyes and promised that she would fulfill her dreams to become a gynecologist and to make a difference in the lives of others. She had held onto this dream ever since she saw blood saturating the grass as her neighbor labored in pain while waiting for the paramedics. Minutes later, the baby rushed out wailing its entry into the world. Unfortunately, Angela didn't hear it. She had died before the paramedics arrived.

Bennett College was a strict and rigorous school for women only and the students there were highly competitive. For some reason, Mrs. Pratt made it a point to drill into Tiffany's heard that Bennett College freshmen were top-notch honor students in high school. Tiffany was determined to give it her all because she couldn't face failure and she definitely didn't want to disappoint her mother or brother.

Hot and humid air poured into Tiffany's bedroom. An air conditioner would have cooled the room, but Tiffany had to settle for "the luxury" of a fan. She had purchased a strawberry candle at the local store, but the wax somehow diffused the strawberry scent, leaving only the smell of burnt wax behind.

She looked out her window, staring at the community kids playing at the park. She would be so far from her mother and brother. A sigh of relief engulfed her as she remembered that her scholarship included a stipend. She could get a telephone card and call her mother at work since they didn't have a house phone.

The little red gift card from the sergeant was propped against the dresser mirror. She would spend the rest of the money on her family. She took pride in her brother's accomplishments in school and in sports. And she was grateful that her mother worked for the Johnsons. A working mother living in the projects was better than a mother who sat around waiting on a welfare check.

Tiffany slipped on a pair of jeans, tennis shoes and a pink tank top. She ran down the wooden steps, strolling into the living room, before scribbling a note that said—I'M AT B&B'S.

B&B Family Store sold everything from candy bars to televisions, just like Wal-Mart. Except things were cheaper here because the items were damaged, opened, old or spoiled—people took a big risk when making a purchase. Eventually, someone reported the store to the Better Business Bureau and people in Cloverdale refused to shop there. The owner, a hateful old man, eventually replaced most rancid items in order to pass inspection.

B&B Family Store was about five blocks away. She wanted to purchase a nice dress for her mother. A shirt and a camera would be a great gift for Tony. Pictures of her family on the walls in her dorm room would help her feel closer to them, no matter how far away. She had time. Tony had basketball practice; he would be there for a few hours and her mother would come in an hour after him.

While sprinting past the community center and the park, she prayed that the store wasn't crowded. Excitement burst through her heart as she thought about making a chocolate cake. The cake wouldn't turn out as delicious as her mother's, but she would give it a try anyway.

When she stepped through the entrance of B&B, the hairs on the back of her neck froze from the cold air blowing out of the vents over the door. He glanced down at the large shopping cart, smiled, then turned on his heels, before sauntering back to his vehicle.

Twenty minutes later, Tiffany hurried toward her house. She looked at her watch. Only three hours before her folks would be home. She took a shortcut through an alley, hoping to have enough time to wrap the gifts, bake a cake, get dressed and decorate the apartment with balloons.

Smith's car zoomed down the street and parked on the other end. Tiffany froze at the mere sight of the man but inched forward.

Stepping through the alley, she brushed aside any misgivings because the bright, scorching sun was still overhead. The prostitutes and junkies who hung out in the alley knew Tiffany was Mrs. Brown's daughter. Many people in the community had respect for Mrs. Brown who was known as a religious and fair woman. When it came to baking cakes, everyone loved her special touch. Mrs. Brown's cakes were so good people in the neighborhood paid her to bake for birthdays, graduations and other special events.

Tiffany passed a hair supply store, a soul-food restaurant and a pawn shop. Pungent wine odors mixed with pee penetrated her nostrils, forcing her nose to twitch. When she turned the last corner, she saw Smith leaning against the graffiti-splattered wall as if waiting for someone. He turned, staring directly at her.

"How are you doing, Sergeant Smith?" Tiffany asked. His lips turned down into a frown as she attempted to pass him. She took a few steps and felt him breathing down her neck. She moved faster and so did he. Every time she glanced over her shoulders, Smith was right behind her.

Her slow pace turned into a rapid saunter. Her heartbeat pounded harder against her chest like a power drill thrusting against cement. Panic set in. She gripped her bag.

"Stop right there!" Smith ordered.

Her heart jumped out of her chest. As she turned to face him, she took a quick look around the alley to see if anyone else was around. For a brief moment, Tiffany thought the sun had blinded her because no one else appeared. People were always passing in and out of the alley, but it wasn't the case at the moment. And somehow that didn't seem right.

"Put the bag down, Tiffany!"

Tiffany lowered the brown paper bag to the ground and slowly stood again.

"There's a lot of drug activities going on in this alley," Smith said, ambling toward her. "I'm searching the area."

"I've never seen anyone selling drugs in this alley."

Loud noises echoed from the other end as the children at the nearby park screamed and laughed. Tiffany glanced around, wishing one of the kids would at least peek inside the alley.

Smith's mouth slightly parted, barely enough to let words slip through. "I'm just checking, that's all."

"People usually pass through the alley to get to the top of The Hill," she said, softly. "That's where the drug dealers hang out. You know that." Sergeant Smith couldn't possibly think she was transporting or selling drugs in the alley.

"So what's in the bag, Tiffany?"

"Gifts I bought for my mother and brother."

He leaned over, peering into the top of the bag. "Can I take a look inside?"

Without a moment's hesitation, she picked up her bag and handed it to him. "I'm going to decorate the living room with balloons," she said, the words gushing out as a nervous tremor settled in her soul. "And I'm taking pictures to put up in my dorm room."

"Oh, really," he said, reaching for the bag.

"Yes," she continued, her gaze following his every move. "I'm making a cake before my mother gets home."

A dark cloud formed in the sky, making the already dim alley darker. Rain was on its way.

Sergeant Smith stared at Tiffany. He then pulled his hand out of her bag, peering at something in his hands.

"You're under arrest for possession of crack cocaine," he stated simply.

A screeching sound of an ambulance's siren roared in the air, causing Tiffany's heart to pulsate rapidly. "For *what*?" Tiffany's eyes widened with shock and disbelief as fear sprang into her soul.

"For these pieces of rock," Sergeant Smith said, holding up a small clear plastic bag.

Tiffany's teeth rattled, her legs wobbled and her hands shook. "I swear I don't know where that came from. I just left B&B Family Store!" Tears rolled down her face as Sergeant Smith pulled out his handcuffs.

"Put your hands against the wall and spread your legs!" he commanded.

Tiffany slowly placed her hands on the brick wall, positioning her feet several inches apart. He ran his clammy hands along her bare shoulders, under her arms and lingered around her breasts.

"Aren't you supposed to call in a female officer to do this?"

He pushed her shoulders against the wall. "Don't you worry about what I'm supposed to do, you need to worry about that rock I found on you." Then he moved his hands swiftly down her back, groping between her thighs, then down to each one of her ankles. Tiffany felt swamped with shame.

"Please let me go home, Sergeant Smith, please," she begged as his strong cologne snatched her breath away.

"I'm sorry, Tiffany," the sergeant replied, pacing around her and scanning her body. "But the only place you'll be going is straight to the police station."

Moisture gathered at the corner of her mouth, but she was too afraid to lift her hand to wipe it away.

"Possession of crack cocaine is a felony," Smith smirked. "You're going to lose that fancy scholarship. They won't even let you into that college."

87

Tears poured out of her eyes faster than a waterfall as her dreams of becoming a doctor shattered.

"God, please help me," Tiffany prayed out loud. "For you said in your *Word*, you would never leave me nor forsake me."

As she prayed, Sergeant Smith yanked her forward thrusting her against the black wall.

"I'm innocent!" she exclaimed, trying to break from his grasp.

He answered in a bored tone, "That's what they all say." Massive hands reached out to stroke her breasts. "You're beautiful and sexy."

She pushed his hands away glancing around in the alley. Stray cats rambled through the trash, looking for food. Tiffany didn't like cats. Tiffany didn't like Sergeant Smith either. Horns honked and tires screeched from a distance. She turned, hoping that someone would cruise past the alley. Her hopes were mere faded wishes.

Small drops of rain dripped on her head, soaking through her tiny curls and falling onto her bare arms and clothes. She gazed at the sky, saying a prayer as the rain sprinkled on her face.

The rain didn't bother the sergeant.

"Being sexy has nothing to do with what's in your hand," Tiffany mumbled, wiping her snotty nose with the back of her hand. "I've never sold drugs and I don't know where that dope came from."

"It came out of that bag right there, young lady, so it must belong to you."

"It's not mine, I swear!"

"I thought you were smart," the sergeant said while grazing her face with a single hand. Tiffany jerked back. "It's a shame you'll have to spend the next few years of your life in a prison cell instead of a classroom."

His tongue swirled around his pale lips. Minutes ticked by before he leaned in. "I can help you, but it's going to require a little *give and take*," he whispered, but his eyes said so much more.

"A little give and take?" she said, instantly sobering. "Sergeant Smith, all you have to do is go ask the cashier who put the items in the bag. That's all!"

A stumbling man, smelling like a liquor factory braced himself against the dark wall, trying to support his puny body, staggering past. Tiffany felt an instant sense of security. But her heart sank when he fell, struggled to stand up, then strolled away to the other end of the alley without glancing at her.

"Place your hands behind your back right now," he commanded.

Tiffany slowly stretched her hands in front, too scared to put them behind her back as the sergeant placed the little silver rings on her small wrists and locked them in place. Smith grabbed her bag and escorted her out of the alley to the patrol car. If someone saw her being placed in the patrol car, the news would get to her mother or brother. That would be a disaster.

She took small slow steps, resembling a person taking the last walk to the electric chair after being on death row for a long period of time.

Tiffany's legs cramped as he ducked her head and put her in the front seat of the car. How could she be on her way to a bright future in one minute and in a desperate position the next? Her life was going into a downward spiral just as fast as the patrol car sped toward the police station—and her future.

As the long, narrow, paved streets of Cloverdale came into view, a sudden pang of alarm settled in her gut. "The police station's back that way," Tiffany said. "Where are we going?"

"Listen, Tiffany, I want to help you get out of this situation." Sergeant Smith reached over and caressed her hand, before lowering it to rub her inner thighs.

"Stop! What are you *doing*?" Tiffany grabbed his wrist and jerked his hand away. She closed her legs, gluing them together tightly.

He reached over and rubbed her breasts. Tiffany jerked back.

"Look!" he yelled, putting his hands back on the steering wheel. "You have two options, sleep with me or I turn the dope in. I didn't give you that gift card for nothing."

Tiffany cried out, "This isn't right! I don't understand why you're doing this."

With a lustful glint in his eyes, he said, "You can forget about your dreams if I turn in this dope, or you can make passionate love to me; those are your two options."

She sank in the seat, squeezing her legs together again. Tears blinded her vision.

Staring out of the window, Tiffany watched the passing cars on Central Avenue, hoping someone would stop the sergeant and ask him for directions or something—anything. She observed every landmark, programming them to memory, so when she had the opportunity to jump out and run, she could get home.

The rain struck the window like small pebbles. But Tiffany continued to count the streets, making a mental note of the stores and churches.

"How many other girls in Cloverdale have you done this to?"

"Now that's none of your business," he growled. "*In fact*, I want you to shut up. You need to tell me what you're going to do."

"I guess you're the reason people told me to be careful if I walk alone from the community center?"

Smith's thin lips curled into a sneer as his blue eyes flashed with anger.

Tiffany felt betrayed and naïve. She couldn't believe that she didn't see this coming! Maybe that's why Tony had insisted that she give that card back. She thought Sergeant Smith was a nice, honest cop like Sergeant Poindexter, who was happy she excelled in elementary and middle school. Poindexter had patrolled Cloverdale for several years before he retired, then Smith took over the position. The more she thought about Sergeant Smith's advances toward her, the more scared she became. He knew she didn't have any drugs on her. He had set her up.

What did she do to deserve this? Was this all about that gift card? Who could she tell? No one would believe a young black girl from Cloverdale over an officer.

Tiffany tried to think of a way to escape. Buying some time, she asked, "Don't you have a wife?"

He slammed on the brakes and pulled the car to the side of the road. "Yes, I have a wife," he snapped, glaring over at her. "What's it to you!"

"I was just wondering," she said in a timid voice. "What's her name, what's going on between you two? Seems like you're not happy."

Smith pulled back onto Interstate 85 South and spilled his guts about how he used to sow his royal oats. He mentioned things he wanted to do to her. Totally clueless, she watched him as a far-off look came into his eyes while he continued to tell her of his sexual exploits with other girls in Cloverdale. The longer he talked, the better her chances of rescue. Then as she looked out of the window, she didn't see anything she recognized. Her hope drifted away.

Tiffany wiped a tear from her cheeks. The cuffs tightened each time she moved.

"Please take me back home!" She kicked the dashboard and banged her hand against the window. Her hands were still in the cuffs which prevented her from striking the window with a hard blow.

Sergeant Smith jerked the steering wheel toward the right, driving down a long, narrow secluded road surrounded by woods. Tires screeching, he forced the car into park.

His eyebrows twitched, eyes narrowed and wrinkles formed on his forehead. He punched the steering wheel and pointed his long white finger in her face. "I'm not taking you home. Shut up and sit still. Don't make me screw you out here in the woods." He unloosened his belt. "You know I will."

She pressed her back further into the leather seat.

Sergeant Smith glared at Tiffany for a few seconds before he put the car into reverse.

Tiffany grabbed the door handle, jumped out and ran. She gasped for air with every step. Her heart pulsated rapidly and her legs pumped up and landed hard on the grass. She couldn't run as fast as she wanted because the cuffs blocked the flow of her stride. It didn't matter where she went as long as she was out of Sergeant Smith's reach.

The wet, muddy grass made her sink each time she planted her feet down. Her clothes were saturated with water. Tiffany felt like she was moving through quicksand instead of charging through the woods.

Sergeant Smith chased after her full speed. Moments later, he grabbed the back of her pink tank top, ripping it as she struggled to get away.

Tiffany screamed and swung her arms. He gripped the back of her neck, picked her up and tossed her over his shoulder. His strong long arms stopped her from moving freely, but Tiffany continued to twitch, trying to get free. She couldn't see his face, but she knew they were headed back to the patrol car.

He breathed hard, his hot breath striking her arms as he carried her. She peered through the woods, wishing hunters would come charging out to save her. Squirrels ran up the trees and birds chirped. They couldn't help her.

Panting for air, Smith slammed Tiffany against the back of the patrol car. He pressed his body against hers to secure her in place, struggling to pull his keys out of a small black pocket.

With tears gushing out of her eyes, Tiffany pleaded, "Please. Please take me home."

"Shut up! You've pissed me off. I have a remedy for that." Smith gripped Tiffany's throat while he put the key into his trunk, opening it.

Tiffany screamed, kicking and swinging her arms again. "Please, let me go!" she yelled at the top of her lungs while tussling with the sergeant.

He picked up Tiffany, shoved her in the trunk and closed it.

Chapter 13

After searching for Tiffany in Cloverdale for at least two hours, Tony finally gave up and turned the car toward Ballantyne Country Club driving down the long stretch of road leading to his cul-de-sac. Every turn meant he was drawing closer to *World War X*. And it was all for nothing. He hadn't been able to find Tiffany. Whizzing past the lake, the community golf course and the tennis court, he wondered what had happened to his sister.

Tony's two-story brick house resembled a mansion on top of a hill. The bay windows protruded out from the den, living room and dining room, giving the house a touch of elegance. The house had a fresh coat of burgundy paint on the shutters and the mailbox. Red scalloped edger blocks marched along his flowerbed, surrounding the yellow, purple and white tulips that presented a dazzling landscape. Ferns lined his driveway, leading to the wood mulch spread around the large Magnolia tree. An undoubtedly beautiful, eye-catching appearance Tony had worked diligently to create.

Approaching the driveway, Tony pressed the keypad on the sun visor to open the garage. He pulled the silver Lincoln Navigator into the three-car garage beside Heather's white Mercedes. He said a quick prayer before hopping out of the SUV.

Strolling in through the mahogany wood door, he dropped his briefcase next to the wooden chest. The scent of Jasmine candles drifted in the house.

Heather stood at the door with her hands on her wide hips.

"Hello, Heather," he said softly, testing the waters.

"Don't hello me, Anthony *Mason* Brown," she snapped. "You have some nerve hanging up on me. I texted you 12 times and you never responded."

94

Heather's gaze followed every move as he took his black shoes off at the door. He glanced at their family portrait displayed above a small brass table in the foyer. A picture of his kids flashed in his mind. Carmen was two-years-old, her hazel eyes and long ponytails made her whole face glow. And Anthony, Jr. with his smooth chocolate skin, long eyelashes and soft brown eyes—a spitting image of Tony—had just turned three. "Where are the kids?" he asked ignoring her comments as he had done with her text messages.

"Robin came and got them," she said, folding her arms over her melon-shaped breasts that nestled softly against her red blouse. "I told her that we needed to talk."

Heather's best friend with her trademark scowl flashed before Tony. The woman had never liked him *or* Tiffany. He whirled to face his wife. "What did you tell her?"

His wife rolled her greenish-brown eyes; her lips curled into a sneer.

"What do you expect me to do?" Tony said, filing past her into the hallway. "My sister's missing and all you can say is that I *hung up* on you."

Heather trudged behind him.

Tony sighed, continuing into the hallway, passing Heather's bridal portrait on the sunflower-colored wall. Finally, he made it to the bathroom where he splashed water on his face, then snatched a towel from the rack.

He strolled into the living room to continue the argument that he knew Heather wanted to finish. The spacious, ocean-blue room was a cozy place for them to talk, instead of the bedroom where they would forget about their issues and end up making hot passionate love. Well, it used to work that way.

The crystal chandelier dangled in the middle of the ceiling. The sky blue wall-to-wall carpet complimented the oversized cream chairs and multicolored throw pillows. The fireplace was once a constant source of sensuous memories that existed before they had kids and before Heather became Tiffany's archenemy.

Tony escorted Heather to the cream chair. He stretched out his hand, taking hers in his. She jerked it back.

Tony squinted. "What's wrong with you?"

She folded her arms, poking out her bottom lip.

How in the world could this woman switch from a loving sweet person to a nagging coldhearted one in such a short period? The first time he saw her on Wake Forest's campus, he nearly lost his mind. Well, what little bit he had left after struggling to pass his chemistry class. Heather was the most beautiful woman on the planet. Forget fashion models and movie stars. Heather should have been crowned as the Queen of the Heavens. Now he would give her a crown all right, but it would be so far from Heaven he couldn't say it out loud.

"I'm sorry for hanging up on you. But no one knows what happened to Tiffany. She ran out of her office, crying."

"Anthony, you have a family now." Heather's lips twitched and her eyes flashed with anger. "I need you. The kids need you. Who do you think your sister is, God?"

He would never make Heather see the reason why he cared for his sister. The rumble of his neighbor's lawnmower swept by the bay window, sounding loud enough to actually be in their living room.

"You're always running to help your sister."

Tony sighed slowly, folded his hands and propped them under his chin. He stared into Heather's eyes, tapping his foot on the sky blue carpet. "Right now, Tiffany needs me. It's not like her to run out of her office and leave her patients behind."

"I need you, Anthony." Heather stormed into the hallway, turned and looked back into the room. "She has a husband. Let him deal with it."

"How can you say that, Heather?" Tony followed her trail to the kitchen. "I can't forsake my family. Why are you so jealous of my sister?"

"*Jealous*? You need to ask her *that*. Why should I be jealous of her?" She flicked her hair off her shoulder, moving it to dangle down her back. "You don't need to call her *every day*." Heather pushed him aside while setting a brisk pace as she made it to the kitchen door. "You've put your sister before me too many times. You can't keep babysitting her."

Tony whirled to block her entrance into the kitchen. "I love you and the kids. You mean a lot to me. But you have to understand that I care for my mother and my sister too. You knew this from day one."

She sucked her teeth. "You need to set your priorities straight." Heather gripped the chrome handle, opening the mahogany cabinets, pulled out a glass and slammed it on the marble countertop. "You spend too much time stressing about a grown-ass woman."

"How?" he said, caressing her small hand in his. "Anytime we go somewhere you're welcome to join us. I have to practically beg you to come with us." Tony rubbed her shoulders. "You get upset when I ask if you want to play cards or if you want to go to my mother's church."

A popping noise came from the microwave. Heather pressed the button, then pulled out a puffy yellow bag. Tony was surprised she didn't burn the popcorn as she did everything else.

She opened the stainless steel refrigerator, moved the orange juice, grabbed a peach-colored container and poured a glass of water. "I want us to do things by ourselves." She put her hands on her wide hips. "I want us to find another church."

"Come on. What are you saying?"

"You heard me," she snapped, walking towards the kitchen door.

Tony jumped in front of her, stretching his arms across the door.

Heather stroked small fingers through her hair. For a split second, she avoided eye contact. Her gaze drifted towards the ceiling, then slowly lowered to meet Tony's.

He pulled her closer to him, running his fingers through the fine strands of wavy hair. "Heather, I love you." He kissed her forehead.

Grabbing her hand, he slid his fingers between the soft curves of hers. Tony embraced her, trying to enjoy the peaceful moment while it lasted. He stroked his fingers across her face, moving strands of hairs that bounced freely.

With every passing second, he caressed her shoulders and neck. Connecting his mouth with hers, Tony's tongue parted her bow-shaped lips. His tongue moved inside of her mouth, hands gently stroked her back, caressing every inch of the length as he sucked on her neck.

Heather moaned softly as she unbuttoned his shirt and licked on the defined muscles of his stomach. Her hands glided down, landing on his black pants. She stroked his erection with one hand, unzipping his pants with the other. His pants dangled on his hips.

Juices pumped into his body. A warm tingling feeling flowed through him. He was on his way to swim in Nookie Lake and couldn't wait to dive in—head first.

His tongue grazed her face as he propped her up on the countertop. His tongue twirled down her sweet jasmine scented neck.

Tony was on his way to love the nest that was bound to finally give him satisfaction.

The phone rang, startling both of them.

Heather inched away, but he gripped her hips and slid her back toward him. Her small hands pressed down on his shoulder. He knew exactly what she wanted. He stroked his hand along her inner thighs, sliding his head under her black skirt.

Clamping his teeth on her silk panties, he peeled them off. He gently nibbled on her thighs as the panties slid down while inhaling her womanly scent. The juices in his body pumped faster and faster, sending a rush of heat to his dick.

Heather pressed her feet on his pants, sliding them down with her toes.

The phone rang again.

Heather glanced at the cordless pushing him away. She hopped down and stormed toward the phone. "Get the phone, *Anthony*."

Tony looked at her like she was crazy. His erection protruded before him like a compass, his pants gathered around his ankle like laundry.

"No, baby. This is *our* time." Tony hopped toward her with pants bunched up at his ankles. "Let's finish what we started."

The shrill ring of the phone pierced the air.

She pursed her lips. "I bet that's your sister calling you to report in." She glanced at her manicured fingernails. "Go ahead and talk to *her*, Anthony." She glanced down at his erection. "Maybe she can help you out, since she's so important and everything."

"Come on, baby. Don't be like *this*."

Heather glistened with anger. "You know what, *Anthony*, I'll appreciate a little peace and quiet with my husband for once in a while. I *know* that's your sister calling. *Answer* the phone."

Heather pulled her panties off and threw them at him. They wrapped around his face like a surgical mask. Tony walked over to the phone and snatched it off its base on the wall. "Now can we finish what we started, baby?" Tony said. He could buy another cord, but he didn't know when the next time Heather would be in the mood. He almost had to make appointments weeks in advance.

This time the phone in the den rang.

Tony reached out for her hand.

"I'm not in the mood anymore," Heather snapped.

The sweet seductive expression that Heather once had quickly turned into a bitter resentful one. She stormed out of the kitchen down the hallway to the bathroom, locking it. "Go ahead, Anthony, take care of your sister!" she yelled from the bathroom.

For a moment, he carried on a conversation with her through the door, trying to get her back in the mood. After ten minutes he gave up, thoroughly pissed off. Swimming through Nookie Lake was the last thing on his mind. He needed a lifeboat. Quick.

Deflated like a balloon, he pulled his clothes up, walking back into the kitchen. He looked at the phone, plugging the cord back in. "Is that how you see it? She's missing and you don't care. What kind of wife are you?"

Heather snatched open the bathroom door and stormed back into the kitchen while sneering as she said, "You can't be that worried if you're trying to get her *rocks off.*"

"Are you serious, Heather?"

Heather frowned. "Let *her husband* deal with that. But then again, I guess I don't have to worry about her calling anytime soon until she *resurfaces.*"

"Heather, what *is* it?" He pounded the eggshell-colored wall. "Why are you so cold-hearted? Why! Tell me, right now. I can't take it anymore."

Heather grazed by him, leaving behind the scent of her expensive perfume. "You're *my* husband," she said, rage blending in every word. "You shouldn't have to talk to *any* other woman but me. I'm your wife."

Tony gripped his head, applying pressure. "Baby, please cut me some slack. Yes, I love you. But right now, I'm concerned about her."

She walked into the den with a glass dangling in her hand and sat down in the black leather chair. "I'm not. You do enough of that for everybody."

"Look, I'm not chasing you around this house." Tony sat beside her placing a hand on his forehead to wipe away the perspiration. "I can't believe how ungrateful you are." He inhaled deeply, a slow throbbing in his temple increasing by the minute. He wished that throbbing was still going on in another part of his body. Wishful thinking.

Heather stared at the carpet, huffing as she said, "Ungrateful?"

Tony slowly raised his head. "Why are you complaining? You have a faithful, loving husband. We have a beautiful marriage. Well, when you're not pitching a *fit*."

Heather picked up the remote and turned on the television. Tony pried the remote from the ridges of her small fingers, turning it off. "I've worked hard to please you." Tony gasped for air. "I've gone beyond the call of duty. What more do you want me to do? You or the kids aren't wanting for anything."

Heather swallowed a big gulp of water, but she didn't respond.

"Please baby. I'm willing to compromise if you are. We're all one family. My family has accepted you with open arms and at every turn, you're rejecting them." Tony stood and paced.

Heather's lips curled into a sneer. "Tiffany doesn't understand what a family is because she doesn't have children." Heather stood, sauntered out and stopped in the hallway. "And while we're on the subject, can she *have* children?"

"You're going too far and I won't tolerate you saying that," he said, shadowing her steps.

Heather propped a hand on her hip. "I'm glad I didn't allow her to deliver our children." She stormed down the hallway to the kitchen. "She isn't a mother, so how would she know how to handle a baby."

"You're out of line. Delivering a baby and having a baby are two different things."

Heather parted her lips, just as the phone rang again.

"I have to answer that." Tony ran down the hallway, trying to calm his nerves.

"Why didn't you answer it in the kitchen!" she yelled after him.

"Hello, Brown's residence?"

Tony listened for a moment, then swung around to face his wife's glowering face. "Where was she? I'll be over in a few minutes."

Heather blew out a gust of air as she stormed past him, heading toward the steps, grumbling, "I can't believe you, Anthony."

He lowered the phone to his chest, pressing it against his chest. "Are you going with me or not?"

Heather pressed her fist firmly onto her hips. "Yeah, I'm going. I'm dying to know why little *Mrs. Saint* disappeared."

Chapter 14

For at least two hours, Smith and June Bug rode around following Morgan. She had a hair appointment, which made it easy for Smith to track her.

Sweet, predictable Morgan. No one would accuse her of living a risky lifestyle, the simple woman that she was. So if someone found her dead somewhere, they would assume she died of natural causes or an accident. Then Smith would get five hundred thousand dollars from the insurance company. If he waited until she died from actual natural causes, he might be too old to enjoy the money. He had to act now.

Smith sat in the patrol car absorbing the cool breeze flowing out of the vents. Morgan left the salon, then traveled to various locations. Smith and June Bug sat in the patrol car, waiting for her to come out of a gift shop.

Just as he had done years before with Tiffany, Smith tracked Morgan, writing down her path to and from work, noting if she attended any social activities that she hadn't told him about. He would continue to gather enough information to give to June Bug.

Morgan carried a shopping bag to her car; her platinum-blonde hair sparkled as the sun's rays pressed against it.

"Man, why do you want to get rid of that sweet-looking white lady?"

"Don't worry about it," Smith snapped.

"What do you mean, don't worry about it? You better let me know something. A man needs to know who he's killing."

"It's my wife, she's been unfaithful to me for quite some time now," Smith lied.

"Now I understand." June Bug wiped a green substance from his hands onto his pants. Smith frowned at the sight of the stuff, refusing to ask

103

him what it was. He didn't want to know. The things he had to do to get things done.

A smile unfolded on his lips. Soon his wife would be gone and he could pursue his passion full-time. Smith's greatest pleasure in working at Cloverdale was having sex with young girls who had reached the legal age. He especially enjoyed preying on single mothers who lived alone. He would stake out their apartments for a while, then set a trap. Black girls, with their luscious breasts, thick thighs and lips made him feel rejuvenated. They were a direct contrast to his aging uninteresting wife, who had refused to get cosmetic surgery no matter how much he insisted.

Over the years, Cloverdale had become his own personal *whorehouse.* He could choose any girl he wanted, depending on what fantasy he wanted to fulfill—and he had some really strange ones, too. Unknown to them, he'd caught most of them on camera, playing the scenes over and over, recreating the height of satisfaction. The fear and disgust in the girls' eyes only turned him on more. Black girls loved sex. They were built for it. The girls were vulnerable and feared being evicted, so they complied with his every command. He felt like a kid in a candy store running wild. After his first dip into a piece of chocolate, a black girl who exchanged sex for a roof over her head when she was busted for smoking weed in her apartment, Smith was hooked and had reached the point of no return. His clientele continued to expand, especially since the Cloverdale population, although it stayed the same on paper, had grown by leaps and bounds in reality—mostly young girls.

The black girls gave him a sexual sensation he had never felt with any woman—especially his wife. They knew nothing about the law, so Smith easily persuaded them. He knew what method to use. They feared being homeless more than they feared God. And that was all right with him.

But after so many easy conquests, he needed a challenge. Tiffany had provided that challenge. She couldn't be bought with gifts or threats of eviction. Everyone in the community loved Mrs. Brown.

He had always strived to have the best chicks in high school and college, but somehow after marrying Morgan, he settled for seconds from Cloverdale. Except for Tiffany, she wasn't like the other girls. She carried herself like a lady. Smith had monitored Tiffany for weeks as if doing a research paper. Exactly the type of woman he wanted to break. How dare she carry herself as though she was as important as his own children.

Tiffany fascinated him even more because she had goals and dreams. His persistent monitoring and patience were worth the wait. Besides, he wanted to take that uppity Tony off his high horse—and he'd done that, too. That summer had been great for him and soon he realized that he would have to go younger and younger to catch the pure ones before they slipped into the darkness of drugs.

The wheels of a grocery cart scraped against the concrete ground, sending a shrieking sound into the air. Smith jerked back into reality.

June Bug sunk in the seat. The heat drifted into the patrol car, amplifying the smell of urine and sweat pouring from the addict like a sieve. Smith lowered the window to allow a breeze to flow through.

"Don't leave the scene until you're sure she's dead. I don't want her to be able to identify you. If she survives, I'll have to kill her myself; then I'm coming for you."

June Bug frowned. "That's what I should've done with my wife."

A horn blew, startling them both. Smith moved the car forward. "Man, road rage is going to be the death of a lot of people." Smith coughed, pulled out his beige handkerchief and wiped his nose. "What were you saying about your wife?"

Smith stared at Morgan as she pulled out her cell phone from her purse and dialed, probably calling one of the little bastards. Sometimes he felt she paid more attention to them than to him. She was nothing like his mother. His beautiful mother. But he couldn't think about that right now.

June Bug sighed slowly. "I had a beautiful wife, a nice house over in Walden Ridge and four children. I had a family. But one day I came home early and caught my wife in bed with another man and a woman. I lost it, man." He gawked at his hands for a few seconds. "I wanted to kill her. I left my house, came to this project years ago, bought some crack and smoked it. The first puff of crack had me hooked. I didn't care about anything else."

"That's *messed* up." Smith started laughing. "Why didn't you just get in the bed with them?"

"Come on, man, how would I look sharing my wife with someone else?"

"Don't get so pious. Didn't you have kids with Zoe while you were married to someone else?"

The addict stared at him. "How do you know her name?"

Smith kicked himself for giving away too much information. He'd have to be really careful with this guy. Smith ignored the question.

"Now you see why death's the only option for Morgan." Smith gripped the steering wheel. "I can't have it any other way."

June Bug moved his tongue around in his mouth, forcing it to press against his cheeks. "So when do you want this to happen?"

Smith's pager went off. He glanced at the number. Morgan.

"I'm waiting for a rainy day."

"Why rain?"

"Don't you remember the plan?"

"Oh."

June Bug held out his hand. Smith dropped a small plastic bag into the trembling brown hand.

The man wanted help. Smith would give him all the help he needed after Morgan was six feet under.

Chapter 15

Tony ran up the wooden spiral steps, passing the guest room, the large crystal vase mounted on top of a three feet column, his children's rooms and went straight to his bedroom, leaving a disgruntled Heather downstairs. Changing his clothes, he reflected on the reasons he didn't want Tiffany to go into Cloverdale alone, especially with Smith still lingering in the area. God, he couldn't wait for that man to retire or die. Maybe then and only then Tiffany would tell him what had happened to her. But until then, he had to find a way to stop the dreadful memories of Sergeant Smith from invading his own mind . . .

The summer sun diminished slowly into the horizon as people from Cloverdale gathered in clusters on The Hill. Mostly the outsiders—dealers that came from as far away as New York, brought drugs and a new sense of hopelessness to the vulnerable. Tony and David came up the grassy area leading to The Hill with a bag in their hands. Some people were nicely dressed and others looked as if they were malnourished, making it easy to distinguish the drug dealers from the addicts. Seventeen-year-old Tony never had a problem with any of them.

Smith's patrol car crept towards them. People immediately dispersed, found another spot to hang out, then came back when they were sure he had left.

The patrol car stopped at the top of The Hill; all eyes turned, anticipating the sergeant's next move. The folks who remained glanced at one another nervously, wishing they'd run earlier like some of their companions.

"Everyone stand still!" Smith yelled from his bullhorn.

Tony nudged David, urging him to turn so they could go back the way they came. David stood his ground. He had to deliver some food to his sister, Star, who would go for days without eating if David didn't look out for her.

Star straddled both sides of the fence, skipping school to hang out with her drug-dealer boyfriend. Later she switched boyfriends but kept her attachment to crack and soon became both an addict and a prostitute. No one in her family would have anything to do with her but David. And he wouldn't come to The Hill without someone watching his back. Normally, that person was Tony.

Smith stepped out of the patrol car. Hastily, he approached the individuals who were still huddled like flies on a turd. Tony scanned the area. Off to the side, girls with short skirts, high heels and thick make-up stood peering at him. Most of them looked as though they were on the verge of dying from drugs or AIDS. Star hadn't had that big of a downhill spiral. Yet.

"All of you need to get out of here or be arrested," Sergeant Smith commanded, glaring at the women.

They picked up the pace, walking back down The Hill while Smith continued his ranting. Tony and David inched back down The Hill. Unfortunately, they were not fast enough.

"You boys stop and separate from each other!" Smith pointed his nightstick at them.

A nervous chill shot through Tony's body. His legs shook even though Smith's gaze was firmly focused on the guys a few feet ahead of them. The men grumbled. Some moved. Others didn't.

Smith's face turned a bright red. "Separate or I'll take all of you to jail," he demanded again. "I know there's dope here and I'm going to find it."

Tony froze. Any movement would cause Smith to turn around. But if he stayed, he would be caught in Smith's web. Tony signaled to David to stop moving.

Smith scanned the ground, then pointed his nightstick at the guys he wanted to stay or leave. After designating his selections, he counted five guys, which, to Tony's dismay, included him and David.

Tony remained calm; they were innocent.

"Here he goes again," Tony said, loud enough for David to hear him.

"I know, man, why is he all up on us?" David whispered as they stood in what soon became a line-up.

"Just relax, man, he knows we don't get down with drugs," Tony replied.

Sergeant Smith whipped around. Tony and David instantly halted their conversation.

"You two sit down!" He angled his stick at Tony and David.

An uneasy feeling settled in the pit of Tony's stomach.

"Okay, if everyone stands still this will be over before you know it."

Three of the guys were fidgety and kept going in and out of their pockets.

"Tony and David, stand up and join the other guys," he commanded.

"Now, who has the drugs?" Smith trailed along the line, his shiny black shoes scraping the dirt-filled areas between the grassy ones. "Everyone empty your pockets and dump the contents on the ground."

One by one he searched the guys, inspecting the ground near them. He told the first three guys they were free to go. Tony and David were searched last.

Tony wasn't worried; they didn't have any drugs on them. He didn't have the slightest idea how to sell drugs and was shocked the sergeant wanted to search them. He stood silently, trying not to show any fear, though his heart pounded in his chest.

Sergeant Smith walked over to Tony and David and looked down, then grinned. Something about that smile didn't sit right. Out of the corner of his eye, Tony looked at the ground. A small plastic bag with a white powdery substance was only a few inches away from where he stood.

"What do we have here?" Smith asked in a patronizing tone, rocking cockily on his heels. Then he reached down, plucked it from the grass, still watching the two boys. Tony's eyes widened to the point he felt they were ready to pop out of their sockets.

"Yes, *Mister there are some good people in the hood*, what do you have to say for yourself now?" Smith sneered, his eyes flashing with deceitfulness as his gaze shifted between the drugs on the ground and the two boys.

Tony rocked on his feet, feeling faint. "That's not ours," Tony said, voice wavering. "We don't sell drugs. One of the other guys dropped that. But you let him go."

Smith's smile widened, but he didn't say a word. The loud roaring sound of a fire truck zoomed down the street. "Shut up and stand still!"

Smith whipped out a pair of cuffs, then read Tony and David their rights. He thought how disappointed his mother would be with him, so he continued to plead his case. "Sergeant Smith, we're good students. We've got scholarships and stuff. We've never had any problems with the law."

"There's always a first time for everything."

"You should have arrested the guys you let go. They're the ones who had the dope. They're the ones bringing it to our neighborhood."

Tony looked around. No one else was in sight. The reality of going to jail was a nightmare. Sergeant Smith ordered him to sit down.

Tony looked toward the dark blue sky, shaking his head. *God, please help us.* The boys, now cuffed, trudged behind Smith to the patrol car. Smith halted, turned on his heels and looked at both boys. "Look, I'll make a deal with you."

Tony stared at the sergeant for a few moments. "What type of deal?"

Smith looked over his broad shoulders. "I'll sweep everything under the rug if you two agree to help me move some things from my cousin's store."

Tony peered at the man. He was up to something. The drug charges were a little too convenient. "When?"

"Tuesday night around 9 o'clock." Smith's face brightened. "The weatherman predicted rain, so that'll be great. But if it doesn't rain, then I'll reschedule."

Smith whipped the keys from his waist, releasing the tight cuffs from Tony's hand. Tony asked, "Why do we have to move things from the store? And why does it matter if it rains or not?"

Smith scowled. "Do you want to ask questions or face charges?"

Tony glanced at David.

"Now, don't interrupt me," Smith snapped, taking a quick look around. "Make sure you guys wear shorts and sneakers. It'll be easier to move things dressed that way."

Tony couldn't help but ask, "In the rain?"

"Yeah, in the rain," he shot back. "I'll pick you up down the street near that abandoned building at 8:30." He pointed his finger at them. "You better not be late, or I'll come to your apartments and arrest you."

With a drug charge, his future was in jeopardy; Tony didn't have a choice.

"Which—which abandoned building," David asked. "There's a lot of them down the street."

Smith squinted. "Are you trying to be sarcastic?"

"No sir," David mumbled.

Smith looked over his shoulders again. "The abandoned building behind B&B Family Store."

Loud barking and growling of pit bulls from a nearby fight echoed in the air.

"God, please help us," Tony whispered. "We can't get involved in *nothing* illegal."

Smith bore down on him. "Listen," he snarled. "Possession of crack is a felony." The cuffs swung on the tip of his finger. "You can cancel your plans for college if I turn you in. I'll give you a minute to think about it."

"Man, my mother's gonna have a heart attack if she finds out about this. She has worked so hard to help my sister and me, I can't disappoint her," Tony said, unable to keep the panic from his voice.

Sergeant Smith added, "Tony, you only have one choice and that's to move those items."

Tony's eyes began to water, but no tears came out. What was the sergeant really asking them to do? He definitely didn't want to disappoint his mother and he was afraid of going to jail, so he swore he would be on time. David chimed in, agreeing to be there too.

Chapter 16

The sun diminished beyond the horizon as clouds clustered together, hiding the bright blue sky. A crystal chandelier dangled from the ceiling above the marble floor foyer. Cherrywood dining room furniture presented an old-world elegance. The white plush wall-to-wall carpet, ten-foot-high ceiling and ancient Greek columns in the living room showcased Tiffany's built-in wall aquarium. Tiffany strolled by pictures of Abraham Lincoln, Harriett Tubman, Rebecca Lee Crumpler and Barack Obama that hung on the wall instead of pictures of flowers.

Tiffany sat on the edge of the king-sized wicker bed with her hands propped under her chin. Vance stomped up the hardwood steps. She glanced at the small radio clock on her black nightstand. It was 4:30.

"Tiffany, where have you *been*?" he demanded, dark brown eyes widening as he wiped his forehead with the back of his hand. "I've been looking all over for you. I had to get someone to cover my court cases."

Vance exhaled deeply when she didn't answer. "How long have you been here?" Tiffany continued to stare at the cream carpet her husband had personally picked out.

"Do you hear me talking to you?" he said, shaking her shoulders. "Where have you been? I was worried about you. Your brother's been looking for you. Why on earth would you leave work like that?"

Tiffany glanced up at her husband. Vance's chestnut-brown complexion complemented a muscular physique for which women lusted. A perfectly trimmed mustache lay smoothly above his kissable lips. Curly black hair, his tamed beard and smooth, unblemished skin defined the dimples in his face.

"I had to clear my mind."

Vance lifted her chin with a single finger. "You *what*?"

She averted her gaze. The sunlight squeezed between the creases of the hunter-green drapes with gold panels into the room. The almond wall was accented with gold trimmed Satin Acanthus Leaf printed border paper that marched along the top portion of the wall.

"I had to get away from the office."

"Why?"

A moment of silence expanded in their bedroom. The air conditioner switched on, breezing past the fresheners in the vents, dispensing a tropical smell into the air.

"What happened, Tiffany? Nurse Patterson told Tony that you rushed out of your office after you treated a rape victim—"

Tiffany slowly slid Vance's smooth hand off her face. "She had no right to tell Tony that."

"Your brother was concerned about you. I'm concerned about you." He sat down on the bed beside her. "She didn't tell Tony the person's name."

Tiffany moved away, curling up on the soft comforter on the bed. She slowly opened her mouth. "I just had to clear my head for a second."

Vance lovingly caressed her arm. "Talk to me. Tony almost had a nervous breakdown."

"I drove around for a minute, that's all. Nothing for anyone to be worried about."

"What are you hiding from me? You've treated rape victims before. What was so different about today?"

She exhaled, letting out a weary sigh. "Nothing, Vance," she said, pushing him away. "I don't want to talk about it right now."

"I need to know, Tiffany. You're my wife. And if you're going to disappear when you treat rape victims then something's wrong." He stood and paced the carpet. "This is what you trained for, so don't lie to me. What's wrong? Why did this rape push you over the edge?"

Tiffany sat up. "Over the edge?"

Vance loosened his tie before sitting beside her. "Honey, I'm trying to figure out what's going on? I almost ran out of gas. They said I couldn't report you missing. It hadn't been twenty-four hours." He pulled off his shoes, dropping them onto the floor. "What's going on?"

"Nothing." Tiffany slid back down on the bed. "All of a sudden seeing that little girl did something to me."

"Why, honey?" He grabbed her soft hand, stroking it lightly. "Talk to me. You can't run off like this again."

Tiffany glanced at the small clock on her nightstand. "I'm okay." She scrambled off the bed, feet landing on the carpet. "We need to get ready for the game."

"Game? We need to talk about why you disappeared today!" Vance stood, blocking her path. "I need to know why you didn't call me if you were so upset. You should've come to me."

Tiffany slowly peeled off her clothes and walked to the shower.

"Tiffany, we're not finished talking," he said, following her to the bathroom.

"I hear you, Vance. Just give me a moment, please."

He followed her into the bathroom as she turned on the water. "What are you doing?"

"I'm getting ready now, so we're not late."

Vance ran a hand through his soft hair. "Look, I don't have a problem having the card game here tonight, but I think we need to talk about what happened today."

She bent over, pulling her socks off. The marble hunter-green and gold floor was a stunning contrast to the princess-cut mirror in the bathroom.

The porcelain Jacuzzi set was not just a luxury but actually a relaxation spot for Tiffany. Today she needed it much more than any other time she could remember.

"Honey, I have to ask you something," he said, unbuttoning his shirt. "And I don't want you to get upset either."

Tiffany's gaze fell on his smooth, bare chest, wishing she could lay her head there and just will the day away.

He paused before speaking. "Did something happen to you before—"

"Vance, I've already told you that I had to clear my mind today," she snapped. "Nothing's wrong." Tiffany rubbed the soft yellow sponge over her arms. "Please get ready. My brother will be here in a little while."

Vance scanned her eyes. "I know there's more to the story than what you're telling me." He pressed his hand on the glass shower door. "I'm going to get to the bottom of this one way . . . or another. I'll call Tony right now."

Vance turned and left out of the bathroom.

She continued to rub the soap over her breasts, a sudden sadness resting deep in her soul—a sadness that began on what was supposed to be the happiest day of her young life . . .

The trunk of Sergeant Smith's patrol car was dark and hot. The smell of motor oil mixed with rubber from a worn tire almost made her gag. She extended her leg, kicking everything in reach. Loud music flowed out of the speakers, elevating louder and louder as she banged on the walls in the trunk.

"God, please help me!" she screamed.

Her hopes for rescue were crushed when Smith started the patrol car up again and pulled away. Within minutes he stopped again, slammed the door and opened the trunk, then forced her into the front seat.

Tears streamed down her face. "Please, Sergeant Smith, take me home. Please!"

His strong cologne mixed with sour sweat nearly burnt the hairs in her nostrils. The sergeant reached over and grabbed her hand, taking off the cuffs.

"Please!"

He stared down at her trembling hands. "I can't do that."

Tiffany tried to stall by carrying on a conversation, hoping someone would walk by. She turned in the seat, trying to figure out what the sergeant was doing when he opened the back door. The brown paper bag was still on the back seat.

She began to shake. "Please take me home."

"Get out of the car and follow me!" he ordered. "If you make a scene, I promise I *will* kill your mother and that precious little brother of yours."

"Please, let me go," she pleaded, gripping the edge of the door.

"Did you hear me?" he asked, putting his hand on the gun. "You better not scream or run when we walk in this lobby. I'm not playing. I'll kill you."

Tiffany glanced out the window, staring at the rain, then dropped her head. With a cramped neck, she strained to look out of the patrol car window.

The man was out of his mind. She couldn't believe he would be bold enough to bring her to the Fountain Spring's Resort Hotel, a hotel for rich people. She trembled with anger as a few eyes focused her way. She didn't want to be seen walking into the hotel with a white man. Somebody would think she was a call girl or something. Her mother worked on this side of town. Oh, Lord.

Tiffany first thought about running. But where?

118

The receptionist, busy registering guests glanced up with piercing gray eyes and made brief eye contact with Tiffany. She flashed a quick look at Sergeant Smith and dropped her head, resuming her duties.

Tiffany let out several rapid coughs, wishing someone would take notice. The sergeant put a vice grip on her wrist nearly dragging her to the elevator. He didn't even stop at the front desk to pay.

"Trust me, nobody's going to help you," he chuckled. "I know all of the dirt that goes on in here." He paused. "As long as they give me my cut, then everybody can stay happy."

Tiffany's eyes locked in on a short girl with ivory skin and sky blue eyes walking toward her. The girl slowly strolled beside a tall midnight black man with her head slightly lowered causing her blonde hair to drape across her shoulders. The girl appeared to be her age. Tiffany could feel fear resonating from the girl from glancing at her trembling small hands. The same level of fear that ripped through Tiffany.

Reaching into his pocket, he whipped out the key.

When did he get the hotel key? Had he planned this all along? Thoughts tumbled through her mind like clothes in a dryer as he slipped the key into the lock, opening it.

He whipped her around, then pushed her across the room and she landed on the bed. Tiffany parted her lips to scream. Sound failed to spring forth out of her dry throat.

A pleasant scent drifted to her the moment he stepped away. Flowers were scattered all over the bed and floor as if this were a romantic date.

The bedroom was separate from the kitchen and the living room. Tiffany didn't know hotel rooms could be so large; she assumed that hotels only had a bed in one room like the ones on her side of town.

The comforter matched the curtains, instead of sheets hanging up in front of the glass. The room was nice and cool, even though it was almost a hundred degrees outside. Air conditioning was a luxury in Cloverdale—a luxury her family would never be able to afford. The carpet looked new and had no burn marks or stains. The pictures on the wall were professionally drawn with paint, a contrast to the ones on the walls in her bedroom, which had been done with pencil or watercolors—with her brother's loving touch.

All of the furniture matched, obviously from one of the fancy stores in downtown Charlotte. Tiffany's mother couldn't afford to buy so much as a pillow out of a store like that.

Tiffany stood, watching Smith out of the corner of her eye. He pulled the sheets back slowly, waiting, looking at her as though she were a willing participant.

She stood frozen at the edge of the bed. Seconds passed before he said, "Your mother and brother will be home in a couple of hours. I want to have you back home before then."

Did he know her family's schedule? She swallowed, trying to keep her fear at bay. Well, at least he didn't plan to kill her. Rumor around Cloverdale was that he had killed her cousin Star. Somehow no one ever proved it.

Sergeant Smith said softly, "Lay on the bed, Tiffany. We don't have much time."

Tiffany frowned as he placed his heavy hands on her shoulders and pressed firmly, forcing her to sit on the cool comforter.

Nervously, she slid forward to the edge of the bed and closed her eyes as if she could teleport herself to the comfort of her home.

"Here, I have something that'll help you to relax." He pulled out a bag of powder, then placed his gun and a pack of condoms on the nightstand, making sure that Tiffany watched every move.

"I'm not taking that stuff."

"Here, all you have to do is sniff a little cocaine. It will take your mind off things."

Tiffany pushed his hand away. "No!"

Smith turned toward the door. Chattering voices became louder and then died away. Tiffany's eyes drifted toward the ceiling as she shook her head, staring at the crystal light fixture.

"Here sniff it," he commanded, pushing the small plastic bag to her nose.

Tiffany shook her head vigorously, covering her face.

Smith shoved the package back into his pocket. "You can lay down on your own free will or I *will* knock you down."

She sat on the bed, helpless, half hoping someone—the maid, room service, anyone—would knock on the door or that he would change his mind. Tiffany slid back, then suddenly jerked up running for the door. His hand reached out, gripping her neck to the point that she couldn't breathe.

"Please, let me go. Please let me go home."

"It's too late for that," he growled, glaring down at her.

Overwhelmed with disbelief and unable to accept what was happening, a devastating sense of shame swallowed every ounce of hope. She had promised her mother she wouldn't have sex until she was married. Evidently, after all her efforts to stay away from the boys in Cloverdale, that promise would soon be shattered—unless she could get away.

He held up the cuffs. "Do I need to use these?"

Tiffany shook her head. If he cuffed her, she would never get away.

Sergeant Smith caressed Tiffany as he peeled off her soaked tank top, pinching her nipples hard through the fabric of her bra. She bit her bottom lip to keep from screaming. Next, he yanked down her jeans and panties at the same time, then reached down fingering the curls between her thighs.

Anger and shame battled for space within her mind.

121

Slipping out of his uniform, he walked to the edge of the bed next to her and whispered, "Slide over, baby and relax."

Tiffany shivered as his cold, sweaty, pale body slipped next to hers. Sergeant Smith retrieved his revolver from the nightstand and toyed with it as he watched her. Tiffany winced when he brought the silver barrel closer to her face. Then he put the barrel of the gun to her mouth and said, "Suck it."

Her breathing stopped for a moment as she hesitated. His face flared into a murderous scowl. The cold metal against her lips chilled her as he slid the barrel in. His fingers lingered near the trigger. The thought of the gun firing while in her mouth almost made her pass out.

"If you ever tell anyone, I'll kill you. Do you hear me?"

She couldn't speak around the silver barrel in her mouth.

"Do you hear me?" the sergeant forced the words through his teeth as he placed his hands on her shoulders and shook her. "If you even peep a word to someone, I'll make sure your mother, *Mrs. Lena Brown*, is kicked out on the streets. Or maybe found dead in a lake somewhere. And I'll do it with this gun. Do you hear me?" Smith waved the gun close to her face brushing it against her nose.

"Yes," she said, the word stumbling out of her mouth.

Sergeant Smith continued to slide the barrel in, out and around in her mouth. The acrid taste on her tongue made her choke. She glanced down and felt sick. His other hand had grasped his penis and stroked it up and down every time the barrel went into her mouth. Lunch rumbled in her stomach, trying to stay in place.

With each move of his hand, the barrel went into her mouth faster. "Girl, you don't know how long I've waited for you," he whispered more to himself than to her.

Tiffany became stiff. Her mind went blank. A sudden burning sensation in her throat made her eyes water. Sergeant Smith removed the gun and rolled it across her breasts, then placed it on the nightstand. Tiffany managed to speak in a broken whisper, "Please, let me go."

"I can't do that, baby," he said, fondling her breasts in one hand and his pink, wrinkled penis in the other. "I've waited too long for you."

"But . . . but you have a wife. You love your wife, don't you? Why do you want me?"

"You're much younger and prettier than she is." He leaned down, taking a breast in his mouth, sucking it before he said, "There are things you can do that she can't do."

"Like—like—like what?" she stammered, inching away from him, glancing once again at the door, judging the distance.

"Hmm." He said, toying with his penis. "You'll see."

He rubbed his groin on her stomach, then grabbed her trembling hand, placing it on the tip. Guiding her hand as he thrust into it, in a slow grinding motion. Moments later, her hand became wet and sticky from stroking him. She leaned over the side of the bed and lunch came streaming out.

He yanked her back on the bed before she had a chance to wipe her mouth. "You ungrateful *slut*! I'm trying to treat you nice and you get sick!" He forced her head into the pillows for a moment. She gasped for breath before he brought her back up.

Then his expression softened. "I understand. It's your first time and all. You'll like it. Trust me. I want it to be good for you too."

Sergeant Smith kissed her breasts, then licked her neck as if she had become an ice cream cone. The rest of Tiffany's lunch almost made a hasty exit.

Sliding underneath the covers, soon his tongue glazed over her stomach, then lower as he put his face between her thighs. Tiffany stared at the light fixture in the ceiling as the cold hand of fear clamped over her heart.

Tiffany drifted off thinking about her future and her family as he reached for the condom on the nightstand. He stared at Tiffany for a split second before he grabbed the condom and slipped it on. "I *hate* to use this, but . . . ."

Fear made her jerk forward, putting one foot on the ground as she twisted her body, trying to escape his clutches. He gripped her thighs and yanked her back into place, prying her legs open with one hand as he reached first for the gun with the other, then waited for her to be still.

She froze as he crawled on top. Moments later, the heavy weight of his body nearly cut off her breath, then pain ripped through her body like a bomb blast, splintering her soul as he thrust himself inside her.

Tiffany gripped the sheets tighter. Turning her head, she pressed her mouth into the pillow as she stifled a scream. As he pulled out and thrust again, ramming inside her like a power drill, she opened her mouth and let out a panicky fragile scream as she sobbed. Blood trickled down her thighs, signaling the end of her virginity. Smith moaned, thrusting wildly, like a crazed animal.

Tiffany tried to block out his loud moaning sounds. He began to shiver and balled up into a knot. A small sense of elation lifted her heart. Was he having a heart attack? Then just as suddenly fear gripped her again and she covered her mouth. If he died, she would probably face a murder charge, too!

He looked up at her, grinning. She swallowed hard.

Relief filled her body when he rolled away. "I'll be back," he said with an even wider grin. Tiffany reached for her clothes, but before she could grab them off the floor, he said, "Lie still."

Smith took her clothes into the bathroom with him. Tiffany lowered her head and cried. She glanced at the sheets and saw blood. Her blood. Going to college was not worth all of this misery. She grabbed the pillow, placing it over her chest, then rocked back and forth. Everything in the world stopped functioning. She couldn't hear or see anything. She prayed for herself. She prayed for her family. She prayed the nightmare would be over soon.

When Sergeant Smith came out the bathroom, Tiffany felt as if she would die when she saw his penis protruding ahead of him. With a grin, he motioned her.

She began to cry as her heart felt as if Sergeant Smith had nearly emotionally drained her soul.

For what seemed like an eternity Smith forced her to do unspeakable things. Tiffany could only whimper in pain or send up a prayer that it would all be over soon.

When finished, he looked at Tiffany and grabbed her chin with his wide pale hand. "Go take a shower."

Tiffany grabbed her clothes, staggering to the bathroom. As the water bounced off her body, she could smell his cologne, a pungent scent that she would never forget. She rubbed the towel over her body, rubbing her thighs. If she scrubbed hard enough, she could erase the dreadful experience. She washed her body repeatedly and thought it was all a bad dream until he came into the bathroom.

"Hurry up, you only have an hour. Don't you have to bake that cake for your mother and brother?"

He must be insane! Baking a cake for her family was the last thing on her mind.

He stayed in the bathroom, gawking at her. He rubbed his chest. Oh, God. Was he going to do something else?

"No one finds out about this," he said, placing his hand around her throat. She gasped for breath.

"Not your mother, not anyone at the community center. Oh, and let's not forget about your *star athlete* brother," he said, sneering. "I'll make sure he goes to prison for life. I know people that'll pull strings for me. Maybe I can have him charged with rape or . . . murder." Placing his finger on Tiffany's mouth, he pressed her lips together. "You better not say a word. Do you hear me?"

Tiffany managed to say, "Yes, I hear you."

Ten minutes later, she sat in the front seat of the patrol car again, tears dripping down on her trembling hands. At the light, he leaned down and licked the tears off her cheek. His tongue felt like sandpaper. He stroked his fingers through her hair and kissed her firmly on the lips.

"This is our special secret," he whispered. "You'll always have a special place in my heart."

This was one secret Tiffany had to take to her grave.

Chapter 17

Smith had dropped June Bug off at the alley near the creek. Meeting the addict earlier that day brought Smith one step closer to getting rich. Glancing at his watch, he realized that he only had an hour before his twelve-hour shift was over. He wanted to spend the rest of the evening with his buddies, sipping on some beers or possibly hitting a strip club.

He shoved the brochure back into the drawer and walked out of the office. Smith had paid the premiums on Morgan's policy for years, not realizing that it would become part of his retirement plan. He had assumed yelling at Morgan would make her a strong-minded woman, would make her obey him. Now it wouldn't matter whether she had a strong mind or not. Now it wouldn't matter if she took that promotion or not.

The sun dipped beyond the horizon as he pulled the black patrol car in front of the police department. The shifts would change any moment and his buddy, Officer Mills, would be at the desk in the evidence lab. Going to the lab was a normal routine for some officers, but Chief Clarence Jones had recently made changes. Materials for a case had to be checked in at the desk for an on-call person to register it. Traffic flow in and out had been restricted to ensure accurate information. This put a little crimp in Smith's plans, but thanks to his buddy, it didn't stop him.

He strolled down the long white hallway with a brown sack in his hand. Uniformed officers were bent over their desks writing reports, reading magazines and shooting the breeze. Smith hurried past the magistrate's office and the warrant squad room.

Mills, with a fresh tan and green eyes, sat behind a long desk surrounded by a bulletproof window. The Community Watch newsletter in his left hand was at least three issues old. Smith tapped on the window with his wedding band.

Spanish words flowed out of the small radio next to the desk clock. Mills reached out and turned down the volume.

The Spanish song took Smith by surprise. Oh, yeah, Officer Mills' wife was from Spain. That would explain it.

"Good afternoon, Smith," Mills said, closing the bright yellow paper.

"Good afternoon to you, too. I need to put this stuff in the evidence lab," Smith said, lifting the brown sack in his right hand.

"What have you got there?"

A bitter smile spread on his lips. "You know, the usual stuff from Cloverdale."

"Man, the crime rate over there is ridiculous," Mills said, shaking his small, bald head. "I don't see how you do it. If I were you, I'd put in a transfer. A lot of officers don't want to work over there."

Smith grimaced, realizing that at first, he didn't want to work there either. Then he learned of the side benefits—and that's what made it worthwhile. "I'm retiring in three weeks. I want to finish up what I started over there," Smith said.

Mills' eyebrows drew in. "Who's gonna take over?"

"Sergeant Clark," Smith said. A sharp pang of resentment cut through his gut.

Mills slapped his hand on his forehead. "Good ol' Brian." He smiled, swinging side to side in his chair. "He's really worked himself up in the ranks."

"Yeah, if you ask me . . . "

"What?" Mills' eyes widened.

"Cloverdale's going to be a real challenge for our little Bible thumper."

128

Mills held out his left hand. "Give me the stuff and I'll register it."

Smith looked over his shoulder, scanning the hallway before he leaned closer to the window, locking gazes with Mills. "I want to put the stuff in there." Smith pressed his nose onto the glass. "You know how the other evidence lab officers are. Stuff comes up missing or gets mixed up all the time." Smith stepped back, scanning the hallway. "I can't risk having my evidence tampered with."

Mills sat up, casting a glance at the screen displayed before him. No other officers were in the area. A black wall directly behind him prevented him from seeing every angle in the evidence lab.

"You know how the crime rate is in Cloverdale," Smith said, lowering his voice. "I'm trying to clean up that neighborhood. I can't afford to lose another case 'cause someone screwed up."

Mills sighed. "Yeah, you do have a point." Glancing at the screen again, he finally pressed a red button. "Hurry up."

Smith nodded before disappearing through the metal doors. The evidence lab was dark. Plaques dangled from the wall and shelves from the ceiling, designating where things should be placed. The floor was stacked with plastic sealed boxes.

Smith ran straight to the narcotics shelves. Huge quantities of dope came into view. He quickly scooped up small portions of crack out of several evidence bags.

"What's taking you so long?" Mills asked, walking up behind Smith.

Smith jerked back. His heart leaped into his throat. Mills was a clean-cut officer.

"I—I was making sure the materials I checked in last week were still here."

Mills' big blue eyes darted around the lab. "Were they?"

129

"No. That's why I had to bring this stuff in," Smith said as he slowly lifted the brown bag, bearing a tight grip. "I'm taking my stuff now."

Mills paused for a few seconds.

"What?" snapped Smith.

"I sometimes wonder about you Smith," chuckled Mills.

A bead of sweat trickled down Smith's face. "I'm sure you have more things to wonder about . . . like your *male* friend."

Mills flinched like he had been busted.

"Don't worry. I know how to keep a secret," chuckled Smith. "So, how are your *wife* and kids doing?"

"Fine," mumbled Mills in a hasty tone. "Hurry up." Mills walked back to his desk, footsteps echoing in the huge room.

Hands shaking, Smith rushed over to the firearms shelves, registered three stolen guns and fake pieces of crack into an evidence lab bag and left.

By the time he finished, there was enough crack in his brown sack to supply the entire Cloverdale community. Morgan's fate was all but sealed.

Smith could continuously play the faithful, caring and loving husband, putting on a front for Morgan and his co-workers. They had fallen for it all this time. Maybe he had Sergeant Clark beaten at his own game.

An hour later, as Morgan packed the last of her things, Smith propped his legs on his coffee table watching the news to keep track of the weather. The murder had to take place on a rainy night. Unfortunately, rain wasn't in the forecast for at least a week.

Morgan had made plans for the weekend. Smith had forgotten all about their anniversary. Plans of spending his Friday night at the strip club had to be canceled.

They pulled in front of the Davenport Bed & Breakfast Inn. The green grass, wooded areas and wild animals brought a touch of excitement. He was fond of the outdoor scenery.

He followed Morgan into a large lavishly furnished room with violet and yellow accented colors. Pictures of historical churches and monuments were framed on the wall, along with different types of flowers.

"Hurry up, Paul, it's time for us to get our massages," Morgan said smiling, her grayish-blue eyes shining with excitement.

Twenty minutes later, Smith lay stretched out on the massage table, with Morgan in the next room. He glanced over his shoulder, speaking to the massage therapist, "You have the best hands in the world, Anna. I could make you feel as good as you're making me feel right now."

Anna giggled as she placed her soft white hands on his back. "Mr. Smith, you're funny. I'm probably young enough to be your daughter."

"You can call me Daddy. I can show you things those young guys ain't learned yet."

Rosemary incense dispensed a soft, enchanting smell into the dimly lit room. Thoughts of his dog, Dexter, flashed across his mind. Dexter was roaming a riverbank where Smith and his father were fishing one day. Smith took him home. He lived on a farm on the outskirts of Ithaca, New York, helping out with the chickens and cows, several miles away from his schoolmates. Dexter was his only friend.

The droplets of water also made him reminisce about his mother. After his mother worked a long day, which was usually a ten-hour shift at Lola's Diner, Smith would fix a hot, bubbly tub of water for her. On a cold winter night in January, a day before his birthday, Smith waited for her to come out of her bathroom. She never did.

The hairs on the back of his neck stood up as the house became eerily silent. Tipping to the bathroom, he inched open the door, only to find his

131

mother stretched out in a tub of red water. Her wrists slit so hard her hand nearly dangled off the porcelain tub.

He was twelve years old. Was that her way of escaping? When his mother was gone, the belt landed on his back. Not to mention the late nights when his father would slip into his bed and hurt him in ways he could never mention. When Smith fought back, the next day his father took Dexter to town and left him. Smith didn't eat for days but found pleasure in killing the chickens. As he held their rubbery little necks wringing the life out of them, he imagined they were his father instead.

Three months later, when his father died in an *accident*, Smith told the police officers that his father liked to listen to music while he bathed and the radio had fallen in the tub electrocuting him. And that was the end of the investigation. Smith bounced from one foster home to the next and refused to see a psychiatrist or therapist which had been recommended by several social workers. Years later, he enlisted in the military; then he went to college. Then he met Morgan.

"Mr. Smith . . . Mr. Smith," Anna said, gently shaking his shoulder.

"Yes, darling." He smiled.

Anna pressed him back down on the table. "Okay, Mr. Smith, what are your problem areas?"

"Right here." Smith rolled over and pointed to his groin. "Together," he said grinning, "we can fix that problem."

Anna motioned for him to turn over. "Now, Mr. Smith, that's not going to happen. Let's get back to this session; you only have five minutes left."

Smith glanced up into her dark brown eyes. "Okay, but you never know, my wife and I might get divorced, or . . ." he caught himself. "Then Daddy could be all yours." The thought warmed him. What would his wife think if she knew how much he hated her?

Later, Smith and Morgan had dinner in their spacious suite, in the small dining area. Morgan had arranged for the hotel to send up one of their best bottles of wine. Halfway through their dinner, Smith turned to his wife. "Morgan, why did you do all this? This must've cost a fortune."

"No, not really. I've been saving it for a while. I just felt we have grown apart in the last couple of years." Morgan plucked a lint ball off his shirt. "You know I love you as much as I did on our wedding day."

Smith didn't respond. Instead, he concentrated on his meal. They ate grilled chicken breasts, asparagus and baked potatoes, Smith's favorite dish. Smooth and mellow tones flowed out of the speakers, creating a nice and cozy atmosphere in the black and gold decorated dining area. The lights were dim with a shimmer from the candle on the table.

"Anyway, I received a big bonus at work," Morgan said as she sliced her chicken.

Sergeant Smith almost choked on his potatoes. "You did?"

"Yeah, I thought this would be the perfect way to spend it." She smiled. "We're gonna have fun this weekend, Paul."

"Yeah perfect, uh-huh." Sergeant Smith tried to focus on his plan as Morgan continued talking.

The red roses in the center of the table released a soft, delicate smell into the air. He plucked one and presented it to his wife. "Goodness, the time has *really* passed. I remember when you were the captain of the cheerleader squad and when you won the college's beauty pageant."

Morgan blushed as she sipped on her wine.

"Gorgeous would be an understatement for that flawless skin, soft blonde hair, long lavish eyelashes that hypnotized a lot of guys on campus and tits the size of ripe melons . . . ."

Morgan's smile wavered as it always did when he addressed her that way. One of the first things he wanted was for her to have those breasts lifted back to their perky domain. She refused.

"You were wife material and I had to snatch you up. I was fascinated by your beauty and graceful personality."

A smile slowly formed on her lips.

Smith slid an asparagus spear into his mouth. "Your skin was soft and filled with the radiance of peaches and cream." He glanced at her wrinkled skin and sags around her eyes and neck and grinned, bringing home the fact that she could use a little help these days.

"You were pleasing to the eyes too, Paul. You swept me off my feet. You *were* a nice, respectful, smart guy. I knew you wanted me when you tried to join the sorority just to be near me. You didn't realize that it was just for girls." She blushed, letting out a small trickle of laughter. "You tickled me when you participated in essay contests. "You never won but the fact that you were chosen as a potential candidate was good enough for me."

Morgan grabbed his hand and kissed it. "In college, a lot of people thought you were a cocky, conceited and flamboyant guy. I saw something different." She grinned. "From the fancy clothes you wore, everyone thought you were from a wealthy family. I hated how people treated you when they found out the truth. It didn't matter to me. I loved you regardless."

He pushed a spoonful of potatoes into his mouth. As much as he had just tried to humiliate the woman, she'd managed to turn the tables.

"I think the other guys on campus were intimidated by you. Your military background seemed to frighten them. None of the guys would speak to me when they found out we were dating."

He squared his shoulders, laughing. "I guess I schooled those young Ivy Leaguers, huh?"

"Yes, you did." Morgan placed her small hand over her mouth, trying to hold in a chuckle.

"I remember the first time I saw you on Cornell's campus, I drooled. You really stood out in the crowd . . ." he said as he gazed at the excess weight she had gained after having their three children. Why wouldn't Morgan get plastic surgery to restore her beauty? He knew Morgan was a Christian woman who believed in allowing God to do his work. But even *God* would have been as disappointed as Smith was at the moment.

"That's not what you told me." Morgan tapped his hand. "You told me my large juicy breasts made your eyes follow me."

"There was more to it than just your breasts." Smith laughed to cover his true feelings. "You were a feisty mid-western chick who didn't smoke cigarettes or do drugs. That's why we are still together after twenty-five years.

"Seems like we made a good decision in life. I love you, Paul," Morgan said as she caressed his hand. "We have three beautiful children."

Smith flinched as the faces of his children flashed before him. Paul, Jr. was the spitting image of him, Crystal resembled her mother and Megan looked like both of them.

Morgan leaned toward him. "I *really* want to work on our marriage and I think this is a good start. We've been tied down with our careers and need a little spice to jumpstart our marriage again. You know it's 'til death do us part."

"That's what they say," he said, lifting his glass. "Til death."

Chapter 18

A disgruntled Tony left the house to go to the garage with Heather marching right on his heels. He pulled out his keys right as Heather walked to her car.

"I want to drive my car to *Snobville,*" Heather said. "So, when I'm ready to leave I don't have to hear you tell me five more minutes," she nearly growled.

Tony looked back at her. "Well, if push comes to shove Vance can bring me in."

Heather glared at him over the roof of the car. "I can't wait to hear why she ran out of her office today."

She cruised down the street as though they'd entered a Thanksgiving Day Parade. He remained silent, listening to the purr of the engine, fuming inwardly, knowing that she wanted to start an argument so they could turn around and go back to the house. He wouldn't give her that satisfaction. She certainly hadn't given him any satisfaction.

Tony put in a CD. A thousand questions for his sister lingered in his mind. The more he thought about his disdain for Smith, the more he remembered she had every reason to . . .

The day after their false arrest, Tony stood next to David at the bus stop for school, afraid to open his mouth. Smith could be watching them. He had to stick to his agreement or face jail time. The bus couldn't come fast enough. At least inside the doors of Independence High School, the Sergeant couldn't follow them.

Hours later, the boys sat in the cafeteria off to themselves. White metal tables lined up along the long, gray painted walls and clustered in the center of the room, leaving a narrow space for the students to walk through. Students pushed one another in the line to get a slice of pizza and fries. The spicy smell of pepperoni floated around in the cafeteria. Tony was too nervous to eat but managed to force a few fries down his throat. "You know we have to do this tonight."

David glanced around, before saying, "I'm scared."

"Me, too."

"Suppose he's one of those sick white men who like young boys? What do you think he wants us to do?"

Tony turned and looked over his shoulders, making sure no one heard them talking. "I don't know. All he said was that we'd be moving some things."

"But what kind of items, Tony?"

Tony glanced at David's large birthmark on his neck which could be seen several feet away. "I don't know, man, but I know we have to do it or else."

"Maybe we should tell somebody."

"David, are you crazy?" Tony closed his eyes and slowly opened them while exhaling. "You know he'll put that charge on us," he whispered. "One day somebody's gonna get him for all the dirt he does."

"I know, but I still think we should tell," David said, barely above a whisper.

Laughter filled the cafeteria as a student fell, splattering his food on the floor. Within seconds a crowd surrounded the kid, taunting and teasing him.

Tony turned to David. "Who's going to believe us?"

"My mama will. Yours, too," David mumbled.

"He knows people in high places." Tony looked around the cafeteria, fearing someone would hear them. "He'll fry us then take it out on our mothers."

David's dark brown eyes widened with fear. "But we're innocent."

"Who's gonna believe two guys from Cloverdale?"

"Yeah, you're right." David sunk into his chair. "I guess we don't have a choice." David shoved a fry into his mouth.

Tony looked at the large clock on the wall, stood, grabbed his book and walked smack into Mrs. Pratt.

Mrs. Pratt pulled him off to the side. "What's wrong?"

Tony glanced down at the books as David pulled up beside him.

"You're not yourself today." Mrs. Pratt stared at him. "You're always so full of life, laughing and joking with the other students. Why are you so quiet today?" She glanced at David. "Something's bothering you. Why don't you come into my office and talk to me?"

Tony hesitated. He felt comfortable talking to Mrs. Pratt, but if Smith tried something underhanded, his future would be jeopardized. "I'm fine. I'm just tired today." He forced a smile on his face, then walked to his class.

At basketball practice, Tony missed several lay-ups, free throws and jump shots. He couldn't remember the plays and had several turnovers.

Coach Johnson, a tall, black and normally mild-mannered man, now wore a serious frown as he shook his head. "Tony and David, you better get it together. Play some defense and run the ball back. Don't come to my practice half-stepping!"

Tony and David were star athletes, starters. They tried to live up to their normal stride.

Coach Johnson gritted his teeth every time Tony passed by him.

Twenty minutes later, Coach Johnson slammed his clipboard on the blue and gold court. "Tony and David, leave right now! If you're not going to practice hard like the other guys you don't need to be here. You are not going to waste my *time* or your teammates' time. Get out right now."

That evening, Tony and David met near the mailboxes, then walked to the designated spot which was four blocks away from Cloverdale. They shared a small flimsy umbrella that could be broken or whisked away if a strong wind came along. The lightning and thundering overhead did nothing to ease their already anxious mood. They were wearing shorts and sneakers as Sergeant Smith had instructed. Although the umbrella barely covered them and the rain pelted their bare arms and legs, the only thing that really mattered was getting things finished so they could put this behind them.

Tony wanted to get home in time to make sure Tiffany was all right. He had a really bad feeling about being away from her and followed her almost every place she went. Smith would comment on that, but not until yesterday did Tony realize that Tiffany really needed that protection. Right now, she was at the house alone and a small shiver of worry filled him every time he thought about it.

Tony had told his mother he had a late practice at the school. He had never lied to his mother so she didn't doubt him. David had used the same excuse just in case their mothers talked—which often happened since both women worked on the same side of the town.

While waiting near the abandoned building, across the street from a run-down used-car lot, the black patrol car pulled up next to the garbage cans just down the street. The headlights blinked twice, signaling to the boys that he had seen them. Tony froze when the lights blinked again.

A chill ran through his body. His clothes were soaked, plastered to his skin. David coughed a few times, rubbing his eyes with the back of his hand. A few seconds later, a tall, skinny, straggly white lady wearing a short red miniskirt and stilettos, scrambled out of the passenger seat while wiping her mouth and fixing her clothes. She disappeared behind a building.

Smith pulled up in his patrol car and told the guys to get in the car. A strong funky scent assaulted Tony's nose. He frowned, closing his eyes slightly to brace himself.

They jumped into the back seat of the patrol car, drenching the warm leather seats. Tony looked at David as the sergeant pulled off in a rush.

While driving, Smith talked to someone on his cell phone. Tony listened closely, trying to get a little inside information.

"Where is he taking us," David whispered as his bottom lip trembled.

Tony placed a long finger on his lip, signaling David to be quiet.

"How many minutes do they have?" The sergeant said, turning down Central Boulevard. "Are you sure that the electrician did his part?"

Tony glanced at David and slid down in the seat. A loud horn blew as Smith ran a red light. He glared at the old lady, flicking his blue lights on and off.

"Yes, it's two black guys."

David leaned forward, resting his head in his hands. Tony tapped his cousin on the shoulders. He shrugged him off.

"No, we don't have to pay them anything," Smith snapped. "What do I look like? How long will it take for me to get my money?" He paused for a few moments before saying, "I'll be the first one on the scene. I told you, I patrol that area." Smith peered in the rearview mirror, staring at the boys. Tony looked away. "Did you scan your credit card at the hotel? They'll need proof that you were out of town. Where did you get the moving truck?"

Sergeant Smith's pink lips broke into a smile. Then just as suddenly he hung up the phone and laid it down next to him on the seat. The patrol car charged down the street like a bat out of hell. He continued to check on the boys through his rearview mirror.

David kicked Tony's foot and squinted. Tony shrugged slightly. He didn't know why the sergeant would talk about his plans unless he was going to kill them. And from what he had heard, Smith wasn't above killing.

David started praying, "God, please protect me and Tony. Our Father which art in heaven...."

Ten minutes later the patrol car pulled up in front of a dark alley near a small bridge. Smith's tall form stepped out of the patrol car, then he opened the back door. "Go stand in the alley by the dumpster. My cousin will come get you."

Tony stepped out of the car into the pouring rain. He didn't bother to open the umbrella for all the good it had done so far. He looked at the piled-up debris.

"You'd better not mess this *job* up or else," Smith said, glowering at the two boys.

Tony and David waited, tucked in the filthy alley like two homeless people hiding from the police. The alley was dark. Rats scurried from the dumpster to the drainpipes, searching for food. The foul smell of an animal's carcass bombarded their noses, forcing them to gag. Rain poured down on them, soaking their already drenched shoes and shorts. Chill bumps broke out on Tony's thin arms as David's teeth chattered a rhythm of their own.

They stood outside in the alley for ten minutes as Smith waited in his nice, warm patrol car. A white truck crept by, then backed into the alley, parking directly in front of a store's metal door. The headlights were off, but from the long rectangular shape and large tires, Tony could tell that it was a moving truck

A short, chubby, white man opened the door and nearly slipped as his feet touched the muddy ground. Tony couldn't see his face clearly in the dark alley but he could hear him talking on his cell phone and assumed from the conversation that Smith was on the other line.

"Yeah, I should've ripped that insurance company off a long time ago," the man said with a harsh laugh, propping up a jumbo green and white umbrella. "Yep, we're going to split the profit right down the middle."

Tony felt a huge sense of apprehension. Not only were they facing cocaine charges but now breaking and entering would be added to the mix.

"Their company's had several false alarms lately because of the wiring system."

Smith got out of the car, phone to his ear, startling his cousin when he appeared next to him under the umbrella. "So, are we good to go, Timmy?"

"What are you still doing here!" Timmy barked, glancing at the two boys then back to Smith.

"Had to make sure these *imbeciles* stayed put. So, we're good, right?"

Tim coughed into his hand, his body jiggling with the effort. "Sure, when it's thundering and lightning the alarm system fails." He coughed again—harder this time. "And it delays the response to the company."

"What are you saying?" Smith shoved the man, then looked at Tony and David. "I thought all of this was taken care of?"

"Calm down. Sometimes, thunder and lightning trigger the alarm system. The alarm company had to send a technician out five times this month. I don't think they will this time."

Smith lit a cigarette, took a long pull and exhaled in the direction of Tony and David.

A bright light flashed across the sky and a loud rumbling noise followed right after. The rain continued to fall as the lightning continued above.

"Did they fix it?" Smith asked, staring at the man.

Timmy glanced over at Tony and David. "It still goes off for no reason now and the cameras are still messed up."

Tony wiped the moisture off his face and rubbed his eyes, then looked at David.

"I'm glad things are still out of whack, Timmy."

"Hey stop using my name. They could tell—"

The sergeant gripped his nightstick. Tony's eyes widened bigger than golf balls. "They're not telling anyone," he said, glaring at the boys. "So don't get your boxers in a twist."

Timmy glanced warily at the two boys. "Well, anyway, the alarm company needs a part to fix the problem. The part's out of stock. It won't be in until next week."

"I just want things to go right."

Tim drew closer to Smith. "I told you my electrician rigged the system for us tonight. No need to worry. I've timed the response time. You better do your part!"

Smith pushed him back with an index finger to his chest. "Oh, I'm going to take care of my part. Everything better go like you said."

After hearing their conversation, Tony's bladder suddenly became full. Then the man walked over to them. "Get in the truck!"

From a distance, Smith yelled, "Tony, you better hurry up." Then he laughed. "No, take your time. I'll look after that precious sister of yours . . . ."

Tony swallowed a big ball of spit. His teeth began to rattle and his hand started shaking. Angered, he turned to follow Smith. The patrol car shot out of the alley and out of reach.

Timmy gripped Tony's collar, saying, "Let's go."

They trudged behind the heavy man and slid into the passenger seat of the van. When Tim got in, he squished Tony and David against the passenger door. At least they were out of the drizzling rain.

"Here, you boys take this stuff and put it on," he ordered.

They slipped on black gloves, black long-sleeved shirts and black masks.

The man was also putting on gear, but he had on dark blue denim jeans.

"Why does he have pants on?" David mumbled.

Tony shrugged, then whispered. "I don't know."

While he put on his gear, Tim's breathing came hard and fast. His stomach pressed against the steering wheel as he leaned down to get something from underneath. Finally, he sat up with a crowbar clutched in his left hand.

"Get out of the truck," he said, gasping. "It's time to start."

They tried to avoid the puddles in front of the brown metal door but soon followed the man to the back of the truck. Tony's socks squished in his soaked sneakers. Tim handed them a dolly.

"There's a dolly near the water fountain." He faced Tony. "You'll see it when you go inside. Grab it and start working."

"I'll move the stuff from the right side of the store," he said. "Stay on the left side and don't come to my side. We've got two hours. Move quickly and *don't* talk. Don't worry about keeping up with the time; I'll do that. When you hear me cough, that's your signal it's time to leave, then grab the dolly and run like hell."

Timmy's cell phone rang and he whispered a few words to the party on the other end. Finally, he turned their way. "Let's go."

They rushed into a large dark room, passing by a staircase, fire extinguisher and water fountain. Big screen televisions, stereos, washers and dryers were all lined up neatly by the back door. Broken glass was everywhere. The awful smell of mildew mop water filled the room.

Tony grabbed the dolly. His heart pressed against his sternum as though it was going to explode. Fear pumped through his veins causing him to tremble. If they were caught . . . .

The boys moved quickly and never said a word. They hauled the items out of the back door so fast; Tony couldn't count how many they put on the truck. But his arms and legs ached as though he had been lifting weights.

Lightning rumbled overhead. The alarm could go off at any minute. The man struggled to carry one little item for every two or three Tony and David managed to ship out. For some odd reason, with every trip to the truck, Timmy managed to stay on the right side of the room.

A quick glance in the corner made Tony freeze. A tiny camera perched in the corner swung back and forth, pointing toward Tony and David. There were no cameras on the right side of the room. Tony yanked the mask down on his cousin's face, making sure the birthmark on his neck was covered.

Moving a big-screen television, Timmy coughed. Ten seconds later a loud piercing sound traveled in the room. Tim's hands clapped over his hand as he stared at the boys. Tony dropped the metal dolly, pulled David by his shirt and ran out of the building with Timmy right on their tail.

The man closed the door then hit it a couple of times with the crowbar.

"I wonder if the cameras saw us."

"Camera!" David shrieked. "*What camera!*"

Tony's heart pounded faster as the alarm continued to ring—panic punched his stomach.

The man jumped into the truck, with Tony and David fresh on his heels. He cranked it up and ran out of the alley. "Keep your mouth shut," he said while coughing to the point it looked like he was about to pass out.

About three blocks away from the store he ordered them, "Take off your gear and put it in the bag on the floor."

Swirling blue lights flashed in front of them. Headlights on an oncoming car went off and came back on.

Tony gripped the door handle as even more police cars whizzed by them, legs shaking as if he were on a roller coaster.

David bit his nails as though eating the meat off a T-bone steak.

Timmy slowed down in front of a patrol car—not a black Mustang like Smith's. They were in trouble. Deep serious trouble.

Chapter 19

Tiffany had a spacious five-bedroom house that overlooked Lake Norman, the largest man-made lake in the state of North Carolina. The cool blue waters had a shoreline of 520 miles that surrounded spacious homes. She had twisted Vance's arm to hire a high-profile interior decorator and the quirky, fast-talking Spaniard had been worth it. Although a major fight ensued when Vance insisted that he should paint the outside; Vance won. And the results were breathtaking.

"Who's ready to get their butts kicked," Tony said, chuckling as he opened the French double doors leading from the garage to the foyer.

The pleasant smell of ocean-mist oils burning in a canister drifted throughout the house.

"Come on. Let's get this party started. A new deck? Please!" Vance said, laughing as Tony waved two packs of cards in the air. "Put the hot wings over there with the chips and dip."

"Where are the kids?" Tiffany asked, peering over Vance's shoulders.

Heather answered, her voice laced with arrogance, "Robin's watching them." Her long, wavy, auburn hair swept her shoulders as she took her shoes off at Tiffany's door.

Tiffany glared at the woman. Before Heather could say another word, Tiffany turned her back, then walked off. She exhaled slowly, hoping Tony wouldn't question why she had run out of her office—especially if Heather was around.

Mixed R&B songs flowed out of the intercoms mounted in every corner of the house, giving it a cozy setting.

Tiffany's white, plush wall-to-wall living room carpet radiated the words, "Don't walk on me," but the house had a warm feel despite the forbidden zones. The white leather chairs in the living room were accented with orange, sky blue and brown throw pillows. An eight-foot custom-made palm tree took its place in the corner near the fireplace. Vance had hesitated to spend so much on an artificial tree, but Tiffany's charming smile and a few hip swivels sucked him in—along with a few other choice items.

Heather froze at the entrance. Her magnetic greenish-brown eyes took in every detail. She had grown up with the cream of the crop, studied in private schools and lived in a prestigious neighborhood. From her long wavy hair to her prissy little toes, she was flawless. She was a great mother and an almost perfect wife even though she could not cook or budget money, but her tiny streak of jealousy blemished that perfection.

"You're always asking about my children. When are you and Vance going to have kids of your own?" Heather asked as a smirk unfolded on her small lips.

Tony paused in his tracks, gaze shifting to his wife. His dark brown eyes glistened with anger.

Why would she ask that if she assumed Tiffany was infertile?

She strolled past him as she said, "You know some professional women become too wrapped up in their careers and overlook the importance of a family."

"In due time, Heather," Vance said as he approached Tiffany from behind and wrapped his long muscular arms around her. "Believe me, we're enjoying ourselves right now."

Tiffany turned, smiling at Heather as she leaned into her husband's embrace. Vance's gaze searched Tiffany's for a few moments before their lips touched. The tension in the room was lightened considerably with just that one enchanting kiss. Hand in hand, they strolled around their imported Italian oval-glassed table.

"Let's get the game rolling," Vance said.

The couples trailed into the solarium.

"Now, don't cheat, Tony." Tiffany licked out her tongue at him. "Make sure you shuffle the cards right. Did you buy new cards again? Let me see them."

Tony winked. "You don't trust me?"

"About as far as I can pick you up and throw you," she replied, holding out her hand for the cards.

"Don't worry, baby," Tony said, glancing at his wife. "We're going to burn them alive tonight." He passed her the cards to shuffle. "Tonight we're the King and Queen of Spades."

Heather's lips were pressed firmly together and she avoided eye contact as she silently dealt the cards.

"How many books are you losers bidding?" Vance asked, reaching onto Tiffany's plate, stealing a hot wing.

Tiffany slapped his hand. "Hey, get your own."

"Yours taste so much better," he said with a wink.

Tony nudged Heather. "Come on, baby. Let's have a good time."

A faint smile flashed on Heather's face, then quickly disappeared.

Tiffany's heart lightened seeing that the worry lines on Tony's forehead had vanished considerably.

"We're here to break you, cheaters, down," Tony said, pointing at Tiffany and Vance.

"Study long, study wrong," Tiffany teased.

Vance grabbed her hand, kissing the tips softly. "Come on, honey, let's give them an old-fashioned butt whipping."

Tiffany snapped her fingers to the beats that flowed into the room from the stereo. Tony stared at her. She knew he couldn't wait to talk to her. Vance kissed his way up Tiffany's bare arm.

"Put us down for seven books," Heather mumbled, peering down at the cards in her hand. "Do we need to get some tissue or the violins?" Her eyes narrowed at the happy couple.

Vance snapped, "If you're in such a rotten mood, why didn't you keep your tail at home? Don't come over here with that nasty attitude. Too much has happened today to deal with your mess too."

"Yeah, you're right," Heather smirked. "A lot *did* happen today." She stared at Tiffany.

Tiffany's eyebrows drew in. This was definitely not the time for her to explain things.

Tony slapped his cards down on the table. The room suddenly resembled a museum with four statues as only the words from Alicia Keys' song, "If I Ain't Got You," traveled in the room.

"Yeah, I should've stayed home," Heather said through her sparkling white teeth as she glared at her husband.

Anger pumped through Tiffany's veins. *Thanks, Heather.*

Tony stood. "Are you ready to go? I'm tired of this."

Heather slouched in the chair. Tony snatched the keys.

"Look, I'm not going to spoil the mood," she mumbled while sitting upright.

Vance mumbled, "Too late for that."

She glanced up at Tony. "Let's play cards."

Tony pulled his chair out, flopping down.

Tiffany reached out, rubbing her brother's hand. "It's all right, let her hold a grudge. I know how much you guys hate to lose."

"I'm gonna pour me a drink," Vance said, walking out.

Tiffany stared at Heather as if her eyes alone could choke the woman senseless.

Vance returned to the room. "Are we playing cards or not?" he asked, sipping on his drink.

Everyone stared at Heather.

"Come on. I'm ready," she replied in a low tone, then slumped in the chair.

Tony gritted his teeth as he tapped his finger on the table.

Heather glanced at him. "I said I'm ready, Anthony." She pulled to an upright position in the chair.

Tony caressed her hand.

Heather smiled and suddenly the dark mood of the evening lifted.

Tiffany knew her sister-in-law thrived on attention.

Tony looked at Heather. Slowly, his frown crumbled and a smile spread across his lips. "You might be feeling lucky tonight, but we're gonna drag you guys through the mud," he said, gently tapping Heather on the leg while looking at Tiffany and Vance.

"Don't worry, honey," Vance said to Tiffany. "Like they say, action speaks louder than words. We're going to bid five books."

"Here we go," Tiffany said, waving her cards freely in the air. She slammed the ace of diamonds on the table. "What you got for this, Tony?"

Tony's lips twitched. "Aw, see, now you're trying to start some mess."

Heather focused on the table. It wasn't just a game for Heather; it was more like a method for revenge. Although each couple played as a team, sometimes Heather cut out her husband to win a play.

As they nibbled on the food and downed a few glasses of wine, cards continued to drop to the table. Hearty laughter filled the air as Tony and Heather quickly took the lead.

Tony glanced at his wife. Tiffany was happy that he had finally done something about that snobby attitude.

Tiffany's face brightened as a smile stretched from ear to ear. *"This is the last* hand," Tiffany grinned. "What? What? I can't hear you talking trash over there," Tony said as Heather totaled up the points.

"One more hand and we can claim our victory," Heather replied, batting her long eyelashes at Tiffany before dipping the last hot wing on her plate in the tiny bit of ranch dressing that had managed to last through the entire two-hour game.

Tiffany grinned, blowing a kiss to her husband, maintaining her composure as Heather sneered.

"Seems like you two need some privacy," Heather said without looking up from her cards.

"Oh, I see the dead has risen," Tiffany shot back. "You were silent all this time and now that you and your lousy husband got a few good hands in, you want to talk junk." She laughed, casting a sly glance at Heather. "How many points are we down on for this last round, Vance?"

"Ninety Points."

Tiffany squared her small shoulders, saying, "And they bid ten this time? We can do this. Come on cards, don't fail us now." Then she glowered at Heather. "It's not like we haven't come from behind to whip your butts before."

Tension swirled in the room. The cards dropped. Heather focused on the cards, then looked up at Tony, her expression grave, eyes sparkling with the need for revenge.

A few cards later, Tiffany jumped up slamming the last one on the table. "Bam. Set! Look at that." Vance stood, slapping both hands on Tiffany's cards. She turned to her brother, patting him on the shoulder. "It's okay, maybe next time you guys will have some luck...." She glanced at her sister-in-law. "At *your* house."

"We're still the champions," Vance sang the old Queen tune as he pranced joyfully around the table.

Tony grabbed the cards, scattered them out on the table and examined them. "I think you two marked these cards. There's no way we keep losing to you clowns."

Heather sat with her arms folded over her ample chest. Not a word came from her lips.

Tiffany and Vance hugged one another, waving their hands in the air as they did a victory lap around the table. "We are the champions. We are the champions."

"Come on, guys, don't rub it in." Tony sighed wearily. "Don't worry, Heather, we'll get them when we host the next game."

The couples filed out of the solarium, passing the dining room, the den and the living room to the garage door. Tiffany hugged Tony and kissed him on both cheeks. "That's for good luck."

"Whatever." Tony playfully wiped Tiffany's kiss off his cheek.

Heather flashed her hand in the air. "Bye." She opened the door and walked out.

Tiffany stretched her arms. "I'm going to take a shower. I need to unwind."

"Again, honey?"

What had actually crossed her mind was Christy on her examination table, followed by Smith's violation. The mere thought of him violating Christy made Tiffany feel dirty as memories of her past stormed through her soul. But when she turned to her husband she said, "A woman has to stay fresh at all times."

Tony said. "You'd better let her go wash those cheating hands."

153

Vance laughed, a soft empty sound. "Okay, honey."

"Goodnight, Tony and Heather," Tiffany yelled over her shoulder as she slowly walked toward the steps.

The doorbell rang. Tiffany stopped at the edge of the steps, peeking at Tony and Vance.

Vance gripped the gold handle and opened the door. Before the door opened all the way, Tiffany head, "Tell Anthony to come on. We have to pick up the kids." Vance slowly closed the door and looked over his broad shoulders at Tony.

Tony leaned in whispering, "Did you ever find out where Tiffany went?"

Tiffany gasped.

Vance scratched his head. "She wouldn't say a word."

Tony's lips slowly parted. "I'll talk to her tomorrow and let you know what I find out."

"If anyone can get information out of her, it's *you*."

At that moment, Tiffany wondered if her bond with Tony would affect her marriage as much as it affected his marriage.

Chapter 20

Tony hopped into Heather's car. She pulled out of Tiffany's driveway and sped down the long stretch of road. "So, what happened to her today?"

Tony peered out of the window. "I don't know."

The moon glowed in the sky.

"I thought that was our purpose for coming over here."

Tony exhaled slowly. "That was part of the reason. The card game came first."

Tony popped in a CD. Instrumental tones flowed out the speakers into the car.

"I was *dying* to find out what had happened." She snickered, begging for an argument. At times like these, he wondered what had he seen in the woman in the first place.

"This is not the time to fight with me." Tony leaned his chair back and tuned her out. Even more disturbing were the images that flashed in his mind as the fear he felt that night during the storm came back full force . . .

Blue lights flashed, then bright white headlights flickered off and came back on. Tony gripped the door handle of the moving truck. Timmy drove toward the police instead of going in the opposite direction.

"Calm down."

Calm down? Tony's legs shook as if he was sitting on a washing machine that had hit the spin cycle. David's teeth rattled.

"Calm down," Timmy snapped. "And stop that foolishness in my truck! You two are acting like little *sissies*. Everything's okay."

Rain splattered the windshield as Tony stared out at the darkened sky. He suddenly remembered that he had left his umbrella behind. It was better off in the dumpster.

Timmy pulled up to the parked patrol car. Smith rushed up to the truck and stuck his head into the driver's window. "The alarm company dispatched the call two minutes ago." Then he glanced at Tony and David. "Drop them off about four blocks from the projects." Smith made eye contact with the boys. "You better not tell a soul or I'll fix you real good! You hear me?" He leaned over Timmy and poked David's chest with an index finger. "I'm not playing neither."

The boys sat like two frogs on a log. Did he really think they *would* tell anyone?

Smith turned back to his cousin. "Follow the plan and don't screw up. I'll go check out the scene and call for backup."

Timmy and the sergeant said a few more words and shared a laugh before Smith rushed back to his patrol car.

The long ride home was excruciating. Consumed with guilt, Tony prayed for God's forgiveness. He had actually committed a crime for the first time in his life.

Tony wanted to throw up but nothing would come up when he gasped for air. Perspiration dripped from his body. He wanted to crack the window to let some air calm his nerves. But he couldn't manage enough courage to ask the man if they could lower the window.

While driving, Timmy reached over and turned on something that looked like a radio, which picked up a lot of static at first, but then a few seconds later someone's baritone voice reported a break-in at Rent & Buy Appliance Store. The person on the scanner said the suspects were two black guys. Tony and David sunk into the seat.

"How did they know it was black guys?" Tony whispered to David, but the man overheard him.

"Don't worry about it." Timmy's eyes narrowed. "The camera only recorded your legs, that's all."

Tony looked over his shoulders as another police car zoomed past them in the direction of the appliance store.

Tim pulled up to the curb while the truck slowly inched forward. Tony and David jumped out. "Keep your mouths shut!" he yelled as he pulled off. They didn't bother to look back. Tony ran toward home. Without a shadow of a doubt, he knew that his sister was in trouble.

"Anthony . . . Anthony, did you hear me talking to you? Anthony!"

Heather shook his shoulder, bringing him back to reality. "Yes. Yes, Heather."

She glared at him.

"I dozed off."

"I bet you did," she snapped. "I'm going inside Robin's to get the kids."

Tony looked around, staring at the porch that he had helped Robin's husband build.

Raindrops sprinkled on the windshield. Tony glanced out the window again, noticing dark clouds moving gradually.

Heather slammed the car door.

Tony closed his eyes and traveled back to that rainy night in Cloverdale . . .

Tony and David hit the ground running when they reached the edge of Cloverdale. They split when they reached the community store. David kept running toward his house and Tony ran towards his own apartment, passing the silver mailboxes, the community center and the park. His clothes were saturated from rain; a cold chill penetrated his body. He gripped the door handle and rushed into the house, forgetting to take off his muddy shoes.

Tony ran through the small kitchen with clustered pictures of him and his sister on the wall and a large picture of Jesus and the Twelve Disciples. The white linoleum floor stretched from corner to corner, except for under the tan refrigerator where water had dripped and deteriorated the tile.

Passing the small empty living room, he ran up the ten wooden steps, straight to Tiffany's room, opening her door. The small black nightstand in her room only had three legs holding it up. The table leaned against the wall, which served as the final anchoring point.

"Tiffany, where are you!" Tony yelled his panicked voice echoed through the tiny apartment.

Gasping for breath, Tony ran back down the steps to the refrigerator, where they kept family notes. He placed his hand on the door, ripping off an orange piece of paper with Tiffany's handwriting on the top.

GONE TO B&B

Tony tore out of the house, passing the alleys, abandoned buildings and The Hill. The parking lot was bright and compacted with cars. The shopping lines were long. There were at least fifteen aisles and only three cashiers. Tony walked up to Genesis, a cashier he knew from school, who lived in an upper-class neighborhood. B&B would never hire people from Cloverdale. Too many families, too many friends. He would never forget when Genesis' parents came to the school complaining that they didn't want their daughter riding the same bus with the kids from Cloverdale. The woman had stormed out of the school when the principal told her that the bus route couldn't be changed since they lived in the district.

"Genesis," Tony said, panting for air. "Have you seen Tiffany?"

"Yeah, she came in here earlier today," Genesis said, smiling sweetly. "Are you going to the prom?"

Tony wiped his forehead. "Can't talk about that right now. I have to find my sister."

"Why? What's up?" Genesis asked, stroking her golden brown hand to remove a bit of the water from his face.

"I can't find her. I think something's wrong."

"She left here about an hour ago."

Tony turned on his heels.

"You know, strange thing, though," she said before he got too far away.

Tony turned, making a puddle right next to the exit door.

"Sergeant Smith followed her in here. He was acting all strange."

A truckload of fear unloaded in Tony's gut.

"I hope you find her," Genesis said as she turned to the next customer.

Tony ran straight to the community center. He almost tore the door off its hinges when he pushed it open.

Laughter exploded from the game room as soon as his soaked sneakers hit the ceramic floor. The large room was sectioned off with several tables. Kids stood in line to play ping-pong while other students played Uno, Connect Four and Dominoes—Tony's favorites. The multicolored room was perfect for the kids, but it was several feet away from the study room.

"Ms. Arlene, have you seen Tiffany?" Tony asked, placing his hand on his chest. A sharp pain pinched away at his heart.

She glanced at Tony with small brown eyes filled with worry. "No, we haven't seen Tiffany all day. And that's not like her." She pointed her finger at a chubby boy who snatched a marker from a short little girl. "Give that back." Then Ms. Arlene turned to Tony. "I walked over to your house earlier and she wasn't there."

"I've got to find her."

She gripped his shoulders. "Why? Is something wrong?"

"I don't know, Ms. Arlene, but I have to go," he said shaking her off.

Tony ran seven blocks down the street to The Safe Haven Outreach Program.

Horns honked and people yelled out of their windows as he dodged cars and flagged people to stop while trying to get from one side of the road to the other.

Tony yanked on the door. It wouldn't give. He leaned on the glass, watching as people walked around inside. He banged on the door like a madman.

"Good heavens," Mrs. Clark said as she approached the door. "Tony," she said in a hurried tone. "What's wrong? Come in out of that cold rain."

Tony stepped inside, placed his hands on his knees as he bent over trying to catch his breath.

Mrs. Clark placed a small white hand on his back. "Tony, what's going on?"

In a weak and shaky voice, Tony raised his head and said, "I—I—I can't find my sis—ter."

"There's no need to panic. I'm sure she'll come home soon." She adjusted her glasses on her narrow face. "You know Tiffany isn't the type to stay out late."

"I have to find her, Mrs. Clark."

A crackling sound pierced the air as the community center's doors opened. The doors needed more than WD-40 oil spray. They needed to be replaced.

"Hilton," blurted Mrs. Clark as her gaze shifted toward a chestnut brown tall kid walking through the community center's doors. "I see you have returned from your long summer camp."

"Yes, I have, Mrs. Clark," smiled Hilton. "I was gone six weeks."

"Did you see Tiffany as you walked here?" asked Mrs. Clark.

"No," said Hilton in a low tone. "Is something wrong?" asked Hilton as he looked at Tony.

Hilton played on the school's basketball team with Tony. He was destined to be a psychiatrist one day. Somehow, Hilton had managed to escape the wrath of Smith's treacherous hands, mainly because Hilton attended summer camps away from Cloverdale every summer. Unfortunately, Tiffany and Tony's mother couldn't afford to ship them off to summer camps—away from Sergeant Smith's evil deeds.

Tony stared at Hilton. Tony knew that Hilton always had a twinkle in his eye for Tiffany. Any lustful thoughts that Hilton had for Tiffany surely would never blossom if Tony and his mother had anything to do with it. Plus, Tiffany never paid Hilton any attention. She was too focused on her school books to notice him.

"I can't find my sister," shrieked Tony.

"Do you need me to *assist* you with finding Tiffany?" asked Hilton in a supportive tone.

Tony paused as he noticed how *proper* Hilton spoke. Tony figured Hilton had enhanced his vocabulary from attending summer camps with white kids every summer.

"Why are you shaking, Tony?" asked Mrs. Clark while walking towards him.

A tear rolled down his face, mingling with the droplets of rain. "I have to find her," Tony said as he ran out.

"If there's anything, I mean anything I can do to help, let me know," Mrs. Clark yelled before Tony vanished down the sidewalk.

A sharp cramp shot through Tony's legs. His chest, heavy and tight, felt as though it had suddenly caved in.

He ran back to Cloverdale, running through the dark filthy alleys asking people if they had seen Tiffany. Most were too stoned to answer while prostitutes tried to offer him a little piece of tail to calm him down.

Tony ran back towards his apartment, clenching his chest.

"Boy, what's wrong with you?"

Tony turned to face an old man around 55. Alcohol leaped from his breath and clothes, contaminating the air. His words slurred as he said, "You're too young to have chest pains."

"Old Man Jeff, have . . . have you seen my sister?" Tony asked, gasping for air.

"Yeah." The man attempted to stand, but his legs began to wobble forcing him to spiral back down on the ground. "I saw the Sergeant put her in his patrol car. She had handcuffs on."

"When! When was this?" Tony asked as he knelt beside Old Man Jeff.

"I'm not good with time, young man," he said, lifting the brown paper bag to his lips, slurping as he sipped the wine nestled inside. "But I do 'member the sun was still out. Matter of fact it was approaching nightfall, right before it started raining."

"Thank you," Tony said, backing away from the man, then breaking into a sprint as he ran up the street. He wiped the tears from his face when he spotted a girl from a distance. She had a shape like Tiffany, although this girl staggered when she walked.

"Tiffany!" Tony yelled. He ran forward.

The girl didn't respond, but as he crossed the distance between the silver mailboxes and the park, he was sure it was Tiffany.

Tony's eyes widened. "I've—I've been looking for you."

Tiffany's clothes were ripped, her face was covered with tears and she was shaking.

She stretched out her arms, wrapped them around Tony and dropped to the ground.

Chapter 21

"Hey, honey," Vance said, gazing at Tiffany's body. "I'm glad we kicked their tails tonight. They can't mess with the true King and Queen of Spades."

Tiffany dried off as she stood at the entrance of the bathroom door. He walked over, embraced her and kissed her on the back of her neck. "Umm, you smell good."

Tiffany smiled as he placed his smooth hand on her face.

"I'm going to hop in the shower, honey." Then he grinned. "I hope you're still awake when I get out."

"I'll try but I'm a little tired tonight."

Vance pulled off his gray shirt. "Tiffany, we need to talk about what happened to you."

"I know but not right now. I'm exhausted." She sat on the bed, slipping her red nightgown over her bare body. "I promise we will talk soon. I want to get some rest. I have a long day ahead of me tomorrow."

Vance cleared his throat. "All right. But we can't keep avoiding this conversation either."

Tiffany slid under the silk sheets and pulled the covers over her as if it were a tent. She could hear Vance walking around the room, in and out of the closet, then stepping into the bathroom. He would be in there awhile.

She couldn't find it within herself to tell Vance why she had run out of her office because it would raise questions about her past. She dreaded revealing what had happened to her.

This was the same issue that had plagued them throughout their three-year marriage. It had started on their honeymoon in Spain and would crop up whenever a problem with intimacy arose. She had almost thought that she wouldn't be able to love him completely. Vance had been so patient on their wedding night; he had been even more patient since.

Tiffany tossed and turned as she slowly pulled the covers off her head. Vance whistled, "We Are the Champions" as the water streamed in the shower. She lay on the bed, allowing her mind to drive down memory lane as she drifted into a deep sleep, cloaked in wonderful memories of Spain and her new husband.

Rustling palm trees and lukewarm beaches expanded on the horizon. The crystal clear Spain waters, large sandy areas and beautiful green hills swept her off her feet—just like her handsome husband had done only two years before. The historical monuments, luxury hotels and ancient churches were all stone and brick sculptured pieces of architecture. However, the friendly people made it a warm, open place and the topless beaches were more than an eyeful. The distinct European culture in Barcelona made their June honeymoon a breathtaking testament to their love. He insisted that he show her The Ramblas—a lively boulevard jammed with tourist centers, entertainment spots and restaurants, the 1992 Olympic Games Stadium and the Music Palace—one of the world's most extravagant music halls. She didn't regret it, nor did she regret accepting his offer to spend the rest of his life with her.

The suite overlooked the beach and fresh pink roses were sprinkled on the light brown carpet. Hunter-green and gold ribbons draped across the king-sized bed. Dark blue chairs with cream throw pillows, brass end tables and elegant silk curtains accentuated the Spanish elegance. The glistening chandelier, Cathedral imprints and marble bathroom floors depicted the décor of European taste. The oversized porcelain Jacuzzi was perfect for the occasion and set the tone for their honeymoon night, which had been delayed by eight hours. The flight had taken that long to get them there.

"I love you, Tiffany, with all of my heart. Or should I say, Dr. Tiffany Brown-Carson? I'm the luckiest man alive." His eyes brightened more than usual. "Look at you, my wife." The warm timbre of his voice enveloped her like a soft caress.

Submerging her naked body under the bubbles, Tiffany said, "I love you too, Vance." Although Tiffany knew she had a flawless caramel brown body, she was too shy to walk around in the nude.

"I can't believe you're finally my wife." He embraced Tiffany, the soft musky scent of his cologne tickling her nose. "You gave me a hard time. But I know you were worth the wait."

She stroked a finger over his smooth brown skin. "I'm the one who's lucky."

The newlyweds sipped on a glass of Dom Perignon Magnum Champagne as strawberry-kiwi aromatherapy candles lingered on the edge of the Jacuzzi. As their bodies glided between the sparkling bubbles, Vance massaged every muscle from Tiffany's neck to her back. A touch of uneasiness vibrated from the depth of her soul. Tiffany prayed that Vance would move slowly. She wanted her first sexual encounter with her husband to be a joyful moment.

Vance flicked foamy bubbles toward Tiffany, which landed on her shoulder-length black hair. Tiffany giggled as she gracefully licked her soft lips. Her spiral curls unraveled from the moisture steaming the mirrors.

"I still remember the first time we met," Vance said, smiling.

"And so do I."

Tiffany was amazed how their paths had crossed. She went to Bennett College during her undergraduate years and Vance went to Morehouse College. It was by fate that they met on Duke University's campus and fell in love at first sight. Tiffany was a first-year medical student and Vance was a second-year law student. Who would have imagined that they would be successful since they both came out of the projects—and the odds that kids like them would not fall into the traps of their environment were slim? Vance had escaped the pressures of the crime-stricken projects in Harlem. He proudly enlisted in the Army while attending college to pursue his dreams to become an attorney—a pathway that his brothers thought took too long to *rack* in cash. Needless to say, his two brothers were serving over twenty-plus years for trafficking drugs.

"Honey, I almost tripped with my books in my hand walking over to you. My heart was beating so fast, I thought I was about to have a heart attack. Even my palms were sweating. And I don't sweat!" He kissed Tiffany on her ear. "Then you smiled at me, though I could still see the pain in your eyes. At that moment, I knew you were going to be my wife."

"Stop it, Vance." She scooped up a handful of bubbles. "See, you've forgotten details already. The first time we met we were in the library. You came over to my table and stared at me." Tiffany giggled. "To be honest, I thought you were crazy."

"I often wondered if that was the reason you didn't call me for several weeks." He poured himself another glass of champagne. "I don't know what came over me." Vance took a sip of his champagne. "You gave me the impression that you resented men."

Tiffany paused, her eyebrows drew in and her forehead crinkled. "I needed time to do a background check on you." A faint smile stretched across her lips. Tiffany's gaze shifted toward the bubbles.

"Is there something you want to tell me?" Vance asked in a low-pitched voice. "Are you all right?"

"Yes, I'm all right."

Vance pulled Tiffany closer against his muscular chest. "Whatever's bothering you, you can talk to me. I'm here for you. You've always given me the impression that you're holding back." Vance reached for his glass. "Anytime you need a shoulder to cry on or a hand to hold, I'm here." He paused. "I'm not rushing you to tell me about your past, but whenever you're ready, I'm here."

"I love you." Tiffany leaned her head on his chest. "You're the only man I've ever loved. The only man I've allowed to hold my hand or hug me. You...you are the first man I've wanted to kiss." Tiffany sighed, running a hand through Vance's curly black hair. People often mistook it for a texturizer, but actually, it was the result of a Hispanic mother and African-American father.

"And I respect you more than you can imagine," Vance said as he caressed the back of Tiffany's neck.

The first time Vance hugged her, she didn't want him to move too fast and she definitely didn't want him to take advantage of her. She felt intimidated standing in front of a six-foot-seven-inch man who towered over her five-foot-five inches. After a few weeks, she realized that Vance was a real gentleman.

The shimmering lights from the candles made Vance's skin sparkle.

"I love you with all my heart." She gathered some bubbles in her hand and rubbed them on Vance's arm. Her hands trembled, sliding down his smooth skin.

"Look at me, honey." Tiffany turned to face him. She slowly maneuvered into the warm, bubbly water. "If someone has hurt you, I need to know. I'll make sure they pay for it. I mean *really* pay."

Tiffany's gaze averted from Vance's.

Vance stroked his long slender fingers along the side of her face. Pulling her closer to him, he cuddled her for a few minutes. For the first time in her life, Tiffany felt a sense of peace, security and love. The events of that painstaking summer were all but swept away.

He charmed her by feeding her grapes, strawberries and pineapples. Reaching for her hand, he slowly guided it to pick up a strawberry and placed it in his mouth. Vance leaned in, inviting Tiffany to share the fruit with him, then gave Tiffany a long and passionate kiss.

He stood, scooping her up out of the water, then carrying her to the bed. As the bubbles rolled off his body and water dripped off him like raindrops, Tiffany cherished every step he made. Trying to sweep away the past and let in new memories of love and hope.

Her husband laid her down on the bed as though she were a precious jewel. Tiffany closed her eyes to avoid seeing Vance staring at her body. Slowly pulling the covers over her unblemished soft skin, he placed a gentle kiss on her breasts.

Tiffany couldn't find the words to tell him that he wasn't the first man to enter her. Let alone, that she was raped. Eventually, she would have to tell someone what had happened, but not now. God, not now.

The plush, feathered mattress nestled her body as if she were a princess. The cream satin sheets clung to her moist skin. She pulled the covers up toward her shoulders, watching Vance's naked body drift around the room.

Tiffany mumbled under her breath, "I'm not a victim. I'm a survivor." She let out a long, slow breath as she closed her eyes and said, "This is my husband. I have to relax. Vance loves me and I love him. I can't allow the past to haunt me." She opened her eyes. "I have to enjoy my honeymoon."

Vance placed candles everywhere, his chestnut-brown body sparkling as he walked past each one. He turned on the little stereo sitting next to the king-size bed and slow, romantic, tunes from a mixed CD flowed out of the speakers.

Caressing every inch of her body with long slender fingers, he followed his touch with a long, searching kiss. Generating smooth strokes, Vance poured peaches and cream lotion on her body. His hands swirled over her body as though he were a massage therapist.

Although Tiffany tensed with his first movements, she enjoyed Vance's warm hands on her body. Her legs began to shake. Her heart beat rapidly in her small chest. She gently gripped his hands and moved them from her body.

"Everything's all right," Vance whispered, hoarsely in her ears. "I love you, Tiffany and I understand how you feel right now. You don't have to be nervous." He kissed her hands. "I want this to be special."

Her breasts pressed against the beat of his heart. "I'm trying, Vance," she said as her lips slowly trembled. She slowly released Vance's hands.

Vance slid his well-sculptured body under the covers. He positioned his body above Tiffany and gently rubbed her as if he was unveiling the soft folds of skin with every touch. He slowly crawled toward her feet, sucking her toes as if they were caramel tootsie rolls. He dangled his tongue along her knees up to her inner thighs. The muscles in her legs jumped in response.

Vance caressed her legs while licking her inner thighs. He launched his tongue inside of her while he continuously massaged her waist, legs and stomach.

Tiffany gently slid toward the headboard. He dangled his tongue to her thighs again, sucking on her hips. She trembled softly.

Trailing his fingers up her arms, he nibbled on each section of her stomach. He cupped her breasts as he licked the soft skin around her nipples. Tiffany closed her eyes, trying to enjoy his gentle touches.

Vance sucked diligently on her fingers. The soft wet tissues in his mouth wrapped around her fingers before his tongue grazed up her hand to her shoulders then to her ears, nibbling on them while whispering softly, "I love you, Tiffany."

Vance slid down to her upright nipples, gently sucking on them. Tiffany gradually arched her back as a warm sensation rushed through her veins. The feeling encouraged her to release herself to the mercy of his hands. Her juices began to flow and nervousness slowly faded. She placed her hands on his head, gripping it like a basketball and slowly swaggered her hips.

"Yes, baby. Open up to me. I'm your husband. I love you, Tiffany."

She gracefully moved in a circular motion while Vance swirled his tongue against the moist walls in her jewel box. He slowly slid inside of her while caressing the soft flesh on her thighs. Tiffany pressed her hands against his chest, making sure he didn't apply pressure.

"Are you okay?" Vance asked as his body moved in slow motion. "I don't want to hurt you."

"Um. Um. Yes," she moaned softly.

Her body slowly invited Vance inside. Her heart raced away and beads of sweat formed on her breasts. With every stroke, Vance embraced Tiffany's body. He rolled his tongue from the side of her face down to her breasts. Her nipples hardened, becoming flush with heat as the soft pressure of his lips clamped on them.

"Umm, Vance," she moaned deeply.

"Yes, honey. Please, let me show you how you should be treated. I love you. I want to be the man you want me to be. Please, baby. Please, baby."

Tiffany placed her hands on Vance's back. Her soft fingers strolled along his spine.

"Yes, honey. Yes."

The walls of her jewel box cuddled firmly onto his erection. Something warm and milky rolled from her walls.

Vance began to jerk. "I'm . . . I'm about to . . . , " he said as his tongue became paralyzed and his body shivered with ecstasy. Yes, she totally understood.

Chapter 22

Monday morning, the bright and warm rays from the sun streamed inside Smith's office. He sat at his desk looking over a catalog, foot tapping impatiently on the white tiled floor. Thursday couldn't come fast enough; the weatherman predicted rain late on Thursday. Smith's heart filled with excitement to the point that he couldn't focus on the images. He had to keep his same work pattern or his subordinates would suspect something. He definitely didn't need Officers Jenkins and Price trailing him.

Smith rocked back and forth as he sat at his wooden desk. He glanced at the red numbers on the clock on his wall. "I can't wait until this day is over."

Smith knew that June Bug's focus was still on his next high, even if it meant killing someone. He was a junkie and junkies don't have a conscience. There had been no more talk of getting help. No more talk of wanting to go to rehab.

Smith fiddled through the papers, trying to find something of interest to occupy his time, he then breezed through the stack of complaint forms on his desk, ignoring each one while he sipped on his Coca-Cola.

He frowned at the complaint on top, mumbling, "What can I do about the drug problem in this community?"

There were drugs in Cloverdale before he came onboard and drugs would be there when he retired in three weeks. The Mecklenburg Correctional center was like a 'revolving door' for hustlers. They went in and came out even worse than when they first started.

He leaned back in the chair, reflecting upon what had sparked his interest to become an officer. As a child, Smith had enjoyed watching the *Andy Griffith* shows and admired the authority the sheriff had. However, he overlooked the fact that the sheriff was a respectful, law-obeying officer.

Years later, Smith enlisted in the military instead of becoming a policeman. He yearned for a superior level of authority, especially power and control, resulting in his discharge from the Army. Then he went to Cornell University. His chemistry degree rendered several job offers, but he jumped at the opportunity to become a high-ranking narcotics officer in Charlotte. He felt the south was a better place to raise kids.

Ringing bells from an ice cream truck swept by the community center. Smith laughed, picturing the kids chasing after the truck, drooling over a popsicle.

Tossing the catalog aside, he gaped at the next complaint. "What do the tenants want me to do about their little *bastards*?" If the tenants were so concerned about the teenage boys not going to school, they should call social services just like everybody else.

Smith rolled his eyes, pulling a complaint out of the middle of the pile while scanning to a page labeled pit bull fights on Tryon Street. "That's not even my territory!" The tenants in Cloverdale knew they couldn't have animals. Having a pit bull was a violation of their lease and they would be evicted. Even if the officers raided that hang out spot, things would move to another location. Business always came first.

He grabbed the binoculars from his top desk drawer, turned around in his chair and looked out the window. "Why don't these people get a life?" He turned from the window, shoved the complaint forms in a folder and stood to stretch his legs. "They wouldn't have time to be nosey if they were working or in school. They need a productive life. They shouldn't be sitting around waiting for handouts."

He glanced at the clock on the wall. "Man, time's going slow."

Shortly afterward Smith drove to the abandoned building, parked his car behind a row of dumpsters and walked up to June Bug. The man waited in the same spot as usual. Smith winced as a foul sewage smell drifted off June Bug's ashy body.

Smith made him recite the plan and almost got a hard-on when the obviously high June Bug remembered every detail.

The next day, Sergeant Smith smiled as the rain pounded against the window in his office. He picked up his binoculars to scope out The Hill. Rain impaired his vision but Smith managed to detect that The Hill was deserted. Hustlers were probably not too far away. Even twelve inches of snow, a tornado, or blizzard wouldn't keep them away. The hustlers were more dedicated to making their sales than Smith's officers were to stamping out crime.

The minutes seemed to have more than sixty seconds. The hours had more than just a mere sixty minutes. He kept checking The Hill. Every now and then a hustler appeared to make a sale, then vanished. Would the rain keep June Bug from showing up?

June Bug's craving for crack would probably persuade him to run through a war zone if that little white rock was waiting on the other side. Well, at least that's how it normally worked for addicts.

Thursday afternoon, Smith patrolled Cloverdale, then met June Bug behind the abandoned building to go over the plan—again. The rain made it impossible to see any further than twenty feet in front of him. Gusts of wind whipped around, forcing him to stagger at times.

June Bug's clothes were soaked and filthy, his skin was ashy, torn black tennis shoes were muddy, eyes were blood-shot red and a dry, cracked, powdery white substance was on his lips. He stood in front of Smith, squaring his shoulders before looking in the sergeant's eyes—not one ounce of remorse for his sad existence.

As Smith opened his mouth to speak to the man, June Bug's tongue rolled from side to side, then hung out of his mouth before sucking his teeth as if he had food stuck in between them. The man had dropped weight since Smith had provided him his previous dosage of crack. He probably hadn't eaten in days. Was he too high to do the job? Smith could see all of his plans going down the drain.

Smith backed away as a downwind brought a horrible gust of urine his way. How did he get involved with this dangerous walking zombie? He might have to kill him when this job was finished.

The cool breeze, blending with the rain, made the summer afternoon cooler than usual. Winds ripped through June Bug's tight sweater that he must have stolen from someone's clothesline. His teeth rattled and his arms vibrated with every thrust of the wind. He slowly pried his mouth apart, teeth decayed and breath smelling like a meeting ground for flies. "I— I need a fix."

"Wait a minute. I have to make sure you remember the plan."

"I know what to do."

June Bug's black dingy jeans began to twitch as the wind brushed against them. His mouth dropped open again. "Have...have you seen my daughter around here? Her name's Star. I've been looking for her. No one's seen her for a couple of days."

Smith rolled his blue eyes. Star had been dead for at least twelve years.

The sound of cats fighting soared through the alley, which didn't bother June Bug but made the sergeant flinch.

"Where is my dope?"

Raising an eyebrow, Smith said, "*Wait* a minute. Man, do you think you'll be able to do the job?"

"Do you have my medicine?" June Bug asked, holding his dark brown hands in front of him.

"Let's talk about business first," Smith said, inching back. "Now, do you think you'll be able to do the job?"

"*Yeah*, man. You already told me where she works and what street she comes down."

"I know, but do you remember our plan?"

June Bug let out a long, slow, sigh. "I was in the car with you when we watched her. Do you remember that? I might be an addict but I'm not stupid."

"Yeah, yeah, whatever," grasped Smith. "I might have another *job* for you," he paused before parting his lips. "How's Tiffany?" Smith licked his lips.

"Man, why are you asking me about my niece? And . . . why you keep licking your lips like that?"

Smith paused, ignoring him. "Do you think you can kidnap her for me?"

"Yeah, man . . . I told you I will handle your wife."

Smith sneered. "No *fool* . . . I'm not talking about my wife . . . I'm talking about Tiffany."

June Bug leaned toward Smith. "Man, what are you *talking* about now! Don't *touch* my niece."

Smith huffed, quickly drifting down memory lane before refocusing back on June Bug. "Alright . . . alright. I'm just joking."

"You *better* be," snapped June Bug.

Smith glanced around. "Where are you getting the car?"

June Bug pulled a paper bag around his shoulders, trying to block the gust of wind. "Man, I can steal a car faster than you can get in that patrol car."

Smith drew back from him. The smell that drifted off June Bug's body snatched his breath away.

"Wait, I'll get a car out of the parking lot at the store."

Smith leaned in asking, "What store?"

"B&B."

A loud rumbling sound echoed through the alley, shattering glass. Smith and June Bug stopped talking and plastered their bodies against the brick wall. Smith paused to make sure no one was approaching, then continued, "No, that's too risky."

June Bug's scrawny arms folded over his chest. "Are you going to give me a car?"

"No, you told me you'd get one."

"Okay then," he shot back. "I'm telling you I can get it from B&B."

"Man, I thought you'd have the car by now."

"Are you out of your *mind*?" June Bug's eyes darted around the alley. "Why would I steal a car and *keep it* all day?"

Smith shook his head. Maybe the man was smarter than he looked.

"Man, why are you worried about where I get the car from anyway?"

"I think B&B's too risky."

"Then drop me off at the parking lot where she works, I'll take a car from there."

Smith grinned. "That sounds better."

June Bug brightened as he held out his hands. "Where is my . . . medicine?"

"You'll get it when the job is done."

The man grimaced, glowering at Smith. "So, what time are you picking me up?"

"I'm not picking you up," Smith spat. "You have to get a car and go over there yourself."

"What?"

"You heard me."

"Whatever, man." June Bug's white lips parted in an alarming smile. "But she works on the other side of town. I might not get there before she leaves. We could do it tomorrow. It might not rain tomorrow though . . . ."

Smith paused for a moment, summing up the situation. A few seconds of smelly discomfort or a long-term plan of luxury? "All right, I'll drop you off a few blocks away from the clinic. She's working second shift this week. Here, take this dope." Sergeant Smith passed the crack to him. "There's much more where that came from. Meet me right here at 10 o'clock. I'll drop you off, then I have to meet some buddies of mine."

June Bug cast a sly glance in his direction. "Yeah, you want me to do your dirty work while you cover your tail."

"What're you talking about?"

June Bug folded his arms in front of his flimsy chest. "Man, I'm not stupid."

"Look, just finish the job," Smith snapped. "And here, take this gun. Stick with the plan, then wait a few minutes and see if she's moving. If she's not, then shoot her."

"Man, what are you getting out of this?" he asked as he leaned against the dumpster.

"Don't worry about that. Meet me right here at 10 o'clock." Smith turned and walked away. As an afterthought, he said over his shoulder, "Hey, don't sell that gun for dope. You better have it when I pick you up." Then Smith returned and took the gun back. "As a matter of fact, I'll keep it until I return."

Later, Sergeant Smith met his friends Raymond and Vincent at the Night Owl Bar. The rain poured down faster than a waterfall. He stayed there until 9:50 p.m.

"Come, let's down a few shots of Vodka," Smith said, passing Raymond four shots.

Raymond stretched out his pale, wrinkled hands. "Yeah, it is your time to buy the drinks, Paul."

"Don't be stingy, Paul, pass one this way," Vincent said as he wrapped his pinkish black lips around a cigarette. "I want seven shots."

"Seven. That's a little too much," Raymond said as he stared at the red freckles on Vincent's face.

"Let the man enjoy himself, Raymond. I'm sure someone will take him home." Smith sipped on his beer and took a long drag of his cigarette.

Loud laughter flowed while cigarette smoke drifted in the air as though the bar was on fire. Alcoholic beverages spread across the bar like a common cold, everyone had one. Large speakers were in every corner, pumping country music all night. People danced on the small, black dance floor, moving like stiff puppets. The walls were cluttered with posters of country singers and the bar was crowded with loyal customers.

"Smith, you sure you have enough money to pay for these shots?" Raymond chuckled as he downed his third shot. "Aren't you still locked into that *crappy job*?"

"Yeah, he's right," Vincent said with his words slurring while he brushed some ashes off his expensive shirt. "Hanging with the *darkies*."

"Sure, I can afford the drinks tonight," Smith said while lifting his glass.

"Look. Look, fellows, there's Mary Beth," Smith said. His head turned 180 degrees to follow the path of her long brunette hair.

"Look at the tits on her," Raymond blurted as he downed another shot.

"Looks like we're running out of shots," Smith said as he continued to sip on the same beer he'd been nursing for an hour.

Raymond laughed, shifting his gaze toward Vincent. "Smith, I hope we aren't tapping into your lunch money." His friends doubled over with laughter.

Smith told them, "I'm going to the bar to get more drinks," but he made it a point to let them know that the bar was swamped before he left the table.

Rushing out, he sped out of the parking lot and down the street. The abandoned building was only five minutes away from the bar. June Bug shifted from leg to leg, in the cold chilly rain, trying to cover himself with a plastic bag.

Smith pulled up, checking his rearview mirror to make sure that the coast was clear, then lowering the passenger window. "Get in."

June Bug gripped the door handle and jumped in. Smith had come prepared; he pulled out a nice piece of crack. June Bug's eyes enlarged to the size of quarters as he licked his lips and snatched it from Smith's hands.

"When you're finished, I'll meet you behind this same building. You'll get a larger package of dope. Enough to keep you high for the rest of the year." Smith continued to look in his rearview mirror. "If I'm not here, don't get pissed, I have to make sure I cover my tracks. I'll meet you tomorrow after work." Smith tapped his long fingers on the steering wheel.

June Bug stared at him.

Smith grumbled, "You have my word. Haven't I come through every time?"

The rain beat against the hood as if someone was striking it with a stick.

"Yeah. But I want my dope when I finish the job, man!"

"I understand. But I have to wait until the police department contacts me about Morgan. Let me take care of all of that first."

"Whatever, man!" June Bug opened and closed his hand, staring at the crack. "I hope you're not trying to get over on me."

"I'm not trying to jerk your balls." Smith handed June Bug the gun, then put the car in drive. "Listen, just meet me tomorrow in the alley around noon."

"You better be there," June Bug said as he sneezed, a slimy substance spilling out on his face.

"I will."

Smith handed him a little going-away present. "Here, take an extra piece. This will keep you nice and right until I meet you tomorrow."

Then he lowered his windows and gulped in a breath of fresh air.

Chapter 23

Smith dropped June Bug off a couple of blocks away from the Piedmont Family Clinic where Morgan worked, then pulled between two cars, keeping a watchful eye on his assassin.

June Bug shivered from the heavy rainfall; he didn't have an umbrella to cover him—just the crack for comfort. He raveled his hands up in his sweater as he strolled up the street. Smith watched as June Bug kneeled in a corner and smoked the crack. A few minutes later, the man headed to the clinic and stared at the parking lot.

Piedmont was open twenty-four hours a day but came to life after 5 every evening—the time when working people could arrange to see a doctor. Patients didn't need to make an appointment; the clinic would treat people even if they didn't have medical insurance. And most of them didn't.

Morgan, the head nurse, cared about everyone, regardless of the color of their skin. She treated patients with respect and kept everyone's information confidential. And there were times Smith needed that information, but she wouldn't budge.

Smith drove closer, switching off his headlights. June Bug was too spaced out to notice the patrol car was cruising at least two blocks behind him. Smith glanced at the clock in his car, trying to make sure he was still on task. By now Raymond and Vincent should be on the verge of passing out.

June Bug stood in a dark area across the street from the clinic, staking out the parking lot. He peeked his head around the corner, scoped the security, the exit doors and then cars in the wide-open area. A quick turn of the man's head and his gaze lined up with several guards standing inside. June Bug's neck craned as though he was trying to get a better view around the corner. Seconds later he ran across the street like a Navy Seal creeping up on a target.

June Bug ducked and ran from vehicle to vehicle, pausing in front of a black Mercedes S600 parked in a reserved spot. Twenty-inch chrome rims and shiny black tires were begging to be stolen. The addict stood beside the car as if someone had a camera off to the side, ready to snap a photo.

"What is he *doing*?" Smith watched as the deranged man positioned his body in several different poses as if though marketing the car for a catalog. "He's crazy," Smith said as June Bug kissed the hood of the Mercedes. "He's wasting time."

Smith coasted down the road, parking near a pickup truck to get a better view of the parking lot and his crazy, well-paid assassin. Tapping thick fingers on the steering wheel, he bristled as June Bug danced from car to car, trying to select a vehicle. Five minutes later the man stood in front of a black Ford F-150 and grinned.

June Bug ducked beside the truck, out of Smith's sight. A few seconds later, the truck pulled out of the parking lot, then parked in a wooded area across the street from Morgan's Toyota Avalon.

The rain beat down on the vehicle and the trees moved gracefully. The wind whipped and snapped against the Ford's windshield, hurling leaves and paper in its path. Streetlights flickered on and off before the power went out down the street. June Bug surely couldn't see anything because it was pitch dark. Smith picked up his binoculars equipped with night vision to monitor things from a distance.

The truck began to shake as if the ground had opened to pull it in. The door handles rattled and the hood vibrated with every gust of wind. June Bug's gaze was focused on the front door of the clinic. Smith put his car in gear and rolled back toward the Night Owl Bar.

Less than five minutes later, Smith got back to the bar before Raymond and Vincent finished their last standing drink. By the time he slipped into his seat, his friends were nearly passing out but wanted more drinks.

He sat at the table laughing and joking loudly with his buddies.

"Hey buddy, you have to calm down," Big Earl uttered as he stood over Smith with his broad shoulders and bear shape arms.

"All right. All right, Big Earl. We'll keep it down," Smith said loudly, trying to get everyone's attention.

"I'm not joking. You guys are on the verge of getting kicked out of here."

Big Earl, the manager of the Night Owl Bar, had fallen into his trap.

Smith had a plan for everything but kept looking at his watch. He leaned in towards the green candle on the table and blew it out as if he had made a death wish for Morgan.

"Hey guys, I'm going outside to take a smoke," Smith said, grabbing his jacket and cigarettes.

"Another one? What are you doing out there, growing weed?" Raymond asked as he tossed down another shot.

"Go ahead and smoke your lungs out," Raymond slurred as the pungent smell of alcohol swirled out his mouth.

Smith checked his watch, glancing back at his buddies as Raymond slumped down in the seat. He slipped some money to the bartender to keep the drinks coming. "Tell them this is from their friend who went outside to smoke his cigarette," Smith said as he handed the slim, white guy the money.

A quick decision had him running to the car, then rushing back to the scene. His cell phone fell out of his pocket. He smiled as he reached down to pick it up. Earlier that day the police dispatcher had informed the officers that the storm had damaged power towers satellites signals, which would interfere with their communication channels, tracking devices and cell phone frequencies. He knew this would happen. He had timed it perfectly according to the weatherman's report. Anytime the heavy rains, thunder and lightning swept through the town, the system was bound to fail for a couple of hours.

He smiled. Whenever the tracking device had technical difficulties, it threw off the readings at least for a two to three-mile radius, instead of a normal one hundred yards and wouldn't show his cell moving towards the target location. Night Owl Bar was within a two-mile radius.

Smith pulled beside a U-Haul truck to prevent anyone from seeing the patrol car. A black Mustang with the number thirty-four written in the back window and on the side of the door near the door handle was rare.

June Bug sat in the truck waiting for Morgan. His head swayed back and forth and fingers snapped in the air.

Smith rolled down his window and frowned. The music blasting out of the truck made it shake. A full dosage of anger clenched Smith's gut. "That fool's going to blow his cover."

Smith glanced down at the dashboard, displaying ten minutes past 11. Morgan was late and probably had to wrap up a few things, but the real concern was June Bug drawing unnecessary attention to the stolen vehicle.

Smith grabbed his binoculars and watched as he extracted a pipe and took a few puffs of crack. Morgan strolled out of the building wearing a bright white pair of pants and a green top, her purse clenched to her side and keys dangled in her hands. June Bug was in such a daze. He didn't see Morgan pull off in her car.

"Snap out of it, you moron. She's getting away!" Smith yelled, hitting the steering wheel, missing the horn.

Morgan vanished down the street. Smith laid his hand on the horn. June Bug jerked and turned in the direction of the parking lot, then sprang into gear.

Chapter 24

Tony stretched out on the black leather sectional chair in the den in front of the television. Heather sat in the chair with Tony's legs resting on her thighs. He placed the cordless phone on the cradle, simultaneously glancing at Heather as she rolled her tiger eyes.

Tiffany had called to make sure that they had arrived home safely through the storm. Tony and Heather took their kids to the Ice Escapades, a Thursday night family event Heather had planned. She was great at planning family activities since family time was a high priority on her list. She'd rearrange her entire schedule at the drop of a dime to take the kids someplace—even if it was only a minor request from their two little darlings. The kids were in bed and from that point on was considered quality time for Tony and Heather. A quick glance at her flushed skin and flashing eyes said time was plentiful; quality had flown out the window.

"Anthony, why did you answer the phone?" She pushed his legs off her lap. Her voice drowned out the television.

Tony almost fell off the chair. "*Look now*! I'm not up for this tonight."

Her lips crumbled into a frown. "This is our time. That's why we have an answering machine."

Tony cradled a bowl in his arms, swiped the remote off the table, searching for a sitcom to spice up Heather's sour mood. "You need to calm down."

Heather snatched the bowl of chips out of his hands and slid to the other end of the sofa. "Anthony, did you hear me?" She turned the television off.

Tony gnawed on his lip. Her snotty attitude was taking a toll on their marriage. He shoved the last chip in his mouth and sipped on his ginger ale before he answered. "Tiffany wanted to make sure we had arrived home safely. Plus, she was upset, Heather. She talked to my mother tonight." He slumped in the chair. "You know she doesn't want to move from Cloverdale and that bothers both of us."

She sat on the edge of the chair. "What does she want you to do? What, Anthony? Where is your cape? Forget Superman. You need a cape that says Super-Tony."

"What are you talking about?"

She angled her feet toward the door. "I guess now you're ready to rush out of the house to rescue her."

Sooner or later, she would dash through the doors. He wasn't in the mood to chase her around the house.

She swung her neck around, facing him. "Why did she run out of her office? I'm still dying to find out."

"Do you hear what you're saying?" Tony ran a hand through his hair, taking a breath before lowering his voice. "I'm sorry you're not close to your siblings. I'm sorry that you only talk to them during the holidays and that's only when *you* call them. You need to tell me what's *really* going on with you and your so-called close-knit family. And why you resent that I'm so close to mine."

Silence took over the room as if the conversation had been sucked up in a vacuum.

"How *dare* you! My family's too busy to worry about one another. We have our own careers and we don't need to babysit one another." She lifted her chin. "We're all rich and successful and have our own families. And we stick to that."

Tony peered at her. "I'm confused, Heather. Help me to understand. 'Cause what it really seems like is that you all are too busy to care." He snatched the bowl back from her, chips spilling onto the floor. "None of them ever picks up the phone to call you. You could be drowning in the Atlantic Ocean for all they care and they'd never know it unless I called to tell them." Tony rammed a chip in his mouth. "Yes, I come from a poor family but we ate and slept off love. We didn't have all the *fancy stuff* you grew up with but we did have each other and that's why we're close—not because material things mattered. *We* mattered."

Tony stood and paced the grayish-black carpet. "I think you're jealous of Tiffany because she's a secure, successful young woman who commands a lot of respect from everyone. Maybe if you'd start thinking of someone other than yourself, you wouldn't be so intimidated by our relationship."

Heather stood, placing trembling hands on her hips and walked toward the steps. Her turquoise camisole revealed every curve.

"You're *my* husband, Anthony, not hers."

"I'm sick of this insecure, nagging *mess*."

"You're not going to stand here and insult me like I'm some *slut* off the streets." She glared openly at him. "I'm not one of those lowlifes you hang out with in Cloverdale."

"Lowlife!" It took every ounce of strength from him to keep his cool. The bowl went flying into the wall. Chips scattered on the carpet. "*I* came from Cloverdale, Heather. You have to accept that."

"Just because you came from there doesn't mean you have to hang with those people." She poked him in the chest with her index finger. "You're better than they are."

Inching away, Tony flashed back to when he met Heather. He was a star athlete, but still had dreams of being a dentist. He stayed focused on his dreams until he met Heather. She had a difficult time accepting his past, but Tony's charming, respectful demeanor swept her off her feet. As far as he knew, Heather still hadn't told her parents he was from Cloverdale—a serious bone of contention between them.

Tony's heart pounded a river of blood to his temples. "Am I better than they are, Heather? How would you know? Just because they don't have a college education doesn't mean that they are less of a person."

She smirked, every ounce of beauty trickling away with the move. "You don't have to justify your weakness for those people. You and your home-wrecker sister can keep pacifying *those* people. Don't take *my* children with you."

"Heather, I need to know what's going on. When I met you, you were not like this. You were a compassionate, loving person. Who are you? And what have you done with my real wife?"

She tilted her chin toward the ceiling, then walked away. "I'm not in the mood to listen to a speech, Anthony."

Tony grabbed her elbow. "We're gonna sort this out tonight."

She jerked away. "I don't have time to listen to a lecture about your sister."

"You and Tiffany got along well before we got married. What's changed that?"

"What's happened is that I learned that you and your sister are joined at the hip." Then her soft lips curled into a hard sneer. "Or are you joined by something else?"

Tony gritted his teeth. "I'm leaving. I'm tired of putting up with your *stank attitude.*" He grabbed his keys and headed towards the door.

"*Anthony,*" Heather said in a soft tone, trailing him to the door.

Tony turned, sharply. "Apologize."

"I didn't mean it."

He held open the door. "You meant it, all right."

"I apologize. Please don't leave . . . let's go back to the den." Heather walked back and sat down, looking up at him.

Moments later he closed the door. "You'd better talk. I'm serious. I'm gonna walk out that door." Tony paced in front of her. "I'm getting migraines from stressing over little things." He applied pressure to his temples. "You need to tell me something right now or I need to go somewhere where I can have peace of mind. I love you, even with your *nasty* attitude and I love my children. But I can't take it anymore. Do you hear me, Heather?"

Heather paused before letting out a soft wailing sound. It seemed like an eternity before she spoke. Tears flowed from her greenish-brown eyes as she said, "Yes, I'm jealous of the relationship you have with your family." Her olive hands covered her face. "I don't know my real parents."

Calmness quickly replaced the overload of anger. Tony sat down on the sofa next to her. He turned off the television.

Tears formed in her eyes as she spoke. "My biological mother was on drugs. I don't like being around drug addicts because they remind me of her and the way she was when she had me. That's why I don't like going to Cloverdale to visit your mother. I don't know who my father is or anything about my background." She buried her face in his chest. Barely audible, she said, "I wonder sometimes where this long, wavy hair came from. Or these greenish-brown eyes and this olive skin tone. No one else in my house looked like me. They made me feel . . . different."

Tony's arms wrapped securely around his wife. Tears dripped onto his silk pajama shirt. "Oh, baby. Why didn't you tell me this before? You made up all that stuff about your family?"

Her tears soaked through his pajama shirt. "Yes. I mean, *no.* Someone left me on the doorstep of the fire department when I was three days old. Social Services placed me with my adopted parents a month later. My adopted mother couldn't have children, so she adopted four of us." She laid her head against his chest. A single hand came up to stroke her hair. "No, we aren't close. I cried a lot because I didn't understand how my mother could forsake me." She shook like a bowl of Jell-O. "I get upset when I see people strung out on drugs. Sometimes I wonder if one of those cracked-out women is my mother."

Tony kissed Heather's forehead as he wiped her face. He couldn't believe how smoothly she had portrayed the role that she had a close-knit, well-to-do family. If the clues were there, he had overlooked them.

"My adopted parents never had time for us." She clutched his hands. "They were surgeons and became so wrapped up in their careers, they were hardly ever home." Her chest heaved with a weary sigh. "We called the nanny mama and the gardener daddy. They deserved those names. We lived in a nice sized house but we weren't loved—not like you and Tiffany. We fulfilled a dream that our adopted mother wanted. She had an image to prove and was ashamed to tell people she couldn't bear children. I remember when she moved to Baltimore she told her parents and friends in Miami that she was pregnant. We didn't visit them for at least ten months. By this time, she adopted my brother and took him to Miami to show everyone."

Tony embraced Heather as she slowly placed her head on his chest. Though Heather had finally unleashed the truth, it was going to take a major overhaul to change her attitude toward his family and his past.

Chapter 25

June Bug tore down the street after Morgan. Smith trailed behind.

"Don't let her get away," Smith whispered, struggling to keep the car on the road.

The roads were slippery and the rain poured down faster. Morgan inched along the treacherous road, handling each curve cautiously. Smith grimaced.

June Bug caught up with her at the O'Brien Turnpike. Then there was only a mile to get to Silver Stream Curve. Smith swallowed hard, wanting to turn the car around and go back to the bar. Curiosity kept him trailing behind the two cars to see that things were carried out as planned.

Silver Stream Curve, a sharp curve surrounded by woods, had caution signs posted for at least five miles before the turn, cautioning drivers to slow down.

After countless accidents and several deaths, the city had finally started the process of putting stronger railings or a steel wall to prevent drivers from going over the cliff but hadn't completed the project. Anyone driving at full speed took their lives literally in their hands. Most people took fifteen miles of back roads to avoid the place, but Morgan always drove slowly and it had been part of her route to and from work for years. Thank God.

Smith stayed several car lengths behind them, keeping Morgan's taillights within his range. Streetlights were the only source of light along the narrow one-way road.

Morgan drove gradually through O'Brien Turnpike. Smith grimaced. She was probably listening to gospel music or praying. The music wouldn't help, but she could definitely use the prayer. If her habits held true, Morgan now had one foot on the gas pedal and the other on the brake, with a firm grip on the steering wheel as she braced herself for the turn into Silver Stream.

Her car idled around the curve.

The rain pelted his windshield, making it nearly impossible for him to see twenty feet in front of the car. He turned the wipers up full throttle as Morgan approached the slippery points of Silver Stream Curve.

June Bug rammed the Ford truck into the back of the little Toyota Avalon.

Trying to maneuver the curve, Smith struggled to hold the binoculars.

Morgan gripped the steering wheel, glancing in the rearview mirror before the truck rammed her again.

Smith's heartbeat quickened. He dropped the binoculars as the patrol car swerved out of the lane.

His cell phone rang. He whipped it out from his front pocket and saw Morgan's cell number in the display.

"*Crap!*"

Smith reached down, turned the radio up to full blast, pulled over to the side of the road then turned off the car. She wasn't dead.

"Hello," he said, nearly yelling over the music. "Here Raymond, take this beer, man." Country music blasted in the car.

"Please help me!" Morgan shrieked. "I'm on Silver Stream Curve. Someone keeps ramming the back of my car. He's trying to force me off the road!"

"What are you talking about, Morgan?"

"Paul," Morgan yelled. "Where are you?"

The screech of tires echoed through the line.

"*Jesus Christ*, that person doesn't know how dangerous this curve is!" Morgan screamed.

"Honey," he said sliding down into the leather seat. "Calm down. Maybe it's someone who's losing control of their truck. Move off to the side."

Smith moved the phone from his face, covered a portion of the mouthpiece as he yelled out, "Next round of drinks is on me."

Her voice became frantic and reached a high pitch. "Paul, move away from that loud music!"

Tires screeched in the background—again. Smith smiled. Morgan was having a hard time keeping the car on the road. He could hear her panting.

Smith said calmly, "You know it's Thursday night and I hang out with the fellows at Night Owl Bar."

"I need you to come right now."

"I'll call for backup—they might get to you sooner. I'm leaving now!" Smith yelled at the top of his lungs, then paused for a second. "I'll see you, fellows, later. Morgan's in trouble." Then to Morgan, he said, "I'm on my way. I'll call you when I get close."

"Please don't get off the phone!" she shrieked. "Paul, I'm scared."

"I'm coming, Morgan," Smith said while cranking the car up and pulling off to catch up with the two cars.

"It looks like Dr. Chris' truck. Why would he want to kill me?"

"Hang in there, Morgan," he said calmly. "I'm on my way."

June Bug rammed the truck again.

"Paul, please help me. He's trying to kill me!"

"Don't talk foolishly, dear. I'm driving as fast as I can." Why was it taking June Bug so long to do the job?

"If I die. . . I know you can cope better than the children."

A bloodcurdling scream surrounded the air.

Morgan gasped for breath, but said, "Our Father, who art in Heaven . . . hallowed be thy name."

"Calm down. Try to think about something other than death," he said with a grin. "I'm coming."

The car shifted from side to side.

"Forever, Amen. Heavenly Father, please watch over my children and my husband, keep them safe within your word and in your loving arms," she said between gasps for breath. "If it's my time to join you in Heaven, I accept that. I love you, God, with all of my heart and thank you that your son Jesus gave his life for me and my sins are forgiven . . . ."

Smith growled at the mention of the name Jesus . . . or God. He wonder how could the woman be thinking about Jesus or God or any spiritual divine being when her very life was at stake? "Can you see the person, Morgan?"

She continued praying which angered him even more.

"Can you see him!"

The tires screeched trying to hold onto the paved concrete road.

"No," she said softly. "He's wearing some sort of mask and it's really too dark to see much else. He has brown skin, I think. Paul, where are you?" Her voice had taken on an irritatingly serene quality.

"I'm coming. You know it's raining." Smith drummed his fingers on the steering wheel. "I'm doing at least seventy miles per hour." He placed his hands over his mouth as he chuckled. His car idled around the curve at about ten miles per hour, but he still could see Morgan and June Bug's taillights. If he didn't hurry up, they would soon be out of the curve and further from Night Owl Bar. Then it would be too late.

Morgan's car jerked forward.

The last words that Smith heard from Morgan were, "God, please send your guardian angels to protect me."

June Bug drove like a maniac, pounding into the back of the Avalon, trying to finish her off before she came out of the curve.

Smith's eyes widened as he watched the car flip over the curve. Morgan screamed in her cell phone. The crushing of metal pounding on the rocky ground fifty feet below the curve echoed through the phone.

June Bug pulled the truck to the side of the curve, then jumped out and ran to the edge of the cliff.

Red lights beamed flickering from below. Smith leaned back in the seat, watching as June Bug fired three shots at Morgan's car, then jumped into the truck and vanished.

Chapter 26

Tony strolled into the bathroom while Heather remained in the den flipping through pictures of her adopted parents, sisters and brothers that she had hidden in the attic. Tony insisted that she look at the pictures.

He closed the glass door to the walk-in shower. The Jacuzzi brought back memories of him and his wife spending countless hours making love in the water.

Pulling the towel off the gold handle, Tony patted the soft cotton on his skin.

The bathroom was spacious with accents of black and gold diamond shapes etched into the marble floor. A wide strip of gold border paper assembled around the point where the ceiling met the wall, creating a distinctively modern look. A wide mirror with oval-shaped light bulbs bonded to the off-white painted wall.

Tiptoeing behind Tony, Heather's hands connected at his navel. Startled, Tony applied a firm grip on the towel and looked over his shoulder. Heather's magnetic eyes held a twinkle that was a common occurrence when they first got married. Gracefully sliding her hair behind her ears, revealing the diamond earrings Tony had gifted her on Valentine's Day, Heather twirled her tongue along the defined muscles of his stomach.

Inching the towel away, she licked his chest while simultaneously kicking off her slippers, tossing them in the corner. Tony prayed that the telephone didn't ring.

His erection lifted the towel, creating a nice bulky print. A small sigh escaped her lips as her soft tongue trailed across his extended member as if licking chocolate icing from a birthday cake. It was somebody's birthday— his.

Dropping the towel to the floor, Tony pulled Heather toward him and walked over to the porcelain black Jacuzzi. His heart pulsated with an intense rush of anticipated pleasure.

The warm water flowed out of the gold faucet. While Tony dimmed the lights, Heather lit a few Jasmine candles that had been held hostage in the cabinets for months, since her birthday in April. She reached up, pinning her soft, wavy hair in a bun.

Fresh, pleasant scents of Jasmine candles quickly dispensed in the bathroom. The shimmer from the candles cast a shadow of their bodies against the wall.

With their busy schedules, quickies were always on the bedroom menu. But now a full-course meal was needed to keep the spices flowing in a marriage that had become mired in routine and jealousy. An affectionate man, Tony had always sought to rekindle the precious moments they used to spend making passionate love until beads of sweat dripped from their bodies and tears of joys followed close behind.

Tony caressed the soft curves of Heather's body as he slowly peeled away her clothes. A throbbing sensation flowed through him as he slipped her black panties over the soft flesh of her hips, down her silky legs; he gently caressed her thighs while sucking on the flesh that stretched up to her soft folds of flesh.

The water merged with shower gel, forming a massive layer of bubbles on the surface. She stood in front of him with bubbles only covering her knees. Her face sparkled from the glow of the candles. Tony pulled her closer.

He wrapped his lips around her right nipple, sucking gently while simultaneously caressing her left one like a sculptor crafting a masterpiece. Heather's eyes fluttered each time his tongue grazed the hardened mounds of flesh.

She gripped the back of his head pressing him closer. "Umm, Anthony. Yes, like that."

He lowered, burying his head into the soft curls covering her treasure. Her head tilted back as another breathy moan echoed above the sound of bubbling water.

"Yes, Anthony," she murmured, wrapping her arms around his neck and straddled her legs around his hips. Bubbles drifted between them as Tony braced himself, keeping her in place. He licked her ears as she caressed the muscles in his back. His tongue trailed along her face to her moist lips where their tongues finally met and twirled around each other.

Heather kneeled; grabbed his erection and thrust it into her mouth. She sucked and nibbled on the skin surrounding his velvet rod. He could feel it pressing against the soft tissues inside of her mouth.

"Oooh . . . Heather." Tony's hips moved forward with the caress of her tongue. He stroked his fingers through her hair, down her back as the muscles in his stomach quivered. The water covered almost to her shoulders.

Tony lifted her, pressing her back against the wall as her legs dangled across his arms. His head squeezed between her thighs. He gently bit on the flesh that stretched her thighs up to her treasure box. Licking the delicate skin surrounding the outside, Tony slid his tongue inside. Her hips moved in a circular motion keeping up with his rhythm.

"Yes. Anthony. Like that."

She caressed his shoulders and neck. Moisture flowed onto his tongue. Heather clamped down on his hand with her fingers, pressing her nails into his head.

He had to pry her hands away. He slowly lowered her body toward his, letting the water flow around them. He stroked her butt and hips, then parted her thighs with his head, slowing entering her creamy center with a long, sure stroke.

Carefully sliding every inch into Heather, Tony parted her lips with his tongue, exploring the soft depths underneath. He trembled. Her skin glimmered in the glow of the candles. Passionate moaning sounds filled the air.

Tony cupped her breasts with the palm of his hand, sucking on the soft flesh and gently nibbling on her nipples. He buried his face into the soft swell of her breasts.

Heather gripped his back as he gently stroked her wide, voluptuous hips, thrusting inside her.

She went limp, nearly lifeless as he pulled out and thrust in again and again.

"I love you, Anthony," Heather whispered.

Tony thrust in again, sinking deeper and deeper.

"Ohh, Anthony," she moaned as he pumped faster and faster.

Tony thrust deeper and deeper.

Warm water splashed against their bodies, blending in with the beads of sweat that had formed on their foreheads.

"I'm sorry for the way I act sometimes. I love you so much." She moaned deeply. "Please don't ever leave me."

"Shh, baby," Tony whispered as he slid one of Heather's nipples into his mouth.

They moved in a synchronized, heated rhythm. The rise and fall of their passionate thrusts made the water splash against Heather's back and onto her hair.

Every muscle in Tony's body contracted as his hips shifted. Gently gripping her soft buttocks, he guided her towards each thrust, increasing the pleasure with every stroke. Tony tilted his neck, burying his head in her breasts. Heather melted like butter every time Tony nibbled on her shoulders and breasts, creating enough juices in her body to fill the Safari Desert.

"Oh, Anthony. I love you." Her eyes fluttered and her hips swayed.

"Shhh, Baby."

Tony gasped deeply as his heartbeat pressed against the soft flesh of her breasts.

He shook as his legs became numb, mouth opening as his eyes rolled in the back of his head. He stroked his fingers along the flesh of her ribcage and her flat stomach.

"Heather," he said as a warm tingling sensation flowed through his body.

The warm water splashed over them like a tidal wave.

"Heather." He gripped her hips, sliding his hands around to her buttocks.

"Ahh! Heather."

"Yes…Yes, Anthony," she whispered tenderly.

Water splattered on the floor.

Tony jerked. His muscles stiffened as he applied a tight grip on Heather's hips and buttocks thrust coming harder and harder, faster and faster.

"Ahh! Heather." His eyes rolled to the back of his head.

Gradually, the muscles in his body relaxed.

Heather nestled her head on his chest, a wide smile on her lips as she asked, "Again?"

Chapter 27

At the bar, Smith sat at the table shooting the breeze with Raymond and Vincent. The Night Owl Bar was closing in an hour, so the bartenders had stopped taking orders. Why hadn't the police department or the hospital contacted him yet? Someone had to drive past the area and notice her taillights shining. Someone would have to run her license number.

His pager buzzed. Smith didn't recognize the number. He shifted his gaze between his buddies, then to his pager. After passing his pager around, he asked, "Do any of you recognize this number?"

"That's Charlotte Medical Hospital," Raymond said, holding the little black device in his slim fingers.

"How do you know?"

"Man, my daughter had my grandson there last week. I know that number like my social security number. The receptionist called me from that same number to let me know Cynthia was in labor."

"You sure?" Smith paused but then continued. "I'll be right back. I can hear better outside."

"Yeah, you've been out there enough tonight."

Smith ran to the car and called the number. "Hello, this is Sergeant Paul Smith. Someone from this number paged me."

"Yes, Sergeant Smith. This is Faye Tillery, the patient intake manager in the emergency room at Charlotte Medical Hospital. We need you to come to the hospital as soon as possible. Your wife was admitted about an hour ago. She's up in surgery right now."

Smith smiled but closed his eyes as he said, "No. No. Please don't tell me this. Please."

"Sir, please calm down."

"What happened!"

"Sir, we will explain that to you when you arrive," she said in a rushed tone. "Please come to the emergency room entrance. I'll be waiting at the triage desk."

"I'm—I'm on my way." Forcing a tear out of his eyes, he strolled back into the bar.

Vincent perked up. "Hey Smith, what's wrong?"

He paused, swallowing before taking a deep breath. "It's Morgan!" Two hands whipped out to cover his face. "She's at the hospital. They said she was in a serious car accident."

"What happened?" Raymond asked, throwing a hand over Smith's shoulder.

"I don't know. The nurse wouldn't tell me. But it sounds pretty serious."

Raymond's bloodshot eyes widened. "Man! You'd better get over there."

"Yeah, I know. Here's some cash for the drinks." Smith tossed a few bills on the table.

Raymond stood, pressing his hand on the back of the wooden chair. "We'll meet you at the hospital. I gotta let my wife know what's going on." He grabbed his coat. "She's on her way to pick me up. Hang in there, man."

Smith managed a few more tears as Raymond and Vincent walked him to his car.

While driving, he rehearsed a few bewildered facial expressions so they would come naturally. Five minutes later, he burst through the emergency room doors, scouting the area. He was hoping he saw Tiffany strolling the corridors of the hospital. He knew that she delivered babies there. A glance of her was all he needed to spark memories.

"I'm Sergeant Smith. Where is my wife! I just got a call saying she was brought here." His face was so wet with rain that he hoped they would mistake it for tears. "Please, hurry up. She's all I have."

"Morgan Smith?" Nurse Tillery, the intake manager, gazed up at Smith. "Yes, we have her here. But I'm sorry, you can't see her right now; she's in the intensive unit."

Sirens pierced the air inside of the hospital as ambulances pulled up to the door.

"What do you mean I can't see her!"

"If you wait a minute, sir," Nurse Tillery said, handing him a Kleenex, "I'll call a nurse to take you to the waiting area."

Two minutes later, a short, stocky woman with a white uniform approached the receptionist's desk.

"Hello, I'm Nurse Logan. Follow me."

The nurse rushed through the metal double doors with Smith shadowing her steps. They hopped on an elevator and she took him to the intensive care unit where Morgan would end up for weeks if she survived. He prayed she didn't.

The nurse then led him into the sterile white area, where she tapped on the window and another nurse opened the curtains. Morgan's near lifeless body had been strung up to several machines. Tubes ran through her nose and monitor pads were pasted on her forehead, neck and chest. Her skin was even paler than he could ever remember. He wiped his eyes and buried his face in his hands.

The nurse led Smith to a small, private waiting room with peach-colored walls.

Smith rehearsed his routine again. He glanced out of the small window. The rain was finally easing up. Somehow it hadn't helped as much as he wanted. June Bug would have to pay for any mistakes.

Five minutes later, a tall lady with a white medical jacket came into the room with a chart in her hand. She looked at him, sighed, then sank into the seat beside him. Nurse Logan sat upright, plucked a tissue from the canister, offered it to him and left. "I'm Dr. Elizabeth Rankin."

The sound of wheels rolling and shoes tapping echoed on the floor.

Smith swept the Kleenex across his eyes. "What's going on with my wife?"

"Sir, I'm sorry you're facing this predicament." She sighed as her light brown eyes locked onto Smith's face. "I wish I could tell you her chances of survival were good. She's lost too much blood and she was shot three times."

Smith dropped his head, staring at the floor.

"Can I go in the room with her? I want to be alone with my wife."

"At this time, we can't allow anyone to enter the room other than medical staff. We must prevent all potential germs from coming into contact with her." Dr. Rankin reached for another Kleenex and placed it in Smith's trembling hand. "We had to rush her into surgery to remove three bullets and give her a blood transfusion." Dr. Rankin patted his hand gently. "The respirator's keeping her breathing even. At last check, her heart rate was slowly dropping and brain waves were fluctuating a bit." Dr. Rankin exhaled slowly. "She's not responding at all. We've done everything we can do. I'm so sorry, sir. We don't think she'll survive much longer on the respirator. Do you want to contact your minister or someone else?"

"For what! She isn't dead," he said, gripping her white coat. "Don't tell me my wife's about to die!" Smith covered his face with trembling hands but peeked out of the corner to gauge the doctor's somber expression.

"Sir, please, calm down," she said, prying his fingers from her jacket. "In a situation like this, people usually call their ministers or ask us to contact the hospital chaplain." She inched forward on the edge of the seat. "Sometimes after receiving prayer, the patients do better."

"I don't know what to do. I'm so confused. I don't know what I'll do without my Morgan."

"She's not gone yet, let's keep praying for her," Dr. Rankin whispered, patting his hand softly.

Smith slumped in the seat, letting out a loud wail that traveled through the long, mint green hallway. Dr. Rankin tried to comfort him and finally Smith agreed to allow the hospital chaplain to pray with him. By this time, Smith's children, Raymond and Pastor Bob, the minister of their church rushed into the intensive care area. Crystal, Megan and Paul Jr. didn't utter a single word. Not even a weak hello. The bastards. Normally, it didn't bother him when they ignored him, but he at least expected them to be civil in a case like this—especially in front of strangers.

"Everything's gonna be all right," Raymond said with a low tone as he patted Smith on the shoulder.

Smith eyeballed Raymond's wife, Joyce, letting his gaze fall on her big, melon breasts. Boy, what he wouldn't give to wrap his lips around—

Raymond glared up at Smith, clearing his throat.

Dr. Rankin directed everyone to the glass window where Morgan's frightfully pale body rested on a long, padded bed inside of a bright room.

Glowering at his little bundles of joy, Smith thought, I could've collected on their policies too. Four for the price of one piece of crack.

Pastor Bob went straight to the window, placing a pale, weathered hand on the glass, touching it as if he could send healing powers to Morgan's body just by that action alone.

To Smith's dismay, the minister began to call on the angels from Heaven to help Morgan. While he prayed, Smith felt a strong sense of fear, stabbing his heart and burning his soul. He should put an end to this. But how?

Smith couldn't bear the sound of the machines beeping; he wanted to burst through the doors and disconnect the tubes from her body.

Pastor Bob began to shake, then babbled in some language Smith had never heard. The old man gripped the window and held it as if he could teleport himself into the room next to Morgan. He wasn't loud, but his actions amplified through the small area. The nurses watched from their spot behind the brown table but didn't stop him.

Smith walked over to the minister and stood dutifully beside him. The man took two steps away, probably needing more space to perform his little rituals.

"Let God do his work," Pastor Bob said, opening his green eyes, then turning to face the three children crowded together in a corner near the nurse's station. He walked down the hallway without saying another word. The man's lean frame suddenly seemed weak and tired as if he had given Morgan a part of his own life. Then the minister vanished behind the double doors. Good riddance!

Dr. Rankin turned to Smith and his children, "You'll have to go back into the private waiting room for now."

Smith leaned against the peach-colored wall several feet away from his children as they cried and took turns reminiscing about the good times they had with Morgan as if she were already dead.

Paul Jr. gripped his curly blonde hair, tears rolling down his narrow, ivory face. Tears streamed out of the corners of Megan's baby blue eyes as her legs quivered like jelly. Smith sneered, rolled his eyes, then flopped in a seat near the end of the table. Crystal opened her small pink lips and released a weeping sound as she prayed. Her body trembled, causing her platinum-blonde hair to vibrate.

Smith joined them in prayer, inwardly asking for God to take her home.

Two hours later, Raymond and his wife went home, leaving Smith in the room for a little quality time with his children. That didn't last long. They turned on their heels, leaving him to venture off into the intensive care area—again.

Smith wanted a smoke so bad that he'd give his right arm to take a few puffs. He certainly didn't want to leave until a white line stretched across the monitor pronouncing that his wife was dead.

He slumped in a heap onto the sofa and dozed off.

Hours later, a slight tap on his shoulder startled him. He glanced around, noticing his kids were staring at him.

"You're snoring," his youngest daughter said, angrily. "Hard."

His gaze shifted to the only window in the room. The rain had ceased and the sun was rising.

Dr. Rankin rushed into the room and yelled, "Come, look. Hurry up! It's a miracle."

Chapter 28

Classical tunes flowed out of the intercom in the medical center pressing against Tiffany's ears. The marbled lobby was filled with radiant pink and beige colors with small pyramid-shaped imprints. Women with skin tones varying from pale white to peaches and cream and from light caramel brown to chocolate brown waited patiently for Tiffany to examine them.

Pap smears were the worst part of the examination for some women, but Tiffany managed to get all of her patients to relax and understand their importance. Early detection could be the difference between a quick treatment or a life-threatening surgery.

Every staff member of Brown Medical Associates came highly recommended because they were bilingual, just like Tiffany. She was an exchange student in Spain for two years. When she hired Maria and Pilar, her clientele in the Hispanic community increased tremendously. Now English and Spanish conversations flowed as patients waited for their names to be called.

Strolling down the long brightly lit hallway, slipping her white jacket over her arms and shoulders, Tiffany smiled with each step towards the last room in the corridor. Childhood friends from Cloverdale and word of mouth had increased her practice from low-clientele-intake to a double booking of patients on some days. But somehow, she managed to give everyone undivided attention. She understood her clients and treated everyone with the same level of respect that some doctors reserved only for their high-level patients.

Tiffany had chosen an office building situated only three blocks from the bus stop, making it convenient for clients who didn't have a car. Plus, graduating with honors from Duke Medical School drew many new patients from more prestigious communities. Although the waiting room could be a bit precarious at times with the upper levels looking down their noses at the less fortunate, the staff soon set them straight, preventing any incidents.

In each examination room, butterflies in different developmental stages hung on the wall. Tiffany compared a woman's body to a butterfly. From birth to womanhood, she believed that all women went through changes in life—some drastic and painstaking and others were enchanting and vigorous. She had certainly had enough in her lifetime. In some ways, her wings were a little clipped and in others, the color had rivaled the rainbow.

Antiseptics, latex gloves, cotton swabs and gauges were neatly arranged on the counter.

"Hello, Tiffany. I mean, Dr. Brown-Carson." The tall patient with light brown skin giggled. She sat on the edge of the table trying to smooth the blue and white gown around her naked body.

"How are you doing, Karen? Or should I say KeKe?" Tiffany asked as she washed her hands, dried them off, then threw the paper towel in the small silver trashcan.

"Look at you in that white jacket. Is that Gucci?"

Tiffany opened Karen's chart. "So now you're a comedian," she said, laughing. "No, this isn't Gucci. You said the same thing last time you were here. Gucci is out of my range."

"Girl, stop playing. You know you're rich." Karen swept her hand across Tiffany's jacket. "You're wearing it like it's a name brand." She threw her head back and roared with laughter. "You know me. I'm not wearing anything that doesn't come from Dillard's with a *five-finger* discount."

Tiffany smirked. Why did so many people prefer to invest their money in clothes instead of an education? Timberland knockoffs from Payless or Nike imitations from Kmart were the only shoes Tiffany's mother could afford. Clothes were temporary garments; education was the future.

Glancing over to the *Cushnie* outfit draped across the chair next to the small changing area and the *Fashion Fair* makeup kit poking out of an *Ashya* bag, Tiffany said, "Karen, I see you're still trying to keep up with the latest fashions." How did Karen squeeze her wide frame into such a tiny outfit? Karen hadn't been a size six since their days at Independence High School.

"You know how *we do* in Cloverdale." Her soft brown eyes glittered. "I have to keep up with the young girls . . . and that means top-of-the-line, baby."

Tiffany peered at her. "Not me. My mother couldn't afford it."

"None of us could." Karen's glittery, gold painted lips tightened. "But you know how I roll."

The morning sunlight streamed in between the slats in the blinds.

Yes, everyone knew how Karen rolled. She had a reputation for dating drug dealers—exclusively. Her motto: "If the dealer isn't paid, he ain't getting laid." Tall, with long legs that every schoolboy and hustler dreamed of slipping between, she wore her hair in a bobbed hairstyle with blonde streaks. She talked a good game, which lured the money out of a hustler's pockets faster than a rocket blasting off. But that greed led her down a road that straddled between promiscuity and prostitution, which, for a teenager, also led to the dangerous road of drug trafficking, running up north to collect dope to keep the Cloverdale junkies supplied.

Shrieking sounds flowed out of the intercom before the receptionist announced, "Nurse Patterson, you're needed in the lobby."

Tiffany glanced at her notes in Karen's chart. She drew a deep breath. "Karen, you know that at some point in your life you have to give up this lifestyle and get back in school."

Karen crooked her mouth a little in something that wasn't quite a smile. "Girl, I'm proud to be Jason's main chick, it's almost like a medal of honor."

"Yeah, hustlers will spoil you and you get the best clothes, jewelry and hairstyles, but every time you get pregnant, they disappear."

"We ain't gonna talk about that," Karen said, folding her slender arms across her small chest. Karen laughed, just like she did any other time Tiffany brought up the fact that having so many partners put her at risk.

"I'm glad you're a doctor." Karen glanced around the sanitized room. "I think you serve everyone in Cloverdale." She gave Tiffany a tired half smile. "I couldn't do it."

"Do what?"

"Look inside of those nasty tricks." Karen's soft brown eyes widened as she giggled. "Did you hear about Ashley and Monica? They were outside fighting. You know they're pregnant by the same guy." She shook her head. "These tricks will never learn."

Of all people, Karen had the nerve to call the girls in Cloverdale, tricks. She turned hustlers faster than Ashley and Monica could service customers on a daily basis. But of course, Karen couldn't see that.

Tiffany placed a finger over her mouth signaling Karen to be silent as the intercom came on. "Nurse Brooks, please come to the lab."

Tiffany closed Karen's chart. "Everyone needs medical care regardless of how many people they sleep with at a time."

Karen's chest puffed out. "Not *whores*."

"You can't talk, girlfriend."

A faint smile flashed across Karen's face. "Don't even start or I'll whip your tail."

"Please!" Tiffany said chuckling. "Don't let this white jacket *fool* you. I whipped your butt that day when you pushed me in the mud." Tiffany sneered. "I can grease up and take care of your little *hot tail* right now. Vaseline's right over there."

Karen burst into laughter.

"Hey, have you heard the latest about Hope? I heard some sad news about her mother," muffled Karen.

"What sad news?" asked Tiffany.

"Do you remember how bad Hope's mother used to treat her?" asked Karen while shaking her head with her eyes closed as if she could feel Hope's pain.

"Yes," mumbled Tiffany while exhaling slowly as she reflected upon the memories of Hope's repeated crackling voice telling her about the unbearable abuse she endured from her mother. Tiffany sighed recalling how she and Hope were close as kids. A shaft of uncertainty flowed through Tiffany as she recalled Hope had vanished without a trace the day they graduated from high school as if she were a fugitive running from the law. People in Cloverdale believed she was either kidnapped or ran away to escape from her mother.

"You two were close," Karen snapped rolling her eyes as if a streak of jealousy overtook her.

"Yeah, we were," Tiffany sighed. "I was surprised she never contacted me after she left."

"I was surprised, too," Karen paused. "She vanished just like Julie did."

"Yeah, you're right," Tiffany exhaled.

"Hope's mother used to treat her like *trash*. But her mother treated Hope's sister, Ivey, like a pot of gold."

A sense of remorse filled the air.

"Now, I heard her mother is sick . . . almost on her deathbed."

"Really," said Tiffany.

"Yes, I heard her mother need something from Hope to stay alive," muffled Karen.

"Are you serious?"

"Yeah . . . and whatever it is, Ivey can't give it to her. I think it is a kidney or bone marrow or something."

"Come on, Karen, are you serious?" Tiffany stared at Karen.

"Yes, I am serious," sighed Karen. "Her mother told somebody and the word spread like fireworks," sighed Karen. "Karma is something. What goes around comes around."

"Is Hope going to help her mother?" asked Tiffany in a remorseful tone.

Karen crooked her head to the side.

"I don't know. But the way Hope's mother used to treat her . . . Hope might let her die," replied Karen.

Tiffany exhaled slowly, taking in Karen's words.

"Hey, what about Mrs. Ruth. She's about fifty-five years old and still getting her freak on," laughed Karen.

Tiffany was grateful that Karen had ceased the conversation about Hope.

"Leave Mrs. Ruth alone. She gets her routine exams unlike *some* people I know."

"Paging, Nurse Brooks. You are needed in medical records."

Karen pursed her lips. "Are you trying to talk about me?"

"I'm not *trying* to do anything," Tiffany shot back.

Karen grinned. "You know Mrs. Ruth still hasn't changed. She's still messing with the young men in Cloverdale. She swears she can get any guy between twenty-one and thirty-five."

Tiffany's leveled eye made contact with Karen. "She's a smart lady. At least she makes sure her men are of legal age."

Karen dipped her head. "Mine are legal."

"Legal enough to land your tail in jail."

Karen inched her plump butt to the center of the table, then leaned back. "Mrs. Ruth looks like she's about thirty-five; I'd still be working it, too."

Tiffany and Karen chuckled in unison.

"I wonder what happened to Mrs. Ruth's daughter, Julie," Karen said. "Mrs. Ruth used to cry all the time after her daughter went missing."

"I know," said Tiffany. "Mrs. Ruth loved Julie."

"The police didn't bother to search for her. They assumed she ran away." Karen cleared her throat. "They think all poor black girls run away."

Tiffany paused before speaking. "Julie wouldn't do that to her mother. She wasn't that type of girl." Tiffany paused. "She's been missing since we were in high school."

"I know," Karen said. "But you know *Rock* used to like her. He was a big time drug dealer." Karen paused.

Silence filled the room for a few seconds.

"Stay still, Karen. I need to check the baby's heartbeat."

As Karen positioned her body, she lifted her neck and said, "By the way, Mrs. Ruth said your husband's fine as *hell*. She said she saw him when you came to your mama's place." Karen waggled a finger. "You better watch her."

Tiffany smiled as she walked over to the small white sink, washed her hands again, dried them, then slipped on a pair of gloves.

The conversation came to a halt when Tiffany spread K-Y Jelly on top of Karen's stretch-marked stomach. She reached for the fetal Doppler placing it on Karen's stomach, listening to the baby's heartbeat.

"Okay. Sounds good."

Karen reached for Tiffany's hand, saying, "Don't ever change, Tiff. Doctors around here know they're working near the projects and won't accept *public aid insurance.* They don't want poor people sitting in their lobbies, even the ones who have a job." Karen paused, staring into Tiffany's eyes. "One doctor told me they had an 'image to portray.' Didn't keep him from whipping out his *python* and trying to slap me some cash for a little head, though."

"Which doctor?" blurted Tiffany. "It better not be from here."

"Girl, no, not here. I'm not telling you his name. I'm not letting you mess up my cash flow. This might be his baby." Karen winked.

Tiffany laughed, nearly dropping the chart. "I'll compile a directory."

Karen pulled herself up to the level with Tiffany's eyes. "What do we need that for? We've got you."

"I know, but it'll be nice to have the names of other places to go. And you know, Tony's a dentist. He'll fix up that tooth that you've been nursing for six months."

Laughter surfed off Karen's tongue. "Your brother's fine. I don't know why I didn't give him a little taste of honey back then. I could've been Mrs. Tony Brown if I could turn back the hands of time." Karen grinned. "You know he thought I was cute. But he wasn't paid back then."

"Karen, you know Tony was into basketball and books. Money wasn't everything to him and he turned out okay." Tiffany pulled her ink pen out her pocket. "I'll write down the list of doctors for you before you leave."

"Girl, it must feel good to have white folk's insurance." Karen's lively expression crumbled. "I bet you don't have a problem getting an appointment. With your insurance, you could be seen by a doctor on Mars."

Tiffany grinned. "There's no such thing as white people's insurance."

"Whatever. Call it what you want." Karen failed in an effort to smile. "I can't wait until I push this one out," she said, stroking a small brown hand over her round belly. "She's been kicking a lot lately. And I eat everything in sight. I stay hungry."

"I'm glad to hear that your appetite has improved." Tiffany jotted down the information in the chart. "I remember when everything you smelled made you sick."

"Yeah. But I can't wait to have this one. I'm tired of being pregnant." Karen's gaze fell. "I sleep all day and night. I can't fit any of my clothes. Plus, I'm ready to get back in my tight jeans."

"Don't rush things. The baby will be here sooner than you know it. You only have six more weeks. You can keep it tight until then, right?"

Karen frowned; her soft brown eyes flashed with pain. "I hope those weeks hurry up."

"Come on, be honest with me. What's really going on?"

"Look at you. You're a successful doctor. But you came from the projects, which shocks a lot of people. We all know how hard you worked in school." She shrugged hopelessly. "Sometimes I hate that I dropped out."

"You still have time, Karen," Tiffany said slowly. "The doors are always open. They're still offering GED programs at the outreach program down the street where I volunteer."

Folding Karen's right arm behind her head, Tiffany examined her breasts, then Karen switched to her left arm when Tiffany directed her to do so.

Tiffany took a slow easy breath. "How's Christy?"

The woman closed her eyes and exhaled a gust of air. "Her therapy sessions begin today." Karen's eyes grew moist. "You know . . . I used to think therapy was for—" Karen glanced toward the white ceiling. "I used to think only *crazy* people needed therapy." She paused. "You know stuff like that is taboo in our black community."

218

Tiffany paused before speaking, knowing a few therapy sessions would have benefited her—especially considering the secrets she had tried to bury as a child. "I know. But I've learned therapy is beneficial for everyone. I think everyone needs someone to talk to sometimes."

"Thanks for visiting Christy at the psychiatric hospital." She paused. "I'll probably do a few therapy sessions myself," Karen sighed. "I've got to make sure these screws are still tight," Karen said pointing at her head. "But I don't want no therapist spreading my business. You know I'm already famous" Karen laughed.

"Girl hush, everything you talk about in therapy is confidential. But there are a few exceptions."

"Like what?" Karen's right eyebrow arched toward the ceiling.

"Calm down," Tiffany smiled. "I'm sure the therapist will go over all of that with you."

Silence flowed through the room for a few seconds.

"Thank . . .Thank you, Tiffany. It hurts me to know that my daughter was raped. I—I wish I could do things over and go back to that day. I would have picked her up from school."

Tiffany opened her mouth, then closed it. She sighed and patted Karen on her shoulders. Her mind flashed back to when she saw Christy stretched out on the medical table. Nothing would wipe the memory away. Her heart slammed against her chest knowing Christy's traumatic experience erased details from her mind—even the name she inaudibly whispered in Tiffany's ears. There was no evidence in or on her body. But Tiffany had no doubt who had violated Christy—even though the police acted clueless. Tiffany hoped Christy's intensive outpatient therapy would help her regain her memory. Regardless, Tiffany was no fool. She had her suspicions. She had no doubt that Smith knew something.

Footsteps tapped on the floor in the hallway.

"How are you holding up?"

Karen's lips slowly parted. "I'm doing all right, Tiffany. I'll make it." Karen looked toward the ceiling. "I've got so many problems."

"Like what, Karen?" Tiffany asked. "Talk to me."

"I have three children already. This will be my fourth child and I'm only twenty-seven. What man's gonna want me?" Karen winced and drew back, muttering something Tiffany didn't quite catch. "*Hell,* even their daddies don't want me. That's why I think I need therapy. I need to find myself. I need to build up my confidence to do more in life. But I don't think no good man is going to want me."

Tiffany propped her hands on her hips. "Do you hear yourself? You're a beautiful girl and you can find a good man." She slowed the flow of the words. "But first you have to start loving yourself and stop looking for a man to take care of you. Then a good man will come. You'll find out."

"Where? I'm dying to find out and please don't tell me in the church." Karen rolled her eyes. "I remember when your mother used to make you go to church every Wednesday and Sunday. I thought you and Tony were going to grow up to be ministers."

"I think going to church kept me out of trouble."

"I still can't imagine a good man wanting a woman who has four kids, especially if he's not their father. I don't know why I'm so fertile. It seems like every time a man breathes on me, I get pregnant."

"First of all," Tiffany began. "You always miss your appointment for your Depo Shot. It's only every three months."

Karen sucked her teeth, fumbling with her acrylic fingernails.

"Nothing is one hundred percent, Karen. But you'd run a less likely chance of getting pregnant if you stay consistent."

"I know. I know. I don't want all of those chemicals in me." Karen averted her gaze to the poster displayed in the room showing the different contraceptive methods. "It seems like the government's always trying to experiment on people."

"I want you to come to the outreach program. There are a lot of programs I think would benefit you. There are still ways to make your life even better."

"I hear you, *Sister Soldier*. Gone with your bad self." Karen laughed. "You sure do know how to say the right words at the right time."

Tiffany sat in her green roller chair and slid to the end of the table. "Now are you ready to get down to business?"

In a low and nervous voice, Karen asked, "Did my results come in?"

"Yes, I received them yesterday. I was waiting until you came in today to discuss it with you."

Karen avoided eye contact. "Listen, if I'm HIV positive I'd rather you tell me than anyone else. I know I took risks. Some of my boyfriends wouldn't sleep with me if I asked them to use a condom. You know I was good at juicing those hustlers out of their money—when I had sex with 'em. I couldn't believe it when I found out Jason was bisexual. He played hardcore to the max. Girl, he even fooled me. Hell, he fooled a lot of people."

"But you're still with him."

"Yeah, he still treats me right, so why do I have to give him up."

Tiffany smiled and said, "So far, you don't have anything to worry about. You're not HIV positive. But you have to be careful because HIV is one of the leading causes of death in the black community. Anybody, anywhere, can contract it. And it doesn't help matters if you don't use a condom—every time."

"Yes! Yes." Karen waved her hands in the air. "I feel like I've won the lottery. I was sweating bullets over here. "Make that examination real quick. I've got some celebratin' to do." She laughed and lay back on the table.

While sliding in the green chair at the foot of the table, Tiffany reached out pressing a round button that was mounted on the wall. "Nurse Patterson, I'm ready in room six."

"Tiffany, why does she have to come in here all the time," Karen said, rolling her eyes.

"It's something I have to do with all of my patients for insurance purposes and if I need an extra pair of hands to assist me. But if you're not comfortable, please let me know."

"I don't care if she comes in here. But make sure she's not looking at my goodies." Then Karen winked. "Unless she's paying."

"Girl, please. You're still crazy," Tiffany said as they both laughed.

Chapter 29

Tony strolled from one examination room to another with a smile plastered across his lips. After a hot passionate night with his wife, he was ready to conquer the world. Stress and tension had flowed out of him each time they rolled over and made love again. And he made up for the lost time. Who knew when he'd get that opportunity again?

He sat at his desk, eating an apple. He had thirty minutes before his next patient arrived. The morning sun shone brightly into his office, beaming onto his desk. He glanced at pictures of his wife and children. His heart melted with joy. No matter how much she nagged and complained, he still loved her.

He reached over and picked up Heather's picture and kissed it. Right as he lay her picture down, his gaze shifted toward a picture of Tiffany and Vance. A warm feeling entered his soul knowing that his sister was happy with the lawyer. Cheater though he was. Teaching Tiffany how to cough and all that other mess during the games. Hmph!

Tony slumped down in his chair, trying to piece together why she ran out of her office. Perhaps it had something to do with what had happened to her that long, painstaking summer. He leaned back in his chair and tried desperately to remember the details of what happened when she collapsed in his arms that day . . .

Tony's soul trembled as he searched Tiffany's eyes for answers. The rain pelted down on them as he tried to keep his sister from falling to the ground. His heart sank and he knew at once that Smith had done something.

"Come on, Tiffany, you have to get up." He stroked a soft hand over his sister's rain-splattered face. "We have to get in the house. Mama will be home soon; she can deal with this."

"No, Tony, I don't want anyone to know." She trembled, vibrating against him.

"Know what, please tell me."

She gripped his shirt. "Please, promise me. Please. Smith threatened that he would kill you and mama if I told."

"Now you know mama's not gonna stand for that." His teeth rattled. "You have to tell her. Or at least tell me."

"I can't do that. Just help me get in the house, please."

Tony hesitated.

"Please, Tony. Please."

Cars inched by, the drivers stared out into the rain-filled evening, staring at the two figures sitting on the curb. A tear rolled down his face.

"Okay. But you'll have to tell me what he did."

"I'm scared, Tony. I—I think he'll come after me again."

"I'm getting you out of here." Tony's forehead wrinkled with confusion and desperation. "I'll sell some drugs to make the money."

Tiffany gripped his arm. "No. Tony, please don't do that. Daddy made you swear you wouldn't get into that."

"I'll do it for you, Tiffany. I know I promised, but I don't care." He helped Tiffany to her feet. "Come on. I've got to get you out of Cloverdale. Let's go and talk to Mrs. Clark before she leaves."

"No, we have to get *home*. I have to clean out the refrigerator before mama gets in." Tiffany gasped deeply to breathe. "We'll have to go tomorrow."

Tony stared at her.

"I promise, Tony. Tomorrow."

The next day Tony walked with Tiffany pinned to his side. The outreach program seemed as though it were miles away, although it was only seven blocks.

Addicts and hustlers stood boldly on The Hill waiting for customers. Tony urged Tiffany along, hoping he could get her to the center and talk with Mrs. Clark alone.

With Tiffany's arm entwined in his, he knocked. A tall white police officer came to the door. Tiffany began to shake and turned to run.

"It's okay, Tiffany," Tony said catching up with her. He led her back to the door.

The red-haired man asked, "Can I help you?"

"We're here to see Mrs. Clark," Tony said, peering around the man, scanning the hallway.

"Come on in," the officer turned and yelled. "Lindy, you have two people to see you."

Mrs. Clark peeked around the corner. The outreach program was empty and only the humming of the water fountain filled the hallway.

"Yes, let them in. That's Tiffany and Tony. They're regulars here." Mrs. Clark's mouth dropped as her gaze traveled the length of Tiffany's body, clothes in disarray and her hair untamed.

"Lord, what's happened to you?" Mrs. Clark asked, signaling the officer to help Tiffany to her office.

The moment the officer touched her arm Tiffany began to tremble. She jerked her arms away and hugged Tony as he escorted her to the small, yellow room.

"Tiffany, it's okay." Her eyes widened more than usual. "This is Sergeant Brian Clark, my husband." Mrs. Clark glanced at Tony, then to Tiffany, waiting for an explanation. When none came, she asked, "What's wrong, Sugar? You weren't at the community center yesterday and you didn't make it in time to tutor here at the outreach program. I was worried about you."

Tony drew a deep breath, slowly releasing it as he planted his butt on the wooden chair. "Mrs. Clark, Tiffany has to get out of Cloverdale. Can you help us?"

Sergeant Clark leaned next to the small brown desk. "*Why*, Tony?"

Tony avoided eye contact with the man. "Anywhere. I don't know. Anywhere but Cloverdale," uttered Tony while refusing to answer Mrs. Clark's question. Tony's gaze drifted between Mrs. Clark and Tiffany. "She has to leave as soon as possible."

Sergeant Clark propped his hand under his chin. "Tiffany, are you in trouble?"

His sister didn't move or respond. The bright lights in the office beamed down on Tiffany's face, highlighting the trail made by her tears.

"No, she's not in trouble," Tony replied. "But I will be if she doesn't get out of this community. I'm willing to do what it takes for her to get out of here—one way or another."

Silence streamed through the room. Mrs. Clark stared at Tiffany. "If someone has hurt you, you need to report it."

"No," Tony replied, his sharp tone making Mrs. Clark wince. "She has to get out of here." His heart pulsated rapidly.

Mrs. Clark glanced out of the small window.

Sergeant Clark cleared his throat. "Lindy, what about the Pre-College Summer Program that the universities are hosting? The program started last week, but they may still have space available."

Mrs. Clark's face brightened. "Yes, I saw the advertisement on the church bulletin board. Sister Campbell is the coordinator for our county."

"I think we need to call her now," the sergeant said while staring at Tiffany's trembling body. "The program helps high school students to see

226

what college life is all about before they start. Would you be interested in that program?"

"Yes," Tony answered for her.

"Your sister will have to answer for herself."

A rapid silent beat of his heart penetrated to the depth of his soul.

Tiffany clutched the ends of Tony's red shirt. She slowly raised her head and paused for a few seconds before speaking. "Yes, ma'am. Can I go soon?"

Mrs. Clark drummed her delicate fingers on the edge of her desk. "Let's see if we can get you into the summer program at Bennett College since you're going there in the Fall."

A cardinal landed on the windowsill, chirping as the sun shone inside the small room. Tiffany looked up at it.

Mrs. Clark leaned back in her chair. "I don't think there'll be any problems." Her round face brightened with a smile. "I'm sure my church will sponsor you."

"A *white* church?" Tony gripped Tiffany's hand. "And what do we have to do in return."

"Nothing, Tony. It's not about what color you are; it's about helping people who need it most. Your mother might need to fill out the forms."

"That's not a problem," Tony said, rubbing Tiffany's hand gently.

"If she gets accepted, my husband and I will take her. You can ride with us."

"No one can know where she is," Tony said as he stared at Sergeant Clark. "Especially Sergeant Smith."

Tiffany started shaking again and leaned her head on Tony's shoulders. Soft sobs escaped, tearing into his heart, splintering his soul.

Sirens resonated in Tony's dental office. He jumped out of his chair, knocking his patients' charts on the floor. He glanced out of his window, staring at a fire truck speeding down the street.

Tony's heart pounded rapidly. He sat back in his chair and looked at his watch. He still had a few more minutes before the next patient will need to be prepped. He was determined to figure out what had happened to his sister. The clues were there and deep down he didn't want to accept the truth. But he needed to hear it from Tiffany, even if he had to drag it out of her. Then maybe she would get some help . . .

Tiffany packed quietly, their mother helping, knowing something was wrong, but hesitating to pressure them for an answer—again. The only sound in Tiffany's bedroom was of prayers flowing from their mother's firm brown lips. At some point, Tiffany and Tony joined in. Sergeant Clark drilled Tony on what had happened, but Tony really couldn't say anything. He didn't know anything.

Mrs. Brown escorted Tiffany to Mrs. Clark's black Oldsmobile. Sergeant Clark opened the trunk for the Samsonite luggage that Mrs. Brown had worked overtime to buy. She didn't want Tiffany to be embarrassed walking on campus with a second-hand suitcase from a thrift store.

The moment Tony and his mother arrived back in Cloverdale and walked back into their apartment, a sense of peace flowed through him. He lay on his narrow twin bed. The thin, flimsy mattress barely supported his back. His long legs dangled off the edge. He reached out, moving the purple sheet from in front of his window, allowing a warm breeze to drift in. *Flintstones, Scooby-Doo* and other animated cartoon characters lined the wall next to the white nightstand, drawings Tony had sketched in his free time between classes, basketball and volunteering at the community center. The white walls near his window and closet were bare. Before the summer was over, he would decorate them with more images of Tiffany, his mother and Genesis, the girl who worked at B&B Store and who was dying to go to the prom with him.

Tony stretched his hand to reach Tiffany's picture that was thumb-tacked to the wall. He smiled. Tiffany had saved his life. When Tony was seven years old, he was walking along the edge of McAlpine Creek and his uncle June Bug had scooped him up and tossed him into the chilled waters, yelling, "You gotta learn sometime." He looked at his children, David and Star, who were soaking their feet in the shallow water and ordered them not to help Tony.

As Tony struggled in the water, the current picked up speed, sweeping him away. Tiffany, who couldn't swim either, jumped in, clothes and all and paddled unevenly across the waters to reach him. Tony went under, gasping for breath. Tiffany struggled in the water but paddled, stroked and dipped, trying to imitate others she had seen, crossing the distance to find him.

They surfaced minutes later struggling to get back to the grassy shore. Mama had nearly beat the black off uncle June Bug. And Tony had been forever grateful that his sister had risked her life to save him. Then their father passed away, drawing them even closer. Mama worked so hard and was gone so much that she was like a ghost. All they had were each other. And no matter what uncle June Bug did, they still loved him. He was their *Santa Claus* on Christmas—most of their presents came from him. They'd receive a second-hand coat from mama. Uncle June Bug received a big paycheck—at least that's what Tony and Tiffany's mother called it. He was in the military and received a monthly from his retirement. He always had money. Well, he did before he caught his wife having an affair which led him to get strung out on crack.

Tony didn't care where Mrs. Clark and her husband, Sergeant Clark sent her as long as she was safe and away from Sergeant Smith. One day she would tell him what happened. Speculation alone was killing him.

The smoky scent of burning charcoal drifted in his room. Hot dogs and hamburgers were cooking on somebody's grill. Glancing out the window, he smiled at the neighborhood kids playing cards on the sidewalk. He slipped on his black sneakers, aiming to find the person behind the wonderful smells drifting in his room and hopefully grab some for himself. Tony loved grilled food.

As he tied the last loop, mama yelled from downstairs in the kitchen. "Tony!"

"Yes, ma'am."

"I need you to go to the store for me."

"Okay."

Tony slipped on a white tee shirt but nearly tripped on the threshold of his door. The heel of his sneaker had worn out and the front of his shoes were scuffed. As long as he could make it around a basketball court, it didn't matter much to him. His mother couldn't afford new sneakers right now, but this summer Tony planned to get a job at the B&B; then he could help out around the house and send Tiffany some money if she needed it.

Tony ran down the wooden steps.

"What were you doing?"

"Nothing."

Mrs. Brown handed Tony a white sheet of paper. "Here, take this list. We need some flour, eggs and milk."

"I can remember that, mama." Tony grinned. "I don't need a list."

"Here," mama said as she handed Tony some food stamps.

"Can I keep the change?" Tony asked, hoping it would be enough to buy him a grilled hot dog. People used food stamps instead of real money all the time.

"Yes. Run along and hurry back." Mama grabbed her rolling pin to press out her dough. "Go to the store down the street. Don't go to the B&B Family Store. At this time, the lines there are too long."

Tony dashed out the door, passing the row of mailboxes and the community center, then cut through the alley. He walked into Lee's Curb Market, a small cold store. The air conditioner had been turned up full blast. Chill bumps spread up his arms as he reached into the cooler to get the milk.

"What's up, Ton?" Lee, a short Asian man asked, peering over the counter at him.

"Hello, Lee."

"I heard your sister was valedictorian," he said in short broken, clipped words. "Yes, she was," Tony replied, with a big smile as he handed Lee the food stamps.

The tan hand slipped into the register and came back with cash, something that almost never happened.

"I'm proud. She a good girl, that Tiffany." He grinned. "She a good girl just like Tony."

Tony turned, thanked the man for the cash and walked out of the store. He ran back toward The Hill, snuggling the bag of groceries against his chest, making sure he didn't crack the eggs.

The sun beamed on the back of his neck, causing beads of perspiration to gather on his forehead. Hustlers on The Hill argued with addicts; prostitutes called out to him that they'd like to spend a little time with the "basketball star" as he ran past.

Tony cut through the alley. He turned the corner and ran smack into Sergeant Smith. Tony's legs slowed to a complete halt.

"Come here, Tony," Smith said, glaring at the scrawny people standing defiantly at the opposite end of the alley. They gathered their things, bodies gyrating like zombies, some storming out of the alley, others staggering right behind them.

The sun shifted behind the clouds, causing a shadow to form in the alley.

Tony glanced at the open end of the alley, then back to Smith. "Man, I have to take my mother this stuff."

"Where is Tiffany?" he asked, gritting his teeth.

Tony trembled with fear but found a way to open his mouth. "Why?"

"Don't why *me*, boy," Smith snapped, thrusting Tony against the brick wall. A gust of air escaped his lungs and he nearly sank to his knees under the blow.

Tony gripped his bag, praying that the eggs had survived the hard blow.

"I'm going to ask you one more time. Where is she?"

Tony paused, then leveled his eyes to Smith's. "I don't know."

"Don't give me that bull, Tony," he said shoving a nightstick into Tony's ribs.

The overpowering scent of cologne nearly singed the hairs in Tony's nose. He coughed and turned his head, trying to avoid the pungent scent, but quickly realized that the awful smell of pee, wine and trash in the alley made cologne smell a lot better.

"You two are always joined at the hip. You *always* know where she is. Don't lie to me, boy."

A strange glint flashed in Smith's eyes. His pink tongue snaked out wetting thin lips. The man was obsessed. They had gotten Tiffany out of Cloverdale just in time.

Sergeant Smith stared at Tony for a couple of seconds then gripped his face with one hand while pushing the nightstick into his stomach. "So, you mean to tell me you don't know where she is?"

A stroke of uneasiness swept through Tony. "I don't know."

Smith turned, scanning both ends of the alley. "What did she tell you?"

"What do you mean, what did she tell me?" Tony asked, trying to ease away from the sergeant.

"Are you trying to be smart with me, boy?" Smith growled.

"No, sir."

"Oh, I'll find her. She'll have to come out of the house sometime." Then he leaned in close enough that their noses nearly touched. "Or maybe, I'll just have to take a little stroll down to that fancy college of hers and pay her a little visit."

The light in the alley dimmed, leaving only a tiny ray of light.

Smith grabbed his groin and smiled.

Fear instantly swept through Tony, but he pushed it aside, pulling up to his full height as he said, "You lay another hand on my sister and I *will* kill you. You can threaten me, you can throw me in jail, but all I'll have to do is tell someone at the outreach program and you'll go to jail right along with me. It may take some time, but somebody's gotta believe me." Then he leaned forward. "I'm sure your cousin's insurance company would really like to know what happened that day. *They* wouldn't think I'm totally lying, now would they? How about that, Sergeant *Paul* Smith?"

Smith stared at Tony, then turned his head slightly toward the left as a group of kids approached the alley. Their loud laughter echoed. Tony gripped his bag, pushed the sergeant back, then took off running.

Chapter 30

"What's a miracle?" Smith yelled, his high-pitched voice echoing through the corridors of Charlotte Medical Hospital. "What's a miracle!"

He scurried down the hall to intensive care. The curtains were still open. All three children were praying and thanking God.

The monitor on Morgan's heart rate picked up. Her brain waves increased with every passing moment. Long, black eyelashes fluttered against her pale skin slowly turning a flushed pink. *No! Please, no!* He sank to the floor, holding his face with trembling hands. Anger ripped through his gut.

Swallowing as he looked at his wife, then to his children who were hugging each other and jumping for joy, rage shot through him. If they weren't standing right there, he would suffocate the woman.

Shut up, you imbeciles.

Paul Jr. brushed past Smith, aiming for the door. Smith's hand snaked out, grabbing his arm. "Where are you going, boy?"

"I'm going to call Pastor Bob and everyone!" Paul Jr. shouted.

"For what?"

Paul Jr. snatched away and kept running down the hall.

Smith yelled after him, "Wait a minute!"

Crystal and Megan glared at him, then inched further away. They had surely never told anyone what he had done to them. And if they were smart, they never would.

Smith stood frozen in the center of the room as life flowed through Morgan's veins. He let out a long, weary sigh when Morgan opened her eyes and focused her gaze on him. A small smile, which he mistook for a smirk, settled on her thin lips. Morgan looked around the room, slowly moving her head from side to side. She blinked against the light, then tried to speak, but Dr. Rankin told her to relax.

"It's a miracle you're alive, Morgan," Dr. Rankin said with a wide smile on her dark brown face. She turned to the glass window. Her voice could be heard as if the glass wasn't there. "I have to close this curtain to examine her."

Fifteen minutes later, the doctor stepped out of the room. "You all can see her now."

The children rushed past her, into the room, leaving their father staring through the glass window, speechless.

Moments later, Smith, realizing that the hospital staff and the doctor were watching him, slowly moved towards Morgan. He reached for her delicate pale hand, grabbed it and then kissed it. The hairs on the back of his neck rose as his children's hot gazes focused on his every move.

"Don't worry. God has a purpose for me. There's a reason he spared my life," Morgan said softly, turning to her children. Then she stared at Smith for about twenty seconds. For a moment his heart stopped beating. Did she know? Oh, God!

"Everything's okay now. God knows what's best for us," Morgan cleared her throat as tears trickled down the side of her face, landing on the white pillow. Her words slurred as she spoke. "God was with me in the car. But he was with me even more right here in this bed. I believe I experienced a touch of death as if someone was wishing that I pass away on this very bed. I could feel my life slipping away."

Dr. Rankin insisted she rest, but Morgan said, "I have to say this to my family, just in case something else happens." She gasped for air. "My heart stopped beating and it felt like my blood froze and wouldn't flow through my body," she said, barely audible. "The air inside of me was sucked out and I lost my sight. I couldn't hear or feel anything! I could hear someone saying that I should just let go and die . . . ." Her gaze locked on Smith's. His children followed. The room seemed hot and unbearable.

"My body became cold, but through it all, I kept praying. I knew God would never leave nor forsake me. It felt like I was in a deep trance but then I felt someone praying for me. Out of nowhere, angels came and laid their hands on me and I knew I would live and tell the story of God's mercy."

Smith's heart pounded away. Did she remember what happened?

Those stupid prayers!

Two other doctors appeared next to Dr. Rankin. They were astounded to see Morgan moving, talking, smiling and sitting up in the bed.

Sergeant Smith stood by the head of the bed, stroking Morgan's forehead. Noting the machines Morgan was hooked up to, he shook his head.

The slow chirp of the machine continued to increase each minute as life restored into Morgan's body.

She glanced up at him, smiling sweetly. "What day is it?" she asked, in a low, weak voice.

"It's Friday morning, mama," Paul, Jr. replied.

Smith fumed, watching his son hovering over Morgan.

"You should leave now, Paul. We need to let the doctor take it from here," Smith said as his eyebrows connected.

Paul sneered. "I'm not leaving my mother. I want to make sure she's okay before I leave."

"Go on home, Paul. I'll call you if anything changes."

Paul stared at his mother with big blue eyes. "I'm not leaving her," he snapped as he caressed his mother's pale hand.

A tall, slender-built guy with curly blonde hair and broad shoulders like his father, he had first started to move to another state but said that he didn't want to be too far from his mother. Paul was an accountant. His wife,

Amber, was a therapist at the local mental-health agency. Now, Amber was a piece of vanilla candy he could really sink his teeth into.

Morgan flanked up at him, smiling sweetly. "Go home, Paul and get some rest. Come back this afternoon," she whispered drowsily.

"Are you sure, mama?" he asked as he rubbed her arm.

"Yes, baby," she said to Paul, though her gaze focused on the machines. "Mama will be just fine."

"But I don't want to leave you."

"Go on home to your wife." She strained to cough, the white sheet whistling with every movement.

"Amber's fine. She didn't want to bring the children out so late last night. The weather was bad."

"I understand, baby. Give her my love."

Crystal grabbed her mother's hand and kissed it. A tear rolled down her face. A short, skinny girl with platinum-blonde hair and grayish-blue eyes, Crystal resembled Morgan more than any of the children. She was a dance instructor as well as the director of the Salvation Army, a place where several poor families from all ethnic backgrounds came for services. When did he raise such humanitarians?

"Mama, are you sure you want us to go home?"

"Yes, Crystal. I need to rest, darling."

"I'll sleep in the chair over there." She pointed, waiting for her mother's approval.

"Pumpkin," Morgan said patiently. "Please go home."

Crystal dug in her heels. "I'm too tired to drive back right now. I've been here all night."

"You can leave your car here." She patted her daughter's small hand. "Your father can give you a ride home."

Crystal cringed. She cast a glance at her sister, then back to her mother. "No! I'll drive home."

Morgan's eyebrows drew in. "Are you sure, baby? Your father can take you home."

"I'm sure, mama. Or, I can get Blair to come and get me." Crystal stroked her mother's hair.

"Being an attorney is hard work," Morgan said as her chest slowly rose.

The beeping noise on the monitors continued to accelerate.

"He doesn't get much sleep. That man sure does love the law," she said, glaring openly at her father. "Unlike some people I know."

The tension in the room intensified as Smith glared back.

"Look at your stomach, Crystal," Morgan said with a smile. "How many months are you?"

"Five months now."

"I think it'll be a good idea if you call Blair. I certainly wouldn't want anything to happen to you or the baby."

Crystal moved out of the way and Megan took the spot right next to the bed.

Megan, now a social worker, had always been a quiet child—so quiet that her father had feared she would never speak. Megan had grown into a short, medium-built girl with platinum-blonde hair who could out talk even the most babbling mouthed commentator. Whenever Smith looked at his youngest, he didn't stare long. Big green eyes of his father looked back at him. Megan had inherited his piercing gawks along with the unsettling color.

Smith hated his father. Ah, the beatings he endured for most of his younger years and the late nights his father slipped between the sheets with him, doing things to him that still made it hard to sleep at night as memories flooded his mind.

Thankfully, Morgan had never questioned the girls when they constantly asked her to enroll them in after-school programs. Morgan was too busy in church and doing charity work to notice much of anything.

Smith glared at the heart monitor, which signaled Morgan's full return to Earth.

"Why are you rushing us off, mama?"

"Come here, Megan," Morgan said, holding out her arms, but soon dropping them back on the bed. "Give me a kiss and stop crying."

"I can't, mama. I don't like to see you like this."

"Everything's going to be all right, baby. Don't worry." Morgan gave her children a hug and a kiss. She slid down and Crystal pulled the covers over her shoulders.

Smith's fingertips glided through her hair.

"Listen, children, Mama needs to get some rest. My body's tired. I don't want you to worry about me. Go home and get some rest. I know you're concerned about me but I'm pretty sure the doctor will keep you informed. I don't want to sound rude, but I need time to myself to think about a few things."

The children left out of the room without saying a word to him. Rage pierced through his heart. "Ungrateful, selfish brats."

"Paul, don't talk about my children that way. Actually, I need a break from you, too." Morgan closed her eyes. "I'll see you later. Much later."

Smith moved strands of hair out of her face. "But what about you? I don't want to leave your side."

"Don't worry about me. I'll be okay. Trust me; God has a purpose for my life."

"I don't mind staying here with you, Morgan. I can ask the doctors to bring me a bed in the room." Maybe overnight he could finish what June Bug had started. Thoughts of tampering with the medical equipment marched through his corrupted mind.

She took a slow easy breath. "That's okay, honey. I want to get some rest. Make sure you go to work today."

Smith lapsed into silence for a few seconds. Morgan had never rejected his presence.

"No, Morgan, I can't do that."

She averted her eyes to the machines. "Please go to work, Paul. I'll be fine. Just stop by and check on me throughout the day."

A faint glimmer of what might have been guilt rushed through him. "I don't know, Morgan."

She slowly closed her eyes. "Look at me, go to work." She licked her dried lips before continuing, "I'll be fine. I want you to find out who did this to me."

Yes, he would make sure someone found out who did it. But he'd make sure June Bug was dead before he could tell anyone the truth.

Chapter 31

Tiffany sat writing notes in her patients' charts. The phone rang, causing her knee to jerk and bump on the drawer.

"Good morning, Dr. Brown speaking."

"Tiffany, are we still scheduled for lunch today?"

"Boy, do you have any etiquette or professional telephone skills?" Tiffany giggled. "That should've been the first thing you learned in that communication skills course." She chuckled. "Introduce yourself when you call my office."

"I'm not doing all of that," Tony said. "You know my voice."

"I guess I've got to block your number then," Tiffany said, giggling.

"All I have to do is bribe Maria and I'll still get through. Hey, are we still meeting for lunch today?"

"I forgot you wanted to meet today. I have a client who's coming at noon. We'll have to reschedule."

He paused for a moment before saying, "What about after work?"

"I haven't thought that far ahead." Tiffany checked her watch. "But I'm going to work out and go jogging."

"What about the card game tonight at my place?"

"Um. Yes. I'll be there."

Tiffany felt a pinch of guilt. She didn't like lying to her brother, but she wasn't ready to talk about the past either. It was over and done, she'd moved on, why couldn't he do the same?

"Why are you avoiding me? I'm your brother and I love you." Tony sighed deeply into the phone. "We really need to talk. There are some things I want to tell you that happened back in Cloverdale."

Tiffany stared out of the window.

Kimberly Morton Cuthrell

"Why are you trying to avoid the issue?"

"What issue?" Tiffany paused for a few seconds. A tear formed in the corner of her right eye. She pulled to an upright position in her chair.

"Every time I bring up the community center, you shut down. Every time I want to talk about that summer, you brush me off."

Maria poked her head in the door, pointing to her watch. Tiffany waved her away.

"What is it, Tiffany? I can't stand the ground Smith walks on, but that's not going to keep me from mentoring the kids in Cloverdale. They need us. They need *you*."

"I don't want to get into all of that. You don't understand."

"Why did you run out of your office last week?"

Tiffany slowly exhaled while placing her head down on the desk.

"You're hiding something and it's starting to affect you. It's starting to affect your relationship with your husband. It's starting to affect your job. Talk to me."

"I have to go now. I'll call you when I get home this afternoon."

"*Please* don't hang up. We promised Daddy that we'd always stick together and that we'd take good care of mama. I know I messed up somewhere along the line, but I want to make things right."

"Making things right might jeopardize your career." Tiffany pressed her lips together, firmly. "I know how hot-headed you can be." Making things right would be a matter of life or death if Tony knew what had happened to her.

Tony gasped.

Tiffany glanced around her office, looking at her cherry wood executive desk, bookshelves that were swamped with reference books and pictures of the female anatomy on her wall. She tried her best to withhold the anguish and pain she had shielded for years. Tears streamed down her face like a faucet. She covered the receiver so he wouldn't hear the sniffles.

She closed her eyes. "I don't want to talk about that now."

"I'm coming over for lunch."

"No, you don't have to do that." She would take care of things in her own way, in her own time, without involving Tony.

Tiffany could hear Tony gritting his teeth.

"Listen, Tiffany. He forced me and David to rip off his cousin's appliance store. He threatened to run us in for drugs . . . ."

A single tear trickled down Tiffany's face. The bright sunny rays that once glistened in her office vanished. Tiffany looked over her shoulders, glancing at the clouds that drifted in front of the sun.

Tiffany glanced at her watch. "You know, I'm proud of David. I wish he and uncle June Bug could patch up their relationship."

"Me too. But June Bug's on that crack and David still can't let go of how the kids in Cloverdale used to tease him about his father."

Although she knew her secret would be safe with Tony, she didn't think talking about it now would make a difference. It certainly wouldn't bring her virginity back. It certainly wouldn't bring back the naïve view of the world she once had.

Tony paused again before his voice echoed through the phone. "I know he hurt you, Tiffany. But how?"

Finally, Tiffany parted her lips to say, "Please don't ask me that."

A loud crashing vibrated into the phone. Had he dropped the phone? Her hands shook, her neck cramped from holding the phone between her shoulder blade and her ear. Things plunged to the floor and pounded against his wall.

"Stop it, Tony!" she screamed through the phone. "Please stop. You're at work. Please don't jeopardize your career."

Tony panted as he spoke a deep deal of anguish in every word. "I'm going to kill him."

Tiffany pressed the phone closer to her ear, trying to listen as someone knocked on Tony's office door.

"Dr. Brown. Dr. Brown, are you all right in there?"

"Yes, Mrs. Spinks," Tony said.

"Can I come in, sir?"

Tiffany took a slow easy breath. Tony had surely knocked down something in his office. "Tony, you have to answer her," Tiffany said.

"Yes, come on in, Mrs. Spinks."

Mrs. Spinks said, "Good heavens. What happened in here? It looks like a hurricane ripped through your office."

Tiffany slumped in her chair, with the earpiece glued to her ear.

"Excuse me, Dr. Brown, are you sure you are all right?" she said in a panicky voice.

"Yes, I'm okay. I fell out of my chair. I tried to catch myself. But . . . my hands slipped off my desk, which made everything fall to the floor. But I'm all right. Thanks for checking on me."

The door thudded to a close.

"Tiffany, you there?"

"Yes, Tony. Please calm down."

"I love you, Tiffany. Deep down, I—I knew the truth. But I couldn't accept it." He paused. "I would do anything for you. Anything! Someone's going to kill him one day."

Tiffany placed her hand on her forehead. "Stop it, Tony!"

"Did you hear me, Tiffany? I'll give my life for you."

Tears rolled down her cheeks. "Yes, I hear you."

Chapter 32

Two hours later, Sergeant Smith returned to the hospital to visit Morgan, who had improved considerably from the night before. The doctors had run several tests, but couldn't find anything on their printouts detailing how or why Morgan was able to pull through. How had she survived? He sat in the room with his wife for about two hours.

The bright morning sun shone inside her room.

"How are you feeling today?" he asked.

"Better than yesterday." She glanced around at the machines. "An officer came in here questioning me about the accident."

Smith sat on the edge of the chair, feeling like a criminal being interrogated even though Morgan wasn't asking any questions.

"I told the officer I couldn't see the driver of the truck."

"Who were the officers who came?" Smith asked, without even looking at her. His gaze fell on the machines, the nurses passing by and the clock on the white wall.

"I don't remember. But I told him that the car belonged to my worker, Chris."

"What did they say?" His voice wavered. His hands begun to sweat.

"The officer said Chris reported the truck stolen."

The machines continued to beep. Why didn't they shut off!

"Did he see anything?"

Morgan paused, blinking against the bright light above the bed. She pressed her finger on a button, dimming the light. "I'm not sure," she said as she turned on her side.

"I've got to get back to the office." He slid the chair back in the corner. "I'll stop by here later."

Smith then turned and looked at her as she said, "Be careful, honey. Maybe it was someone you arrested before. Maybe the attacker found out where I worked or where we live. You need to get to work so you can get to the bottom of this. If that person is still out there, he'll come after you too."

As Smith walked into his office, conversations died away as his officers stared at him. They were curious about Morgan but were too polite to ask.

Officer Jenkins said with a deep baritone voice, "Smith, Clark was by a little while ago. He asked about Morgan and said to give him a call."

Everyone focused on Smith.

He walked over to the officers, forcing a tear out of his eye—something his officers had never seen.

The fresh scent of Lysol drifted past his nose.

"How's Morgan?" Officer Price asked with a low-pitched voice. "What happened?"

Smith covered his face with his hands, then slowly dropped them. "Morgan was forced off the curve." He paused. "Someone shot her a couple of times." A feeble tear glued to his eyelid. "Morgan thinks…." He sniffled, chest heaving with the effort. "Morgan thinks my life is in danger."

"The vehicle was found," Officer Price said. "The detectives ran the fingerprints in the truck."

Smith wiped his face. He drew a deep breath, then swallowed. "Did…Did they come up with any prints?

Officer Jenkins said, "Yes. They said the prints belonged to Lamont Brown, AKA June Bug."

"I'm going to walk around the projects for a couple of minutes." Smith strolled toward his office, then turned back to the officers. "Then I'm going back to the hospital to check on my wife."

On the prowl again, looking for June Bug, he kept the alley under surveillance. About three hours passed and he finally saw the addict poking his football-shaped head out of the alley.

Smith stormed out of his office.

June Bug spotted him the moment he came out of the community recreational center. He whistled to get Smith's attention but Smith kept walking. He scanned the area, making sure the coast was clear before signaling the scantily dressed man to walk to the other side of the alley.

Smith continued to walk. June Bug strolled toward him. Smith turned and went in the opposite direction.

Rain had fallen for the past couple of days and people were now outside on the first clear day washing and polishing their cars. Children were getting off the summer school bus and running directly into the community center. Others ran across the street to the park which had only a single sliding board left to play on. Smith tried to walk faster, getting away from any witnesses. He definitely didn't want his officers to see him with June Bug.

Barking echoed up and down the alley. A pit bull fight was going on somewhere.

Smith turned just in time to see June Bug running toward him. "No!" Smith shrieked hoping June Bug would go in a different direction.

Some of the tenants stopped. Probably curious about June Bug in full speed sprinting *toward* the sergeant instead of in the opposite direction.

"Where is my dope, man?" June Bug yelled as he ran toward the sergeant,

Smith grabbed the man, banging him against the brick wall, growling, "I told you to kill her."

"I did, man!" June Bug yelled.

"No, you didn't. She's alive and well. She's coming home in a couple of days."

Loud music pumped out of a black jeep. Tenants huddled around the vehicle, dancing.

June Bug stiffened. "Stop lying, man. She hit that ground hard and I opened fire like you said."

"It didn't work!"

"So *what*? I still want my dope!"

Smith glanced over his shoulders. "Where is the gun?"

"In my pocket."

"Why did you park the car down the street from the projects? Why didn't you park it somewhere else?"

June Bug scratched his head. "Man, we didn't go over that part."

Smith turned. The music no longer traveled out of the jeep. "I figured you would have enough common sense to know not to park it near here."

"Man, I needed a ride back here. It was raining and you weren't there." June Bug shrugged him off. "Now where is my dope?"

"Give me the gun first."

"We can make an even exchange." June Bug squinted. "The gun for the dope."

"Haven't I always kept my word?"

Some of the tenants were walking toward them. The tenants knew they had to stand at least fifty feet away. If they didn't, they would be charged with interfering with police procedures—which would have been grounds for eviction. So, he wasn't worried about them getting too close. At the same time, two of his officers had crept up on them. Now that would be a problem. He had to think fast and either send a signal to his officers that his life was in jeopardy or for them to stand down. Played right, this could be an opportunity to get rid of someone linking him to his wife's attempted murder, or a chance to get a medal.

Think, Smith! Think!

Black uniformed men ran toward June Bug. The addict took off running like a bat out of hell. He jumped over a fence, dodged cars and cut through an alley. The officers couldn't keep up and Smith surely wasn't really trying to catch him.

Chapter 33

Friday evening, the fresh soft smell of tulips whizzed through Tony's nostrils as he pulled his lawnmower out of the storage room. The sun's rays bounced off his house as a cool afternoon breeze swept the ground. Tony challenged the thick grass as he pushed the lawnmower across. Rain in the past couple of days had rendered ample time for his grass to grow. The gusting winds during the storm had even ripped leaves off the Magnolia trees in his yard.

The leaves had all but taken over the yard and had started a massive spread toward the tree-lined street. Overhead, the Magnolia tree limbs tilted as though trying to embrace his house, causing leaves to drop on his bay windows and gather on the roof. He had a hard time cleaning the gutters.

Tony's muscles contracted with each power push of the mower, then with every thrust of his rake. Maintaining an upscale appearance in his yard was a priority.

Housework was something he did daily when he lived in Cloverdale. His father believed that every household should have a balance of responsibilities and that belief carried on, even after his untimely death. Now Tony was a jack-of-all-trades; he helped with cooking, cleaning and repairing everything in the house. Although Heather thought they should have a repairman, a maid and a cook, Tony preferred that his children work alongside him and that his wife appreciate the value of teamwork in a family. Now a cook might be in order. Heather could burn boiling water. Although their incomes surpassed the middle-class status, Tony liked being outside, working all of his limbs and enjoying the fresh air.

"Anthony, didn't you hear me calling you?"

"No," he said, pausing to turn to her. "Now, you know what they say, you can't interrupt a man when he's working."

Heather's face glowed as if the afternoon sun had finally found a way to shine directly on her. "Your sister and Vance will be here in an hour. I know you want to take a shower before they arrive." She smiled. "I ironed a shirt and a pair of jeans for you. I'll bathe the kids and get them ready for bed."

"Thanks, Heather. I'll be in there in a few minutes. I'm almost finished. It took me longer than I thought because I had to get all of the leaves off the roof and out of the gutters."

"I heard your crazy self up there. You'll break your neck and then what will happen to us."

"Life will go on, dear. Life will go on."

Heather stepped back inside yelling over her shoulder. "Don't forget to put the ladder in the storage. It's still behind the house."

"All right, *Drill Sergeant Heather,*" Tony said as he strolled across the yard. "I'm coming now."

Ten minutes later, the phone rang. Heather reached out, snatching it on the first ring. "Good evening, this is the Brown's residence."

Tony picked up the telephone upstairs.

"Hello, Heather, we're on our way." Tiffany's soft voice came through. "I hope you guys are ready to lose again."

"Are those fighting words," Heather said, anger slowly creeping into her tone. "I guess we'll have to go to war when you guys get here."

Although Heather presented it as a joke, Tony knew she meant every word. There was no mistaking the emotion behind the words.

"Where is Tony, Heather?"

"He's taking a shower."

Thirty minutes later, the couple strolled through Tony's front door. Tiffany wore a pink jogging suit with a green tee-shirt peeking out and her hair pulled back into two ponytails. Vance had on jeans and a gray polo shirt.

Tony opened the door. "Come on in, Vance," he said while signaling for Tiffany to stay on the porch. "We'll come in a few minutes."

Tony stepped outside, closing the door behind him.

"We're not finished with our conversation." Tony sighed. "I need to know one day, Tiffany." He closed his eyes. "It hurts my heart to know that Smith did something to you . . . and you will not talk about it."

Tiffany gasped for air. "Tony, this is not the appropriate time."

"When is?" He clenched his teeth. "You know I promised dad I would protect you and mama." He reached for her hand. "I feel like I failed dad."

"You didn't, Tony," shrieked Tiffany as she opened the door nearly bumping into Heather.

"I started wondering if we were going to play the card game on the porch." Heather chuckled.

"Are you two ready?" Tony smiled.

"Tiffany told me there's a battlefield in your house," Vance said, chuckling.

"Man, what are you talking about?" Tony turned to face Heather. "What battlefield?"

"Hmmm, Friday night card game." Tiffany grinned, rubbing her hands together. "I wonder who's gonna win."

Vance laughed loudly. "We're here to claim our throne. Where are the cards?"

"Hey, guys, let's change the game up," Tony said as he walked around his cherrywood table. "Why don't we make the game more exciting." He glanced at Vance. "Let's switch partners."

252

"I'm down," Vance said as he gave Tiffany a peck on her cheek and walked to the other side of the table directly across from Heather.

"When did you come up with that idea?" Heather asked, eyebrows lifted and luscious lips poked out. The lively twinkle in her eyes had vanished.

Back to ground zero. He knew eventually her jealous streak would spring forth. Tony sat across from Tiffany and shuffled the cards. No matter what Heather said he had his mind made up to be Tiffany's partner for a change. Maybe a win for Heather would brighten her mood.

"Daddy, I want some water." The muffled voice of his son interrupted Heather's glaring stare. Tony glanced at the stairs just in time to see his son rub his eyes.

Anthony Jr.'s body swaggered as he waited for his father. Navy blue pajamas with bright red and yellow cars all moved with him. "I want some water."

Tony looked at Heather. She had Anthony Jr. on a schedule to prevent him from wetting the bed. And so far, it had worked

Heather nodded but still frowned.

"Sure thing, little man. Daddy's coming to the rescue."

"Hello, Anthony," Tiffany said, kissing her nephew on the forehead.

"Hi, Aunt Tiffany."

"Is that all you see in here?" Vance teased, tickling Anthony Jr.'s stomach.

"I said hi," he shot back with a little attitude, trying to avoid Vance's long fingers.

"Can I have your pajamas?" Vance asked. "I think I can fit them."

"No!" Anthony gripped his pajamas, pulling the cotton material around his little frame.

"I'm kidding."

"So!"

"Anthony, Jr., what did I tell you about that word?" Heather said, pointing her finger at him.

"Don't say it," he mumbled, lowering his head.

Tony scooped up his son and walked into the kitchen. His son's eyes lit up when he saw the Hi-C Punch in the stainless-steel refrigerator.

"Daddy, can I have some cook-aid?"

"That's not cook-aid. Little man, it's Kool-Aid." Tony smiled. "We'll make a deal. If you don't wet the bed tonight, then you can have a big glass in the morning."

Tony poured only one-fourth cup of water.

"No, Daddy! I want some Kool-Aid now. Pour that out."

"You can have a glass of water and that's the end of that, little man."

The little brown-skinned boy sulked. Although only three years old, Anthony Jr. knew by that tone, that argument was over.

Minutes later, Tony tucked his son in the little black Lamborghini bed which cradled his body. The sky blue wall displayed colorful images of a basketball, football, baseball and a soccer ball and a couple of paintings that Tony had painted especially for his son.

Tony slowly opened Carmen's door to check on his daughter. She was snuggled under her yellow comforter holding a bright white teddy bear that traveled everywhere with her. Her wall was covered with clouds, birds, butterflies and a few of Tony's sketches of his youngest child. More teddy bears assembled along the edge of her white canopy bed.

"Okay, guys, where were we?" Tony asked, strolling down the stairs. "What did I miss? I hope you guys didn't mark the cards—again."

"Why do you want to switch partners, Anthony?"

"Come on, Heather. This will make the game exciting and give one of us a chance to win tonight," Tony said, staring into Heather's fierce tiger eyes.

Folding her arms tightly across the lavender tee-shirt covering her breasts, Heather grunted as she stared at her husband. Tension filled the air. "Whatever. I guess being my partner is boring."

"You didn't say that last night."

Heather glared at him as Vance and Tiffany busted out laughing. With a deep sexy voice, Tony said, "Heather, don't take the fun out of the game."

"Okay. Shuffle the cards. I don't want to spoil the mood." Heather gasped, tiger eyes widened with horror as Tony smiled and winked. "How dare you bring up our sex life in front of them," she whispered, loud enough for him to hear.

"Now that that's all squared away," Vance said, cautiously watching her reaction. "Let's get this game rolling, Heather. How many books are y'all bidding?"

Tony smiled, saying, "We have six and a possible."

"Man, you can't bid a *possible* book." Vance peered over his cards.

"Stop whining and play," Tiffany said, blowing a kiss to her husband. He caught the imaginary kiss in his hand and put it in his pocket.

"Oh, so I don't rate having my kisses go on your lips anymore?"

"Keep talking trash and I'm gonna put it where it really will do some good," Vance said, patting his butt.

"Forget you."

Tony clapped his hands. "Come on, Tiffany, we're going to drag them through the gutter."

"Oh, before I forget, there's a new Jazz spot in town," Vance said.

Tony covered his cards. "Really. Where?"

"Uptown near the Adam's Mark Hotel. It's called Classic Touch. It's only open on the weekends."

Tiffany rocked in her chair. "Seems like someone has done his homework."

Vance winked, whispering, "There's something else I'd like to study *real hard*."

Tiffany blushed, looking back down at the cards.

"Let's go tomorrow night then. Our Saturday night is flexible," Tony said, staring at Heather.

After a moment she said, "All right. Sound good to me."

"Oh, yeah. Tony, don't forget we're going to visit mama in the morning."

Heather's eyes narrowed.

Tony grimaced, almost glowering at Tiffany for bringing that up now. "I know. I'll pick you up."

Heather stole a glance at Tony.

The cards started falling faster on the table as laughter filled the air.

"Bam!" Vance said, slapping a card in the center of the table. "Let's see if you guys can beat my ace of hearts."

"Slow down. Don't get too excited. We've got something for that." Tony laid a three of spades on the table. "Tiffany, I see your husband likes to arrive early."

"Yeah?" Vance said. "Just as I long as I . . . *come* late."

Tiffany almost spit out her wine.

Heather remained silent, slowly dropping her cards on the table as she gazed out the window.

"Look, Heather. Are you going to play tonight or what?" Vance snapped as he closed his cards in his hand.

She turned back to the game.

"I'm not used to having a partner who's not involved." Vance leaned back in his chair. "Hey, I still want to win tonight."

"All right. All right, I hear you." Heather spat. "You don't have to get uptight about a card game. It's only a game."

"That's not what you said last week." Tony exhaled, grunting. "Let's get these next books." He sipped on a glass of cranberry juice. "We can't show them any mercy," he said as she stared at Heather. "How many books are you bidding on this time?"

Physically, the woman he married was sitting in her chair across from Vance, but mentally her mind had drifted somewhere near Pluto.

"Heather, do you hear me talking to you?"

"Oh, sorry. Yes, Anthony, I hear you."

"Is this part two of last Friday's saga?" Tiffany snapped.

Heather squinted, slapping her hand face down on the table.

Vance cleared his throat. "What do you have, Heather? We're partners, you can tell me." Vance raised his eyebrow, a wide smile on his lips.

"Hey, you know you can't show him your cards," Tony said, slipping a chip in his mouth.

"Oh, I forgot," Heather said. She looked at her hand and a slow grin spread across her plum-colored lips.

Tony released a gust of air as if blowing out candles.

"What are you bidding, Anthony?" Heather asked, hovering a pencil over the table.

"Wait a minute. We bid first in the last game. You go first."

"I know you're not talking about the game *last* week," Heather shot back. "Besides, the rules have changed. It was *your* suggestion to switch partners. So how many are you and Tiffany bidding?"

Tony dipped his head sheepishly. "Um. We have to go *board*."

"Are you serious, man?" Vance chuckled. "You guys can only get four books?"

"Don't rub it in Vance. You and Heather better play your cards right. Or we're gonna set your trifling behinds." Tiffany winked at her husband.

Vance sat up straight. "Awwww, yeah, talk the talk, honey, but can you walk the walk?"

"Let's start with this." Vance slipped an ace of hearts on the table.

The cards fell. With every good hand, Heather's face glowed and a smile periodically flashed as if she had won the lottery.

"Yes, give me five, Vance. We're beating them." A smile stretched across her lips. "I think I like being on the winning team."

"Yeah, weeeeell," Tiffany said, winking. "Maybe you may want to rethink that." Tiffany spread the last three cards in her hand.

Tony jumped from his seat. "Set! Set, baby. Now that's what I'm talking about!"

Heather's smile disappeared. Vance's eyebrows twitched as he frowned.

"Cloverdale strikes again."

Heather slumped down in her chair.

Chapter 34

Slowly driving past the massive crowd, trying to avoid the potholes and broken wine bottles, Tiffany and Tony cruised through Cloverdale to their mother's one bedroom apartment as smooth beats soared out of the speakers. The office manager, Mr. Floyd, had automatically transferred her to a one-bedroom when Tiffany and Tony moved out.

Heads turned as the rims from his truck sparkled from the rays of the sun. The musty smell of marijuana drifted in the air like pollen. Sidewalks were covered with crayons marks as if they were a community poster board.

Tiffany scanned the crowd, locking her gaze on a guy named Ace who was known for trafficking drugs from Maryland to the Cloverdale projects. Did Sergeant Smith know? Of course, he did. But Smith valued dirty money more than upholding the law.

"What's up, Tony!" a guy with a long sterling silver necklace yelled. "Give me some money, man."

"Tony, look at Pee Wee still wearing that necklace. He still wants people to think it's a platinum chain. I'm surprised his neck hasn't fallen off from gangrene," Tiffany said as she waved at some of her childhood friends. "If that necklace had legs it would've jumped off his neck years ago."

Laughing, Tony said, "Leave Pee Wee alone. You know that necklace is his pride and joy."

"Are you kidding me? I remember when he stole that mess from the jewelry store. He had the audacity to brag about what he had done." She glimpsed out of the window. "I can't believe you told him you wanted one, too. When mama found out I thought she was going to kill you. I guess she beat you good because you stopped hanging with him."

"Girl, stop bringing up old stuff. I hope you didn't tell Vance what some of my boys used to do. I don't want him to indict me for a conspiracy," Tony said.

"Vance doesn't have room to talk about us. He has three brothers. Two of them are in prison and the other one's strung out on drugs. No one expected Vance to grow up and become a lawyer. He used to live in the projects in Harlem and did whatever it took to survive. He knows first-hand the life that the streets can force poor people to live."

"Yeah, he's a cool dude. I still remember when he walked you down the aisle. He was smiling so hard I thought he was going to pass out."

"What about Heather?" Tiffany asked. "She skipped down the aisle and tried to rush service just to get you to the point of saying I do."

"You know my wife's a good woman. I love Heather but we have different viewpoints sometimes." He lifted his finger to his temple. "She has a good heart and doesn't mean any harm."

"Yeah, well, I hope her nasty attitude and outlook on life doesn't affect Tony, Jr. and Carmen. You know she doesn't like stepping her precious feet on project soil. She has issues."

Tiffany drummed her fingers on the dashboard as the Jazz tunes drifted into her ears. Would Tony start questioning her again? Tiffany hoped that he wouldn't.

"I can't believe she feels like I'm stealing you away from her." Tiffany paused. "What's wrong with that picture?"

"I've told her over and over to calm her nerves. I'm beginning to sound as though I have a speech impediment or she's deaf. The other day I almost left the house . . . . Hey, look at mama hanging out clothes."

The clothesline was old and wilted. The poles were bent making the fiberglass lines droop in the middle.

Mrs. Brown wobbled from side to side as she moved. Her unblemished dark brown skin sparkled as the rays pressed against her face. A warm and lovely smile was permanently painted on her heart-shaped face.

As Tony and Tiffany walked closer to their mother's apartment, some of the tenants stood on their porches, pointing as if the brother and sister team were celebrities.

"Mama, go inside and sit down." Tiffany rushed over to grab the clothes basket. "We'll take care of this." She pried the woman's weathered fingers off the basket.

The sweet smell of peach cobbler drifted out of mama's apartment.

While raising her small brown eyes to look at Tiffany, mama slipped the clothespins into her pocket and put her hands on her waist. "Child, I'm not that old. I still can get around and hang out my own clothes."

Tony said, taking the basket from Tiffany. "We know, mama, but we want to help you."

"Now *that* sounds better. You two can help me. But I don't want you to do it for me."

Mama never did like handouts. It took her forever to finally sign up for food stamps—and only because they had missed a few meals. Sometimes her independent streak was frustrating. She loved her children beyond life itself, but she wanted her children to enjoy their lives and not worry about her.

Twenty minutes later, Tony wiped his forehead with the back of a hand. "Goodness. I'm glad we're finished."

"Go stand in front of the fan to cool down, Tony. You're sweating faster than butter melting in a hot skillet."

Hot humid air circulated through the fan, creating a cool breeze in the living room. The navy blue sectional chair stretched along the eggshell-colored wall. Pictures of Tiffany and Tony were assembled neatly on the black entertainment center. With their first paychecks, Tiffany and Tony had refurnished their mother's apartment. If she wanted to stay in Cloverdale, they wanted her to live in style.

"Mama, you need an air conditioner." Tiffany joined Tony in front of the fan. "We'll buy you one today."

"Pumpkin, I don't want an air conditioner. I'm used to the hot air. All I need is my fan. I ain't had an air conditioner in twenty summers so why will I need one now? 'Sides, I reckon an air conditioner would shake up my arthritis."

"Mama, we can adjust the air so it's comfortable," Tony said.

The gray-haired woman turned to the television when T.D. Jakes' sermon came over the airwaves. She stretched out her weathered hands, connecting with her children's hands as each bowed their heads to pray.

Slowly opening her eyes, Tiffany held onto her mother's hand as they walked into the kitchen. The peach cobbler sat on the round glass kitchen table. The crust was crispy and brown and the peaches looked juicy and sweet.

"Sit down, mama," Tony said as he pulled her chair out.

Mama slid her gray hair behind her small ears. "Where is Vance, pumpkin?"

A warm feeling flowed through Tiffany's body. "He's at the office preparing for a tough court case in the morning."

"That's a good young man. I remembered when Tony walked you down the aisle. That big old man was crying more than me." Tiffany and Tony joined her laughter. "I remember the first time I met him. He sat right there in the same chair you're sitting in now." Mama pointed at the black padded chair. "Tony was acting like a detective." She grinned. "But Vance answered all of your questions. I finally had to tell you to leave the man alone."

Tiffany smiled as she looked at her brother. "Yes, he's a good husband. I wouldn't trade him for nothing."

"He'd better treat her right," Tony mumbled. "Or I'll rough him up good."

"Tony, Tiffany's a grown woman now, son," Mama said, smiling. "You can't go off fighting her battles all the time."

"I know, mama, but she deserves the best and to be treated like a princess."

Mama pulled the clothespins out of her pocket and dropped them into a plastic bag. "Heather's a lucky woman, too." Mama exhaled slowly. "I'm sure there're a lot of girls who wish they were your wife."

"Yeah, right," Tiffany quipped. "I don't know why."

"Stop teasing your brother." Mama turned, facing Tony. "Tell Heather I said hello. Oh, before I forget, here's Carmen's hair bow. She left it the other day." Mama placed her elbow on the table. "I think she thought she was too good for you at first." Mama raised one eyebrow.

Tony didn't say a word.

"I hope she appreciates you for the good man you are . . . ." Mama perked up. "You know the circus is in town, baby, you should take the kids."

"We did, mama. We took them last Saturday. Carmen was scared of the clowns, but Tony Jr. wanted to touch the lions."

"Why didn't you push Heather into the lion's den?" Tiffany chuckled. "That would have brought that witch to life."

"Be nice, Tiffany," mama said.

Tony shoved Tiffany as she nearly doubled over, laughing.

"I'm glad you're able to take your kids to different things." Mama's gaze fell on the magazine covered table. "Give those kids things that I wasn't able to do for you."

Tiffany's laughter came to a sudden halt.

"That's okay, mama," Tony said, reaching for her hand. "You did your best and look at us today."

"Mama, please move out of Cloverdale. We'll buy you a house." Tiffany's soft voice was laced with worry. "I don't feel comfortable with you living here. We live way across town and it saddens us to know you're still living here. It's getting dangerous now with more of those outsiders selling dope over here."

"Baby, I know Cloverdale isn't the best place in the world to live but I feel comfortable here. I'm used to the problems over here."

"What do you mean you're *used* to the problems?" Tiffany asked.

"I have lived here for at least twenty years. I've made a lot of friends here."

"And you can visit them whenever you want," Tony said, handing her a steaming bowl of peach cobbler.

"I don't want to leave my friends. Everyone knows me and I get a lot of respect around here. I'm old. I have lived my life." Mama slid a spoonful of peach cobbler between her brown lips. "Don't worry about me, I'll be all right. My life is here in the projects. Besides, I don't know how to survive outside of Cloverdale."

"Please, mama," Tiffany said, her eyes flashed with worry.

"Who's going to fix my toilet when it overflows? Who's going to cut my grass?" She shrugged. "I don't have to worry about that over here."

"We'll help you, Mama. You can live with me and Vance if that makes you feel better."

Mama glanced at the stove, refrigerator and around the small kitchen as if taking a last minute view of the scenery.

"If I move to another community, I will feel lonely. What if I moved to a so-called better neighborhood and feel left out?"

The thought of walking out of her mother's apartment once again without extracting a promise for her safety made Tiffany's heart ache.

Chapter 35

Saturday morning, Smith strolled the corridors of Charlotte Medical Hospital, heading toward Morgan's room. He crept quietly across the tile making sure no one spotted him. He scoped the nurse stations, noticing that Nurse Logan was reading a chart. Her light blue and white uniform could be seen from a distance.

Smith dashed across the hallway to Morgan's room. Inching the door open, he hoped his wife was still asleep. Quietly, he closed the door, making sure it didn't startle her. The room was dark. He paused for a few seconds as he contemplated his actions.

The white cotton sheets covered Morgan's pale body. Her eyelids were pressed firmly together as she snored as if she hadn't slept comfortably in years. Tubes were still inserted into her frail body and the machines continued to beep signaling a strong sign of life. Hopefully, he could change that.

Smith tiptoed toward Morgan and gently pulled the firm white pillow from under her head. Morgan's head slowly shifted off. He gripped the pillow, raising it over her face. A tap on the door made him freeze in place.

Smith quickly propped the pillow under Morgan's head, waking her up.

Morgan's eyelids fluttered for a few seconds as she glanced around the room. "Hello, Paul."

"Hey, Morgan," Smith said, giving her a forced smile.

"Good morning Mrs. Smith," Nurse Logan said, turning on the light. "I've got to do your 7:00 a.m. check-up."

Morgan slid her blonde hair behind her ears, then sat up. "Okay."

265

Nurse Logan turned. "Hello, Mr. Smith. It sure is a beautiful Saturday morning, isn't it?"

"Yes, it is," the sergeant said, his heart racing a hundred miles an hour. Perspiration formed around his neck. He wiped it away while kicking himself for not getting there earlier.

The nurse stared at the machines, then jotted down notes in Morgan's chart. "How are you feeling, Mrs. Smith?"

"I feel much better than yesterday. Seems like I'm healing more and more as the days pass by."

"That's great."

Smith stared at Nurse Logan's round butt as she stood in front of Morgan but inwardly anger had gripped his heart.

Nurse Logan picked up the chart, jotted down more notes. "Dr. Rankin will examine you in an hour," she said, closing the door.

Morgan leaned back. "Paul, how long have you been here?"

"I walked in a few seconds before Nurse Logan came in. Have you eaten breakfast?"

Morgan glanced up at the yellow clock on the wall. "The dietician will be in at 7:30."

Smith walked to the blinds, opened them and grabbed a chair. The sun peeked between the ridges, shining into the room.

Morgan slowly pulled herself to an upright position. "Do the police have any leads?"

"Yes." Smith cleared his throat. "The fingerprints belong to a guy in Cloverdale."

Morgan's eyes widened. "Who?"

Smith hesitated to answer her. "Lamont Brown. But they call him June Bug."

"Do you know him?"

"No, but I heard he was a drug addict."

"Why was he trying to kill me?"

Smith shrugged, then shifted his gaze from Morgan to the machines. "I don't know. We found him in Cloverdale, but my officers let him get away."

Morgan winced. "How is that, Paul? Where were you?"

The door opened. A short lady in a green uniform walked in, then placed Morgan's food on a tray behind the bed. "Good morning," the lady said.

"Good morning," Morgan said, pulling her tray closer as she watched the lady leave.

Smith stood. "Well, gotta go, Morgan. I need to go to the office in thirty minutes."

Morgan slid her tray to the side. "Wait a minute, Paul. I've been meaning to ask you something."

Morgan's sharp tone struck Smith across the heart. He wasn't used to her addressing him that way.

Smith turned, snapping. "What is it, Morgan. I can't be late."

"I've had a lot of time to think about a few things." She paused. "What's going on with you and the children? For the life of me, I don't know why the girls hate you so much. And why won't Paul, Jr. talk to you?"

Smith's eyes twitched. His blood seemed as though it had frozen. "I—I don't know, Morgan. I've wondered the same thing."

"It's unnatural for children to hate their father, Paul. I don't understand what's going on. You were a great provider for them."

"Yeah, but I don't get credit for it." Smith's lips tightened. "I've told you they're ungrateful, Morgan."

"No, Paul, it has to be more than just that. Their relationship with you is so . . . strange. It's been like this since Crystal was ten and Megan was nine-years-old."

For a split second, Smith reflected upon the late nights he crept into his daughters' rooms. The warmth of their young, tender bodies trapped under him felt better than Morgan's—not to mention the tightness of their . . . .

Smith sneered as he gritted his teeth. "I don't know why you're such a *concerned* little mother now. I don't know why those ungrateful bastards act like that!"

Morgan flinched. "Paul, please don't call our children that."

Smith walked toward the door, gripped the knob. "I hate that I wasted my money paying for them to go to college. They don't have the decency to show me any respect."

"And that's a good point. Why don't they?" Morgan coughed. "The girls won't come to the house if you're there and Paul, Jr. acts like he's covering up something for them." She squinted, casting an icy glare. "What is it, Paul? They don't even want our grandkids around you."

Smith placed his hand on his holster. His pager started beeping. He glanced down. A blank line flashed across. Smith had turned his pager off then back on. "Gotta go, Morgan."

"We've got to finish this conversation, Paul," she said as Smith closed the door.

Not if he could help it.

Chapter 36

Mellow Jazz tunes flowed out the speakers in Classic Touch. The lights were dim. Candles were lit on every cloth-covered table. The audience nodded, tapping their feet and fingers to the melodies.

"I like this," Tiffany said, caressing Vance's hand.

"I'm glad, honey." Vance planted a kiss on her cheek. "Now we have a place to go on the weekends when we're not swamped with work."

"I like this place, too," Heather said, looking around at the well-dressed crowd. "I think it's a great idea to have a place for Jazz, oldies but goodies, poetry reading and karaoke. Seems like the owner was trying to attract the mature younger folks and the older crowd."

"Ladies and gentlemen. I'd like to introduce myself. I'm Devin Fuller, the owner of Classic Touch. We hope that this will be a place you'll return to on a regular basis. Hopefully, you'll hear something tonight that will melt your hearts, ring in your ears and linger in your minds."

"I know that guy," Tony said, peering up at the short, stocky man on the stage.

"Who, the owner?" Heather asked, perking up. "He looks like an intelligent brother."

"Yeah, that's Devin," Tiffany said, peering across the dim room. "He lived three doors down from us."

Heather cringed as if someone had sucked the life out of her.

"Why don't you go and speak to him," Vance said, rubbing his wife's hand. "He's mingling with the crowd."

Tony said. "Maybe we will in a little bit."

Heather's tiger eyes widened as her gaze shifted toward the ceiling. "Wait until he comes over here, Anthony. There's no need to run the man down."

"Now, he's truly a success story," Tony said to Vance.

"Why do you say that?" Heather asked, raising a single eyebrow.

"He had dreams of becoming a child psychiatrist. He was the only kid in our psychology class who had an A-plus." Tony looked up at the guy as he mingled with the crowd. "He served a little time in prison. Sergeant Smith had him framed. We were at the bus stop waiting for the school bus one morning and Smith wanted to know who Devin was." Tony huffed. "Weeks later, Devin went to prison."

"Prison?" The olive-skinned woman turned up her nose. "Tony, you sure know how to pick friends."

Tiffany yawned, casting a bored gaze at Heather.

A tall waiter with long legs placed their food on the table.

"Come on, Heather," Tiffany said, slicing into her steak.

Heather sighed deeply.

Tony glared at her. "Give the man a break."

"Heather, three minutes ago you said he looked like an intelligent brother," Tiffany blurted out. "Now, that you know he was in prison, your thoughts have changed. Just because a person's been to prison doesn't mean they should be an outcast."

Heather's lips curled into a sneer as she sipped a Strawberry Daiquiri. "Seems like both of you have a thing for ex-cons . . . . "

Vance parted his lips to speak. Tiffany gripped his hand, patting it softly. His expression softened instantly. "Not all ex-cons return to the prison system. Some of them learn from their experience. My brothers are in prison and I seriously doubt they'll go back there once they get out."

Heather almost choked. She stared at Vance as if he were an alien.

Music nearly drowned out conversations.

Tony leaned back in his chair. "I was with Devin that night he got arrested."

"What!" Heather shouted.

"It's a long story," he said, patting her hand. "Believe me when I say it was definitely a case of mistaken identity."

"What happened?" She reached for her drink, taking a long swallow. "I'm *dying* to hear this one."

Tony paused trying to gather himself to speak over the jazz music. Heather tilted her head as a frown slowly formed on her small lips.

"We were about sixteen years old. Devin and I were walking home from the football game; we were playing around, wrestling and stuff. It was about 10 o'clock that night and some of the streetlights were blown out. Devin tripped and fell on some glass; his hand was bleeding and he panicked. I took off my tee-shirt and gave it to him. We were about two blocks from home. We split up to go in different directions."

Heather's eyes narrowed. "So what happened to him?"

Tony exhaled. "The next day my mother told me that Devin was arrested for breaking and entering which was impossible because he was with me during that time. The police saw Devin running home with his hand bandaged and stopped him because a call was dispatched about a break-in at a store blocks away from our house." Tony sighed. "The owner was shot as he stood in front locking up the store. The front glass of the store shattered. He told the police that the robber busted the window with a brick but the robber's hands had been cut."

Vance asked, "Did anyone investigate the case?"

Tony nodded. "Yes. A detective questioned me and I told him what had happened. The owner of the store said Devin *looked* like the person who broke into the store and shot him. Of course, Devin was found guilty and served time in prison."

"What about the gun?" Vance asked. "They had to have the gun to convict him." Vance's eyes widened.

"The police said that Devin dropped the gun. It was a *lie*." Tony frowned.

"Didn't he have a lawyer?" Vance blurted.

"Yeah, the one the *courts* gave him," Tony said before taking a sip. "He didn't do anything to help Devin." Tony sneered. "Devin was guilty *just because* he was black."

"That's messed up," said Vance.

"Goodness." Heather slouched in the vinyl chair. "I'm sorry to hear that. I wonder how much time he served in prison?"

"I'm not sure but he's been gone for a long time." Tony looked at Tiffany. "We lost contact because he didn't want to talk to anyone . . . not even his mother."

"Here he comes," Vance said, cutting his eyes to the left.

"Hello, I hope you all are enjoying yourselves." The heavy-set man paused. "Oh my God, Tony! What's up, man?"

Tony stood.

"Man, give me a hug."

Tony embraced him.

Then Devin smiled at the caramel-brown woman sitting next to Vance. "I know that *is not* Mrs. Brown's daughter, Tiffany."

"Hello, Devin," Tiffany said in a sweet soft voice. "This is my husband, Vance."

"You're a lucky man, Vance." He grinned. "Tiffany wouldn't even look my way."

Tiffany stretched her long slender arms around Devin's beer belly to hug him then sat down.

"Man, I see you're doing well," Vance said. "I like this spot man."

"Thanks. I had plenty of *time* to think about this joint," Devin said as he elbowed Tony in the side.

"Yeah, it's great that you opened this place." Tony leaned back in his chair.
"Devin this is my wife, Heather."

Heather's gaze leveled on the table.

Devin smiled. "Man, you hit the jackpot."

"Hello," Heather said unenthusiastically. A fake smile flashed across her face as she waved instead of shaking Devin's extended hand then turned in the opposite direction.

A frown rippled across Devin's face before quickly vanishing.

"Look at you, Tony, trying to look buffed," Devin said, chuckling. "Don't tell me you're still doing three-hundred sit-ups before you go to bed."

"And two-hundred push-ups." Vance chimed in, ribbing Tony.

Tony laughed. "No, I'm going to a fitness center now."

"I need to sign up, man," Devin said while rubbing his pouch.

"Let me know when you want to go, man. We can go together."

Heather sighed wearily.

Tony glared at her.

It was going to be a long night.

Chapter 37

Later that night, Tiffany sprawled across the cream satin sheets with her eyes closed. She curled her hands around Vance's as he slid his body next to hers. His warm skin against her breasts, heating the temperature under the covers.

Vance's moist tongue teased the walls of her mouth. Her soft flesh snuggled nicely under his warm body. A warm sensation flowed through her body like ocean waves. The shifting of their hips and the arching of their backs created a cyclone of moisture between them. Sweat dripped from Vance's muscular chest onto Tiffany's full, ripe breasts and rolled onto her flat stomach.

Peaches-and-cream scented candles filled the air mixing with the array of body chemistry they created.

Vance's long, pleasurable strokes into her creamy center drove Tiffany to maneuver in a slow grinding motion. The king-sized wicker bed provided an abundance of space.

The shaft from the moon flowed through a crease in the ruffled hunter-green curtains onto Tiffany's face. She closed her eyes as her tongue slithered inside his mouth.

Straddling her legs around him, she thrust toward him as her toes curled and hands gripped the silk sheets.

"Ohh, Vance," she moaned.

The anticipation alone was worth the excitement of pulling her panties off. Tiffany never imagined that she would crave for a man inside of her. But her husband, gentle and patient, made coming together a spectacular thing.

"Yes, honey, I'm all yours," he mumbled.

Beads of sweat dripped off his body onto her breasts. Her heart melted with joy, sending a sensational warmth of arousal throughout her body.

Vance circled each breast with his tongue, pausing for a split second to catch his breath in the crease of her cleavage. Her nipples hardened against his soft lips. His warm, moist tongue dangled across her breasts.

The more he licked and sucked her breasts the more she could feel her insides boiling over with moisture. Vance cupped her then, gently nibbling on her engorged nipples. She gripped his head, forcing it to clamp down on her nipples, a feeling she enjoyed. Pulling him deeper inside, her heart bubbled with joy with every inch he slid in.

"Awww," she moaned softly.

Closing her eyes, releasing herself at the mercy of his strokes, she swirled her tongue around her lips while running her fingers through his curly black hair.

Her breasts jiggled each time Vance thrust forward. She twirled her finger down his back as his muscles contracted and his body jerked.

Tiffany spread her legs further, propping them in the air, granting him more space to work his magic. Vance's hips shifted like a swing on a playground, moving back and forth.

"Yes, like that." Tiffany gripped the sheets as an explosion of passion ripped through her.

His long slender fingers caressed her waist, arms, and hips. His tender touches sent a nourishing feeling through her like the morning sun on a bright summer day.

Vance's kiss trailed across her cheekbones down to her neck. Tiffany pumped her hips up and down as her garden of love satiated him with moisture.

Their lips locked in a deep, passionate kiss. Her hips rose toward him as he massaged her spine. His long, deep strokes sent waves of pleasure

275

through her. Vance embraced Tiffany, thrusting in and out at a rapid pace. Her moist, tight, heated center clenched around the hardness of his velvet rod. Her heartbeat pounded against his chest.

The moment her thighs trembled, he thrust again and again, burying his head between her breasts.

"Ooo, honey," he grunted.

Vance applied a powerful grip around her body as he thrust faster and faster and faster.

"Yes. Yes. Yes," Tiffany said in a loud moan.

She could feel the rapid beats of his heart against her breasts. His legs stiffened and the muscles in his butt tightened with every thrust.

"Oh, yes. Oh, yes." Vance's body went from a fast pace to a slow grinding motion as his chest glued to Tiffany's breasts. The temperature in the room rose by several degrees. He caressed her soft hands, licking her fingers as he laid breathless on top of her.

Tiffany curled into her husband, holding on for dear life as a wave of heat flooded her being and splinters of her soul slowly found their way to a peaceful existence.

Chapter 38

An ivy leaf trimmed with pearls was framed on the wall in Tiffany's office. She was a proud member of Alpha Kappa Alpha Sorority, Incorporated. The elegant colors of salmon pink and apple green in the picture were representative of her character, sense of pride and perseverance. She kept in touch with her sorority sisters at their monthly meetings.

Vanilla-scented oils burned a stainless-steel container, giving her office a soft, pleasant smell. Tiffany stared at the items neatly displayed on the wall next to her degrees and licenses. She laughed, remembering how her calculus class used to kick her tail. Sipping on a cup of herbal green tree, she looked at a picture of Vance. He was God's gift to her. Last night had been wonderful. Her little jewel box still throbbed with precious memories.

Looking at a picture of her mother, Tony and herself, Tiffany leaned back in her chair. She had the perfect husband and a loving family who accepted him. God, the man could make her laugh.

The phone rang. "Good morning, Dr. Brown speaking."

"Can I speak to the most beautiful woman in the world?"

Tiffany chuckled. "Sure you can. How are you? I thought you had a lot of cases this morning? You know how busy your Monday mornings are."

"I did, but most of my clients wanted me to request a continuance. People will never learn that they can't commit a crime, then brag about it and expect to get away," he said, snickering. "So, how does lunch at Olive Garden sound today?"

"I think I can squeeze you in my busy schedule." Tiffany giggled as she picked up her husband's picture on the edge of her desk, trailing a single finger around his lips.

"You know you want to see me," Vance said.

"Yes, but you know how *crowded* the medical center gets sometimes. We don't have an official lunch break like you fancy lawyers at the courthouse." She crossed one leg over the other.

"If you can't escape from the center, then I'll pick up something and we can eat in your office."

"Now that sounds good."

"Did you deliver the twins this morning?"

"Yes, Laura pulled through like a champ. Everything went well."

"I know it did," he said smoothly. "You didn't graduate top of your class for nothing."

"Allen might need you to take over his caseload while he celebrates the birth of his twins."

"You're kidding me, right? Allen knows my cases are already kicking my tail. Besides, he handles murder cases and I'm not up for that this week— that's way more paperwork." Then he sighed wearily. "But if I have to, I'll help him out."

"I'm joking, baby," Tiffany said, twirling her fingers through her black hair. "He only told me to tell you the good news. You'll probably see him next week."

"I'm glad his wife finally got pregnant. They had been trying for five years. One visit to you and boy oh boy did she get pregnant. What do you have over there? A magic wand?"

"I'm no miracle worker," Tiffany replied, placing a hand over her heart. "But what can I say? I guess I *am* good at what I do."

"Do I detect a little arrogance in my baby?"

"Not arrogance, pride, my brother." Tiffany chuckled.

"You have every right to be proud, honey. Who do the twins look like?"

"They have their father's green eyes and dimples. But they have a lot more hair." Tiffany laughed. "You should've seen Allen. He smiled from ear to ear the whole time, rubbing his bald head."

"Hey, was he scared to cut the umbilical cord?" Vance asked in a rushed tone. "He told me he would be."

"I'm not telling. Ask him." Tiffany glanced at a chart on her desk.

"He told me he wanted *you* to do it."

Tiffany cackled. She wanted to tell Vance how the famous attorney Allen Pierce panicked when she told him he had to cut the cord. He nearly passed out when Laura let out that first shriek of pain. Nurse Patterson had to slap him to get him out of a trance. But she was certain that he wouldn't tell Vance all of that. And she wouldn't either.

"We have one more year before we experience that, honey," Vance said with a soft, pleasant tone. "I think we should shoot for three children."

Tiffany's soft features spread into a smile. "I'm ready whenever you are, Vance.
I love you."

"I love you too, honey . . . more than words can say."

Tiffany allowed his words to simmer in her heart.

Sirens from a police patrol car zoomed past her office window.

"Don't forget, I'm going jogging this evening. I won't be home when you get there."

"Okay, baby. You're serious about this jogging thing. You do it at least three or four times a week now."

She hesitated, glancing at the chart on her desk. "I need to jog so I can stay nice and slim for you."

"Hmmmmm. I'm glad your karate classes ended. We already don't spend enough quality time together."

Tiffany slid down in her office chair.

"What are you training for," he asked, with curiosity trailing in his voice. "With all of this martial arts and conditioning, you've got me thinking that maybe you think someone's going to do something to you."

Tiffany laughed it off. "Hey, don't forget my brother wants to take you to Dave's Pool Hall, tonight."

"What are you gonna do while I hang out with your brother?"

"I have to work late."

"Dr. Brown we have a code yellow in progress. Another little girl has been brought in . . . ."

Vance sighed softly. "I'll see you when you get home, Baby."

Chapter 39

Friday afternoon, the sun disappeared behind the clouds, casting a dark shadow over the Cloverdale community. The corners were deserted and the traffic had slowed to a crawl. The cold chilly night forced a lot of tenants to stay in their apartments. Hustlers held their ground on The Hill.

Smith strolled out of the alley with hopes of finding June Bug before he spilled the beans. He didn't have a choice but to allow June Bug to flee the scene because his officers were approaching and too many tenants were watching.

Still angered by his earlier conversation with Morgan, he knew he would still have to take her out. If she started questioning the girls, then he was in for a hard time. Maybe with the girls being so emotional about almost losing their mother, they might say something. His threats to them wouldn't mean a thing.

Walking to his patrol car, he brushed away a few crumbs from a late afternoon snack that had fallen onto his shirt. He pulled off, driving around the abandoned buildings and dark alleys, searching for June Bug.

On Friday evening, he cruised to an obscure corner from the main alley with the highest traffic flow and the park came into view. Sooner or later June Bug would peek his head out the abandoned building, like a groundhog trying to determine the onset of Spring.

Listening to the daily news, Smith picked up his camcorder, flipping on the night vision.

A scrawny figure staggered out the alley. June Bug. Smith loosened the buttons around his thick neck, slipped on a pair of black gloves, pulled a stolen gun from under his seat, put the silencer on and then waited for June Bug to walk further away from the alley.

He galloped down the street, heading in the direction of The Hill. Dingy jeans, ripped shirt and dirty shoes fit the characteristics of a man on the deep end of addiction. Even from a distance, the calloused, flaky skin made Smith cringe. The man's eyes were wider than a quarter and his hair had become even more matted.

June Bug strolled through a long alley consumed with rubbish, wine bottles and rats. His long dark brown arms swung rapidly back and forth as though this would force his legs to get him to The Hill even faster. Smith drove slowly, lights off, trailing behind June Bug, catching up to him before the man got out of his reach.

Smith craned his neck out of the window, flicking his headlights off and on. "Come here, June Bug."

June Bug jerked around with a frantic look.

"Come here, right now," Smith commanded, getting out of the car, palming the gun.

The addict picked up speed. "What you want?" His arms and legs moved at a brisk pace. "I did the job."

"It didn't work!" Smith broke into a brisk gait, running after him.

"So what!" June Bug whirled to face Smith, creating a foul breeze. "I'm not doing anything else for you. You sold me out! You didn't give me the rest of my dope."

Smith struck the man's brown face. "Shut up. You're useless, you pathetic piece of *trash*. You can't follow simple instructions. I gave you the gun to finish the job." He gripped the man's shirt with his hands. "Yeah, you were right," he said, slapping the man again. "You do need help. Look at you."

June Bug's hand balled into a fist. "Man, you better get out of my face. I'm not playing, Smith." June Bug turned and walked off, then he turned back. "You know, at first I didn't believe the rumors about Star. People said you killed my daughter. If you can kill your own wife . . . maybe I should tell somebody what you're doing." June Bug turned on his heels and ran.

"Get back here. I'm not finished with you." Smith caught up with him, grabbed the man, nearly plunging both of them to the ground. "You're better off dead like your *slut* of a daughter."

June Bug stopped in his tracks and slowly turned to face the sergeant.

Smith grinned, holding the gun in his hand. "You should have seen Star begging for her life."

The man's eyes became glazed with anger.

"And I screwed her brains out before I put her to *sleep*. I killed her in this very same spot. Where was Daddy, then?" Smith sneered. "I guess you were out getting high."

Twelve years earlier, Smith had trailed behind the short, golden brown girl with hazel eyes and long, dark hair. Her juicy butt and plump breasts enticed him just as they did most of the men in Cloverdale. She had been on her way to a bright future at Howard University and commanded everyone's respect, until one of the men who wanted her gave her a sweet taste of that evil white substance. Soon all anyone had to do was feed her drugs and she'd spread those legs for whoever was on the holding end. She dwindled from a Coke bottle to a skeleton. Her breasts sagged, butt caved in and her skin, once so smooth and flawless, had a crust that would put out most fires but that didn't stop others because she still had a wide smile and some semblance of the beauty she once had.

That warm night in June, after his search for Tiffany had proven fruitless, Smith thought he'd teach those little uppity chicks a lesson. Star was related to Tiffany and Tony and *word* was bound to get back to Tiffany that her cousin had been killed. Maybe that would loosen Tony's tongue. Tiffany would have to come home for summer or some type of break. Then he'd show her how gentle he'd been with her before.

Smith loosened his belt buckle and unfastened three buttons on his white shirt. Watching Star's wide gait brought him an erection he hadn't had in days. Star came out of the alley, holding a beer can and staggered three blocks down the street to an abandoned building. Sergeant Smith followed her, parking on the opposite side of the alley so no one could see him. Slowly, he walked into the building and looked around. The coast was clear. He inched quietly inside, unsure if someone was waiting for Star. He paused, listening for a moment.

The old ravaged building was small and only had one floor. All of the windows were shattered and the steps had splintered and cracked. The cement tile had peeled away. Deterioration and neglect had rotted parts of the roof. The walls were covered with mold and the building smelled like garbage. But what was a little thing like mold going to do to him? That never had stopped him before.

Star sat in a corner with her head tilted back in a daze as the cocaine flowed through her flimsy body. Smith drew closer, but she didn't look up. A few seconds later, Smith stood directly over her with his pants unfastened.

Star slowly opened her droopy, drug-glazed eyes; in her own world. Her normal customers were white businessmen who'd creep through the ghetto late at night in search of a little black pudding. She managed to open her mouth, although it was dry and sticky from the cocaine, gazing up at the man standing before her. "What do you want?"

"You know what I want!"

"I've served my last customer. I'm going to the rehab tomorrow."

Smith roared with laughter. "That's what you all say."

"Look, I'm serious. I just took my last high."

Smith pulled the drugs out of his pocket, dangling them in front of her. "Now, you were saying . . . ."

"What do you want," she said, her gaze following the little plastic bag as if hypnotized.

"You know what I want."

"No," she said, wiping her face with the back of a shaky hand. "You have to *tell* me what you want."

He rubbed his growing erection. "What do you think I want?"

"Look," she slurred, "some want me to play with it. Some want me to suck it. Some watch me dance while they play with themselves. Some even get a thrill out of watching me finger myself."

Smith perked up. "Are you serious?"

"Yep! So what do you want? And how much are you going to pay?"

"How much do you want?"

Star laughed, the sound grating on Smith's nerves. "Cash or dope?"

"Money? I'm not giving you any *money*!"

"Okay. How much dope do you have?"

"I've got some crack, cocaine, weed and heroin. What do you want?"

"I don't mess with heroin or crack." She sniffed. "You can give me the powder."

"Powder?"

"Yeah. That's what we call cocaine."

"Oh, I knew that."

"Yeah, right." She glanced up, grimacing as he stroked his groin. "Who are you anyway?"

"Don't worry about all of that."

She cast a sly glance his way. "Give me my powder first. I don't like to play games. Besides, I have to make sure it's the real deal.

Smith reached into his pocket and tossed a small plastic tube of powder to her. She grabbed for it, attacking like a lion after bloody meat. She ripped the plastic tube open with her teeth. Some of the cocaine splattered into her mouth. Moments later she smiled.

She sat for a few seconds before hopping to her knees and wrapped her lips around his condom-covered erection. She sucked hard, slurping it like a lollipop. Smith's eyes rolled in the back of his head.

The girl had skills. Maybe he could meet up with her again. Star rolled her tongue around his rod as though it was a vanilla Popsicle. He liked that. He wanted to take the condom off and let her really do the job, but he didn't know if the girl had a disease. He would never be able to explain that to Morgan. She gripped his narrow hips and caressed it as if giving him a *special* treatment. The juices in him pumped. Star rubbed his legs, stroking his butt as though they were lovers. Maybe he could get her to serve him at least three times a week. Then the world almost went black as the hot sensations built up and nearly released.

The shaft of light from the moon penetrated through the shattered windows, shining down on the badge lying next to her. Star continued to perform oral sex on him and glanced at the badge. She gagged. By this time, Sergeant Smith was erupting into the condom, his eyes completely closed, in the heat of passion.

When he opened his eyes, fury sent boiling rage through him. The badge had disappeared from the ground. A professional knew how to do at least three things at one time without creating a distraction, but Star had definitely messed up his plans of having a skilled addict always ready to serve him.

He reached out, grabbing her neck, wrapping both hands around it.

Star's hands flailed, scratching at him. He wasn't worried that forensics could match the skin found under her fingernails. Murders of prostitutes were low on the list of the department's priorities.

Her eyes went from a drug-induced glaze to that of one slipping from life to death.

Minutes later, he let her lifeless body drop from his hands.

Shocked at the intensity of his rage, he fastened his clothes and ran out of the building. As he reached the patrol car, he realized he had left the badge. A group of voices made him scramble into the car and close the door. Three bony men strolled past, eyeing the patrol car suspiciously.

When they were at least thirty feet away, he ran back into the building to Star's lifeless body. She had the badge gripped tightly in her hand. Smith had to pry open her hand to get the little silver piece. The badge cut her hand and blood splattered on the badge, spraying on his clothes before pouring out on the concrete ground.

Smith ran out of the building. Had he covered his tracks? He had used a condom. He didn't have to worry about evidence in her mouth and the wrapper was still balled up in his pocket. No one saw him leave the building. Everything was squared away.

Now twelve years later, he looked down at Star's father and said, "That was one less addict in Cloverdale. I hate that I had to kill her. Man, she could suck a mean one. I had plans for her, but she messed up a good thing."

"You say what?" June Bug forced air out of his nostrils. He staggered forward, dropping to his knees. "You—you killed my daughter. Is that what you are telling me?"

"Look at you. You were never a father to her. You're a junkie. She was a junkie." Smith laughed bitterly. "I guess it runs in the family. You're better off dead yourself."

"I know my ears are deceiving me. I know you aren't telling me you killed my baby." A tear rolled down June Bug's ashy face as he sank to his knees.

Smith sneered. "Yeah . . . go ahead and shed your last tear. You'll be one less person spreading rumors about me and one less person I have to worry about setting me up."

"*Oh, God*," wept June Bug.

"Go ahead and say your last prayer. I guess I can let you do that," Smith chuckled. The nerve of the man to feel something now. "Oh, by the way. That perfect little son of yours broke into an appliance store. I guess you weren't around for David, either," Smith said, unzipping his pants. "Maybe there's something you can do for me. Hopefully, you're as good as Star."

The shriek of tires made both men look up. Car lights zoomed into the alley and a silver Smith & Wesson was aimed at Smith.

Chapter 40

Tiffany left the police department. They had done nothing despite her efforts to bring that treacherous man to justice. They didn't believe the residents of Cloverdale and though she came to them in a professional capacity, they didn't believe her either. What a way to spend a hot Friday evening.

As she had done every day for the past week, Tiffany had trailed Smith from the moment he left the community center. Now she sat in her car with her black jogging suit and tennis shoes and her hair pulled back into a ponytail. The more she thought about what he did to poor little Christy, the more anger stirred her soul. Although Christy had only said the word Sergeant before passing out, Tiffany was certain that Smith was the one who had attacked her and the other little girls. There was no way she could have been talking about Sergeant Clark. Clark was one of the good guys.

Smith had strolled out of the building toward his patrol car as if he were the king of Cloverdale. People who were standing on the corner scattered, tenants scurried to their apartments and hustlers strolled back toward The Hill out of arm's length.

Smith got into his car and pulled down the street. Tiffany waited until the coast was clear before she swerved, trying to pull in front of the patrol car, blocking him from driving away. A little girl stepped out in front of her.

Tiffany slammed on the brakes, shrieking to a halt. Her heart stopped and for a minute she blanked out, praying that she hadn't hit the little girl.

Her auburn ponytail bobbed up and down, torn jeans sagged as the little girl turned and waved, not realizing that she had come within a hair's breadth of death.

Fear settled in her gut. Smith's car had vanished from view. She couldn't keep lying to her husband, telling him she was jogging when all she wanted to do was get enough evidence to put Smith away. She had a tape recorder and knowing how the sick man's brain worked and how he liked to brag, Tiffany was certain she could get something—anything that would make the police look into what had happened to the little girls.

Intuition made her drive past the alley near the creek, then the abandoned buildings near the hair supply store and soul-food restaurant. She knew, from living in Cloverdale, that these were the places Smith ventured to when he wanted to do shady stuff. Then she saw Smith. Then she saw her uncle kneeling before him. A faint glint of light beamed on the gun in Smith's hand. Her uncle would die if she didn't act fast.

And she did, aiming the 9mm Smith & Wesson straight at the sergeant, hoping that he suffered before hitting the pavement.

"Who is that?" Smith aimed his gun.

Tiffany hopped out of her truck, holding the gun steady in her hand. She kept her truck running. With rage boiling in her soul and retaliation ripping through her mind, she forgot all about justice, wanting to take matters into her own hands and leave the police totally out of things.

"*My oh my,*" Sergeant Smith said with a grin as he put his gun back into its holster.

That bastard! She wasn't a threat to him.

"Aren't you a brave little soldier now?" He squared his shoulders in a cocky stance.

"Shut up," she snapped. "I'm not scared of you anymore."

His gaze trailed over her body, causing her to shiver with disgust.

"Look at my little honey bun," he said softly. "You don't have to be feisty, baby. You didn't have to go out of your way to stop me, sugar. You know I'll squeeze you in my schedule at the drop of a dime." He grabbed his groin. "Wait in line. I've got plenty to go around."

The overcast sky promised rain at any minute, making it difficult for Tiffany to see Smith's hands.

June Bug stood, eyes drenched with tears. "What you doin', Tiff? Give me that!"

Tiffany stepped closer as the anger rushed through her body. "It's time for him to pay for what he's done to the women of Cloverdale."

"Look, Sugar."

"Stop calling me Sugar!" she shrieked. "I am not your sugar and never have been."

"Come on, baby," he said, coming toward her with arms spread. "How can you forget the hot passion we shared? I remember it clear as day."

"Now you're having men suck your little-shriveled dick," she spat. "Get away from my uncle, you sick bastard."

"I'm not going anywhere. But if you don't want your uncle doing the job, I'm all for you putting those luscious lips around it." Smith winked. "You liked it before."

Tiffany felt ill. It took every ounce of strength she could muster to stand her ground.

June Bug whirled to face her; eyes wide with horror. "What's he talkin' 'bout, Tiff? What's he saying?"

Tiffany swallowed hard.

Smith leaned forward. "By the way, did you tell your husband that he's getting sloppy seconds?" Harsh laughter filled the air. "I see him at the courthouse, arrogant little cuss, strutting like a proud peacock. Wouldn't be so proud if he knew I broke that lovely cherry." Smith rubbed his cleft chin, winking. "Maybe I should tell him sometime."

Tiffany lunged, landing a hard left on Smith's nose. Blood spurted, splattering her clothes and the gun. She jumped back, looking around. The alley was clear.

She gripped the gun she'd brought from one of the people on The Hill in exchange for medical services.

June Bug eased next to her and she said, "He raped me." She nodded as tears welled up in her eyes. "Before I went off to college, he raped me."

Afraid to pull the trigger, Tiffany lunged again, throwing a hard blow across Smith's face, simultaneously kicking him in the ribcage, a technique she had learned in karate class. This time he bounced off the brick wall and landed in a hard heap between the dumpster and broken glass.

"I know he's the one raping those little girls, too."

"I don't know what you're talking about," Smith said with a mouth full of blood. "You don't have to do this. I'll give you some lovin', sugar, you don't have to force me to go through all this trouble," he said cupping a hand over his mouth, glaring up at her. "And I didn't touch any little girls. I like 'em legal," he said, grinning. "Like you." Then he turned to June Bug. "Like Star."

"I wasn't legal!" Tiffany shrieked.

Smith leaped toward them. A gun went off, the shot echoing in the alley like a death toll.

Chapter 41

Puffy blue clouds stretched across the dark sky. A warm breeze on a hot summer night whizzed past Tony and Vance as they strolled from their cars to a large glass door, trailing a crowd entering through Dave's Pool Hall.

Dave's Pool Hall was spacious with two bars, four televisions and ten pool tables. The famous spot hosted pay-per-view sports events and had the best hot wings, hot dogs and fish sandwiches in town. Well, at least according to loyal customers. Friday night specials as well as the pool hall's rules were posted on the large black billboards. Cigarette smokers had a designated spot out on the patio. Drugs were never welcome—*never*.

Dave, a tall, midnight-black man with large biceps that protruded menacingly out of his tight shirt, was enough to make even the toughest thug think twice. If he caught a person smoking or selling dope on his premises, he would ban them. If they gave him some flack, he'd turn them over to the authorities. And that was after he whipped their asses. He worked hard to establish a good reputation.

As Tony and Vance moseyed through the doors, a few appreciative glances of the women closest to the entrance swept over them. Hip Hop and R&B music pumped out of the large speakers in the corners. Tony's eyes danced as he absorbed the music.

"I'm glad I did take Tiffany's advice to hang out with you," Vance said, smiling at the woman who winked at him.

"Yeah, me too. We needed a break from the card games. Heather was killing the vibe."

"Who you telling?" Vance grinned.

"We're meeting my boys here." Tony glanced in every corner. "You know Heather would have a fit if I brought some of my friends from Cloverdale to our house. God, the things I do to keep peace in my house."

"I hear ya."

"I've even started cooking, man. Unreal!" Tony huffed as Vance laughed.

Hot wings on a tray passed in front of Tony, making his stomach grumble because he wasn't sending the food down fast enough.

Vance's gaze swept over the bar. "Where are your boys, Tony?"

"They'll be here. They're practically part of the furniture. Travis and Terrence hang out here a lot. They're identical twins."

"So, you grew up with them? They played basketball, too?"

"Yeah." Tony nodded. "They gave me a run for my money in practice. Man, they had potential, but between the girls and the streets they got sidetracked."

"What's up, Tony?" Terrence said, punching Tony's arm as he appeared next to the two men.

Although the lights in the pool hall were dim, Terrence's pinkish black lips could be seen across the room. Travis was a tall mocha-brown guy with locks.

"This is my brother-in-law, Vance. Where is Travis?"

Terrence eyed Vance up and down. Everyone in Cloverdale wanted to meet the lucky man who had swept Tiffany off her feet. Didn't mean they would be friendly about it.

"What's up, man?" Vance said.

"Come on. Travis is waiting for us."

They walked through the crowd to a table in the corner. Tony spoke to a few guys he played with on the courts.

"Look at you, *Mr. Dentist*," Travis said as he stood and hugged Tony. His dreads were longer than Terrence's, making it easy to tell the twins apart.

"Go ahead and get all of your jokes out."

"You know it wouldn't be me if I didn't make jokes."

Squinting, Travis asked, "Who's this cat?"

"Stop tripping, man," Tony said. "This is Vance, my brother-in-law." The man stared at Vance.

"So, that would mean he's married to Tiffany," Terrence said with a smirk.

Vance glared back. "Yeah, man, I'm Tiffany's husband."

A sense of unease washed over Tony. Terrence thought he was the man in Cloverdale. Tiffany stripped his ego when she had turned him down several times.

"That's cool," Terrence said as he sucked on his teeth. "Where you from, man?"

"Harlem."

"Hey, the game's about to come on," Tony said, trying to redirect Terrence's attention to the game.

The guys mingled for a few minutes and ordered their food as they waited for the game to finish. Streaks of jealousy turned to a highway of laughter as music filled the pool hall.

"Aw, man, did you see how Lebron dunked on those clowns?" Terrence said as he gulped down his glass of Long Island Ice Tea.

"He dominates the paint," Tony said, quickly reflecting on the days when Terrence was considered the "King of the Paint."

"Charlotte is growing. We have an NBA, WNBA and an NFL team here." Travis said, biting his hot dog. "Next thing you know we will have an MLB."

"Man, forget all of that. I can't wait until Shaq comes to town." Terrence threw his hands in the air as if shooting a ball. "I'm going to have a seat out on the court or up in a booth. Tony, I bet you can't ball anymore. I remember when I blocked your shot," Terrence said, gripping his stomach to hold in the laughter.

"That's nothing." Tony smiled. "Do you still remember how I dunked on you in practice? Everybody talked about *that* for a week."

"Oh, I see you want to bring up old stuff," Terrence said with a wide grin. "Man, that was when we were in high school. You haven't seen my skills now."

"Tony, you've got jokes," Travis mumbled, sinking his teeth into a hot wing. "Do you remember when you went up for a dunk and got hung?"

Vance laughed, turning to his brother-in-law. "You say what? Not Tony?"

"He didn't tell you about that? Man, we have a lot of stories we can share with you." Terrence pulled his locks behind his ears, showcasing his platinum chain and earrings. He'd argue you down if you tried to tell him the chain wasn't real.

Tony put his beer on the table. "Okay, you want to go there? What about the time you stole the ball and missed an open layup? My grandmother could've made that shot."

Vance roared with laughter.

"Oh, so you find that funny, huh? What's that in your hair?" Terrence asked, pointing at Vance's head and laughing. "I thought S-Curls went out in the 90s."

Raking his hair with long slender fingers, Vance tilted his head toward the floor. Travis' short, stubby, fingers tapped on the table as he laughed.

"What's up with your boy, Tony?" Terrance asked. "What's he doing?"

"Stop tripping, Terrence." Tony gawked at him. "He's showing you that it's not chemicals. That's that man's hair."

"Yeah, that's what they all say." Terrence's lips curled into a sneer. "I don't know why people won't go natural. People waste too much money buying perms and all of that mess."

Vance paused before he spoke. "There are a lot of brothers up north with locks. So, I feel you. But this is the texture of my hair. I don't have to pay anyone to get my hair like this. You did those locks without any help, right?"

Terrence glared at him.

Tony said, "What about the time we were down one point and you took a long three and missed? Coach Fisher wanted to kill you."

"Man, I think he bet some money on that game."

"You would know, Tony." Travis pulled on his locks. "You were his boy."

The music continued to play as conversations filled the pool hall. The four men ate their food and sipped on their drinks.

Terrence stuck a toothpick in his mouth. "A lot of things change but some things stay the same. You know Sergeant Smith is still tripping, man."

"He'll never change." Travis slumped in the metal chair. "I don't know why he's still over there."

"Who is Sergeant Smith?"

Travis guzzled his beer. "Vance, you don't want to know. He's trouble. He patrols the area in Cloverdale. Has for years."

"Tiffany's never mentioned him."

Tony lowered his gaze, glaring at Travis hoping he would take the hint and shut up.

"Man, Smith has screwed a lot of chicks in Cloverdale," Terrence said as his gaze trailed the path of a girl's big butt as she walked past the table.

Travis peered at Vance. "Tiffany ain't never told you about him before?" His eyebrows rose as a smirk spread across his lips.

Terrence added, "Tiffany didn't tell you about the *Almighty* Sergeant Smith?"

Tony turned his head, glowering angrily at Terrence.

"Tony, you know he used to make people do a lot of crazy stuff," Travis said, pressing a wine cooler on his lips.

"I know."

But that all ended for Tony the day he stood up to Smith in the alley; the man hadn't bothered him anymore. After a few angry stares and verbal threats, he no longer made Tony feel like a weak, timid little boy—if only Tony had done that much earlier.

"You know," Terrance said in a sly tone, "I heard that Tiff—"

Tony stood, rage building inside him as he realized Terrance was so jealous of Vance that he would shed a negative light on his sister.

Vance was getting an earful and would raise questions as to why Tiffany never mentioned Smith's name. Tony reached for his Long Island Ice Tea, sipped it and said, "Let's play some pool."

Chapter 42

Vance slipped his naked body in the bed next to Tiffany. She was curled up into a ball with the cool satin sheets draped across her body. Vance inched closer to her, gently stroking her back. Tiffany lay stiff and in a daze.

Slowly caressing her body, he nibbled on her ear as he said, "Are you awake, honey? I had a nice time with your brother at the pool hall."

The fresh, crisp scent of his cologne drifted into her nose. But sex was the last thing on her mind. Normally, the passion that flourished between them took her mind off things.

Rain bounced against the window, echoing into the quiet room.

"Tiffany, are you okay?"

Not a muscle in her body moved.

"*Tiffany.*"

Silence seeped out of every pore in her body.

Vance nudged her. "Honey . . . are you all right?"

Leaves rustled outside the window.

Vance gripped her shoulder, rolling her over to face him. His eyebrows drew in as he touched the pillow beneath her. The pillow was saturated with her tears.

"Honey, what's wrong?" he asked, pulling her closer.

Tears tumbled down her face, forming a puddle under her chin.

Vance slid toward the headboard and sat up. He cuffed his arms under Tiffany's back and slid her towards him.

Tiffany nestled her head on her husband's chest. The rapid beats of his heart pounded in her ear.

"What's wrong, honey? Please talk to me."

Tiffany trembled. Her heart stopped, then fluttered like a butterfly. Every degree of guilt flowed through her soul. How could she find the words to tell her husband what had happened?

The rain continued to pelt against the window.

Vance stroked his fingers through her hair, then tilted her face towards him. He pressed his palm against her cheeks and wiped away her tears. But too many were coming out for his bare hands to dry up; they kept flowing.

The wind whirled, causing leaves to brush against the window.

Tiffany's head slowly lowered, burying into his chest—again.

"Please talk to me," Vance said as he reached down, kissing Tiffany on her forehead. "I'm your husband. You have to talk to me, honey."

Tiffany slowly lifted her head, establishing eye contact with him. A gust of air escaped her lungs as if it were her last breath.

Vance caressed her shoulders. "What . . . what is it, honey?" The words slowly rolled off his tongue. "Please tell me."

Tiffany folded her arms in front of her stomach as she curled up again. Stricken with a mixture of anguish and self-defeat, she began to sob and shake.

"*Oh God*, Tiffany what's wrong?" Vance said, wrapping his arm around her and holding her tight.

A cool breeze drifted out of the vent, striking her wet cheek.

"Honey, you've got to talk to me."

Tiffany's eyelids joined. Somehow, the tears managed to squeeze through.

"Talk to *me*." He tilted her chin.

Prying her lips apart, Tiffany mumbled softly as she curled into him, saying, "Just hold me, baby. Just hold me . . . ."

Chapter 43

"Good Morning, Charlotte Viewers. We're sorry to interrupt this broadcast but we have a Channel 23 News Flash," Kelly Moore's monotone voice broke into Tony's Saturday morning breakfast with his family. He had made waffles, which Heather preferred over pancakes and strolled out the kitchen into the den, turning the volume up.

"We've just received shocking news about a gruesome murder of one of Charlotte Police Department's own. Barry Snow is on the scene." She turned her head to the screen behind her, saying, "Barry, can you fill us in?"

A portly man with blonde hair and small green eyes came into focus. "This is Barry Snow and I'm reporting live from an alley where the body of Sergeant Paul Smith, a community patrol officer in Cloverdale Assisted Housing Community, was found after a city trash collector called the police station. Sergeant Smith has been shot, dismembered and mangled."

"Do the police have any leads?"

The cameraman panned the area. "Kelly as you can see . . . there are a lot of officers with hound dogs on the scene. They're still searching the area. But I can tell you that a small case containing heroin, fentanyl, cocaine, and cash was stashed in a hidden compartment in the trunk of the patrol car.

Barry paused, lowering his head, listening to his earpiece.

Kelly swirled in her chair, then turned back to the camera in the studio. "We'll be keeping track of this story throughout the day." She adjusted her earpiece. "Now back to the—"

"Wait, Kelly! More information has come in. We're finding out that Sergeant Smith has been the subject of an ongoing Internal Affairs investigation for the past four months."

"Didn't you say that he was a community patrol officer in Cloverdale?"

"Yes, that's right, Kelly."

"Viewers," Kelly said, turning back to face front and center. "Cloverdale is a community with one of the highest crime rates here in Charlotte and—"

Tony groaned. Another round of false speculations would result from this newscast. He reached for the phone and dialed Tiffany's number. She didn't answer. "Hey, you two," he said to the frisky little kids. "Go upstairs with your mother."

"Kelly, I just overheard Detective Wayne Jackson say that this alleged murder is the work of more than one person."

"Do they have a suspect?"

"At this time, they're still investigating the matter." Barry lowered his head. "Wait, Kelly information is coming in." Barry turned to look at the crowd behind him, aiming the mic toward the police, zeroing in on what they were saying.

"Kelly, it seems like they have two eyewitnesses with conflicting stories. One is stating that she saw what happened out here in the alley. Another witness apparently called in to report what happened on the other side of the town."

A burly man with jet-black hair and piercing brown eyes shoved his hand over the microphone. "Excuse me, Mr. Channel 23 news you're interfering with a police investigation. Move on."

"Everyone," Barry said, ignoring the officer and speaking into the mic, "This is Detective Jackson from the Charlotte Police Department. What can you tell us about the alleged murder of Sergeant Paul Smith?"

"No comment, and you know you're not allowed behind the police tape." The detective reached out, covering the camera lens with a wide bronze hand.

"Sorry Kelly, I'm not able to disclose that on the air at this time," Barry's muffled tone came through the airwaves."

"Barry, can you interview the witness?"

Barry trudged away from the scene. "At this moment, no. The witness is downtown at the police department. But he wants to remain anonymous for safety reasons." He grimaced as he looked into the camera again. "I'll keep you posted as information unfolds."

Moments later, Morgan made a public announcement on the news as she sat in a wheelchair in front of Charlotte Medical Hospital telling the public that her husband was known as a strictly-by-the-book policeman. She said he was a good man and a loving, kind, husband, who cared for the safety and well-being of people. As she spoke, her children appeared to be disinterested.

The camera switched back to Kelly. "Viewers, once again Channel 23 will keep you updated. Switching to the sports headlines, tonight the Charlotte Bobcats...."

Tony slumped to the sofa. He shut off the television and looked up at Heather who stood at the door watching him.

Chapter 44

The morning sun peered through the curtains, allowing the rays to shine on Tiffany's face. She pulled the covers over her to block the sun. Saturday mornings were the days she could sleep until noon. Today, with a heart as heavy as hers, she could sleep forever if anyone would let her.

The scent of pancakes, turkey bacon and hot maple syrup drifted from the kitchen into the bedroom. Tiffany pulled her body up to sit on the edge of the bed. A skimpy purple lace nightgown was draped over her body. A smile spread across her face while she looked at Vance's picture on the nightstand. Then a pang of worry filled her heart. Hopefully, June Bug could keep his mouth shut. No one would have to know.

Thirty minutes later, Tiffany walked into their spacious gourmet kitchen. Vance grinned from ear to ear as his gaze traveled the length of her body. A black strapless shirt outlined her breasts and her flat stomach. The sight of him made her heart melt. Tight black denim jeans and a green polo shirt were a startling contrast to the bright gold and cream in the kitchen.

The breakfast table had been neatly arranged with fluffy pancakes, cheesy eggs, thick slices of turkey bacon and buttery grits. A crystal vase filled with yellow roses took its place in the center of the table. Tiffany admired the glistening appearance of the fragrant flowers.

"Here you are, my queen," Vance said with a flourish of his hand. "I thought I would surprise you and make you breakfast. I was going to bring it upstairs."

A fruit tray on the other side of the table was filled with strawberries, apples and oranges.

"I hope it tastes as good as it looks," she said.

Vance pulled Tiffany toward him. "Let's hope *you* taste as good as you look." He kissed her on the forehead and on her cheek, embracing her gently. Tiffany dropped her head onto his massive chest, his muscles rippling against her face. Vance trailed his fingers up and down her spine.

Caressing Tiffany's hand, he pulled her toward the table. "Come on baby, let's eat," he said while pulling a chair for her.

"I love you, Vance." She smiled. Then it disappeared as she looked at him, eyes brimming with tears. "If something ever happens to me, Vance, please don't forget about my mother."

"What do you mean, honey?" he asked, sliding his chair closer to her. "We're going to be together for at least the next 150 years. You're not going back on your promise, are you?"

Tiffany's lips lifted in a slight smile. "I'm serious, Vance."

"Honey you sound like you know you're going to die soon or go to prison for the rest of your life."

Tiffany's eyebrows twitched.

"What are you trying to tell me, baby?"

Her lips parted but the phone rang at the same time. An uneasy feeling grew in the pit of her stomach.

She stood quickly. "I'll get it."

"We have an answering machine, Tiffany." He gently grabbed her hand, pulling her back toward the chair. "I think it's more important that we talk right now."

The phone rang again. Tiffany glanced over her shoulder to the cordless resting on the cradle.

Vance grimaced. "I'll get it, Honey. I don't know who could be calling this early on a Saturday. Even Tony doesn't call this early."

"Good morning," Vance said, in a deep tone, then paused. "I'm doing all right . . . Wayne. What's up?"

She slumped on the chair and couldn't hold back a sniffle.

Keeping his gaze on Tiffany, Vance cleared his throat before saying, "Did I miss a court appearance today or are you trying to play some golf this morning?" Vance turned to face the calendar, lifting the orange clipboard. "Sure, but for what, Wayne?"

"What witness? How can she be a suspect?"

"Wayne? You're jerking my leg, right?"

Chapter 45

The interrogation room was a cold and dreary place to be on such a beautiful and sunny Saturday morning. The spacious, closed-in room was filled with electronic equipment. Several chairs stretched in front of a wide black window and along the wall. Cold air gusted out of the air conditioner and bright lights aimed down onto Tiffany's face. The acrid smell of cigarettes lingered in the air from the vents and in some of the officer's clothes.

In a room filled with stern, hard noses, on top of a sleepless night, the tension that had built up at her temples and the smell in the interrogation room triggered a migraine.

Tiffany sat at a long back table, positioned in front of a dark mirror. A tape recorder perched in the middle of the table had been turned on and several notebooks and pens were arranged on the opposite end. Tiffany glanced at the dark glass, certain that more officers were on the other side of the mirror listening in. She was accused of killing a police officer. They wanted her to fry.

The solemn expression on Wayne's face made her even more nervous. But she felt a sense of security that Vance and Allen, now her attorney, were sitting beside her.

Tiffany had a flashback to when she had delivered Allen's twins. Tears of joy ran down his face as Kaylee and Haylee made their entrance into the world. A far cry from the hard-edged professional sitting next to her. Not once had he asked her if she had killed Sergeant Smith. She wasn't sure if that was a good thing or not.

Detective Wayne Jackson read Tiffany her rights, which were waived by Vance and Allen, then he proceeded with the interrogation. Detective

Jackson clenched his wide brown hands together, starting with, "Please state your name."

With a soft shaky tone, she said, "Tiffany Michele Brown-Carson."

Then he asked where she lived, what she did for a living—the usual drill, with minor objections from Vance and Allen.

"What is your marital status?"

Someone on the other side of the table cleared their throat. Tiffany's gaze fell on the table.

Vance blurted out, "That information should be off the record for now."

"Do you know Sergeant Paul Smith?"

"Yes."

"How?"

"He was the community patrol sergeant for Cloverdale Projects."

"When was your first encounter with him?"

Allen waved his hand. "Tiffany, you don't have to answer that."

The detective grimaced, eyeing Allen with a smirk, before continuing. The tapping sound of Wayne's pen landing on the pad echoed in the room. The other men gathered on the opposite side, almost looked like a choir.

Tiffany felt like a child in time-out. Every question forced her to remember her painful experience with that sick bastard and how Christy's small body draped over the examination table. Shaking her head, bracing herself to go on, she tuned into Wayne.

"So, you admit that you did have an altercation with Sergeant Paul Smith on a side road here in Charlotte, North Carolina."

Tiffany craned her neck over the table to speak in the tape recorder. "Yes."

"Did you kill Sergeant Paul Smith?"

Before Tiffany could answer, the interrogation door swung open and a deep croaking voice said, "I killed Sergeant Smith."

Tiffany turned and her eyes widened in shock. She never wanted to involve this man in her troubles.

Never.

Chapter 46

Vance followed fast on Tiffany's heels as she trudged out of the interrogation room. They strolled to the parking lot where he opened the car door and she slid into the passenger seat. As she waited for Vance, she glanced back at the police department, observing the glaring eyes of several uniformed officers. She rubbed her arms which now had an array of goosebumps. Vance stood outside talking to Allen, making plans to meet early in the office on Monday.

The sunny scent of citrus wafted around the car from a freshener dangling in front of a vent in the Mercedes. Vance hopped in and pulled off, hitting Trade Street a few moments later. Vance's soft brown eyes constantly darted from the road to Tiffany.

"Do you want to listen to some music, honey?"

Tiffany shrugged.

He reached down and within moments mellow tones floated out of the speakers.

They drove past Church Street and Graham Street, merging onto Interstate 77 North to their house in the Lake Norman Community.

Vance had held his ground and his tongue up until now, but he suddenly switched off the music. "You've got to talk to me."

Butterflies swarmed her stomach as her heart pounded in her ears. The thought of telling Vance the truth made her soul cry out to the heavens above.

Vance cleared his throat while placing a cuddling hand on top of Tiffany's trembling ones. She slumped down in the seat as she bent down to tie her tennis shoes.

She took a slow, deep breath as she raised her head. Vance stared at her.

A horn blew as Vance swerved into another lane. He gripped the steering wheel, jerking it to the right to get back into his lane.

Tiffany fumbled with her fingers as she glanced out of the window at the trees, trying to avoid eye contact with her husband. A faint smile spread across her lips as she watched a bride get into a limousine in front of University Park Baptist Church.

"What were you thinking, Tiffany?" he asked. "You went looking to kill that man while you had me hanging out at the pool hall with your brother."

Tiffany sighed, closing her eyes. She had expected this storm a little earlier. On the way to the station, Vance was too busy trying to track Allen to really question her. He had all the time in the world now.

"Do you know what that's called? Do you?"

She shrugged hopelessly.

"*Premeditated* murder. The kind that will land you on death row."

She didn't say a word.

"What else are you hiding?" He gawked at her. "What did he do to you?"

Shaken by the harsh tone of his voice, she didn't know if she was between a dream or a nightmare.

"And why do you and your brother keep so many secrets?"

Tiffany felt a sharp pain in her lungs like ice and fire as words struggled to escape her mouth. "He was an evil man, Vance. He did a lot of terrible things."

"But why did *you* have to go after him?" He punched the steering wheel. "Out of all of the people he's hurt in Cloverdale, why *you*?

Tiffany's heart rate escalated.

"All of a sudden you're a killer now? That's who I married? What are you hiding, Tiffany?"

Vance laid a hand on the horn and cut in front of another car. He had almost missed their exit off the highway. Tiffany jerked forward, gripping the seatbelt.

"You've jeopardized your career and our marriage."

Tiffany turned to face her husband, the first time she had made eye contact with him all day.

"You can't take matters into your own hands," Vance snapped. "Did you consider how this would affect me? My career? My reputation? My wife being tried for murder?"

"Is that all you can think about right now?" Tiffany shot back. "He's done more than you could ever imagine! He's worth me doing time in prison."

A gust of air shot out of Vance's mouth. "I'm tired of being in the dark. I need answers."

Tiffany folded her arms. His abrupt tone caused her to bristle. "Now isn't the time for answers."

"Then when is the time, Tiffany? First our wedding night, then last week. You can't keep avoiding my questions," he said, gripping her arm.

Tiffany snatched her arm away, hitting the dashboard with her fist.

Vance pulled the car over to the side of the road in front of their house.

"What do you want to know, Vance! What!" she screamed, the tension finally unraveling.

Vance turned off the car, slumped in his seat, his eyes widening as he looked at his wife.

"Go ahead, Vance. Ask me."

They stared at one another with their lips pressed together.

Vance sighed. Lowering his tone, he said, "Honey, please tell me what's going on? What did he do to you?" He placed a gentle hand on top of hers and caressed it. "Do you want to go inside the house and talk?"

Silence took over her for a few seconds.

"I will prefer to tell you in the car. I don't want to discuss this in our home." Tiffany braced herself against the seat before allowing words to drift out of her mouth. "He raped me," she said in a resigned whisper. Three simple words, but her body felt as if a ton had been lifted off of her.

Vance covered his face with his hands while applying a firm grip to Tiffany's. She could feel his hand trembling. His hand dropped; his face twisted with rage. "You should've told me this a long time ago. Does Tony know?"

Tiffany gaped out of the window at the black mailbox. The one her husband insisted on having. "Yes...well, not really."

"I'm your husband." He stroked his long fingers through her hair. "That's something you should've told me. I never could understand that bond you have with Tony."

"What did you expect me to do? If I would've told you I was raped, would you still love me?" she asked, turning to stare at their house. A tear inched down her face.

"Of course, I would love you. I married you for you, *not* for what happened to you." He covered his face with both hands—again.

Tiffany gasped for air. "How *could* I tell you, Vance?" She lifted her hand to her temple. "You walked around saying how you were the luckiest man alive to marry a virgin." A tear rolled down her face. "You thought I was a virgin."

"I *thought* I had married a woman who would never lie to me."

She glared at him, saying, "Everyone lies at one time or another. All of us have to tell lies one day." She stared out at her neighbor's mangy dog.

313

"My lies are all out in the open now. Whether you like it or not. Whether I like it or not."

Chapter 47

Sunday morning, Tiffany sat in her sunroom, reading *The Charlotte Observer* and sipping on a glass of green tea. "Peace," one of Juanita Bynum's songs, flowed out of the little clock radio by the flower vase on the table. A blue jay flew past the window, perched on the ledge of the bay window and began chirping its morning song. Boat engines on the lake revved up as they zoomed past her house.

The sunroom was the perfect place for her to relax, read and look out at the lake. Eastern Whitebud trees, blue petunias and pink and yellow roses outlined with the crystal clear water combined for a stunning view in her backyard.

The phone rang. At first, she didn't bother to get up, thinking Vance would answer, then remembered that he had left out earlier.

"Good morning, Tiffany. How are you?"

"I'm doing much better. How about yourself?"

"I'm glad somebody's ended the nightmare in Cloverdale," Tony said. "Have you read the morning paper?"

"Yes, I saw the article on Smith in there. Just because some of the truth is spilling out, doesn't mean the nightmare's over." Tiffany snapped the obituary section out in front of her. "Who knows? Maybe another officer will pick up where he left off."

"I heard Sergeant Clark is going to take over," Tony said. "That's the best news I've heard all day."

Tiffany looked down at her wedding ring. "I've been through a lot the last couple of days."

"I know," Tony said, breathing deeply in the phone. "When the news said you were brought in for questioning, I rushed down to the station."

315

Her bay window vibrated as the hovering noise from her neighbor's lawnmower bounced against it.

"What possessed you to walk in and lie like that?" Her flow of words stopped, then slowly returned. "How could you turn yourself in and you didn't even know all of the facts, Tony?" She snapped. "You didn't even consider that falsely confessing to Smith's murder could lead to you going to prison and your children growing up with their father!"

Tony paused before speaking as if Tiffany's words had forced him to accept the reality of his actions. "Why didn't you call and tell me you had to go in for questioning?"

Tiffany closed the newspaper and sipped her tea. "I didn't want you to get involved."

"*Involved*? You know I couldn't take seeing you in prison."

She winced. "You knew they would find out you were lying."

"That was a chance I was willing to take."

The sunlight streamed in through the window. Tiffany leaned back in the chair, propping her foot on the armoire.

"I'm going to Smith's funeral."

"Why?" Tiffany pulled herself to an upright position.

"I want to see them put his trifling behind in the ground."

She gnashed her teeth as she stared at Sergeant Smith's name printed in bold letters on the paper. Her mind flashed back to when Smith's blood spurted on her and June Bug. She shivered in disgust. "I might go to the funeral too," she snapped while sneering.

"What!" Tony flinched.

"I need to make sure that *piece of trash* doesn't resurrect," she grappled.

A puzzled look stretched across Tony's face before he asked, "Did you kill him?"

316

Silence flowed from Tiffany's lips.

"Did you dismember and mangle him?" Tony's eyebrows connected.

"Medical school taught me a lot about bodies. But his body wasn't *worthy* of any surgical procedure." Tiffany glanced at her hands.

"Don't *play* games, Tiffany. I have no time for your rhetoric." Tony snapped. "I'm trying to help you."

"I'm sure there were probably a lot of people *competing* to slice up his *corrupt body* in that alley." Tiffany sneered before a small chuckle leaped from her mouth. "Maybe the wild animals had a feast with his body," she said while glancing out the window. "I heard the city has a big issue with the wild animals attacking people near the park and alley."

Tony frowned. "I guess you're not going to answer my questions."

Tony's head shifted from side to side. "Where is Vance?"

"He's downtown taking care of a few things."

"On a Sunday?"

"He has a meeting with the detective and the district attorney tomorrow."

Silence filtered through the phone. Depression settled on her shoulders as if bricks were on them, causing her lips to grow slack and her gaze to level with the floor.

"I'm on my way over there."

"You don't have to, Tony." She propped her elbow on her knee, pressing her hand onto her forehead. "I'm okay."

"No, you aren't. I'm on my way. I'm bringing mama with me."

Good Lord. Just what she needed.

Chapter 48

An hour later, a knock on the door startled Tiffany out of a catnap.

As the French door slowly opened, Tony glanced up at the crystal chandelier dangling in Tiffany's foyer.

"How are you, baby?" mama asked, wrapping her arms around Tiffany's small frame.

Mama sighed, holding in her tears.

"I'm doing much better."

"I don't think so," mumbled Tony. "I know you better than Vance does," Tony said as he drew closer. "I can see it all over your face."

Tiffany buried her face into her brother's chest. He walked her over to the sofa.

Rocking back and forth on her brown leather sofa, she gripped a soft cream pillow in her hand. Tiffany told her story, releasing the pain and fear she held for years. Tears dripped onto Tony's linen shirt.

Mama leaned forward, grasping her daughter's hands. "Baby, you should've told me." She tilted her head toward the ceiling. "I'm your mama."

"I was ashamed," she mumbled in a soft low voice.

"Ashamed, precious? There's nothing under the sun that you can't tell me."

"Shhh, it's all over now," Tony said, grabbing their hands. "If I were you, I would go to the funeral. You need closure."

"I don't think I can do that."

"The man's dead now, Tiffany. He can't hurt you anymore," Mama said as tears fell onto her white dress.

Tiffany's gaze fell on the backyard, following a rabbit hopping along the freshly mowed grass. She couldn't imagine leaving her husband and family, much less serving time in prison. But if the district attorney had his way, she would do just that for the next eighty years. Only with Vance's expertise and pulling a few strings was she permitted to go home. They had to put up the house to do it.

"Tiffany," mama called out, shaking her shoulders gently. "Tiffany."

"Yes, mama?"

Mama dropped her head as she reached for their hands. "Lord, I need you right now," Mama said as tears sprinkled down her brown face. "My children need you. We need you to move in favor of our lives. The devil is trying to attack my family." Mama stretched her hands in the air, lifting both of her children's hands as well. "Lord, I'm calling to you beyond the gates of heaven for you to help my daughter through this tribulation and to comfort my son."

Minutes later, mama sat down, leaned back in the chair and mumbled another silent prayer. She raised her head and dried her tears. "Don't worry. I can feel God's presence, baby."

Tony walked to Tiffany's photo stand. A grin spread across his handsome face when he looked at one picture in particular—a picture that he begged her to cut up more than once. Thirteen-year-old Tony stood in the center row of his basketball team. His legs were ashy, he had an Afro the size of a watermelon and his tennis shoes were ripped on the side.

"Don't try to take that picture like you did last time," Tiffany uttered as her lips lengthened into a smile. "I'd hate to have to string you up to get it back."

He looked down at the photo again, a bitter smile on his lips. "All of our lives, we have worked hard for everything we have. We didn't deserve to be treated like trash. Especially by the likes of Smith." Tony paused as though searching for the right words to say, then poured out his own pain, sharing his

319

dreadful story about Smith. "Tiffany, I'm here for you. It shakes my soul to know that you were taken advantage of ...."

Tiffany spaced out again, wondering how she would tell Vance the full story.

"Tiffany. Tiffany." Tony shook her back to the present. "Don't do this to yourself. It wasn't your fault what he did to you."

"I know. Both of you are right." Tiffany fumbled with her slender fingers. "I went to counseling and I thought I had gotten over my pain and fears. But when they brought Christy in that day, everything came back. And every time an innocent little girl was brought in, the nightmares came back, too." Her heart seemed to melt with pain. "The rapes got worse and worse. I was afraid that soon I wouldn't be able to keep the next one alive."

Mama planted a kiss on her forehead. "Tiffany, did you kill him?"

Silence.

"Did . . . your uncle June Bug kill him?"

Silence.

"Tiffany, just tell us." Tony blinked as his eyebrows gravitated toward his hairline. "If you did, I'll find a way to put it off on me. If you didn't, I can start looking for the real killer."

Tiffany flashed back for a few seconds. She remembered standing over Smith's body, watching his blood flow onto the ground. The gun dropped out of her hand. June Bug slowly stood, holding Smith's gun in his hand. Smoke wafted from the barrel. Her uncle's eyes were stretched wider than saucers and his jaws separated in disbelief.

"Don't say that," Tiffany said as she balled up on the couch.

"You mean more to me than anything else," he said softly. "I don't want to see you behind bars. He stole something from me. He stole something from you. You didn't deserve that. You weren't like all of those other girls in the projects. The thought of knowing that Sergeant Smith . . . that Sergeant

Smith . . . raped you, makes me want to dig him up after he's placed in the ground...."

Once again silence drifted in the air.

Mama mumbled another prayer as she grabbed Tony's wide hand.

Tony exhaled slowly as he stared at Tiffany. "If you . . . if you killed him, tell me."

Tiffany closed her eyes. "You have a wife and kids. Don't do anything stupid."

"I'll do whatever it takes to clear your name." Tony stood, extended his hand to their mother and they left.

Chapter 49

"Good morning, Heather. What brings you over here this early?" Tiffany asked.

Heather glared angrily. "I'm looking for *Anthony*. I shouldn't have to search for my husband on a Sunday morning."

"He's not here. But you're welcome to come in."

Heather stormed through the French door with one hand on her hip.

"How are you doing?"

"*I'm* doing well," she said, her tone even snappier than before.

"How are the children?"

"They're doing all right. Enough small talk." She said in a short tone. "Where is Anthony?"

Heather would explode if she knew Tony had left an hour ago to take their mother to Cloverdale.

"Why would I know? Isn't he at home?"

Heather followed Tiffany to the kitchen. "No, as usual, he's probably out taking care of something for *you*."

Tiffany turned to her sister-in-law. "I'm sorry. Did the world catch you in a bad mood?"

"Listen, Tiffany," the woman snapped. "I don't mean to rain on your parade but Anthony's married now. He has a new family."

"I know he's married, Heather. I was there when he made that mis—
"

Heather's head whipped up.

"—when he did the deed," Tiffany replied, grinning. She leaned over on the counter.

"You know, you need to stop calling our house so much."

Tiffany pulled out a brass chair from the table and sat down. Her gaze fell onto Heather's mismatched tennis shoes.

"I didn't think it was a problem for me to call him. He's my brother," Tiffany said, pressing a glass of orange juice to her lips. She didn't waste her time offering breakfast to Heather, knowing the ungrateful woman would reject it.

"Calling every *day*? That's ridiculous."

"Heather, what do you have against my relationship with my brother?"

Heather paused, took in a deep breath and blew it out as if a birthday cake had materialized in front of her. "You don't have to check up on Anthony *every* day and you don't have to report to him like some little kid." She rolled her greenish-brown eyes. "You have your own life to live now. You *are* married." She sneered. "Unless there's something you're not getting from your husband …."

The timer on the oven started beeping. Tiffany stood, turned off the oven, pulled out her biscuits and returned to her seat. "Excuse me. I know I'm a married woman. Do you?" Tiffany forced some eggs into her mouth. "Don't try to jump down my throat because you can't find your husband. Maybe if you'd learn to cook that might keep him home."

"Maybe I could if you'd stop calling him *all the time*. You take up too much of my husband's day. He's always running to rescue you." Heather banged her fist against the glass table. The crystal vase jumped in response. "Now there's this new *saga* with the police. I will not allow you to drag my husband into your problems."

"Excuse me?" Tiffany dropped her fork. It clattered on the plate. "What's wrong with you, Heather?"

"I don't owe you an explanation."

"You know what? I've gone out of my way to keep peace with you. We used to get along so well, especially when you were trying to get Tony to the altar. What's changed that? The fact that he said, I do?"

"Like I said before," Heather snapped, "I don't owe you an explanation. Anthony's not your father, he's not your husband, and he's *certainly not* your lover unless something's going on here that I don't know about . . . ."

"Well, there's something that you don't know," Tiffany said resuming her meal. "I betcha I know where my husband is. Do you?"

Hopefully, Vance would come in and rescue her from this deranged woman.

Heather gnashed her teeth.

Tiffany slid a forkful of grits into her mouth.

"I would know where mine is if you stop calling *my* house. You need to stay out of my marriage. Anthony doesn't need your advice on what goes on in *our* house. He doesn't ask for your two cents when he wants some *nookie.*"

Tiffany rolled her eyes. "I'm sure he could've found better."

Heather winced. "I'm sick of this *mess.* Do you know why I can't stand you?"

"Please enlighten me," Tiffany said with the wave of a hand.

"Anthony communicates with you more than with me. He can't even *fart* without asking for your opinion. That's *why* I can't stand your ass. Who does he think you are?"

Tiffany picked up her napkin, dabbed at the corners of her lips and balled it up, clenching it with a tight grip. "I've been holding back, but I'm not going to bite my tongue anymore. Tony is a good man. You treat him like he's a child. He goes out of his way to make you happy. You'll never find another man that will put up with your *foolishness.*"

"What!" Heather stood and forced her chair under the table, scraping it against the marble floor.

Tiffany stood right with her. "Heather, I feel sorry for you because you aren't close to your sisters and brothers, but I've known Tony a lot longer than you have. And I'll be here after you're gone . . . ."

"Whatever." Heather waved her hand in the air.

"If your family was close, then you'd understand that family is always there for each other. Maybe if you didn't have such a *nasty* attitude, you'd figure that out."

"What . . . what are you talking about?"

"Come on, Heather, stop playing games. I see right through you. Tony might not see it, but I know deep down inside you wish you had the same type of relationship with your siblings."

"You're crazy."

Tiffany squinted. "Am *I,* Heather?" She clamped her jaws together. "Easy enough for you to hide behind the fairytale life you had as a child. With all of the money, private schools, nice cars and fancy house your parents had, it's a shame you turned out this way. I guess money can't buy happiness—or class."

The lines on Heather's forehead wrinkled. "How dare you! How *dare* you! You know what?" She pointed her small finger at Tiffany as she glared. "I can fix *all of this*. Don't call my house *anymore*."

Tiffany shook her head, laughing. "Listen, Heather, I don't know how you were raised. But even though we didn't have all the fancy things you grew up with, we had the one thing that surpasses everything." Tiffany flushed some orange juice down her throat, but still maintained eye contact with Heather. "Unconditional love."

Heather blew out a long, slow breath. "Don't call my house anymore."

"*Your* house? Strange. I thought it was a house that belonged to you *and* Tony. Get your head on *straight*, woman."

Heather headed towards the front door, Tiffany trailing behind.

Tiffany sighed. "Listen, Heather, I don't want to argue with you."

"What's there to argue about?" Heather snapped around as she opened the door. "You know you're jealous of me."

Tiffany whooped with laughter, doubling over in front of the fuming woman. "You could've fooled me because I certainly would never be jealous of you—by any stretch of the imagination."

"You're still holding a grudge because I didn't allow you to deliver your niece and nephew."

Tiffany laughed again. "Heather, you can seek medical treatment wherever you please." Tiffany placed her hand over her chest. "But yes, I asked myself that day why you didn't choose me. When Vance and I have children, I would love for you to be their pediatrician." Tiffany's eyes narrowed. "If you ever stop playing games and get rid of that snobby attitude."

Sunlight beamed past the French door, shining into the foyer. Her neighbor's kids played outside, laughing as they ran through a water sprinkler.

"Your kids? *Your* kids?" This time Heather let out a small, bitter laugh of her own. "Tiffany, you're the one who needs to stop playing games. You know you can't have kids." She sneered. "You need to go to a fertility specialist . . . or find a surrogate mother," chuckled Heather.

Tiffany paused. Anger shot through her like a cannon.

"*Excuse* me?" Tiffany slammed her front door, barely missing Heather's foot, but then it bounced back. "I don't know where you got that information but Vance and I have decided to wait."

"*Girl . . . whatever!*" Heather swung the door open—again and stepped out on the porch. "Maybe you need to examine yourself and find out why you can't get pregnant. That'll keep you busy, *Mrs. OB-GYN.*"

"What needs to be examined is your head. But it may be too far up your *tail* to find. Did you hear what I just said? Vance and I aren't ready for children. I'm mature enough to know that we needed some time to grow closer, rather than springing out children back-to-back trying to get a man to marry me."

The olive-skinned woman flushed red, glaring at Tiffany.

"What's wrong with you? I want to talk to the *old* Heather. The Heather I used to know. The one who was happy and had some common sense. I'm not trying to put you down." Then she paused, saying, "Well, if the shoe fits . . . ."

Heather blinked as sun rays struck the right side of her face.

Tiffany waved her hand in the air as her neighbor drove past her apartment, blowing his horn.

"I wanted us to be close like we were before. But you're making that impossible. Right now, I need all the support I can get."

Heather grimaced. "Whatever. Don't involve Anthony in your *drama*," she said, brushing past Tiffany heading for the front door again.

Tiffany pressed her body against the wall, too angry and hurt to do anything.

Chapter 50

Monday morning, bright clouds stretched across the sky. The thought of Tiffany going to prison made Tony's heart race. His hands began to shake as he sat in his truck. Suddenly he felt as helpless as the day Tiffany had fished him out of the water.

He glanced over at the community center, contemplating his next move.

Tony picked up his cell and called the dental office.

"Good morning, Doctor Brown's Office."

"Good morning, Mrs. Spinks."

"Hello, Dr. Brown," she said cautiously. Tony pictured the old woman checking her Swiss watch, realizing that he was more than a little bit late.

"I need you to cancel all of my appointments today. I have to take care of some things."

"Yes, sir." She cleared her throat. "I'll take care of that."

"Thank you, Mrs. Spinks."

"Are you okay, Dr. Brown?"

Tony shifted in the driver's seat. "Yes, everything's right as rain."

"Tell Tiffany I'll keep her in my prayers."

"I will."

Tony got out of his truck, locked the doors and walked into the community center and soon extended his hand to the office manager. "Mr. Floyd, thank you for meeting with me."

"I can't believe they're trying to frame little Tiffany with the sergeant's murder," Mr. Floyd said barely above a whisper.

"Me, neither." Tony looked down the brightly lit hallway toward Smith's office. "Mr. Floyd, I need to get in his office."

The pale-skinned man with a beer belly the size of an oven, leaned forward, whispering, "Tony, I want to help you . . . but you know I can't do that."

Tony looked around. The small brown desks were empty.

"Mr. Floyd, please let me go inside."

"I'll lose my job."

Tony leaned against the desk. "You know my sister's not a murderer."

"I know."

"Help me, Mr. Floyd. Now you know there's a lot you let slip by when we were kids. You know he wasn't right and you didn't say a word."

The pleasant scent of Lysol breezed across Tony's nose.

"What do you think you'll find in his office?" Mr. Floyd asked, squinting.

"I don't know but it's worth trying. He was a dirty cop and you know that."

Mr. Floyd dropped his head. "Look," he said, glancing around. "I go to lunch at 11 o'clock today. I won't be back until about four hours later. I have a meeting at the main office. I'm supposed to leave my keys in that box for the maintenance man today." Mr. Floyd turned and walked into his office without a backward glance.

Tony strolled down the hall to Smith's office. A yellow strip of tape crossed the doorway, saying, POLICE INVESTIGATION. DO NOT ENTER.

Tony gripped the metal handle, looked over his shoulder and twisted to the right. Nothing. He would need that key.

Tony rushed outside and ran to his mother's apartment. He had thirty minutes before Mr. Floyd would leave the building. He couldn't wait in the car that long. Someone was bound to get suspicious.

"Who is it?"

"It's me, mama."

The door squeaked as she pulled it open. Pink rollers were the first thing Tony saw when she stepped across the threshold. Mama had on her favorite red apron with flour sprinkled on the front. Her weathered hands were covered with dough. The delicious smell of buttermilk biscuits filtered through the house.

"Hey, mama."

She turned to him, smiling. "Hello, baby. Why aren't you at work?"

"I came over here to talk to Mr. Floyd."

She froze, looking up at him. "About what?"

Tony bit his lip. Telling his mother the truth would make her worry. But he didn't want to lie to her. "I have to find a way to help Tiffany."

Mama's lips trembled. Tony wrapped his arms around his mother's small frame. The dough stuck to his black shirt. Heather would have a hard time getting that out.

Gospel music traveled from the living room into the kitchen through the small stereo Tony had bought for her.

"Mama, don't worry." Tony wiped her tears. "I'm going to find a way to help her."

"Tiffany has worked so hard. She doesn't deserve this. She isn't a murderer."

Tony gently placed his hand on his mother's cheekbones. "Everybody knows that, mama."

"Tiffany's a good girl. God, please help her!" Mama shouted, dropping to her knees and saying a prayer. Tony kneeled beside his mother.

Mama pressed her hands on the table as she stood. Tony grabbed her arm to give a little support.

When she ended, she asked, "What's Vance doing about all of this?"

"Thanks to him Tiffany's not in jail. If it weren't for him, they would have her booked and in a cell right now. Vance and Allen are on the case."

Mama wiped her face as she sat down. "Did Tiffany tell you someone threw a brick through the window in her living room?" Tony's jaws slowly parted. Before he could respond, mama said, "And someone put a dead cardinal in her mailbox."

The thought of someone threatening Tiffany made Tony's blood pump rapidly through his veins.

Words leaped out of his mouth. "Why didn't she tell me?" His hand clenched into a fist. "Nobody's gonna hurt her, mama. Nobody. I'll make sure of that."

Mama looked towards her ceiling and held her hands together. "Lord, please help my baby."

"Mama, don't worry about me. I'll be all right."

Chapter 51

Two hours later, Tony rushed out the back door to the community center, a few pounds heavier than when he had come in earlier. Mama had served up a tasty breakfast, enough to make him want to curl up on the couch for a nap. Maybe he'd have to join Tiffany for a jog, especially if he made a visit to mama an everyday thing.

As he passed the silver mailboxes and the park, his heart pounded.

Tony slowly opened the center's door, poking his head inside. Voices from people down the hallway reached his ears. Cautiously, he tiptoed to Mr. Floyd's drop box and snatched the keys. Glancing around, he sighed, trying to calm his shaking hands and wiped a bit of sweat from his forehead.

Tony quickly slid the key into the lock and opened Smith's door, leaving it cracked. Then he quickly returned the keys just in case the maintenance man came before he finished searching the office.

Smith's office was dark and messy. Tony opened the blinds slightly, allowing some sunlight to enter since he couldn't turn on the lights. Magazines and newspapers were stacked up in a corner. Starbucks cups were piled up in the trashcan. The brown desk was cluttered with papers and an empty cigarette pack. The small blackboard on the wall listed community events and monthly meetings. Smith's college degree and certificates from the police department were framed along the wall. The stale scent of Old Spice lingered in the air and for a minute, Tony felt as if he looked over his shoulder, he would find Smith standing at the door.

The desk had been positioned directly in front of the window. The blinds were slightly bent in the middle as if the sergeant peeked out of them a great deal. Tony rambled through the drawers. Files were scattered everywhere. Yellow sticky notes were posted on several papers. Business cards marked with various symbols were in his desks. Tony quickly tried to piece together what the symbols meant, but couldn't. So he put the cards back in place for now.

Searching the files cabinets and trashcan proved fruitless. Scratching his head, he plopped down in Smith's chair and stared out the window. People on The Hill were mingling with the regulars and traffic flowed in and out of the alley like opening night at a talent search convention.

After another search, Tony's gaze darted around the office. His fist struck the desk. Time had moved so quickly and this would be his only chance. Mr. Floyd wouldn't allow him to come in again, no matter how much the man wanted to help Tiffany. He stood, kicking the side of the desk, causing it to slide. Pain shot through his foot, forcing him to double over. But that paled in comparison to the disappointment weighing on him. He had failed Tiffany again.

He winced, holding Tiffany's pain deep in his heart.

As Tony dropped down to take off his shoes and give his aching foot a little relief, he noticed a tiny piece of paper poking out of a small crack in the ceramic tiled floor. He lowered to the ground, forgetting all about his aching foot. Yes, it was from *under* the tile, not just lying on the floor.

A ray of sunshine whisked away his disappointment.

With all of his strength, Tony pushed the wide brown desk away. The ceramic tile had a small hole about the size of a quarter, enough for someone to stick a finger inside and lift it up. Tony ran over to the blinds, opening them all the way, before peering down into the hole.

Sticking a slender finger inside, he lifted the tile, opening to show a small drop box below. Tony lifted the large metal box, barely taking a breath as he opened the inside, finding surveillance tapes, receipts and log-sheet. Tony looked at the index on the tapes, some were as old as five, ten and fifteen years ago. Although the log-sheet was written in code, someone had to know how to figure it out.

Tony rushed over to the trashcan, searching for a bag. Cigarettes and stale coffee odors leaped out the trashcan into his nose, causing him to draw back.

Finally, he ripped the plastic off the newspapers that were stacked up in the corner. Tony dropped the tapes and log in the bags, put the tiles back in place, slid the desk to a point that it totally covered Smith's secret hiding place, and strolled away without a backward glance.

Chapter 52

Wednesday morning, the sun peeked through the trees shining onto Tony's porch as a warm gentle breeze swept the leaves.

The doorbell rang, echoing from a white box mounted in the hallway. Tony ran down the stairs to greet his guest. To Heather's dismay, he had stayed up all night waiting for David to arrive. Even though he and his cousin had not seen each other much since they left Cloverdale, they still managed to keep in touch, often discussing joyful times and glossing over painful memories.

David was now the director of a computer engineering company in Chicago.

Every time they talked, David would try to extract a promise that Tony, his wife, and children would come visit him. It hadn't happened in three years and Tony doubted if Heather would ever consent to the trip.

David's honey brown complexion, trimmed mustache and faded haircut almost mirrored Tony's.

"What's up, David?" Tony said, hugging his cousin. "Man, I'm glad you came. There's so much that's been going on I don't know where to begin."

"I know, man." A faint smile flashed on his face. "I'm here to help," David said, his voice much deeper than Tony remembered.

"You got a cold, man?"

"I've got a toothache."

"Oh, well, I can take care of that."

"Not on this trip," David said, pressing his hand against his jaw.

Tony groaned. "Not you, too. I get enough of that from people who don't know me."

David grinned. In college, his looks automatically granted him entrance to panties on North Carolina A&T State University's campus and the surrounding suburbs. But now he was a married man with three kids and lived a faithful, committed life. At least that's what he told Tony.

"You know I have to support you and Tiffany," he said trailing behind Tony. "You guys are family."

"They're still questioning Tiffany about his death."

David paused, casting a hasty glance at his cousin. "Do you think she had something to do with it?"

"If you asked me a couple of weeks ago, I would've said no. But after what I just found out, I'd say I'm not sure."

"Man, I dropped the telephone when you told me Smith had hurt her." David stared at Tony for a few seconds as he stood motionless. "Did she tell you everything?"

Tony could feel his heart slowly beating.

"Smith did some cruel things to people," David said.

"Don't *we* know?" Tony exhaled slowly. "I went to his funeral yesterday."

"Yesterday? Why so quick."

"Man, you know they have to put white folks in the ground before they start changing colors."

David let out a little laugh.

"Tiffany went too."

Silence flowed from David's mouth as if disbelief had stolen his words for a few seconds before he asked, "Why?"

"I wanted to make sure that sick *monster* was dead. I guess Tiffany did too. A lot of Cloverdale tenants were there. Somebody said his children refused to come. There's no telling what he did to them."

David's eyes widened. Tony escorted him to his living room.

Glancing around, David held his fist out for Tony to give him some pound. "Man, you're living in a palace."

"What can I say," Tony said with a slight smirk.

"What's on the tapes, Tony? I brought my equipment so I can make copies and a web link."

"I couldn't see all of them because some were beta and others VHS."

"Don't worry; my equipment can work wonders."

Tony frowned. "Smith was a weird person. He filmed himself having sex with girls in Cloverdale and with prostitutes."

"Is Tiffany on there?"

Tony closed his eyes, exhaling deeply.

David stopped in his tracks.

The burnt, scorching smell of grits drifted to the living room. Tony dashed to the kitchen. David followed. Tony snatched the pot off the stove, pressed the circulation vent and threw the grits away.

"I see you're still trying to cook." David giggled.

Tony glanced over his shoulders. "Man, that's a long story."

"Where is your computer?"

"Come on. Let's go downstairs."

The large flat-screen television, surround-sound system, wet bar and pool table brought a grin to David's lips. "Technology has certainly improved since the days when your mother had two televisions sitting on top of one another."

"Yeah." Tony chuckled. "We had to listen to one and watch the other." Tony yawned. "Mama still uses them. She barely looks at the new one we've bought her." Tony reached behind the sofa. "As soon as we can archive what's on these tapes, I'll feel a lot more comfortable turning them in. Evidence comes up missing all the time and we *are* talking about one of the

Charlotte police department's own. They'd certainly want to cover this up, too."

Tony pulled the tapes out of the bag. "Check this out. He has surveillance tapes of his officers committing crimes."

"Like what, Man?"

"Drug trafficking, rape, robbery and so on."

David glanced at all the tapes, shaking his head. "Yeah, I've got to archive them first." David assembled his equipment. "Don't worry; when I'm finished these tapes can be seen all over the world. It'll only be a matter of clicking on a link to the hidden pages on my website."

"Let's hope it doesn't come to that."

"Yeah, Officer Jenkins is on one of those tapes," Tony said, flopping on the black chair. "He's messing around with Courtney Foster."

"Are you serious? He's about fifty now. She's about what? Sixteen? I remember when she used to come to the community center. We were seniors when she was in first grade. We used to tutor her at the center."

"I figured I could talk to him." Tony raised one eyebrow. "You know, make a deal with him."

David squinted. "You mean blackmail him?"

"I've got to help my sister. Now, I'm sure Officer Jenkins doesn't want his wife to find out." Tony grimaced. "Officer Jenkins is in love with Courtney. I'm not kidding. Wait until you see how he's hugged up on her. I couldn't believe it. You should see how she's kissing him on the tapes. You remember he used to be fat. He's lost a lot of weight. Probably trying to stay in shape to keep Courtney under his wings. But he still has a low-cut hairstyle and a round dark brown face."

David released a gust of warm air. "His wife is white, right?"

"And she's the mayor!"

"Man, this is getting deep," David said. "What about the other officer who patrols Cloverdale?"

Tony turned on the radio. Jazz vibrated out of the speakers.

"Man, you better get some real music up in here. Turn on some R&B." David giggled. "Hey, what about the other officer?"

"I'm not trying to turn in the other officers on these tapes. Officer Price is so heavy in drug trafficking he might have us killed if we put this out. I figured Jenkins is the only one I can talk to."

"What about Officer Clark? You remember how he used to act like he was a Saint."

"He's a sergeant now." Tony scratched his head. "He's the only officer that isn't on these tapes."

Tony handed David another stack of tapes.

"Maybe Smith never caught him doing anything wrong," David said, sitting at the computer. "Maybe he really did have a clean nose. If so, he's the only one so far."

"If you ask me, after looking at some of the tapes, I think Officer Clark probably was the *only* good officer patrolling Cloverdale."

"He should've been the sergeant for Cloverdale."

"Oh, yeah—Smith was crazy. He would talk to himself as he watched his officers commit crimes. Man, check this out—he would stand in front of the camera and brag about crimes he committed as if he was counseling himself, making a confession."

"Sick bastard."

Fifteen minutes later, Tony and David started watching the tapes. Tony sat on the edge of the chair. He gnawed on his lips. Blood rushed through his veins. David's eyes widened as his mouth hung open.

David popped in another tape.

"I can't believe Smith's gonna make Pee Wee suck his . . . Ah, noooo." Tony pounded his fist in the chair. "I didn't know he smoked dope. I remembered when he stole a chain from a jewelry store. The owner said a lot of items were taken. Now, I see who Pee Wee gave the jewelry to."

"I remember." David pressed a button on his computer. "Seems like Smith enjoyed blowjobs no matter who was giving them."

Gray lines flashed across the screen. David pressed another button to adjust the perception.

"Who is this lady, Tony?"

Tony squinted. "That's Mrs. Ruth. She has a thing for young men. She's about fifty-five. But she likes guys between twenty-one to . . . thirty-five. At least, that's what I heard."

David winced. "I don't remember her. Why is she handing Smith money?"

Tony stood, pointing at the screen. "Look...Look, he's handing her a bag of weed."

David leaned back. "That's *a lot* of weed."

Tony shook his head. "I can't believe this. Mrs. Ruth sold dope?"

"Look at this. She's not the only tenant Smith forced to sell dope for him." David sighed. "Just like he pulled us into that robbery." He scratched his head. "Why did Smith record all of this stuff?"

Tony handed David another tape. "Who knows? Seems like he was psychotic or something."

David continued to record the tapes. Smith was definitely a treacherous man.

"Look at this . . . why is he monitoring Classic Touch?" Tony asked. "What's that?"

"A place that Devin owns. You know Smith framed him."

"Yeah, I know," David said. "He's walked around there three times. Is he gonna rob it or something? What's that black thing in his hand?"

Tony squinted. "I'm not sure."

Tony and David viewed several tapes. Tony slumped in his chair. Smith had filmed them stealing the appliances out of his cousin's store.

A few hours later, Tony sat on the sectional chair in the den staring at the blank television screen. "You know, when you first came, you asked me if I think she killed him and I said I'm not sure. But if you asked me now, I'd tell you I'm sorry she beat me to it."

David leaned back on the chair. "Why didn't his officers realize he was on the edge?" He shook his head. "I guess they were too busy doing their own dirt."

Tony exhaled deeply. "Tiffany said she believes he's behind the rapes of the little girls and I believe her. You saw how many high school girls he raped? Going younger wouldn't be a stretch for him."

"I still can't imagine Tiffany killing him." David popped his knuckles. "Not Tiffany. Maybe another girl or dude from Cloverdale."

"Me neither. But you know me, man. I even went in and tried to take the blame so that they'd send her home while she gave her husband enough details to find the truth."

"Man, they could've locked your *crazy* tail up for giving false information."

"I know. But I had called the station and I could hear it in the voice of the officer that they were going to railroad her."

David slipped back onto the leather sofa. "Everybody knows how crazy you are about your sister. Where are the kids? I know they are spoiled rotten."

"They're over a friend's house. And they're no more rotten than your three rugrats."

"Hey, I can't help it if they turned out like you," David shot back. "So where is the boss lady?"

Tony turned the television down, grinning, "I sent her to the spa and told her I had to take care of some things. I ordered the house special so she'll be gone for at least three hours."

David looked around the room. "I'm surprised she wasn't tripping," David said, taking a small sip of lemonade.

"You know she had her words." Tony winked. "Until I told her about the spa."

The phone rang.

David grimaced. "I hope that's not your better half saying she didn't like the services."

Tony laughed, answering.

"Hi, baby," his mother's voice came through. "Did David make it there safely?"

"Yes, mama. He's here."

"Does he still look like his father?"

Tony glanced at David. "Yes, he still looks like uncle June Bug when he was younger—much younger."

David flipped Tony the bird.

Tony giggled, covering the phone whispering, "I'm telling."

David waved him off with a laugh.

"Tell him I said hello. I won't keep you long." Then she paused.

Tony knew that bad news was on the way.

"You know the fingerprints on the gun and the car were matched to Tiffany."

A torch burned in the pit of his stomach. "I'm sure Vance's working to find the truth. Tiffany didn't kill him." But an inkling of doubt lingered in his mind.

"I'll talk to you later, baby."

"Okay, mama. I love you. I'll call you tonight. Do you need me to bring anything over there for Sunday dinner?"

"We'll talk about that later, baby. Go ahead and take care of your business."

Tony turned to his cousin.

David's eyebrows connected. "How's your mother taking all of this?"

"She's handling it okay. All those little girls, the robberies and now murders, I can't believe she won't move."

"Yeah. I can understand how you feel about that. If I had moved June Bug from Cloverdale years ago, maybe he'd be all right by now."

"You still call your dad June Bug?"

"Yes." David's gaze fell on the grayish black carpet. "When has he ever been a dad? Between the family he had with his wife, he never had time for my mother, me and Star." Then David rubbed his massive hands along his navy blue slacks. "But you have to understand after a person has lived a certain lifestyle for a long time it's hard to adjust to a new environment."

"I know, but we're willing to help her learn how. She won't even ask us for money when she needs it. We have to slip it into her purse like criminals in reverse."

David laughed. "Is she still cleaning houses?"

"No, she stopped last year because of the arthritis. It's been bothering her for years. But somehow she manages to keep a smile glued on her face."

"That sounds like the Aunt Lena I know," he said, lifting a black tape off the coffee table. "Now, let's see what's on these tapes."

Chapter 53

Friday morning, Tony strolled down the long, white hallway into the interrogation room Tiffany had been in only a few days earlier. Harsh, staring eyes followed his trail as he passed the bulletproof window. Fingers pointed in his direction and whispers trickled down the hallway as he carried a little black box.

The black uniformed men positioned themselves to get a good look at Tony. He took a seat and waited for Detective Jackson to come for him.

Cold air drifted out the vents onto the back of Tony's neck as he sat in the small padded chair, placing the box on the gray and white ceramic tile floor. Tension crackled in the air, hovering over him like a rain-filled cloud as he slowly raised his eyes. Several officers were glaring down at him. Tony glared right back. He'd already spent the early years of his life being intimidated by one corrupt officer; these knuckleheads didn't have a thing on Smith. Every day, more stories about him were coming out. Things people had suspected for years were now found out to be fact. The officers knew. The chief knew. Everyone knew. But no one did a thing.

"Anthony Brown, Detective Wayne Jackson is ready for you," said a short plump lady who avoided eye contact with him.

Tony grabbed the box, following the woman whose shoulder-length red stringy hair bounced with every step.

"I can't believe he has the audacity to destroy the name of one of our officers," said an officer from a distance.

"This is a bad image for our department. Who does he think he is?" another replied.

The short lady came to a halt, pointed at a door, turned abruptly and disappeared down the hallway. Tony gripped the cold metal doorknob and turned. His heart rate increased. He didn't know what to expect or who would be in the room.

"Good morning, Mr. Brown. Have a seat," Detective Wayne Jackson said in a short, clipped tone. Then the well-built man cleared his throat and picked up an ink pen with his dark brown hand. "Mr. Brown, I have to turn on this recorder. And the cameras are rolling."

Tony stared at the small white machine before nodding.

The detective pressed the button on the recorder.

Tony scanned the dreary and gray interrogation room. A big screen television was off to the end of the room and pairs of blue, brown and green eyes were glued to Tony's brown ones. Everyone from uniformed officers, those in plain clothes and the ones wearing business attire stared fiercely back at him. The bright lights in the back of the room obscured the images of the two men sitting in the far corner. He could only imagine that one of them was Chief Clarence Jones and the other was Mayor Catherine Jenkins. The news was giving the department a hard time.

"Thank you for coming today," Wayne said as he positioned his slender body in the chair.

"I'm glad to be here," Tony said, glancing around the room as he sat down. "But it seems like someone wished I would've stayed home...all four of my tires were *flattened* last night."

The detective leaned back in his chair. "We'll begin when you're ready."

Tony paused, noting the detective's small, bitter smile. "I'm ready now," Tony said, sitting upright.

The door burst open. Bright light streamed in behind two new figures.

"Don't say another word," said a familiar voice.

Angry murmurs rose from others in the group. Tony tried to match the voice with a face, but couldn't right away.

"We're here to represent you," Vance said while walking in behind Allen Pierce, then reached out, trying to take the black box in Tony's hand.

Tony gripped the box. How did Vance know he was coming in today? Only Heather knew that he was coming forward to help Tiffany.

After the detective asked a few preliminary questions, which were answered to his satisfaction, the interrogation continued.

Detective Jackson said hastily, "State your name, please."

Tony paused. Vance glowered at him, dark brown eyes hovering somewhere between deadly and strictly business. A small pinch of anger settled in the pit of Tony's stomach. Why was Vance angry with him?

Tony knew that he would have to pay when this was over. Vance didn't look like he was in much of a mood for explanations. And Tony couldn't tell him everything—not with Tiffany displayed on one of the tapes. That was one tape he and David hadn't watched all the way through. As soon as Smith ripped the blouse from her trembling body and her tear-stained face flashed across the screen, Tony shut it off. As much as he thought he wanted to know, he didn't need to know.

Now he was in the middle of a war zone; the police department versus him. Stepping forward with the tapes was a life-threatening decision. And if he hadn't been sure before, the officers watching him with intense eyes let him know he was on dangerous ground. The officers would never forget his name. God help him if he ever needed them.

"Tony, *give me* the tapes," Vance growled loud enough for him to hear.

"If it's all the same to you, I'd rather keep the tapes for now."

A tall, thin man slammed his hand on the table at the opposite end. "Let's get this show on the road. What's the difference? You'll have to turn them over to us sooner or later." Then the man grinned. "And we'll take good care of 'em, too."

Tony squared his shoulders, leveling a stony gaze at the cocky officer. "I'm sure you will. You've been *covering up* for him for years. You have no idea how much he didn't trust his fellow officers . . . . "

"Tony, shut up!" Vance snapped as a collective groan went up from the people in the room. "That's what we're here for."

Tony flinched. "I didn't call you."

"No, but we're here," Vance shot back. "And if you don't keep your mouth shut you can make things worse than they already are."

"How can I do that? I didn't *do* anything."

Vance leaned in, whispering. "How did you get the tapes, Tony?"

Tony stared at him.

"That's what I'm talking about," Vance flopped in a chair, his navy blue suit tightening around his muscled frame.

To tell the truth, things were a little worse than they were a few minutes ago.

"Hey, are you gonna hand over the tapes or are we just gonna sit on our asses all day?" Chief Jones's gruff voice bellowed in the room. "We've got work to do."

The chief reached over with his long white arm, turning the recorder off as several officers walked out of the room.

"Then go do it," Vance snapped. "We'll take the tapes and give them to the media and you can sort things out later."

"Those tapes don't leave this office," the mayor uttered through her arched pink lips. "This is nonsense and a waste of time."

Tony glared at the mayor. "You won't think that after you see who's on them."

The mayor glanced around the room as she slowly tapped her pen on her notepad. The lines on her white forehead wrinkled with confusion. Her tone of voice changed to a soft one. "What's on the tape?"

"Give me a moment to confer with my client," Vance said. "And if we don't reach some understanding…then I'll let you know."

Vance pulled Tony to a far corner. Allen trailed their footsteps. "What's on the tapes, Tony?"

Tony hesitated a brief moment. "Girls from Cloverdale—little girls, high school girls, prostitutes and surveillance tapes catching some of the officers in this room in the act.…"

Vance gasped, sucking up all the air in the hot room. "Is Tiffany on one of those tapes?"

Tony drew a deep breath, weighing how much to say. "Not on the ones I have here."

"There's something you're not telling us," Allen said, pulling up next to Vance.

Tony grimaced, before saying, "Mayor Jenkins' husband is on one of those tapes."

"Doing what?"

"You don't want to know."

"*Look!*" Vance turned, making eye contact with the mayor. "If we weren't in mixed company, I'd rip you a new asshole, Tony."

Tony glanced across the room. "Stand in line."

They maneuvered back into their chairs. The detective turned the recorder back on. Bright lights turned on when the cameras started rolling.

"What is your name?" the detective asked.

"My name is Anthony Mason Brown."

"Where do you reside?"

Tony sighed wearily. "You guys already know where I live. Let's not waste time."

The detective looked at the chief who said, "Move to the next question."

348

"What's your occupation?"

"I'm a dentist."

The mayor steadily tapped her ink pen on her notepad.

"What's your marital status?"

"Wayne, that's not relevant at this point," Allen said, placing his hand over the microphone.

"What's your purpose of coming in today?"

"I have evidence of Sergeant Paul Smith committing crimes." Tony slowly slid the tapes to Vance.

"How do you know Sergeant Smith?"

"I grew up in Cloverdale. Sergeant Smith was the community patrol sergeant there."

Mitchell Langley, the district attorney asked in a deep voice, "Why would you bring in evidence? What do you hope to get out of this?"

"The department is so out to get my sister that you're slandering her name and ignoring the truth." Tony's gaze fell to each person. "The department needs to know how dirty this man was. I'm not seeking recognition. I want the truth to be told. There's no need in the department to continue to paint him out to be a strictly-by-the-book officer on the news. You all are depriving people of the truth." Tony gritted his teeth. "There have been too many innocent lives destroyed because of this man and you all did nothing. Nothing!

"The people in Cloverdale deserve an apology. I don't think an apology will heal the wounds that are too deep. Those people have been manipulated, blackmailed and tortured." Air filled his jaws as he squinted. "How do you think they feel when they turn on the television and see Sergeant Smith displayed as a hero?"

The chief leaned in, jowls flapping as he asked, "Do you have a personal issue with Sergeant Smith?"

"You don't have to answer that question," Vance said, staring at the detective.

Tony glanced around the room again. A coldness settled into his soul. He could feel the officer's anger directed at him.

"When you think about our police department what comes to your mind?"

"Come on, Detective Jackson. What are you really trying to ask him?" Allen stood, grabbed the box with his thick Ivory fingers, signaling to the district attorney to play the tapes.

As Vance nodded, Tony quietly slipped the tape logs to him. "No, I have no hard feelings about police officers in general. There are some clean-cut officers and some crooked ones. Some of them right here in this room."

Detective Jackson bit down on his pen. He glanced around the room.

"Who do you consider as a clean-cut officer?" Clarence Jones, the chief of police asked, sliding his fingers together so that they pointed under his double chin.

"Sergeant Brian Clark."

Someone in the room coughed, then another and yet another. A code for something. But what?

"How do you know the suspect Lamont Brown?" the district attorney asked.

Tony had to think for a moment. "Lamont Brown? That's my uncle. We don't call him that, though."

"How do you know the murderer, Tiffany Michele Brown?"

Vance jumped up. "Murderer! Detective Jackson, I believe you need to restructure your sentence."

The detective paused for a few seconds, biting down on his ink pen again as he glared at Tony. "How do you know Tiffany Michele Brown?"

"She's my sister."

The room was silent. The chief glanced at Vance, then at Tony. Everyone in the room certainly knew Vance was married to Tiffany. Tony could see in their expressions that they thought Tiffany had killed Sergeant Smith.

"Why do you want us to look at the tapes?" the detective asked.

"The truth must be told. You'll see why you really need to find the real killer and stop trying to frame my sister. You're blasting her in the media and painting Smith to look like a saint. None of you acted on her tips when she said that he was raping and torturing those little girls. We have copies of the reports she filed—"

"Is this why she killed Smith?" the detective asked.

"She didn't kill him!" Tony shouted. "The tapes will show you something you've known about for years."

"Where did you get the tapes?" the district attorney asked.

"Wait a minute." Vance leaned over, whispering to Allen. Then he turned back to Tony. "You can answer."

"In Smith's office."

The chief glowered at his subordinates. "When? That's strange. I have a report stating that the officers searched his office three times."

"Yeah and I bet they reported they *didn't* find anything," Tony said. "To be honest, I don't think they *wanted* to find anything."

"This is worth a thorough investigation," the mayor said, staring at the chief.

Chief Jones swiveled in his seat, glaring openly at the officers and detective who had written the report. "Where did you find the tapes?"

"Out of the floor in his office. These tapes will show everyone the truth."

Wayne asked, "Did you break in his office?"

"Don't answer that," Allen said, glaring at the detective.

Vance cleared his throat. "Detective Jackson, enough with this line of questioning. Can we review the tapes?"

The detective stared at Tony. "Did you break in his office?"

"No, I got the keys from the office manager's tray."

"So, you stole the keys?" the detective asked with a smirk on his thick lips.

"I volunteer at the community center all the time. I've been all over the place. *Anyone* could have picked up those keys at any time. Like the officers who searched the office and missed the evidence in the first place. They didn't need the keys, did they?"

"How did you know that the keys would be there that day?"

Tony looked at Vance and Allen. Vance nodded. "They're there every day. No big deal."

"If you went out of your way to find this evidence how do we know you didn't fabricate the tapes?"

"I'm sure an expert can authenticate them," Allen said as he handed Vance a working pen.

"Look, you can think what you want. But I guarantee when you look at the tapes you'll find out what Smith was up to—what some of the other officers were up to . . . ."

The chief leaned over Detective Jackson's shoulder, whispering. Then the burly man looked at Allen, Vance and then Tony before asking, "Do, you have copies of these tapes?"

Tony looked at Tiffany's husband and winked. Vance smiled and turned to Allen whispering something Tony couldn't quite catch.

Allen then straightened to his full height, twirled his fingers as he grinned at the detective, signaling: move it along, man, move it along.

The tension in the room went up another notch when neither of the men answered the question.

Splinters of My Soul

Tony slid back in the chair. It was gonna be a long Friday morning.

Chapter 54

Tony rushed out of the police department ahead of Vance and Allen, sprinting towards the parking lot. A brisk warm wind wafted by, trailing a delicate scent from the carnations that were lined up on the edge of the sidewalk in front of the police station.

He stood at the curb, waiting as a transit bus passed. A sudden glance left and he froze. Police officers joined him at the curb, keys dangling in their hands. A few of them cut their eyes at him and the ones in the back didn't bother to hide their blunt comments. Tony shrugged as he pulled out his keys. Their reactions didn't surprise him.

The traffic light flashed green. Tony took one step off the curb when a voice yelled behind him, "Wait up, Tony." He pivoted, peering over his shoulders as the officers trailed behind him.

"What's up, man," Vance said, clenching his briefcase. "Why didn't you call me?"

Tony drew back, turning to face oncoming traffic. Muffled conversation among detectives took place as they huddled near a fire hydrant. Tony could see one of them with a notepad and pen, waiting.

The sun blazed against Vance's navy blue business suit, the hot rays caused beads of sweat to form on his chestnut-brown forehead. The day was too hot to deal with foolishness.

"Let's move over here," Vance said, strolling toward a shady area near a large pine tree. "Now, why didn't you call me?"

Tony shrugged. "I didn't need your help."

"Evidently your wife felt a little differently."

Rage shot through him so quickly it took a great effort not to curse. "Why did Heather call you?"

"I'm a lawyer, Tony!" Vance nearly growled his left eyebrow twitching. "Why *else* would she call me?"

His outburst sparked a nerve in Tony. "When I need your help, I'll let you know," Tony said pushing past the man. He'd heard enough of Heather's *bull* that morning. He certainly didn't need more of the same from his brother-in-law. A man who for all the talk in the world wasn't getting Tiffany out of trouble fast enough.

"You needed someone to represent you. Those *bastards*," Vance shouted pointing an index finger towards the police station, "want to fry you right alongside with your sister."

Tony winced.

"So if you have any bright ideas or information that may help her case, you need to come to me not ride off and do *things* on your own."

Tony swallowed hard.

Vance poked a finger in his chest. "Do you know they could have got you on breaking and entering? No matter how you slice it, Tony, you didn't have permission from the investigation squad to go into that office. As a lawyer, I could've helped formulate a better plan for turning those tapes in and used it as leverage to help Tiffany—legally."

Tony glanced over at the officers mingling in a huddle, staring at him. Waiting. But for what? Two officers stood behind his truck with a notepad, writing something. His tag number, of course. Something Tony knew they would do.

Vance rotated a briefcase to his left hand. "Man, I'm only trying to help you. I love Tiffany and I'm trying my best to find out what happened."

"You haven't done enough. Why didn't you have your own team to go into Smith's office?"

"Because there are procedures we have to follow. Legal ones."

Kimberly Morton Cuthrell

"And by that time the tapes would have been long gone and no one would have known about them. They're not playing it legal," he said, nodding to the officers. "They're playing it close to the chest."

Vance punched his briefcase. "You've got to let me know what's going on." Vance drew in closer. "If not, she's going down for this one. Between fingerprints at the scene and God knows what on the rest of the other tapes you're still hiding at home, this is making it harder than it should be." Vance's briefcase slipped out of his hand. He reached down to pick it, casting a wary glance at the men standing across the street. "These cops aren't playing."

"What do you want from me?" Tony said through his teeth. "What do you want me to tell you that Tiffany hasn't already told you?"

Vance paced the grass in a circular motion, one hand in his pocket and the other gripping the briefcase as though it contained top-secret information. "I'm trying to help my wife. But it seems like she's not telling me everything. I need you to help me, man. She seems closer to you than she is to me . . . ."

The musty smell of weed drifted by Tony, his nose twitched. The gall of some punks to smoke that stuff so close to the police station.

"First your sister and then you run off trying to handle things on your own. What's really going on?" Vance stopped long enough to look at Tony. "There're too many secrets between you two. Eventually, I'm going to get to the bottom of this."

Tony shoved his hand into his pockets, pulling his keys back out.

"What's on the other tapes, Tony?"

Tony hesitated.

"You've got to tell me if you want my help."

A quick flash of the images of Tiffany and Smith yesterday made the blood in Tony's veins pump rapidly, causing his heart to pulsate to the point

356

that he felt he was about to pass out. Vance could never know about the tapes. He could never *see* the tapes. Men didn't always take too lightly when their wives have been raped and although Vance was a good man . . . .

Vance stared at Tony. "I've read some of the complaints that Smith raped young girls in the community, among other things . . . ."

Tony turned his head, wishing the pedestrian light would change so he could walk back across the street to his car. As bad as he wanted to tell Vance the truth, he couldn't. Keeping his bond with Tiffany was more important.

Tony bit his bottom lip. "Let me handle this."

Vance snatched his hand out of his pocket. "I, her husband and a lawyer, can't help Tiffany if you don't talk."

Tony squared his shoulders with Vance's. "I said I'll *handle* this."

The men stood like two trees. Not a word passed for a few seconds.

"I'm going to find out what's on those tapes," Vance said as he took four steps away from Tony.

Not if I can help it, Tony thought, exhaling.

Vance stopped in his tracks, slowly turned to face Tony tears welling up in his eyes as he asked in a feeble voice, "How bad did he hurt her? Is that why she's so hard to reach sometimes . . . ."

Tony, tears streaming down his face, reached out and embraced his brother-in-law.

Chapter 55

Tony stormed through the mahogany wood door running past the foyer, the den and the living room.

"*Heather*, where are you?"

The soft scent of Jasmine aromatherapy candles flowed through every room in the house. This time, they did nothing short of irritating him.

"I'm in the kitchen, Anthony."

The one place he didn't expect to find the woman who couldn't cook, clean, or do laundry but could easily shop until they had nothing. Also, the woman who could go behind his back when she felt like it.

Tony walked down the long sunflower-colored hallway, passing her bridal portrait, strolling straight into the kitchen. Clothes tumbled in the dryer, creating a clicking sound that competed with the sounds of the evening news.

Heather sat at the glass rectangular table wearing an orange and royal blue sundress, sipping on a glass of iced tea; *The Charlotte Observer* in her delicate hands. A shaft of light poured in through the window into the kitchen, illuminating her olive skin and tiger eyes. Normally he would consider that illumination a beautiful thing. Right now he was too busy trying not to go off to care.

"Why *did* you call Vance!" Tony forced air out of his nostrils.

Heather turned the page in the newspaper, failing to give him an answer.

"Do you *hear* me talking to you?" he said, gritting his teeth.

She turned another page, took another sip of tea and placed the glass on the soft purple mat a few inches in front of her.

Tony snatched the newspaper out of her fingers. "Why did you tell Vance I was going to the police department!"

Finally, she stared at him, a blank expression in her normally expressive eyes.

His fist pounded the table, causing the tea to splatter over her thigh-high dress. "Answer me!"

Heather pushed away from the table, stood and walked over to the sink. She plucked several paper towels off a spindle, went back to the table and wiped up the mess all without establishing eye contact with Tony.

"What's wrong with you?" Tony inched closer to her. "Do you hear me talking to you?"

"Anthony, you need to lower your voice before you wake up the kids. They're taking a nap." She pressed the latch on the garbage can with her foot and tossed the wet napkins inside. "I called Vance because you rushed off without weighing the consequences. You were in such a rush to help your sister that you didn't think about the consequences of turning in those tapes. What if something happens to you or your family?"

His eyes closed as he shook his head. "Did I ask you to call him?"

"Do you know how much danger you've put yourself in...and me...and the children? Do you?" Heather huffed, propping her hands on her hips. "Your tires were flattened last night and while you were gone this morning someone set a Magnolia tree on fire in the woods behind our house!"

Tony walked to the kitchen window staring at the woods behind his house. He clenched his hand into a fist.

"You needed some type of protection, Anthony."

"*Protection?*" Tony turned sharply, facing his wife. "I've protected myself and my family all of these years and I didn't need Vance." He exhaled. "I'm capable of protecting you and the children."

"How, *Mr. Superman!*" Heather snapped.

A river of blood rushed through Tony's veins.

"Listen, Heather! Yes, I want you and *our children* to be safe." He paused, seriously considering what Heather was saying. "I think I need to send you and the children out of town for a few weeks until things calm down."

"Do you hear yourself, Anthony!" Heather huffed. "We're not going anywhere. This is our home! I didn't know I married an *action-packed* villain. If that was the case, you need to wear your *costume* every day and play with our kids. I'm sure they'll like having a real action figure in their house. Hell, they'll probably want to invite their friends over."

"I see you've got jokes," Tony huffed.

"You're not *Batman* . . . or *Ironman*." She paused. "You are a dentist. You are a husband. You are a father." A tear rolled down her face. "You're about to ruin all of that."

"What do you want me to do, Heather?" Tony asked, softening his tone.

Heather glared at Tony. "I want you to allow your sister to deal with her own problems!"

"Are you serious, Heather?" Tony exhaled. "I have to help her just like I'm aware that I have to protect you and the children."

"That's the problem. You and your family act like you don't need anyone else." She twitched her small lips. "I don't know what to think these days. You've lost sleep, haven't eaten since Tiffany was arrested."

"What do you expect me to do?" Tony leaned against the marble countertop. "You expect me to act like everything's all *right*?"

Heather placed her hands on his beige shirt, pressing them softly to his chest. "Baby, please believe me. I didn't mean any harm by calling Vance. I was scared. I thought you would need Vance to represent you. I didn't know what those officers would do to you."

Cold air drifted out of the vent above Tony's head, cooling his body. "Why did you tell him I found some tapes in Sergeant Smith's office?" Tony applied pressure to his temples. "Why, Heather? Why?"

"I—I thought it would help him defend Tiffany."

The rush of words stopped for a moment.

Tony looked up at the ceiling before taking a deep breath. "How? You don't know what's on those tapes. And since when did you care so much about helping Tiffany?"

She pressed her lips together before wrapping her arms firmly around his waist.

"Please don't get upset." She dropped her head on his chest. "I watched the tapes last night when you were asleep."

Tony pried her slender arms away from his body. He gripped his head and yelled, "You had no right to look at those tapes!" He sat down and placed his face on the table with his hand pressing on the back of his head.

A loud beep echoed into the kitchen from the dryer, signaling that the timer went off.

"*Why* did you look at them?" he said, his voice muffled by the glass on the table. His heart skipped a beat. Now Heather had found out something that Tiffany would practically die if she knew.

"Anthony, I didn't tell Vance what I saw." She placed her palms on his shoulders and slowly caressed them. "I promise, I didn't...I wasn't trying to be vindictive. I just wanted to help. I wanted my husband to come back in one piece," she said, kissing the back of his head.

"I can't believe this."

"I'm sorry for everything, Anthony." She paused for a few seconds while she stroked her fingers along his hand. "We have to help Tiffany."

Tony was silent. He slowly raised his head, turning sharply to her.

Heather grabbed a napkin and wiped the tears from his face as she perched on his lap. "Tiffany needs everyone's support. Not just yours."

Chapter 56

Wednesday morning, Tiffany pulled up in the parking lot in front of the medical center. Her eyes widened. At least a hundred or more people clustered in the parking lot and crowded around the front of the door. Even on a good day, she never got *this* many patients. What was going on?

As Tiffany cruised through the parking lot, heading towards her reserved spot, the crowd dispersed on both sides of her truck, granting her entrance to pass as they all began to clap.

"Tiffany! Tiffany! Tiffany!" they chanted as they waved posters in the air. *You're our hero.*

Tiffany scanned the crowd, trying to identify the people as she slowly pressed on the gas and pulled into her parking space. Several Cloverdale tenants, whose ages ranged from eighteen to seventy years old, mingled with the rest of the crowd. Some hadn't been to the office in ages.

Slowly planting her feet on the freshly paved parking lot, she continued to scan the crowd.

"Tiffany, we're here to support you," Karen said as she wobbled to the vehicle, glancing over her narrow shoulders with her hand gripping the handles of a stroller. Little Nicole waved up at Tiffany. The little brown-skinned girl, with a wide smile and sparkling brown eyes, looked just like Christy. Tiffany looked at the crowd. Smiling faces stared back at her.

"You've given the people in Cloverdale strength to speak out against the things Smith has done for years." Karen tilted her head toward the bright blue sky. "He treated us like animals. He raped my daughter. Christy didn't deserve that."

"Now that the truth is out, those bastards will have to do something about it now!" Mrs. Ruth said, folding her redbone arms across her melon-sized breasts. "We've been protesting in front of the police department every day since we found out that you were arrested." Mrs. Ruth pressed her tiny hands on her wide curvaceous hips. "The media's been there every day, too."

Tiffany blinked. She took long, slow breaths as the words finally penetrated.

"The news reporters keep saying that Sergeant Smith was a good officer, but we've been telling them the real deal. Now people are hearing both sides. All of us can't be making this stuff up!" yelled an old lady in a wheelchair. "I've lived in those projects for over thirty years. Out of all of the police officers who have patrolled there, I've never seen one as cruel as him."

Sirens roared as blue lights flashed from patrol cars that zoomed into the parking lot. The presence of the officers didn't keep the tenants from talking.

Overwhelmed with gratitude, Tiffany covered her face with trembling hands as she pressed her back against her truck. Relief soared through her as she realized it wasn't just about what had happened to her. It was about what had happened to poor people living in the ghetto. Tears dripped onto her white medical jacket. Nurse Petrina rushed through the crowd and wrapped her arms around Tiffany as Nurse Brooks trailed behind her, dabbing Tiffany's face with a tissue.

"We're going to stick by you," Nurse Petrina said, smiling.

"If anyone in the world would understand these people's pain, it's you, Doctor Brown," Nurse Petrina said as she continued to hug Tiffany.

"We've filed at least ninety complaints since yesterday," Mrs. Ruth said, rolling her eyes at the officers who were trying to blend in with the crowd. "Thanks to Tony, now we have copies of all the old ones we put in before." She sneered. "Now they have to believe us. Smith always threatened that he would have me evicted if I spoke out. Well, that bastard can't stop us now, can he?"

The sun shone brighter as if the heavens had opened up and poured every degree of light over the crowd. Tiffany closed her eyes and said, "Thank you, God."

The crowd continued to reveal their secrets as if they were in a support group, encouraging one another.

"I've . . . I've been telling people for years that Smith was an *evil man*." Old Man Jeff said as his words floated out his mouth smoothly for the first time. Old Man Jeff wasn't drunk for the first time that she could remember. "Nobody believed me when I told them that he killed Star. People thought I was a crazy *old drunk*. But I've finally got some help with my drinking problem," he said while pulling a napkin out of his blue jeans and wiping sweat from his wrinkled brown forehead. "And . . . it's about time we tell the world what he did."

A warm breeze swept past her. Tears of joy glided down her cheekbone. A sense of peace flowed through her body. Things will turn out right. Now the man couldn't hurt another little girl. He couldn't hurt anyone anymore.

At the door of the medical center, she turned to address the crowd. "I'm glad you all have the courage to speak out." Her lips lengthened into a faint smile. What she had done was worth it. She could spend her life behind bars, knowing that she had, in some way, helped the people who had supported her for years.

The clapping continued.

"We're on our way to file more complaints," yelled a tall man in the crowd with a deep voice and a scraggly beard. "Thanks to that website and those fangled computers at the center, we've seen some of those tapes."

Tiffany took in a deep breath. Tapes? What tapes? Smith had tapes! Oh, God, she might be on one of those tapes!

"There's no way we'll let you go down without a fight!"

Chapter 57

Saturday morning, Tiffany banged on the mahogany door. The glass above the door and in the bay window rattled each time her fist landed.

"Who is it!" Tony yelled, before swinging the door open. A smile appeared on his brown lips.

Tiffany pressed her hands on her firm hips. The muscles in her face twitched as she frowned.

"How *could* you turn in those tapes without telling me first, Tony!" she shouted, glowering angrily at her brother. "You've exposed me to the world. I wouldn't do you like that."

"Come inside, Tiffany," Tony muttered, trying to pull her inside.

"I'm not staying long." She huffed, folding her arms over her chest and moving out of his reach.

"Calm down."

Her heart was trapped between two brick walls, caving in on her. On one side she had never thought that Tony would betray her, but on the other, she understood his reasons but felt her life had been invaded.

"Calm down and come inside." He scratched his head as his brown eyes narrowed. "You look pissed off. It's too early in the morning for that."

"Don't patronize me, Tony."

Tony took several steps away from the door, tightening the belt on his white robe.

Tiffany stormed past him into the foyer, slamming the door behind her.

The delicious smell of French toast and ham and cheese omelets swept past her. A breakfast that she was sure that Tony had cooked because that wife of his could burn a frozen dinner.

"Tiffany, listen to me."

"For what," she said through clenched teeth. "How could you do me like that?" She glared into his eyes. "Why didn't you show me those tapes before you turned them in?"

"Calm down!" Tony yelled.

"Calm down? How!" She pushed him. "You've allowed the police and everybody to watch something so painful to me. Something I hid for years." Tiffany gasped for air as her eyes filled with tears. "How could you let them see me on that tape." She blinked her eyes. "*How,* Tony?"

"Please calm down. I promised Daddy I would protect you and that's what I did."

"How? By sharing my pain, my humiliation with the world?" Tiffany gazed around the foyer knowing that Heather would soon pop her nosey tail around the corner. "Did you expect me to be *stronger* now as an adult to talk about it? Did you expect me to share my story like the courageous rape survivors you see on tv?" Tiffany spatted. "I respect them. Yes, *indeed,* I do. But nobody, *nobody,* experienced my rape but me!" she shrieked through her teeth. "I was a *poor black* child who was raped by someone who took an oath to protect the public! Who was going to believe me?" Tiffany sobbed. "But I'm not that little, *weak* child anymore. So I don't need you running around like you're some type of warrior for me," she said waving her finger toward him.

"I…I just wanted to help you, Tiffany." Tony exhaled. "I am here for you. I want you to be strong."

"I am *strong*! I don't need you to tell me to be strong! I am a survivor." She paused. "And I *learned* a lot in medical school about trauma. But I dealt with my past in a way that best fitted me." A tear rolled down her face. "Maybe…one day I'll open a program for rape survivors." She exhaled. "But for now, I expect privacy…and I expect respect."

Tony stretched out his hand, trying to pull her closer to him. "I know, but it had to be done, Tiffany. I had to give up those tapes. It was the right thing to do."

Tiffany snatched away. The flesh on her neck and chest heated to an unbearable level. She fanned herself with her small hand.

"Do you *hear* yourself?" She gritted. "Why did you *do* that?" she screamed at the top of her lungs. "*Why*?" Leaning against the burgundy painted wall in his foyer, she trembled to the depths of her soul.

For a split second, her mind flashed back to that hot day in the alley . . .

June Bug stood over Smith's lifeless body. A level of rage pierced through his eyes that Tiffany had never seen before. She had heard about the *war* stories that resulted in him being diagnosed with PTSD while he was in the Army. But nothing, nothing, could have ever prepared her for the *person* . . . *or animal* who her uncle had suddenly transformed into in the alley. Smith's body was treated like a *trapped enemy* in a warzone. She remembered June Bug telling her not to worry while he glanced around the alley as if his words would erase the memories of the events that were unfolding before her eyes. A cold chill shot through her followed by a sense of foreboding.

Tony stood in front of her. Sunlight poured in through the small square-shaped windows above the door.

"Get away from me," she said, voice trembling.

Tony leaned against the wall beside her. Their reflection in the mirror hanging in the foyer stared back at them. Although she was infuriated, the smell of French toast still made her stomach growl. How could she think of food when she was so angry?

He turned and said in a low, calm tone, "I didn't give them your tape."

"Then where is the tape, Tony?"

Tiffany felt like she couldn't breathe as she waited for him to respond.

Tony tilted his head toward his chandelier. "I've got it.... But I don't think you need to see it."

Tiffany lowered her head. Tony placed his slender finger under her chin, lifting her face. "I don't want you to relive that nightmare." He sighed softly. "I cried when I watched that tape. I don't want to give it to you."

Tiffany slowly moved his finger away. "Why not? It's about me. I want to be the one who destroys it."

"No, Tiffany," he said softly. "*I'll* destroy it."

Tiffany dashed towards the hallway and down the steps to his entertainment room, passing the wet bar, the pool table, running straight to his movie collection. She knocked down DVD movies and scattered his camcorder tapes, searching for the tape.

Flapping noises came down the steps as Heather's slippers shifted on her feet.

Tiffany froze, her hair plastered on her face making it hard to see. Her clothes were wrinkled and one of her shoes had somehow ended up far off in a corner near an artificial palm tree over by the wet bar. Her heart pounded away as rage pumped in her veins.

A fragrant wind of Jasmine flowers wafted into the room, mingling with the smell of breakfast.

"Here, Tiffany. Here's the tape," Heather said, stretching her delicate hand, dangling the tape from her fingertips.

369

Tiffany's chest fluctuated rapidly. Her nostrils flared with every force of air pulling through and her blood flowed like a volcano boiling over with hot lava. The man had taped her that day?

Tony glared at Heather. "How *dare* you come between us."

Tiffany stood, smoothed out her clothes, and putting on her tennis shoe. Her feet moved as if she were in quicksand as she walked toward Heather.

"It's her life, Anthony," his wife snapped back. "She has the right to destroy this tape. You can't protect her by keeping it from her."

Trembling hands took the small black tape from Heather. "Thank you," Tiffany said, then ran up the steps leaving arguing voices behind.

Chapter 58

Smith's death was the talk of Charlotte, North Carolina. Stories about his criminal behavior spread like wildfire through Cloverdale. The voices of tenants he had mistreated, tortured and abused had gone unheard for too long.

Monday morning, Tony and several tenants from Cloverdale rallied in front of the police department, demanding to speak to the chief. Tony held his mother's hand. She remained silent and prayed endlessly.

Minutes later, officers pushed and shoved Tony and the tenants, trying to prevent the crowd from entering the building.

The information on the tapes was no longer a secret but the police department still tried to brush it under the rug, continuing to portray the sergeant as a good law-obeying officer in the media.

Now Smith's wife, still recovering from her horrible accident, had suddenly disappeared from the media spotlight when her children wouldn't stand with her. Then the tapes came to light, along with stories that Smith had plotted her death.

Tony would love to find out the reason his children had turned against him.

"Let him in," Chief Clarence Jones yelled.

Tony rushed up the sidewalk and then up the stairs. He brushed himself off as the doors swung open. The lobby was vacant because all of the officers were outside trying to control the crowd. A handful of uniformed officers stood behind the intake desk, monitoring the crowd outside while simultaneously turning up their noses at Tony.

A tall uniformed woman pointed to the room. "He's in room three."

Tony ran down the hall, peeking his head in every room, trying to find the tall white man who had yelled out the entrance doors to let him in.

He entered the large conference room where dark brown carpet stretched from corner to corner. Photos of the chief, sergeants, detectives, lieutenants and officers lined the wall.

"Come on in, Mr. Brown and have a seat," the chief said as he kept his icy gray gaze on Sergeant Clark, who sat in a chair across from him.

Clark looked up at Tony, "I told him he should at least speak to you."

Sliding into the chair next to Clark, Tony maintained eye contact with the chief.

The hefty man cleared his throat before saying, "We were undecided whether we should include you in this meeting or not. This is not a normal procedure. I figured if I allowed you to say a few words, then your crowd will be satisfied."

"Thank you, sir." Tony shifted his butt in the padded seat, wishing he had brought a tape recorder. "The crowd outside consists of tenants from Cloverdale. Now that they know that Tiffany isn't the one who killed him, they're trying to pin it on my uncle, who says he had acted in self-defense. June Bug is being punished for protecting his own life.

Chief Jones glared. "How can you say it was self-defense, Clark?" He frowned. "Smith's body was dismembered and mangled."

"Chief, the coroner and said wild animals done it," Clark responded. "The city has been having trouble controlling those wild dogs over at the park and alley."

"Yeah right . . . maybe Tiffany used her medical school skills to cut him up *before* the wild dogs got to Smith's body," Chief Jones snapped. "Or maybe her uncle June Bug used the *military cutting tactics* that he learned from the Army," He paused gasping for air as he leaned forward. "Maybe Tiffany and her uncle took turns on Smith. What do you *really* think, Clark?

Clark glanced out the window before shifting his gaze back to Chief Jones. "I *really* believe that June Bug is being punished, Sir." He paused.

372

Tony cleared his throat before blurting, "The crowd outside knows this isn't right. A lot of them have suffered when you put Smith in Cloverdale knowing that the man *hated* black people."

"He's right, chief," Clark said.

Chief Jones glared at the Clark. "Do you *realize* what position you're putting yourself in, Sergeant Clark?"

"Yes, sir. There's too much that has happened to the people in Cloverdale. Even you said that before, sir."

"I said *what*, Clark?"

"You told me when I accepted the transfer that you believed something wasn't right about Sergeant Smith. You questioned the way he handled things in that neighborhood. But since the tenants never reported anything you overlooked even your own instincts."

The chief cleared his throat. "We never caught Sergeant Smith red-handed."

"Chief, everything's on those tapes. What more do these people have to do, take out a billboard?" Tony said, looking out the window at the crowd then to the chief.

"Smith committed a lot of crimes," Clark said as he loosened the top button around his neck. "The truth is the truth. I can't sit back and allow those people to suffer any longer. The people *did* file reports. I found them. Smith and some of the officers swept it under the table."

The chief leaned back in his black chair. "The bureau's cracking down on our department. I'm in the hot seat. The bureau wants to know how this department, how I allowed one of my officers to go on a torturing spree and didn't know about it." Then the man's gray eyes settled on Tony. "*Somebody* sent a web link to the bureau and me, threatening that they would release information to the public if Lamont Brown and Tiffany Brown were not cleared." One eyebrow raised. "Do you know anything about that?"

"Chief, I'm not going to lie to you," Tony replied. "I will do whatever it takes to clear my sister's name and help my uncle."

Tenants continued to yell outside, almost causing Tony to smile. With every yell, the chief turned a hot red.

Clark leaned forward. "Sir, I understand that the department's getting a lot of flack right now, but Tiffany's a good girl. Her uncle may be strung out but he's rarely into any trouble. The stuff he's telling is the truth. The man even paid an addict to kill his wife. That's not something we can overlook."

"I hear what you are saying, but there's nothing I can do." The chief said, dangling his pencil in front of them. "We can't just let this go . . . if one gets away with it, we'll have chaos on our hands."

"You let Smith get away with it. And that was fine because he was an officer?"

The chief pressed his hands firmly on his desk as his head and shoulders tensed. "The district attorney said it's a possibility that Tiffany Brown-Carson, instead of Lamont Brown, killed Sergeant Smith. Word around the department is she wanted revenge."

"What are you talking *about,* sir? My sister is not a murderer. She didn't kill that criminal that you're trying so hard to protect." Tony rocked back and forth in his chair. The little twinkle of hope he had when he walked in the station had now crumbled. The chief wasn't going to help them.

Clark's eyebrows twitched. "Chief, you're aware that we have officers on the force who are not clean-cut. You, yourself, told me that before. If you don't help Tiffany, I'm going to start talking and telling *my* stories. Then you'll really have a problem. People won't have a problem believing me. I've got a good track record, unlike some people around here . . . ."

Chief Jones leaned forward, eyes narrowing as he looked at the officer. "Is that a threat or a promise, *Sergeant* Clark?"

"It is a *promise*, sir. Those people outside aren't dumb. I bust my tail every day trying to make our department look good. I know I'm not the only good officer on the force and I know that the other *clean-nosed* officers will support me."

"What's your *point*, Clark?"

Clark's lips slowly parted. "I appreciate you for promoting me to be the sergeant in Cloverdale." He paused as he cleared his throat. "But I refuse to allow those people to keep living in fear and be mistreated. It's not right, sir. . . it's not fair."

Tony exhaled slowly as he looked out the window. More tenants had arrived.

"Those people standing outside need to see a change," Clark said, sliding to the edge of his chair. "My job might be on the line, but as God is my witness, I know I'm making the right decision by trying to help this family. I had to help get that girl out of Cloverdale years ago. Now I'm learning why. Tony was protecting her from Smith. I mentioned it back then that he should've been transferred, but you didn't listen to me then. I *also* told you somebody needed to investigate things in Cloverdale back then, but you didn't listen to me. I hope you're listening to me *now*."

"*What* do you want me to do, Clark?" The chief placed his elbows on the table. "*What*." He bit his bottom lip, tapped the edge of his desk with his pencil and stared at Clark. He tapped the pencil on the desk harder and harder as the seconds went by, causing it to break.

Clark shook his head. "The truth will come out one way or another. I feel like I'm out on a limb here, but I see the way some of the officers talk to people. It's unfair treatment. You put the most *racist* person in charge of people he didn't respect enough to protect."

"Enough of this! My hands are tied," the chief said as he walked to the door and opened it.

Tony glared at the chief. "Tiffany isn't a cop killer. She didn't help June Bug kill Sergeant Smith. June Bug killed the sergeant out of self-defense. Everything points to that."

"My hands are tied, Anthony."

Clark stood, following Tony out the door. The chief's meaty hand reached out gripping the officer's shoulder. "I need to speak to you for a minute before you leave."

Tony walked to the door. "You can talk all you want. My next stop is the mayor's office. With what I have, I'm sure she'll be singing a different tune."

Chapter 59

Wednesday afternoon, Tony cruised through a large paved parking area, scanning a pavilion of restaurants assembled in a small shopping center on the outskirts of Charlotte. Cars were parked everywhere, leaving a narrow, long red-brick sidewalk for customers to walk on.

Tony pulled his white truck in front of Pizza Hut beside a black two-door Buick. The bright afternoon sun beamed over the area, making an already hot day even more humid.

Pizza, hamburgers, chicken and fish dominated for the right to claim the air. Yellow daisies clustered along each side of the long sidewalks. People mingled under the few scattered pine trees as children laughed and played within eyeshot of their parents.

His meeting with the mayor didn't produce the desired results. She was stalling him and maybe a little *push* in the right direction will bring her over to the right side.

Tony closed his eyes thinking about his wife and children. An unsettling feeling pierced his side as he thought about the potential risks that he was putting his wife and children in. His bond with Tiffany was strong and he was determined to help her. But Tony realized his heart was slightly torn between his love for his sister and his commitment to his wife and children. The thought of taking on the dangerous task of threatening a corrupt police department landed an ounce of fear in Tony's veins. But someone had to do it. Someone had to have the *balls* to put a stop to the madness in Cloverdale. Tony exhaled, knowing he had to be wise with his actions to prevent harm from happening to his sister, wife and children—even his mother.

A red four-door car pulled up from the opposite direction beside Tony, close enough for Tony to pull the driver's seat belt if he had to, but far enough away so that no one would think it was suspicious. Tony kept the engine running, turned down his radio and lowered the window as he tapped once on the horn.

"What's so urgent that you need to meet with me," the man growled, with a deep voice. "I can't be seen talking to you." He glanced around the parking lot and lowered into the seat a bit more.

"Look, Officer Jenkins," Tony said. "Let's not waste time."

He stroked his neatly trimmed mustache. "How did you get my cell number?" he asked, frowning.

"Don't worry about that."

Cars pulled in the parking lot as customers streamed in and out of the restaurants.

"You heard the message. Are you going to help me or not?"

"I'm not getting into that *stuff*." He turned his head out of the car, spitting on the paved parking lot.

"I don't think you have a choice."

The officer grunted. "I *do* have a choice. And I'm *not* helping."

A short husky man cranked up his car, startling Officer Jenkins. He gripped the

steering wheel but settled back down.

"You and *Courtney* are on that tape," Tony said as he peered in his rearview

mirror. "What do you think the media's gonna say about the mayor's husband screwing a sixteen-year-old girl?"

The officer's nostrils stretched and his eyes widened with disbelief.

"What are

you talking about?"

"You and Courtney. *Statutory rape*."

The sun beamed on the man's black uniform. Sweat from his forehead dripped onto his collar.

Officer Jenkins shoved his wide brown hand into the glove department, pulling out a napkin, then wiped his forehead. "Courtney who?" he asked, glaring at Tony.

"Courtney *Nelson* from Cloverdale."

The man's eyes darted around the lot. "What are you talking about?" He licked his big, brown lips and then said, "You've got the wrong officer."

"Oh, do I?" Tony smirked. "Tapes don't lie. I've got one with you and Courtney going to the Hilton Hotel at least three times last month. Smith followed you every time."

Officer Jenkins gripped his steering wheel, nearing twisted the tattered threads. "You're bluffing."

The hot humid air drifting inside Tony's car overpowered the air conditioner. His engine revved forcing cool air into the car.

Tony reached under the seat, keeping his gaze on the officer.

The officer popped his knuckles. "Your sister killed one of our officers and you expect me to *help* you?"

Tony glared at the man.

"I'm not turning my back on the department."

"This'll make you change your mind." Tony dangled the tape out the window. "And I do have copies. This one's for you." He grinned. "Think how this would ruin your career and your wife's reputation if the media gets a hold of this." He tapped his fingers on the tape. "By the way . . . your trips to Fountain Spring's Resort Hotel are on several tapes." Tony sneered. "It makes me sick to my stomach knowing how that resort allowed innocent teenagers to be victimized by people like you and others."

The officer flinched. "What are you talking about?"

Kimberly Morton Cuthrell

"Don't play dumb. Tapes don't lie," Tony chuckled while dangling the tape from the tips of his fingers.

The officer closed his eyes. "Man, I thought dentists were supposed to have *ethics*?"

"I do. I'm just using the type of *ethics* you officers have." Tony wiggled the tape in the air. "Sometimes you have to play the game by the rules you're given."

The officer placed a black glove on his wide hand and grabbed the tape.

Tony peered through his rearview mirror. No one had even looked in their direction.

The officer scanned the label. Air filled up in his jaws as the muscles in his face twitched. "Now exactly what do you want me to do with this?"

"You'll figure it out," Tony said, pulling off.

Chapter 60

Four months later, Tiffany strolled in the outreach program with June Bug. He had a nicely faded haircut, a new outfit and clean shoes that Tiffany and Tony had bought him. The almond-colored walls of The Safe Haven Outreach Program were decorated with Halloween art drawings and collages that the kids had made and certificates that some adults had received from educational and vocational training programs.

"Come on in, June Bug, Mrs. Clark is waiting for us."

"I'm going by Lamont Brown these days. I'm a changed man. June Bug is on his way to a rehab center."

Tiffany chuckled.

Lamont paused as he stared at the pictures on the wall. "Those pictures remind me of when Star was a kid. She always liked to draw pictures of bunny rabbits."

Every door in the center had a different color. Tiffany knocked on the green one.

"Yes, come in," Mrs. Clark said as an inviting smile developed on her small ivory face. She now wore glasses and her hair, once laced with a few strands of black, was now almost totally gray.

"Hello Lamont Brown," Sergeant Clark said as he shook the man's hand. "Mrs. Clark and I are proud of you. You're about to make the most important decision in your life."

"I thought I was gonna rot in that jail." June Bug exhaled slowly. "Those cops wanted me to fry. I got tired of going back and forth to court, repeating that story over and over." He scratched his head. "You should've seen the frowns on the officers' faces. I—I had to protect myself." His eyes closed for a split second. "Smith was trying to kill me. I'm glad my case wasn't dragged out for years. I heard the mayor and the internal affairs people had something to do with that."

Tiffany shifted her gaze to Clark, who pressed his lips firmly together. She knew he had something to do with it. Tony, too. But no one would tell her anything. Hey, it was her life!

"The investigators uncovered a lot of information," Clark said slowly. "They put fire under the chief's feet and pressured the judge and district attorney to give you a speedy trial." He sighed before saying, "The investigators found out that Smith molested his daughters and the little girls in this area. He was a *sick* man."

Silence swept through the room.

June Bug shook his head. "And he killed my daughter."

Chill bumps rippled up and down Tiffany's arms, realizing that death could have knocked on her door that fateful day when Smith had kidnapped and violated her.

"I thought I was dreaming when the Judge said my charges were dismissed." June Bug said with a wide grin. "People from Cloverdale stood, clapping in the courtroom until the judge threatened to lock them up." He chuckled slightly.

"I'm glad I was able to be there," Sergeant Clark said as he stretched out his arms to hug Tiffany.

"Have a seat," Mrs. Clark said in a soft, shaky voice.

Lamont pulled two chairs from the corner and slid them in front of the desk. Tiffany winked at Mrs. Clark, signaling that her uncle wanted to voluntarily commit himself to a drug treatment program.

The older woman turned down her clock radio. Gospel music slowly faded away. "How are you doing, Tiffany?"

Tiffany grinned. "I'm taking it one day at a time. My therapy sessions are going well. I'm almost finished"

Mrs. Clark smiled. "Great. I'm proud of you."

"Me too, Tiffany," Sergeant Clark said.

Tiffany smiled.

Mrs. Clark sipped her coffee. "I'd like to commend you for making this big step, June—uh—Lamont."

"Me too. I need a second chance." He rubbed his arms. "Crack took me on a long dark road. I'm not going to lie I enjoyed the trip but I've run out of gas. I'm tired. I need a change in my life."

Tiffany smiled at her uncle. "You have to take it slowly, uncle Lamont. I'll help you as much as I can, but you're going to have to work hard at it every day."

"I know, Tiffany. I didn't think crack was so addictive. Nothing mattered as long as I was high. I want to go to a place outside of Charlotte. I need to be in a different environment."

"Serenity Psychiatric Center in Greensboro has a psychiatric hospital with inpatient treatment programs," Mrs. Clark said, handing him the brochure. It has a really good treatment program for adults with chemical dependency."

"*Greensboro?*" June Bug flinched. "How will I get there?"

"I'll take care of that," Tiffany said. "Greensboro is only an hour from here."

"I need to go somewhere," he said with trembling hands. "Look at me." He raised his hands. "I know I can do better than this. I have failed a lot of people. Especially Star." His head drooped. "After I get some help, I'm going to try to make *amends* with my son."

Tiffany smiled. "I'm sure David would be willing to give you that chance."

"I pray he does." He sighed. "I'm ready to get my life back on track. I know I can do it. But I need help doing it." His head tilted toward the ceiling.

"I needed help a long time ago. I was too embarrassed to get help because of the stigma." He closed his eyes. "That's way I didn't get help before. But I realized I couldn't focus on the stigma or feeling embarrassed anymore."

Sergeant Clark smiled before speaking. "Lamont, I'm proud of you for taking a leap of faith and doing what is best for you and your family."

"Lamont, you have to look toward the future and pick up the pieces as you go along," Mrs. Clark said while handing Tiffany a brochure to use as a guide as they talked. Tiffany had already met with her to discuss the treatment program and to get a list of the supplies he would need.

"Our church is willing to sponsor you," Sergeant Clark said.

"Thank you." June Bug's gaze drifted toward the floor. "Sergeant Clark, you have helped me to see that there are some good officers out there."

"I try to help people whenever I can. It's my calling. God will bless me."

"Thanks for helping me to get my life on track. I wanted to tell you a long time ago about Sergeant Smith." June Bug frowned. "But I thought all officers were like him."

"It's a shame that the good ones are labeled based on what the crooked ones do," Sergeant Clark said as he walked to the door. "I have to get back to work. I'm glad I'm working in Cloverdale now. Maybe my wife and I can really do some good." He opened the door and left.

Tiffany grabbed her uncle's hand and held it firmly. June Bug's fidgety body shivered.

"When can I be admitted?" His body twitched. "I need to go today. Right now. I don't trust myself out there in the streets."

"We're taking you, today. The application package is completed and I have arranged everything at the treatment program. Since you're voluntarily committing yourself there won't be any problems getting you in."

Chapter 61

A sense of peace flowed through Cloverdale for the first time in years. The tenants were no longer scared to walk through the community or mingle in their yards. Smith had destroyed many lives and embedded fear in the souls of the people in Cloverdale. Now that he was finally dead, they could free their minds from their secrets as Sergeant Clark took new reports on old infractions and brought them to the attention of the authorities.

Standing on the porch, Tiffany could easily look through the window and see mama's room and the dimly lit hallway. The television was turned up and Juanita Bynum's voice bellowed out of the speakers.

The cool November wind swept across her neck as she peeked through the living room window and yelled, "It's us, mama. Unlock the door."

Moments later a shuffling of feet across the carpet resounded through the doors. Mama opened the brown metal door which scraped the ceramic tile floor on its way back. She wiped her floured hands on her red apron.

Delicious smells of beans and cornbread floated from the kitchen to the front door.

"Hello, mama," Vance said, kissing her cheek. "Church service was awesome this morning."

Mama grinned. "Yes, Reverend McCoy sure can preach."

Tiffany stretched her caramel arms around her mother. "Where is Tony, mama?"

The older woman turned the television off when Juanita Bynum finished the sermon. "He's in the bathroom."

"He *stays* in the bathroom," Tiffany said, walking to bang on the door. "Get out of there. Mama doesn't have enough toilet tissue for your big old butt."

"Hush, Tiffany," mama said with a wide grin. "And give him some peace—especially in there."

Tiffany banged on the door again before she turned and walked towards the kitchen. Spicy peppers and pungent garlic scents drifted.

Mrs. Brown paused, looking at Tiffany's face and then at her stomach.

"What?" Tiffany smiled.

Mama grinned. "You've got a *pregnancy* glow," Mama said smiling ear to ear.

Tiffany winced, quickly doing a mental check of her last menstrual cycle. "*Oh, no . . . .*" Tiffany's head shifted side to side while smiling. She and Vance were adamant about taking precautionary methods until they were ready for children. Yet, Tiffany had learned from medical school that there was a percentage of possibility for anyone to get pregnant regardless of precautionary methods. "I'm sure Vance would be happy if I were pregnant. He's been tossing around a few clues like he's ready now." She chuckled. "But I'm not pregnant."

"Okay, if you say so." Mrs. Brown grabbed Tiffany's hand. "Heather and the kids are in the kitchen," she whispered.

"Heather?" Tiffany froze. "I'm surprised she's here."

"Things are much better. God has answered my prayers."

Mrs. Brown walked to the kitchen with a smile pasted on her dark brown face. Her silver hair shined with every move as Tiffany and Vance followed on her heels.

Outside the window, neighborhood kids squirted water guns and chased after squealing victims.

"Hello, Tiffany," Heather said with a tentative grin on her lips.

Tiffany glanced at Vance. "Hi. Heather." Tiffany stretched out her arms to pick up Carmen, whose yellow ruffled dress brightened her light brown skin.

Her niece, with almond-shaped eyes and cupid bow lips, was like a bundle of joy, bouncing up and down in Tiffany's arm. She batted her eyelashes like a movie star, which made Tiffany giggle.

"You look like a little baby doll, Carmen," Tiffany said as she swung the child in the air.

Heather placed the paper plates on the table. "She looks like you, Tiffany." A smile formed on Heather's lips.

Tiffany turned, casting a quick, wary glance at her sister-in-law before staring at her mother. Mama smiled, bending down to take the cornbread out of the oven.

Vance winked as he placed seven glasses of fresh squeezed lemonade on the table.

"What did I miss?" Tony asked, strolling in the kitchen wearing a black suit and white shirt.

"I'm wondering the same thing," Tiffany said, kissing Carmen, then hugging Anthony, Jr. while keeping a watch on Heather from the corner of her eye.

"Look at our family." Tony smiled from ear to ear. "I'm glad we could all get together for Sunday dinner," Tony said as he carried the meatloaf to the table. "Mama, you didn't have to cook all of this food."

"I don't see you putting it back either," Mama shot back as Tiffany laughed.

"Noooo," Tiffany said. "He needs to keep time in the bathroom."

"Hmm. I smell pound cake," Heather said as she handed Tiffany a glass of iced tea.

"Lord, I need to take that cake out," Mama said, rushing towards the stove.

"I'll do it." Hot air blew out of the oven as Tiffany opened it, mixing with the cool breeze drifting through the window in the kitchen.

Tiffany placed the cake on a mat in front of the window as mama sipped on a glass of ice water. "Carmen, baby, *get* away from the stove."

Vance dashed over, scooping up Carmen. "We've got to keep our eyes on you."

"She's curious, like all children," Mama said resting her elbows on the table.

The glass table was covered with food—Meatloaf, mashed potatoes, cabbage, pinto beans and cornbread—Tiffany and Tony's favorites.

Tiffany glanced down at the food. "This must be a special occasion. Mama knows we love meatloaf."

"Always been your favorite."

Tony's gaze swept the kitchen, a glint of sadness in his eyes. "Mama, you need a bigger kitchen."

"My kitchen is the right size for me. I like having everything within arm's reach." Mama placed the knife in the meatloaf and sectioned it. Then she picked up a napkin, swept it across her forehead, wiping the sweat off.

"Mama, Tony and I think you need to move from Cloverdale."

She put down the knife. In a sweet soft voice, she said, "Cloverdale is my home. I know you want to help me but I don't want to move."

Vance and Heather paused. The kids were on the floor coloring. Heather, sensing a sudden tension in the room, picked them up and placed them on her lap. "Do you want me to take the kids out?"

Mama waved her skinny finger side to side. "My life is here in Cloverdale. My friends are here and I'm all right."

Tiffany's eyelids joined. "But, mama—"

"Tiffany, please, baby." Mama pulled the string on her apron, removing it from around her slender waist. "Don't worry about me. I'll be all right here in Cloverdale."

"You know how we feel about this," Tony said.

"Yes, I do. But there's no need for you two stressing yourselves over me." She folded the apron across a clothes hanger. "Believe me, mama's okay living right here in good old Cloverdale. Maybe one day I'll change my mind, but not now."

"Okay," Tiffany said as Tony's expression crumbled. He walked out of the kitchen.

Mama's gaze trailed his footsteps. "Where're you going, son?"

"I'm going to wash my face, mama."

"Back to the bathroom," Tiffany teased.

Mama placed the knife back in the meatloaf and continued sectioning it off.

"I want you to be happy, mama," Tiffany murmured, hugging her mother from behind.

"I am, baby. As long as you and Tony are out of harm's way, I'll be okay." Tiffany leaned into the soft curve of her mother's shoulder. Mama placed her hands on Tiffany's face and kissed her forehead.

Tony strolled back in the kitchen and their mother reached out pinching his cheeks. "Mama's going to be all right, baby. Don't worry." She paused then said, "Thank God, Sergeant Clark helped you and June Bug." She turned, but not before Tiffany saw tears well up in her eyes. Mama spread butter over the cornbread. "I'm glad June Bug's in the rehab."

"Me, too," Tiffany said, staring at Tony. "But I wonder why the mayor launched a thorough investigation into the police department."

Tony shrugged as he picked up his son, walked to the window and pointed at some neighborhood kids who were playing kickball. Anthony, Jr.'s giggles soon filled the air.

Heather joined him at the window. "Look, Carmen, do you see the little girl playing with her doll?"

Carmen stood on her tiptoes in a chair, peering out the window.

"Yeah, they found out a lot about Sergeant Smith," Vance said while rubbing Tiffany's hand.

Mama wiped the sweat off the back of her neck. "A bad apple can ruin the whole basket."

Vance uttered, "But what about Officer—"

Tony turned from the window. "All evidence was linked to Smith only."

Tiffany's eyes widened watching the exchange between her husband and brother. She was certain that the officers were being investigated.

Mama exhaled. "My heart wept when I saw on the news that they had closed a resort because of the terrible things that they allowed to happen to teenagers."

Heather's lips parted. "Yes, that was really sad. It was called Fountain Spring's Resort Hotel."

"I heard Smith was *heavily* involved with things at that resort," Vance grappled.

"Things are going to get better," Tony uttered. "I'm sure a lot of Smith's *dirt* will be exposed."

Mama sat down in a chair. "Now Cloverdale has a chance to heal. I'm glad June Bug's in that rehab." She glanced at Heather and nodded to the woman who hadn't shown an ounce of attitude since Tiffany had arrived. "We can eat in a few minutes."

Heather took a quick sip of her iced tea. "Tiffany, can I talk to you for a minute in the living room?" she asked, placing Carmen on mama's lap.

Tiffany paused. "Umm…Sure." Suddenly Tiffany had lost her appetite.

"Let's sit down," Heather said, pointing at the navy blue sectional chair.

Tiffany slowly perched on the edge of the seat.

"I don't know where to start, Tiffany." Heather exhaled slowly. "I know you've been through so much…and I apologize for the way I've treated you."

Tiffany leaned back in the chair, wanting to pinch herself to make sure she wasn't dreaming. Heather apologizing? Definitely a first.

"I know I've been selfish. I understand Anthony's your brother and nothing can change that." She rubbed her hands together.

Uh oh, here it comes.

"I didn't realize how much you needed his support." She said, lowering her gaze. "And my support," she said, slowly looking up. Tiger eyes flashed with sadness. The woman was actually being sincere.

Tiffany's lips slowly separated. "I understand, Heather."

A cardinal landed on the windowsill, chirping, sending soft melodic sounds into the living room.

Heather crossed her legs. "Anthony's all I have, the only person who has really cared for me. I love him, Tiffany."

"I know you do, Heather, but I'm his sister." Tiffany slid to the edge of the chair. "I know Tony's married and he has a family. But you and I have to come to an understanding. I'm not trying to take him from you, we're just maintaining the bond we've always had. The kind you admired when you first met him . . . ."

"I know. I guess I was a little jealous because Anthony cares so much about you."

"That's the way we were raised, Heather."

Heather's gaze fell toward the floor. "I don't know if Anthony told you or not, but I was adopted and my siblings and I didn't have that bond like you and Anthony."

Tiffany's eyebrows connected. "No, he didn't tell me." Now Tony was keeping secrets from her.

"Yes, my *biological* mother was a crack addict." Heather's gaze slowly lined up with Tiffany's. "She abandoned me when I was three days old."

Tiffany's heartbeat slowed; a small stab of compassion welled up inside.

"I was adopted when I was a month old. I grew up in a place so different from this but I wasn't loved." She cleared her throat. "It was hard for me to understand how Anthony and you could love one another so much, coming from such a poor environment."

Tiffany reached out for Heather's hand. Slowly, Heather placed her hand in Tiffany's. "We grew up on love, shared dreams and slept off hopes," Tiffany said, reaching out to wipe a tear from her sister-in-law's olive face.

A smile stretched across Heather's small lips. "Look at your mother. I would've thought she would pack up her bags and run when Anthony told her that he wanted to buy her a house. But she insisted she wants to stay here." Heather sighed slowly. "You all have shown me the true meaning of a family and that not all people in the poor communities are bad elements in life. I was so wrong."

A tear rolled down Heather's face. She wiped her cheek with her small hand.

"Don't cry, Heather," Tiffany said, trying hard to hold back her own tears.

"I didn't like coming to Cloverdale because my mother was an addict. When I see a female addict I often wonder if she's my mother . . . " Heather paused, taking in a long slow breath. "I guess I'll never find out. Anthony helped me realize that it's not where you're from or who your parents are that decides your destiny. It's all about what you want out of life."

"Yes that's true," Tiffany said, looking towards the ceiling.

Heather pressed her palm against her face, wiping her tears away. "You're not the only one seeing a therapist. I'm learning how to cope with certain issues in my counseling sessions as well. I had a hard time accepting the bond that you share with Anthony. I wanted him to love me and only me— because it's the first time anyone has been so good to me . . . and loved me." She exhaled slowly.

Heather's gaze shifted toward the ceiling. "I was eight-years-old and I remember Mrs. Brooks, the school psychologist, recommending that I see a therapist. I don't know why, but my adopted mother, Olivia, didn't stay in Mrs. Brooks' office long enough to find out what she could do to help me. She stormed out the door, dragging me with her." She leaned back. "No matter how much Mrs. Brooks insisted that I see a therapist, Olivia wouldn't take me. I wish she had taken me instead, she drilled in my head that black people *don't* need to talk to a shrink and that the ones who do are insane."

"That's not true," Tiffany said, patting Heather's hand. "You're not insane and I'm not. Besides, I know a lot of people, not just black folks, who get counseling. Some people need counselors to help them cope with certain issues . . . or just an objective voice that can help them realize things."

Heather steepled her fingers under her chin. "I know. But counseling was taboo in my house. Olivia's denial caused more harm than good. Even as an adult, I've put it off for years. But Anthony insisted two months ago that I see a therapist or . . . ." Heather closed her eyes.

Tiffany's lips slowly parted. "Tony's not gonna leave you."

"I hope not, Tiffany. I'm glad that Anthony's gonna come to the next counseling session with me." She paused. "Dr. Reed has helped me see that I have a fear of abandonment and that I've always had a problem expressing my emotions and bonding with people. But when I eventually open up and develop a bond with someone, I want that person all to myself."

Tiffany smiled. "Seems like we both have a few things that we have to smooth out in our lives."

"I want us to pick up the pieces, Tiffany. I'm willing to put forth an effort."

Tiffany stretched out her arms, wrapping them around Heather's slender frame. "Things are going to work out for the good, Heather." Tiffany patted her on the knee. "You're a part of our loving family." She grinned. "Even when you're giving us attitude."

Heather's face brightened. They stood, walking into the kitchen.

Smiling faces greeted them. A warm feeling flowed through Tiffany. If only she could convince her mother to move out of Cloverdale, then one more splinter of her soul would be removed. But for now, the main ones were slowly dissipating and being replaced with new hopes for the future.

Mama stretched out her hands to Heather and Tiffany. "You see, children, God does answer prayers."

Chapter 62

Two weeks later, Tiffany glanced around the green lush picturesque grounds
marching around the Grandover Resorts & Spa. The evening sun inched behind the clouds allowing only a small shaft of light to beam on the enclaved cathedral-designed resort making an enriched presence for its 36 holes of championship golf, luxurious spas and pristine guest rooms and suites. A large cascade waterfall positioned in the middle of the sandal gold marbled floor provided a ray of grace throughout the oversized lobby. The pure elegance of the art gallery showcased with a rich deep culture of art from the artists of North Carolina provided a perfect collection of art, pottery, sculptures, wood and other fineries.

"This is nice," Vance said, sipping on a glass of white wine while glancing
around.

Cream high-back luxury décor chairs aligned oval shaped Mahogany tables
trimmed with gold accents in the large grand dining room. Large architectural windows allowed natural light to flow through to balance against the saffron painted walls creating an astounding view of the terrace and floral garden.

"I figured we needed a change in scenery." Tiffany glanced around the dining
room. "So I thought we'd get out of Charlotte for the weekend and come to Greensboro."

"Well, I must say this is a great way to start off the weekend," said Vance while planting a piece of lemon baked salmon in his mouth. "You're right. There has been a lot going on lately." He took a small sip of wine while locking his gaze with Tiffany. "I'm glad to finally spend *quality* time with my wife alone."

"Yes, we needed to *unwind* and spend some *quality* time together." Tiffany

smiled. "We've been so busy lately…and I wanted to let you know how much I appreciate you."

"I know you do, baby. So . . . don't *ever* worry about anything." Vance

reached for Tiffany's hand, gently rubbing it. "I will always love you."

Soft jazz flowed through the room, mingling with the small candles floating in

oblique shaped glass vases on the tables.

"I love you so much, Vance," said Tiffany while launching her fork through a cluster of asparagus surrounded by rice pilaf and squash—an appealing vegetarian entrée. "I am glad we had this weekend off so we could come here." Tiffany slowly winked, thinking about the *finale* she had waiting for Vance upstairs in their suite on the 12th floor.

Muffled conversations surfaced in the air from the nearby tables. Tiffany and

Vance held moments of silence as they ate their cuisine dinners and desserts.

"Well, I must say that this was nice." Vance paused. "I noticed you didn't order

meat or wine."

"I'm making a few changes in my life." She paused. "I have to make sure my

body is *healthier*." Tiffany grinned.

Vance leaned in his chair, pressing his back firmly against the seams
in the chair.

He slowly rubbed his chin as if he was intensely thinking about something.

"What do you mean *healthier*?" He paused. "Is there something you
need to tell

me?" Vance smiled as his right eyebrow arched toward the ceiling.

Tiffany's lip slowly parted. "I have a gift for you."

Vance leaned forward, connecting gazes with Tiffany. "Are you
going to answer

my question?" chuckled Vance. "And why do you have a gift for me?" He
smiled.

A soft voice interrupted the flow of their conversation. "Is there
anything else I

can get you two?" asked a short caramel lady with light brown eyes wearing
a pristine cream uniform.

Tiffany looked at Vance for a split second trying to determine if he
wanted to order anything else. Of course, she wanted him to build up his
energy for the romantic evening she had waiting for him.

"No, we're fine. I'm stuffed." Tiffany responded in a polite tone.
"Please charge

the bill to our suite." Tiffany never imagined being able to say those words as
a kid growing up in Cloverdale.

A soft noise flowed from Vance as he cleared his throat. "Now, back
to what

we were talking about."

"Patience…goodness." Tiffany grinned. "I'll give you your gift when
we get to

the room."

"What type of gift?" Vance tilted his head to the side. "I hope it is a *special gift* in

the shower." Vance slowly licked his luscious lips.

"Oh, *trust me*…it is going to be *special*. This is a special occasion."

"Okay…okay…what is it, Tiffany?" asked Vance as if curiosity was burning at

the seams of his brown slacks. "You have to at least give me some clues." He spatted. "Can I see the gift now?"

"Goodness, you are so impatient." Tiffany giggled.

"I've always been patient with you," Vance smiled, causing Tiffany to recall the

gentle, caressing touches he rendered throughout her body. "I want to see the gift."

Tiffany reached in her black purse, pulling out a purple small wrapped box

with a white bow on top. "Here, *Mr. Carson*," she laughed.

"What is it?" asked Vance with excitement in his voice while reaching for the

box. "Is it a watch?"

"You'll see."

"Wait." Vance paused. "You said that in a calm voice. . . too calm." He bit his

bottom lip. Now you've got me a little nervous. I hope . . . well I know these can't be divorce papers rolled up in this box."

"No, silly."

Vance chuckled. "Is it a nice watch?" He gently shook the box. "It sounds like a

box of candy."

"Trust me, you're going to need a box of candy after you open it."
She smiled.

"I'd rather you open it when we get in the room."

"Now you've got me curious." Vance strolled his fingers along the
ridges of the

box. "I've got to open it."

"Okay...if you say so," Tiffany whispered in a seductive tone.

"Why are you whispering."

Silence flowed from Tiffany's lips before a high-pitch voice flowed
through the

room. "Yes, yes," said a medium-built lady with long blonde hair as a
chocolate brown man kneeled before her with a small ring box in his hand.

"Go ahead and open it, Vance," said Tiffany. "I know you're going
to keep asking

me if you can." She laughed.

Vance's eyes locked onto the box like a kid preparing to open a
birthday present

His fingers peeled off the layers of the wrapper. He slowly opened the box.

"What is this?" Vance asked while pulling a slender pink stick from
the box.

Tiffany remained silent as Vance's eyes scanned the words on the
stick.

Silence flowed from his mouth as he slowly closed his eyes. A single
tear eased

from the corner of his right eye.

"Say something, Vance, please," Tiffany whispered.

Vance's lips slowly parted. "You're . . . you're pregnant." A smile
stretched

across his face. "I've . . . I've been waiting for this day. Does your mother know?" Vance reached for her hand.

"Yes." A sense of excitement flowed through Tiffany seeing Vance's reaction.

"Mama knew before I did." She paused. "It is funny because I'm a doctor . . . an OBGYN at that . . . and my mama told me before I even knew it." She chuckled. "She told me I had a pregnancy glow." She grinned. "I didn't learn about *pregnancy glows* in medical school."

Vance's smile slowly faded forcing Tiffany to take notice of his sudden shift in

emotions. "I hope I'll be a good father."

"You will be." Tiffany paused. "I'll be a great mother and you're going to be a

wonderful father."

Chapter 63

A month later, the black metal door swung open. A small golden brown girl dashed inside the building. The cold freezing wind trailed behind her. The bright lights shone on her face, highlighting her dimples. The almond painted wall was covered with Christmas decorations, certificates and announcements in The Safe Haven Outreach Program.

The fresh smell of disinfectant cleaning supplies filled the air. A soft, nice breeze whizzed by Tiffany's nose each time the door was opened.

"Hello, Mrs. Tiffany," Christy said, wrapping her small arms around Tiffany's waist. Her lips lengthened into a bright smile.

A sense of peace and happiness filled Tiffany, seeing that the little girl could still wear a smile after being raped—enduring a major operation and intensive outpatient therapy. She had a smile that should have been framed in an art gallery. Tiffany was relieved knowing Christy eventually recalled details of her rape, confirming that Smith had raped her.

Tiffany grinned. "Hi, Christy. How are you? How was school today?"

Christy's face beamed brighter than the morning sun. "I made a hundred on my spelling and math test. But my teacher didn't give it to me. She said I have to wait until tomorrow."

"That's great. Make sure you bring it tomorrow so you can get an extra treat."

Extra treats ranged from a free bag of chips to a free cheeseburger. Tiffany would write the prizes on pieces of paper, place them in a bag and have the children draw out a slip. Christy enjoyed when she pulled out the gift for McDonald's because that included one-on-one time with Tiffany.

The outreach program was an outlet for kids. Children came to play games, get snacks and escape the pressures of the Cloverdale projects. Although Cloverdale still had a community center, some of the kids liked the outreach program because it had a larger game room.

"Good afternoon, Tiffany," Mrs. Clark said while walking towards Tiffany.

Tiffany turned. "Hello, Mrs. Clark."

"Can I see you for a minute?" Mrs. Clark said.

"Christy, can you please excuse me for a minute?" asked Tiffany.

"Yes." Christy said in a low tone.

Tiffany smiled. "Go ahead and put your book bag up and join the art group."

After Christy left, Mrs. Clark said, "I want to commend you for opening the program for rape survivors."

"Thank you." Tiffany slowly exhaled. "I'm glad I opened it. I've hired several therapists."

"I've heard that the therapists are bilingual. I'm sure they'll help a lot of people." Mrs. Clark said with slight excitement in her voice. "Just like . . . I'm sure your story will help a lot of people." Mrs. Clark reached for Tiffany's hand gently tapping it.

"I hope so." Tiffany closed her eyes for a split second. "I wish I had started the program a long time ago."

Mrs. Clark's eye glanced at Tiffany's stomach. "How's your pregnancy coming along?"

Tiffany paused before speaking. "Great. I can't complain." Tiffany smiled, knowing news traveled fast in the community.

"I heard that you are having twins."

"Yes, fraternal twins. Vance and I have been blessed with a boy and girl," commented Tiffany as she proudly rubbed her stomach.

"What a *huge* blessing."

Shoes tapped on the floor as kids entered the building.

"Excuse me, Mrs. Tiffany, can you come and color with me?" Christy's voice echoed across the room.

Tiffany turned. "I sure can, Christy." Tiffany smiled. "I'll talk with you later, Mrs. Clark," said Tiffany while walking towards Christy.

"I don't have homework," Christy said, dropping her sack into a small box.

"Christmas break is next week."

"Excuse me, Christy." Tiffany turned to face a staff member. "Mr. Kirk, please let me know if you or the other staff need help. You can send some kids over to the arts and craft table when they finish their homework."

While booting up the computers, he turned and said in a deep voice, "We have everything under control over here. I think Christy's the only one right now who doesn't have homework."

The doors swung open again. Children ran up the long, narrow hallway to the homework room, laughing aloud but quickly mellowing out when they entered the large spacious room. Children with white to dark brown complexions took off their winter coats and book bags, pulled out their homework and sat down at the circular tables. They were aware of the program's rules and knew that they would get a treat if they completed their homework and maintained good behavior.

Tiffany joined Christy, then moved the little girl away from the other students to avoid distracting them as they did their homework. The small wooden table sat in front of a square-shaped window, allowing the sun to peek in.

Christy flipped through the coloring book.

"Here's something I colored for you, Mrs. Tiffany—butterflies," Christy said, tearing out two brightly colored prints, then handing one to

Tiffany. "Why do you like butterflies, Mrs. Tiffany?" she asked, eyes glittering with anticipation.

Tiffany thought about that for a moment before replying, "I think my life has developed just like a butterfly. Do you know butterflies go through a lot of changes before they blossom into something beautiful?"

Christy shook her head.

"They start as squirmy little caterpillars then go into a shell and come out with wings and beautiful colors. That's how life is." Tiffany poured the crayons and the markers on the table. "These butterflies are going to be beautiful, just like you, Christy."

Tiffany smiled, turning to monitor the other kids. Homework time was a quiet

time, which lasted for at least two hours. The kids were good at occupying their time by reading or coloring until the other students were finished.

"Mrs. Tiffany, I'm glad you're here." Christy picked up a blue crayon and handed it to Tiffany.

A book bag fell on the floor, breaking the silence on the other side of the room. Mr. Kirk rushed to help the little boy.

Placing the crayon on the table, Christy turned and whispered, "Thanks for helping me . . . to learn how to read."

For a split second, she thought Christy was going to bring up her rape incident.

Tiffany exhaled slowly.

"I'm proud of you. You've worked hard. Your grades have been really good."

"My teachers asked me who helped me. They didn't believe that I did it by myself." Christy placed her small hands on her little hips. "I told them— Mrs. Tiffany."

"Take your hands off your hips, little lady." Tiffany giggled, picking up a yellow marker.

Christy grinned as she slid her hands off her tiny hips, then picked up an orange crayon. "That's only because you helped me. The kids at school used to pick on me because I couldn't read. They can't do that anymore. I'm glad you're my friend."

"You are welcome. I enjoy being with you."

Tiffany glanced out the window at a pine tree. A cardinal jumped from limb to limb, making snowflakes sprinkle onto the ground. She detected a pinch of nausea settling inside her body reminding her that she was pregnant.

"Did you have any adult friends when you were younger, Mrs. Tiffany?"

Tiffany sighed as she reached for a purple crayon. "Yes, Mrs. Lindy Clark and her husband, Sergeant Clark."

Christy's eyes widened. "You *knew* Mrs. Lindy when you were young?" She said, grinning. "She must be *real* old."

Tiffany giggled. "She has been here a long time."

Another stream of students stormed through the doors talking loudly interrupting the students in the study room.

"Shhhhh," a voice said from a long rectangular chair.

"I want to be a ginny doctor just like you when I grow up."

"A *what*, Christy?"

"A ginny doctor. You know . . . like you. I want to do what you do."

Tiffany grinned. "*Ohhh,* a gynecologist."

"Yeah, that's the word. How do you spell that, Mrs. Tiffany?"

Tiffany wrote it on a piece of paper.

Christy picked up the paper. "I'm gonna be . . . that . . . when I get big." She smiled from ear to ear.

Tiffany smoothed back Christy's hair, looking into the light brown eyes filled with as much pain as hers had been. She embraced the little girl saying, "You can be anything you want to be."

Author's Quotes

"We tend to seek the obvious in life, instead of the impossible, due to chance of failure."

Kimberly Morton Cuthrell

"Wisdom is Key."

Kimberly Morton Cuthrell

"You do not have to be smart to do what I have done. You have to be wise."

Kimberly Morton Cuthrell

"We do not waste time by making mistakes. We waste time by not learning from mistakes."

Kimberly Morton Cuthrell

"Never underestimate the benefit of constructive criticism."

Kimberly Morton Cuthrell

"Success should not be determined only by what you have achieved. It should be determined by your ability to pave a path forward for others to learn and achieve."

Kimberly Morton Cuthrell

"Our accomplishments should not define us. It is our learned experiences that matter the most."

Kimberly Morton Cuthrell

About The Author

Kimberly Morton Cuthrell is an attorney, mediator, clinical therapist, and currently a medical student with a quest to create new inroads to suspense novels with behavioral health twists to destigmatize perceptions.

She was born in Greensboro, North Carolina and spent many years residing in Portugal, Greece, Turkey and Spain where she became proficient in Spanish before returning to the United States of America where she lives with her family.

Kimberly's interest to write evolved from reading books, crafting her dissertation, writing proposals for grants and contracts, composing corporate compliance and policy/procedure manuals within provisions of state and federal laws, and developing behavioral health accreditation manuals whereby she secured a corporation's Three-Year Accreditation three consecutive times with an international accrediting body.

In her fiction work, she draws from thought-provoking imaginary situations, the art of wisdom, and diverse viewpoints. Kimberly, a member of Alpha Kappa Alpha Sorority, Incorporated, writes to intrigue readers' minds about *potential* real-life situations and inspire them to advocate for positive change and make meaningful impacts in their communities.

When she is not writing, Kimberly can be found playing her favorite board game, mentoring individuals to pursue their greatest potential, and spending time with her family. A lifelong learner, she enjoys promoting confidence and wisdom in others.

www.kimberlymortoncuthrell.com

kimi@kimberlymortoncuthrell.com

Made in the USA
Middletown, DE
08 August 2022